"Llywelyn's work is known for its skillful blend of historical fact with interesting characters." —*Richmond Times-Dispatch*

"Morgan Llywelyn is known for giving life to Irish myth and history in novel form. . . . She presents history in a most readable fashion." —*The Charleston Post & Courier*

"Rich, masterfully told." —*The Hartford Courant* on *Lion of Ireland*

"Mary Stewart has a worthy rival." —*The Baltimore Sun*

"Magic and words and war. It makes a wonderful book." —*The Washington Post* on *Bard*

"An old Irish proverb maintains that 'a good story fills the belly.' *Pride of Lions* does more than that; it totally fills the mind and the soul. Morgan Llywelyn once again displays all the talents found in century-old traditions of revered Celtic bards. . . . Llywelyn, the consummate storyteller, smoothly weaves many threads into the rich tapestry of this novel that continues her Irish saga begun with *Bard*." —*Rocky Mountain News*

"Powerful . . . Llywelyn has created a lusty, poetic, and legendary world." —*The New York Times Book Review* on *Red Branch*

By Morgan Llywelyn from Tom Doherty Associates

Bard
Brian Boru
The Elementals
Finn Mac Cool
Lion of Ireland
Pride of Lions
1916
The Horse Goddess
1921

FINN MAC COOL

MORGAN LLYWELYN

TOR®

A Tom Doherty Associates Book
New York

FINN MAC COOL

Copyright © 1994 by Morgan Llywelyn

Book design by Lynn Newmark

A Tor Book
Published by Tom Doherty Associates, LLC
175 Fifth Avenue
New York, NY 10010

www.tor.com

Tor® is a registered trademark of Tom Doherty Associates, LLC.

ISBN 0-312-85476-5 (hc)
ISBN 0-312-87737-4 (pbk)

First Hardcover Edition: March 1994
First Trade Paperback Edition: May 2002

Printed in the United States of America

0 9 8 7 6 5 4 3 2 1

For Michael

I

THE RED STAG BROKE COVER UNEXPECTEDLY. FINN AND his hounds were taken by surprise. The two dogs froze, waiting for his command. He had one glimpse into huge liquid eyes, pleading eyes; then the stag bounded away down the mountain, belling a warning.

Light from the westering sun burnished the deer's russet coat. North beyond Galway Bay, thick, pale clouds sagged with the weight of approaching winter. Sleet hissed on the wind.

Hot with life, the stag flickered like flame across a cold grey landscape.

"Red deer, red deer," Finn murmured, immobilized by beauty. A poem rose in him like spring water.

Shouts exploded behind him.

"Stag, a big one!"

"Get it!"

"Kill it! Kill it!"

Men boiled past Finn, waving their spears and howling their hunger. His instincts briefly merged with theirs. His fingers tightened on the shaft of his spear, his muscles contracted for heft and hurl.

But the poem stopped him. The poem, growing in him.

"Hold where you are!" he cried. The two young hounds, Bran and Sceolaun, whined, but stood.

The men found it harder to obey. Momentum had already carried them past him. They were hunters and a stag was running. But they were also warriors of the *Fíanna,* and he was the new leader of their particular *fían* of nine.

He called himself Finn Mac Cool.

Planting their spears on the slope to brace themselves, the *fénnidi* watched with regret as the deer leaped from one limestone outcropping to another. When it disappeared from sight, their eyes turned toward Finn.

"You let a fine fat stag get away," accused Conan Maol, Conan the Hairless. "And us starving."

Dark, slender Cailte added, "I could have run him down and eaten the entire animal myself."

"You could have done," Finn said amiably. "But then he'd be gone, all that grace and beauty destroyed. And you'd just be hungry again tomorrow. A creature that splendid can serve a better purpose surely than swelling your belly."

His men exchanged glances. They were beginning to recognize a certain cadence when it crept into the speech of their newly appointed *rígfénnid*. Fionn son of Cuhal was a dedicated hunter. But when the impulse to poetry seized him, everything else must wait. His band had already learned that much about him.

With a last wistful glance after the lost deer, they formed a circle around their leader, crossed their legs, and sat. The ground was cold. They ignored discomfort.

Finn remained standing. His eyes were turned northward. The jagged peaks of the Twelve Bens were dimly visible across the bay, disappearing into lowering clouds, but Finn was not looking at the mountains anyway.

In his mind, he was watching the red stag run.

His expression grew dreamy and faraway. His hair was as pale as winter sunlight, his eyes as clear as water. But when he was ready to speak, his voice would be deep and sure.

Bran and Sceolaun sniffed out the bed in the bracken where the deer had lain. Some of the animal's warmth lingered in the flattened ferns. Circling three times, the hounds remade the bed to suit themselves and curled up together. Sceolaun rested her muzzle on her crossed forepaws, but her companion's head was propped across her back so Bran could keep watchful eyes on Finn.

The cry of wild geese rang through the sky. Looking up, Finn saw black wings carving lines in silver space.

He nodded. The poem was complete. He recited,

> *Here's my tale.*
> *Stag cries, winter snarls, summer dies.*
> *High and cold the wind.*
> *Low and dull the sun, and brief its run.*
> *Strong surge the seas.*
> *In red-brown bracken, shapes lie hidden.*
> *Geese sing, fleeing south, ice on wing.*
> *That's my tale.*

When Finn stopped speaking, Donn said, "Brrr! That's made me colder than I was already."

The poet smiled, flattered.

" 'Winter snarls,' " quoted Fergus. "A particularly nice bit, that." His mouth worked, savouring the words.

"It's a grand poem entirely," Cailte affirmed, "but it won't fill our bellies. Words are no substitute for a haunch of venison or a fine silver salmon with the smell of the sea on him."

"I'd give my good eye for some badger meat dripping grease," sighed the husky voice of Goll Mac Morna.

Lugaid suggested hopefully, "We could still bring down that stag, the hounds could track him."

"Leave him be!" Finn ordered sharply, unwilling to have the source of his inspiration slain. "We'll find something else, we always do." He brandished his spear and whistled. Bran and Sceolaun jumped up and ran to him, wriggling with the exuberance of half-grown hounds. The hunt resumed.

Except for Goll Mac Morna, all of them were young and exuberant, brimming with barely controlled energy. They had unblunted features and blue-white eyeballs and had only recently begun growing warriors' mustaches. They were brash and merry and thought themselves immortal.

Searching the slopes of Black Head, the fían poked spears into every crevice and hollow, seeking to flush out small game—hares or red squirrels, or even the half-mouthful of a pigmy shrew. They laughed and swore and shoved each other; they traded insults until the crisp air crackled.

Cael challenged his friend, "If you can put one foot in front of the other, I'll race you to the bottom!"

"Done!" cried Madan Bent-Neck, who owed his permanently cocked head carriage to a slight deformity. He wore the round shield slung across his back higher than his companions did, to conceal the unevenness of his shoulders.

Physical beauty was not required of a *fénnid;* only strength and courage mattered in battle.

The two bounded away in exaggerated leaps. Goll said disapprovingly, "Those young fools will kill themselves, running headlong on that footing."

Finn flashed a merry grin. "Then that's two less we'll have to find game for. Think of the effort saved!"

Goll chuckled. One of his eyes twinkled. The other was milky, bisected by a slashing scar that puckered cheek and brow. "It's Conan who'll be the most grateful, he's the laziest."

But in spite of Goll's prediction, Cael and Madan reached the bottom without mishap. They turned and trotted back up at a more leisurely pace, watching their footing. By the time they rejoined their companions halfway up Black Head, they were breathing hard, however.

Cailte said scornfully, "Neither of you knows how to run." He pulled his wolf-fur cloak out from under his shield and tossed it aside, revealing a body as thin as a sapling, clad in a leather kilt and a deerskin tunic. "Mind you, this is what running is," he said. He raced off down the mountain, his shield bouncing against his shoulder blades.

In a voice like thick cream, Fergus Honey-Tongue remarked, "Cailte Mac Ronan is faster than thought."

"He makes Cael and Madan look like old women," said Conan.

Madan bristled. "It's not fair to compare us to him. Cailte won the running championship at the last Tailltenn Fair."

"So he did," Finn agreed. "Therefore he should be the standard you set for yourselves. Go and catch him, you two."

Cael's jaw sagged. "You aren't serious."

"I am serious. And since I would never ask you to do anything I wouldn't do myself . . ." Without pausing to take off his cloak, Finn turned and ran down the mountain after Cailte. Bran and Sceolaun frisked along beside him, barking excitedly.

With a whoop, Blamec set off after them. Cael and Madan felt compelled to follow. The entire band joined in, slipping and slithering down the north face of Black Head, waving their arms and their spears for balance, cursing and colliding and shouting with laughter.

Reaching the bottom well ahead of the others, Cailte sat down on a slab of stone and dug into the leather bag slung from a thong around his neck. He was just taking a bite of hoarded food when Finn joined him.

"Want some of this?" Cailte offered.

"What is it? Och, honey fungus. I'll wait for meat. You'd eat anything though, wouldn't you? Move over."

Cailte obligingly slid over to make room for Finn. "I'd eat anything if I was hungry. And I'm always hungry."

As the others arrived, Finn called out their names. "Blamec. Lugaid the Serious. Donn. Conan the Hairless. Cael. Fergus Honey-Tongue. Madan." There was a long pause while they all waited. Then, "And here at last is Goll Mac Morna."

Goll was gasping for breath and sweating profusely. He had an appalling stitch in his side. He stopped before he got to Finn and bent over with his hands braced on his knees. "I had to bring up the rear," he panted. A fit of coughing ensued. When it had passed, he added, "Someone had to guard the young ones' backsides."

Sceolaun ran to him and began trying to lick his face. He elbowed her away but she came right back. Her tongue slopped noisily across Goll's mouth. He made a strangled sound of disgust. "Finn, call off this wretched bitch!"

Finn whistled. At once Sceolaun left her victim and trotted to her master, mouth agape as if laughing.

Goll followed, clutching his side. "When I was the age of these young ones," he said raspingly, "I was as fleet as any of them."

Finn smiled. "It's not your age that hampers you, Goll. It's your girth. You grow thicker and thicker, like an oak tree."

"And like an oak tree, I'm hard to cut down," Goll growled.

Finn's smile held. "Everyone knows that Goll Mac Morna is unkillable."

Seen together, the two might have been taken for father and son. Both were tall and fair. But while Finn was lean and taut, Goll was bulky, thick through chest and shoulder, short of neck and broad of thigh. Compared to Finn, he looked clumsy and past his prime.

Yet he had his pride. His voice had been permanently hoarsened during long service as Rígfénnid Fíanna, chief of all the Fíanna, commander of the army of Tara long before Finn joined them.

Now, however, he marched with Finn's band and followed Finn's orders. That alone should have made them enemies, though there was another, darker reason for enmity between them. Finn never referred to it, but Goll could not forget that he was one of the men who had killed Finn's father.

Any other man in Erin would have devoted himself to finding his father's killers and exacting a terrible vengeance. But Finn Mac Cool did not seem interested in revenge. He treated Goll as he treated everyone else.

The situation made Goll acutely uncomfortable. He was a professional warrior, accepting a demeaning assignment with the obedience born of long discipline. Finn's apparent friendliness should have made it easier.

But it could never be easy.

Cailte drawled, "I notice none of you bothered to bring my cloak down for me."

"We thought you'd want to run back up the mountain and get it yourself," Finn teased.

"I will of course, no bother on me! And I assume you'll accompany me as a courtesy?"

Cael snorted with laughter, but Finn replied without batting an eye, "I will of course." He was on his feet and running, with his hounds beside

him, before Cailte realized what was happening. The thin man had to
sprint madly to catch up.

They raced up the mountain together. Cailte inclined his lean torso
parallel to the slope. Watching from the corner of his eye, Finn copied
his technique and matched him stride for stride. They ran faster than
Cael and Madan ever could.

The earlier running had been for fun. This was different. Both men
recognized that a serious challenge had been offered and accepted.

They competed on a treacherous slope studded with slabs of limestone and fern-concealed potholes. One misstep could break a man's
leg.

Black Head was the northernmost point of the region known as the
Burren, an eerie moonscape land where plants and flowers thrived that
grew nowhere else in Erin. Wind and weather had sculpted stone into
thousands of time-fissured faces, until the Burren became not a place,
but a Presence. Using the wind off the sea for a voice, grassy uplands
hummed songs of a Stone Age past.

Time circled and spiralled and had no shape. Stone tombs erected
millennia earlier were monuments to forgotten chieftains who still
haunted the corkscrew hills. Natural terraces of striated limestone
shifted colour from grey to violet to rose in the pellucid light of an
Atlantean sky.

Nothing changed and nothing stayed the same—not in the Burren.

Two young men raced up the headland in a ringing silence broken
only by the sound of their harsh breathing and a curlew's cry.

Black Head was steep above the sea.

Under their eyebrows, both youths darted covert glances upward,
assessing the remaining distance. Every fénnid was an experienced runner, but this racecourse was vertical and each footstep potentially deadly.
And by some trick of the light, the summit of the mountain seemed to
be receding even as they climbed.

There are strange tales told of the Burren, Cailte thought. Can the
mountain be growing taller to spite us?

Finn, however, was telling himself, I should have carried Cailte's
cloak down with me. I should have foreseen this and been able to
avoid it.

His lungs burned agonizingly. The air he breathed was liquid fire.

He ran. Cailte ran. Up and up and up they went, and still they could
not see Cailte's cloak waiting above them.

What a stupid mistake, Finn thought, to challenge Cailte. If he beats
me, I'll be diminished in their eyes.

If he beats me.

If.

The word took on new meaning. "If" indicated there was an alternative. "If" meant Cailte might not beat him.

Finn did not tell himself, I will win. He told himself, I will not lose.

His legs pumped and his heart hammered and he matched Cailte stride for stride, refusing to be beaten.

Cailte was not under the same pressure. Already an acknowledged champion at running, he knew that one race lost to Finn Mac Cool would not irretrievably damage his reputation. So Cailte ran his best, but he did not put in that extra effort beyond one's best that can burst the heart.

Finn did. He lengthened his stride. When rocks rose in his path, he leaped over them, gaining ground with every jump. For a time, Cailte kept up with him. Then there was a moment when the rhythm of the champion's breathing faltered, and in that moment, Finn passed him.

Try as he might, Cailte could not draw even with Finn again.

The hounds, running ahead of them, stopped abruptly and dropped their muzzles, sniffing. At their feet lay a puddle of wolf fur—Cailte's cloak.

Finn reached it one stride before Cailte did. Swooping, he brandished the cloak above his head. The men watching below saw him wave the silvery banner and cheered.

"I can't make out who has it," Blamec complained.

"Cailte, of course," said Conan.

Lugaid cupped his hands around his eyes. "I don't think so. That looks like Finn to me."

"Not possible," Conan snorted. "Finn could never outrun Cailte."

"I think he has," Lugaid insisted quietly. He sounded impressed.

All of them were impressed.

Halfway to the summit, Finn and Cailte were each struggling to keep the other from seeing how breathless he was. Finn had clamped his lips together and was trying to make himself breathe softly through his nose. Cailte had bent over the fur as he brushed bits of bracken from it, hiding his flushed and panting face. From that position, he did not see the two men come down from the ridge above.

"Look here, Cailte," Finn alerted him. "We aren't alone."

Startled, Cailte glanced up. Two men, one his own age and one slightly older, were making their way toward them. The older one had a dead deer slung over his shoulder.

Finn tensed, then relaxed. It wasn't his stag, his poetic inspiration, but an old doe. Her head was grey with the frost of too many winters.

It was her time to die.

"You're very welcome, strangers," Finn called in the time-honoured greeting.

The man carrying the deer had a round, pleasant face but hostile eyes. "We aren't strangers. You are. This is my mountain." His speech was clipped, abrupt with anger.

Finn had been in the Fíanna long enough to know that men some-times made unwarranted claims to territory. "Is it now?" he asked with icy politeness.

"It is indeed. I am Iruis son of Huamor, who is chieftain of the Burren. He's given me use of this mountain to build a fort on because I'm taking a wife next Beltaine."

"Huamor!" Finn's voice thawed. "The very man we're looking for. We must have missed his stronghold somehow. Do you know where he is now?"

"I don't know who *you* are."

Finn lifted his chin. In a voice like the ringing of bells, he announced, "I am Fionn son of Cuhal son of Trenmor."

Iruis sniffed. "Fionn means "fair," and your hair's the colour of bleached linen, so that much is true. As for your being a son of Cuhal Mac Tremor . . . he was famous but he's been dead a long time. Who can vouch for you now?"

Finn's lips tightened. He spat the words between them. "No one questions me. I'm a rígfénnid, an officer of the Fíanna."

Iruis was openly contemptuous now. "A boy like you?"

"He is a rígfénnid!" Cailte burst out. "His fían are down below. He has eight armed and dangerous men in addition to me, and when the rest of them learn you wouldn't take his word for his identity, you're going to be in real trouble."

Iruis braced his legs belligerently and thrust out his jaw. Two stran-gers were not going to intimidate him on his own mountain. "Go look," he ordered his companion, "and see if anyone's really down there."

The other man stepped to the brink of the nearest rock ledge, peered over, and hastily moved back. "There are men down there," he reported, "and they're looking up this way."

"Not just men," said Finn. "They're members of the Fíanna, the best army in Erin, and I can summon them with a shout. Every fénnid is an expert with sword and spear. Would you care to see a demonstration?" He smiled disconcertingly, a feral baring of teeth.

Iruis took a closer look at the strangers in the gathering twilight. Confidence began to seep from him like cold sweat.

The one who claimed to be a rígfénnid was rawboned with youth, but massive of frame. Hair like molten silver streamed over improbably broad shoulders. His cheekbones were boulders. He wore a huge, rough mantle of wild-animal skins crudely stitched together with sinew, and a plain deerskin tunic; but a belt around his torso held a gilded and embossed leather scabbard. Thrusting from the scabbard was the leather-wrapped hilt of a shortsword, bound with fine silver wire and set with a pommel stone.

It was unmistakably the weapon of a rígfénnid. To make matters worse, Finn was unslinging his shield from his back and slipping his left arm through its straps.

Iruis began to fear he had made a dreadful mistake. His father would deny him Black Head if he had insulted an officer of the Fíanna—if he survived, that is.

Iruis slumped his shoulders in the posture of submission. The deer slid to the ground. Holding out a weaponless hand, he said, "I accept your word, of course. But one can't be too careful these days. There are outlaws even here in the Burren."

"That's why we've come," Finn replied. "Huamor sent a request to the king of Tara, asking for help from the Fíanna in dealing with your outlaws."

"He did? He never mentioned it to me—not that my father discusses his affairs with me. But I didn't expect him to send for mercenaries."

Ice crackled in Finn's reply. "We aren't mercenaries. We're part of the Fíanna."

Iruis was flustered. "Of course, I know . . . I mean . . . I thought . . ."

"Did you?" Finn asked sardonically, pressing the advantage. "Did you indeed? Is it something you do often—thinking?"

Iruis's companion rescued him. "I'm afraid you took us by surprise, that's all," he said to Finn. "We would like to welcome you so you won't accuse us of a lack of hospitality. But we have only the one deer. If you and your men will share it with us, however, we'll consider ourselves honoured."

Iruis shot his friend an annoyed glance. He muttered, "I was just about to say that."

"Then why didn't you?" the other whispered back.

Finn bit his lip to keep from smiling. He was enjoying their discomfiture hugely. "Of course we shall accept your offer of hospitality," he said, sounding very formal, "and commend you to the king of Tara. Summon the fían, Cailte."

Cailte went to the brink and shouted down. Distance distorted his words, but his beckoning wave was clear.

Blamec groaned. "We have to go all the way back up there? I don't believe it."

"If you're lucky," Conan suggested, "you might burst something in your brain and die on the way."

"You have a nasty mouth, Conan."

"He has a gift for sarcasm," Fergus Honey-Tongue interpolated.

"He has a nasty mouth. Perhaps it's the result of being as hairless as an eel. Conan Maol has an eel's bite."

"Save your breath for the climb," advised Goll. He started up and they followed. No one ran.

Far above them on the side of the mountain, the doe was being gutted and skinned. Finn and Iruis watched as the other two did the work.

"Your friend is good with his long knife," Finn commented. "Where's he from? I don't recognize his accent."

"He's a Connacht man from Mullach Rua. He likes to be called for his birthplace, in fact. Never uses the name he was given at birth."

"Mullach Rua? Red Ridge?" Finn frowned, thinking. "I've heard of it. It was mentioned in one of the poems I learned to qualify for the Fíanna. I must admit, I've never been to that part of Connacht myself, though." He caught a lobe of raw liver that Cailte tossed to him, nodded his thanks and tore it in two with his bare hands, giving half to Iruis. The treat was quickly swallowed.

Iruis resumed, "No one goes to Mullach Rua if they can help it, it's as lonely as a cry in the dark. Red Ridge was glad to come here to spend the winter. He's assigned as a bodyguard to the woman I'm going to marry, who's also wintering with us."

Red Ridge looked up. Coppery curls clung tightly to his skull. There was something friendly, yet uncompromising, in his eyes.

Finn took an immediate liking to him. "I didn't care for the name I was given at birth, either," he confided.

Red Ridge said, "Mine didn't suit me."

"Neither did mine, it could have belonged to anyone. I prefer being Finn the Fair, which describes me."

"I prefer being Red Ridge. That's the place that shaped me. A man's name should fit like his skin, not hang from him like someone else's tunic."

"Absolutely," Finn agreed. He watched as Red Ridge and Cailte completed extracting the organs from the carcass, then cut the hide at neck and ankles, skillfully worked it loose from the underlying connective tissue, and peeled it off the deer inside out. Cailte turned it right side out again, then rolled up the damp bundle and handed it to Finn.

Finn promptly turned and gave it to Iruis.

After a moment's hesitation, Iruis handed it back to him. "Take this as my gift," he urged.

He knew he had lost ground to recover. He was very aware that Finn's band would join them at any moment. Indeed, the first head was just topping the nearest ledge.

Though the others had passed him as they climbed, Goll Mac Morna was not bringing up the rear. He had craftily engaged Cael and Madan in conversation so that the three arrived together.

Introductions were made. Seeing them in a group, Iruis could not doubt they were fénnidi. Though they were very young, they balanced themselves on the balls of their feet like warriors and their eyes constantly scanned the landscape like hunters.

Their tall leader appeared to be little more than a boy, but a boy with a disconcertingly direct gaze. Beneath that gaze flickered something as hard and cold as iron.

Suddenly Iruis was glad he had given Finn the hide.

The atmosphere was quickly established as cordial. The cold quality lurking in Finn's eyes seemed to disappear; he grinned, he laughed, and his men laughed with him.

Iruis told them, "We'll need to gather a lot of bracken and dead brush for firewood. This is an old doe and she'll want a long roasting."

Donn surveyed the deer with a practised eye. "I know about cooking. She'd be better boiled."

"Roasted," Iruis said firmly. "To boil her would mean leaving the mountain and going to the nearest farmstead for the loan of a cauldron. I won't leave Black Head tonight. I mean to choose my building site by the light of the rising sun."

"That meat's too tough for roasting," Donn insisted.

Iruis scowled at him.

"We won't have to leave the mountain to boil the meat," said Finn.

"Why not? Have you cauldrons with you?"

Finn gave a disdainful snort. "Fénnidi are men of no property, we don't burden ourselves with cauldrons. We find what we need wherever we go, ready to hand."

Iruis was mystified. "How?"

"If you plan to build a fort up here, surely you know of some fresh water supply on the mountain."

"I do. There's a spring not far from where we stand."

"Lead me to it!" Finn said cheerfully.

Iruis took him to a small spring that bubbled up in a natural stone hollow fringed with ferns. Crouching on his heels, Finn examined it thoroughly, estimating volume of water and speed of flow with the skill of practise. Then he stood.

"Dig the pool just . . . there," he commanded his men, pointing. "And the ditch from there to there."

Dividing into work parties, his fían dug out a pool below the spring. A channel, which they temporarily dammed with stones, was dug to connect the spring to the pool.

Lugaid and Fergus built a fire beside the pool, using alternate layers of rocks and dead brush to create a draught. With sparks from their flintstones, they lit the fire, while Cael lined the pool with Finn's deer-hide to keep water from seeping away. As they waited for the fire to get hot enough, the others scoured the slope for stones the size of a baby's head.

Meanwhile, Lugaid patiently tended the fire. Its heat grew steadily. A deep red glow began to appear in its heart.

After an interminable wait, Lugaid pronounced the fire ready. The dam was broken and water flooded into the pool. The fénnidi dropped the stones they had gathered into the heart of the fire, waited, then twitched them out again and expertly flipped them into the pool with their shortswords. The water began to steam, then to boil.

Donn had been gathering plants from the surrounding area, finding what he wanted with unerring instinct even after the sun had set. He threw his collected seasonings into the boiling water, adding strands of seaweed taken from the leather pouch he wore on a thong around his neck. Then he motioned to Cailte and Red Ridge to throw in the by-now-dismembered deer.

A heady aroma soon rose from the pool. The hungry men crowded around to watch the hunks of meat tumbling in the roiling water. "This is wonderful entirely!" cried Iruis. "I never expected to have a banquet such as this tonight."

"The Fíanna hunt all over Erin," Finn replied, "and we travel light. But we live well. We carry necessities like flintstones for fire and seaweeds for salt in our neck bags and rely on the land to supply the rest. We may be men of no property, but we want for nothing, as you can see. When we need a cauldron, for example, we simply construct a *fualacht fíadh*, a deer's bath, like this one. You could track the Fíanna clear across Erin by the cooking sites they leave behind."

The night was cold, the men ravenous. They began pulling meat from the pool long before Donn thought it was ready.

Finn would not allow any of his fían to eat, however, until they performed a set ritual.

In spite of the cold, every fénnid had to strip to the waist and wash himself in the icy spring. The men then combed their hair—except for Conan Maol, who had none. When it was neatly braided, they performed a complicated set of suppling exercises. Only then did they re-clothe themselves and sit by the fire to eat.

"What's all that in aid of?" Iruis asked Finn.

"Fíanna discipline."

"I'd never delay a meal just to flex my muscles."

Finn shrugged. "Then you'd never make a fénnid."

The hint of condescension in his voice annoyed Iruis. "Why would I want to join the Fíanna? I have everything a man could want. I have this mountain and the fort I'll build and the woman who'll warm my bed here. I have cattle of my own and ear rings and arm rings and a store-house filled with furs. I have all the Burren to hunt in. I might even be elected chieftain someday, when my father's dead. What have you to compare with that?"

"We have the songs we sing as we march," Fergus told him. "We have the thunder of the *bodhran,* the war drum, and the cry of the trumpet."

Donn said, "We sleep someplace new every night, and the stars themselves are our sentinels. People envy us our wild, free life."

"We chase the red deer in the south and the wild boar in the north," Blamec contributed. "We aren't limited to our tribelands, as you are. We can hunt anywhere in Erin."

"From Beltaine to Samhain, we support ourselves by hunting," said Cailte, "but from Samhain to Beltaine, we're quartered on the people. They vie for the honour of being our hosts."

"They also keep our hounds for the winter," Cael added, "at no cost to ourselves, no matter how much they eat."

"It's because the people are grateful to the Fíanna," Madan explained. "A fine, chest-swelling feeling, that is."

Conan muttered, "They aren't always grateful, the maggots. I could tell you some stories—"

Lugaid interrupted smoothly, "Of course we don't complain, it's our profession. We were born to be warriors, just as others are born to be craftsmen or beekeepers or druids. Or princes like yourself," he said, flattering the chieftain's son.

Only Finn had not contributed to the conversation. Iruis noticed that a gobbet of flesh was dangling forgotten from his fingers. He was gazing into the fire, which set his pale hair agleam and gilded the angular planes of his face. It also revealed an unexpectedly sweet curve to his lips. His was a boy's mouth, merry and vulnerable, in contrast to the brooding eyes.

Iruis sensed a mystery. "You're very young, Finn Mac Cool," he commented. "Why did you join the Fíanna yourself? Because you were born to fight? Or is there more to it?"

Finn had not expected the question. Keeping his eyes fixed on the fire, he swiftly sorted through a range of possible answers. He could simply tell the truth, outlining in a few blunt words the loneliness and restlessness of his formative years.

But on the other side of the fire, Goll Mac Morna had stopped eating and was leaning forward intently, listening.

The fénnidi were listening too. Beside a roaring campfire on a cold night on a lonely mountain, they huddled into their cloaks and looked expectantly toward Finn.

They wanted to be entertained. They were young, and the night was long.

"Blamec," announced their new rígfénnid, "you'll stand the first watch. Go as far as the firelight reaches and circle the edge of darkness until I send someone to relieve you. Mind you stay alert. Enemies could see the fire and try to sneak up on us from below.

"As for the rest of you, keep the soles of your feet toward the fire and I'll tell you something about Finn Mac Cool."

2

Blamec resented having to take sentry duty.
With the possible exception of Goll Mac Morna, none of the fían knew much about their leader. In a race notable for its loquacity, Finn Mac Cool had been closemouthed about himself. His only personal comments were made through his poetry.

But now he was going to talk openly about himself. In spite of orders, Blamec kept edging back toward the fire, trying to overhear.

"You know, of course," Finn was saying, "that the Fíanna is the standing army of the kings of Tara, as the Red Branch once served the kings of the Ulaid. We're sworn to repel any foreign marauders, and to make our services available to those chieftains who give their loyalty to the king of Tara—like your father, Iruis. This was the purpose for which Conn of the Hundred Battles formed the Fíanna when he was king of Tara. He wanted an army capable of keeping peace in his territory and commanding respect from other tribes."

"Not easily done," Conan interjected. "Peace is in short supply with the Gael so fond of fighting each other for sport and profit."

Ignoring him, Finn continued. "Conn was succeeded at Tara by Airt his son. In the reign of Airt, Cuhal my father became Rígfénnid Fíanna, not just the leader of a company, but the commander of the entire army of Tara." His voice rang with the words. They seemed to come from somewhere deeper inside him than his chest.

"How large is the Fíanna, exactly?" Red Ridge asked.

"The Rígfénnid Fíanna commands seven score and ten rígfénnidi. Each rígfénnid has three times nine warriors in his company. You see but one of my bands of nine here. Two more are waiting for me at Slieve Bloom, where we will winter."

Finn's voice underwent a subtle change as he said, "Before I was born, there was a challenge to my father's leadership of the Fíanna. He was murdered by members of another warrior clan, men who had served with him in the army." Finn named no names, however. His eyes did not meet Goll's eye across the flames, though he felt the weight of its stare.

"My mother, who was called Muirinn of the White Throat, bore me on the Bog of Almhain while fleeing from my father's enemies after his death. She gave me into the keeping of two old women, a druid called Lia and a wise-woman known as Bomall. They hid me away in the Slieve Bloom mountains. There I grew; there I learned to hunt and fish and run and hide. I was called Demna in those days," he added with a careless wink toward Red Ridge.

"My mother married another man, a chieftain from Kerry. But after six years, she came to visit me. She took precautions so no one would recognize her and follow her to me." Finn paused to lick the last traces of grease from his lips. With sudden inspiration, he said, "She disguised herself as a deer."

"You mean she was wrapped in deerskin?"

"I do not. I mean she became a deer. My mother had . . . certain powers," Finn said mysteriously, eyes dancing.

His listeners leaned forward. Such a claim was not without precedent. And on a night such as this, a night of windhowl and fireglow, anything seemed possible.

"The two old women trained me, and a hard school they ran. They would put me into a meadow leaping with hares and order me not to let a single one escape, or I should not be fed for three days. They threw me into a river and shouted that I must discover how to swim or drown straightaway. They taught me to survive in a world without mercy, those fierce old women."

"A wise-woman and a druid?" Iruis sounded impressed.

Embellishing his tale, Finn said, "The druid was a kinswoman of mine, actually." He could not resist adding, "She taught me some of her magic. She was that fond of me."

If they laughed, he was ready to laugh with them. But they did not laugh. He saw belief in their eyes. They came of a race with a long experience of druidry. They had accepted Muirinn's transmogrification; they had no trouble accepting this.

That's it! Finn suddenly realized.

Until this night, his youth had seemed an insurmountable obstacle. He looked older than he was. In truth, he was scarcely old enough to lead one fían, much less entertain higher ambitions. But for a man who could do magic—or was believed capable of doing magic—age was irrelevent.

His future opened out before him, richly, goldenly, the gift of accident and inspiration.

The wind blowing off the western sea moaned around Black Head.

The flames of the campfire leaped and writhed. In the wind's voice Finn thought for a moment he could hear *her* voice, urging him on. Goading. Pleading. Tormenting. Or was it the stag's voice, belling a warning?

He could taste deer meat on his tongue.

Shapes shifted in his brain. He fought his way back to his story. "Bomall and Lia kept me with them until I was of an age when no woman could control me, and then I went wandering. I made Erin my pillow and hunted in forests where the trees were as thick as hairs on a hound. I learned to rely on myself only."

"But would you not seek out your own people, your clan?" Red Ridge wondered.

"I didn't know who they were. The old women would never tell me."

"Didn't your mother tell you when she visited you?"

"She couldn't. She came to me as a deer, not as a woman."

"Then how," asked Conan reasonably, "could you possibly recognize her?"

Finn saw his mistake. To cover it, he snapped, "And would you not know your own mother, no matter what she looked like? If not, it's a poor son you are!"

He went on hastily. "On the banks of the Liffey, in my fifteenth year, I saw a group of lads my own age. They challenged me to a swimming race. When I stripped to join them in the river, they called me Fionn because of my fair hair and fair, strong body; but when I outswam them all, they were jealous. So I left them and went away alone again.

"But I kept the name they had given me.

"Soon afterward, my skill at hunting attracted the notice of a chieftain who hired me to hunt one summer for him. It was he who first told me of the Fíanna and their murdered leader. Peering into my face one day, he said, 'If Cuhal had a son, Finn, I think that son would be exactly like you.'

"From that day, curiosity tormented me worse than fleas. I learned that Cuhal's widow had married a chieftain in Kerry, so I made my way south. As soon as I saw her, I knew Muirinn of the White Throat for my mother."

"Marvellous powers of recognition," Conan said dryly.

Finn ignored him. "Muirinn told me of my people, the Clan Baiscne, and also the details of my father's death. But her husband wouldn't let me stay with her. He was afraid Cuhal's enemies would learn of me and come to kill me while I was under his protection, which would have forced him to break battle against them."

" 'The guest in the house is sacred'," quoted Fergus.

"Indeed. So my mother's husband insisted I leave, and she took his part. At the last moment, however, she drew me aside and urged me to . . ." he paused, letting the tension build ". . . urged me to seek out the Fíanna and join them."

A tight voice asked, "Is that all she asked you to do?"

Finn looked up. Across the flames, he locked gazes with Goll Mac Morna. As if the wind had shifted, there was a sudden change in the atmosphere.

"Did you?" Red Ridge asked eagerly. "Did you join the army then?"

Finn relaxed. "Not for a while. First I went looking for my father's brother, Crimall, who was reputed to be hiding out with the last surviving officers from my father's command.

"But on the way, I met an old widow, and she was grieving. Her only son had just been slain by . . . a giant." Finn paused in his narrative to adjust his neck bag, which had become twisted on its thong. "For the old woman's sake, I hunted down the giant and killed him. And on his body I found a . . . a bag made of crane skin. I subsequently found Crimall and showed the bag to him, and he identified it as having belonged to my father. So the giant I had killed was one of Cuhal's murderers," he concluded with satisfaction.

Goll Mac Morna sat up very straight. "You never mentioned this before."

"I never did," Finn agreed. "The giant was called Luachra and the bag he had stolen from my father contained the treasures of Clan Baiscne."

"What were they?" asked a breathless voice.

Finn twisted around to scowl up at Blamec. "You're supposed to be standing watch, so why are you hanging over my shoulder?"

Shamefaced, Blamec scurried back to his post. Finn went on weaving words from smoke and flame. He was lost in them now himself. He believed, so his audience believed.

"The bag was made from the skin of a bird that had once been the beloved second wife of the sea god, Manannán Mac Lir. His jealous first wife turned her into a crane, but the magic killed her. Manannán took the crane's skin and had it made into a bag in which he kept his shirt and knife, and the shears of Alba, and the tools of Goibniu the smith—all of them items of great magical power, you understand? Treasures."

His audience nodded as one, spellbound.

"Because the bag belonged to the sea god, it was full when the tide was full but appeared empty when the tide was out." He was constructing his tale carefully now. There must not be another mistake like claiming he could recognize a deer to be his mother. "The bag was given by Manannán to Lugh son of Evleen. Lugh in turn gave it to Cuhal my father, when he married Lugh's sister, Muirinn White Throat." Finn took a deep breath, satisfied that the provenance of the magical bag was now firmly established.

Iruis asked, "Do you still have it?"

With one forefinger, Finn tapped his neck bag. Fénnidi were called Men of the Bag, *Fir Bolg*, because they carried pouches on thongs around their necks to hold their flints and combs and razors and needles and other necessaries of a nomadic life. The appellation Fir Bolg was an ancient one, predating the founding of the Fíanna, and had been applied to some of the most ancient tribes of Erin, many of them including Finn's ancestors.

Finn's bag happened to be covered with crane skin taken from a bird he had killed with a slingshot on the Bog of Almhain, near his birthplace. He neglected to mention this detail. He merely called attention to the bag and let the others draw their own conclusions.

Conan said doubtfully, "Clan Baiscne must be poor in treasures. That bag isn't exactly bulging."

Finn was ready for him. "Of course not. The tide's out."

Conan glowered.

The others laughed and elbowed him. "The tide's out! Didn't you even know that?"

Finn let himself relax. He had told them enough for now. Give them time to think about it, time to digest and accept. He felt as if he were watching the scene from a distance, a dispassionate observer assessing the advantage Finn Mac Cool had just won for himself.

Until tonight, his skills had been enough to entitle him to leadership of one band of warriors. But to lead the entire army, a man must be extraordinary.

Goll Mac Morna had been such a man. In his prime, he was reputedly the strongest man in Erin, and his hardiness was legendary. The injury that had cost him an eye was minor compared to some of the wounds he had survived. His body was a map of warfare. In addition, he owned the famous Gold and Silver Chessboard and was a master at the game.

Possession of the magic bag of Manannán Mac Lir would bestow a similar prestige on Finn Mac Cool.

He knew that someday he might be challenged to prove his tale. But not tonight. No Gael would ruin a good story on a night like this by questioning it too closely.

He drew up his knees and spread his legs so the fire could warm his private parts. Resting his arms on his knees, he stared again into the flames. One hand scratched the shaggy head of Bran, who lay beside him.

No one urged him to go on with his storytelling. He appeared lost in thought, and out of a new respect, his companions left him alone. From time to time someone would dart a glance at him and quickly look away. Finn was aware of the glances, but he did not react. He concentrated on the warmth of the fire and the fullness of his belly—and on trying to keep his face impassive.

The irrepressible boy just beneath Finn's skin kept threatening to laugh out loud. They believe me. They believe me!

His eyes were itching. The wind had shifted and was blowing smoke into them. He stood up and went around to the other side of the campfire. Bran lifted an ear, looked up quizzically, then rose and stalked after him.

When Finn sat down again, he found himself beside Goll Mac Morna. "So it was you who killed my brother—Luachra the Large," the older man said in an undertone.

Finn reached for a partially gnawed bone and gave it his full attention, tearing off shreds of meat with his teeth.

Undeterred, Goll went on. "Did you really take a bag from Luachra's body? I suppose you thought it belonged to the widow's son and meant to return it to her sometime. But was it Cuhal's bag? I don't recall precisely what his neck bag looked like, though I'm sure I saw it often enough during our seasons in the Fíanna together. I don't even know if he was wearing it at the Battle of Cnucha.

"There was a lot of confusion that day, Finn. You must understand. What happened to your father was no simple thing, one blow in the heat of the moment. There was a long history of bad feeling between Clan Morna and Clan Baiscne, and he'd brought it to a head with his own actions. Cuhal was responsible for his own death, really. He brought it on himself."

Frowning, Finn concentrated on worrying a resistant piece of gristle from the bone.

"If you think we killed Cuhal for his treasure bag, you're wrong," Goll insisted. "It was politics. Mac Con, the Son of the Wolf, encouraged the feud between Clan Morna and Clan Baiscne for his own purposes."

Tilting the bone toward the fire, Finn squinted at it.

"If you really did have that bag, you should have left it with your uncle. It would be dangerous to carry around a bag of . . . jewelry, perhaps?" Goll guessed. "And you with no guards."

At last Finn spoke. "I have the Fíanna."

"You have nine men, for now," Goll corrected. "And the possibility of two more bands of nine if you do well."

Finn dug into the bone with his forefinger, extracting marrow. "Perhaps I did leave the bag with my uncle."

"The bag you're wearing right now is crane skin."

Glancing down, Finn simulated surprise. "So it is!"

"We didn't rob Cuhal, Finn!"

"You took his command. You killed him to get it."

"It was politics!" Goll protested. "And Cuhal's own greed. He was loyal to Airt, and when the Son of the Wolf killed Airt and seized Tara, he naturally wanted his own man to command the Fíanna. But for years he was afraid to demote Cuhal, who was too popular with . . . a certain element of the fénnidi. Then Cuhal stupidly made a mistake that was used against him to stir up the feud between his clan and mine. That culminated in the Battle of Cnucha, when Clan Morna did what the Son of the Wolf wanted done and killed Cuhal. Afterward I was named as Rígfénnid Fíanna by the king simply because I was the best qualified.

"I still am," Goll added.

As if none of this touched him, Finn recited in a singsong bardic chant, "And in time the Son of the Wolf was killed by Feircus Black-Tooth, himself the next king of Tara."

"Feircus, that Ulidian! I suppose you take vengeful pleasure knowing he demoted me to put a northerner in command of the army."

"I take no such pleasure," Finn replied calmly. Then he raised his voice so that his next words were audible to everyone. "I've disavowed all forms of personal vengeance, Goll. When I killed that giant for the widow, it didn't bring back her son. It just left another corpse to feed the ravens. I learned that day that revenge accomplishes nothing. I don't intend to pursue it."

Goll fought to keep the relief out of his voice as he said, "You have an old head on young shoulders."

"Not at all. I'm just mindful of the oath I took when I joined the Fíanna. I'm supposed to pursue the king's interests, not my own."

In the firelight, Goll studied Finn's face. The younger man looked earnest, sincere. Devoid of guile.

But is he? Goll asked himself. He's Cuhal's son, and Cuhal was unpredictable.

To distract himself from his doubts, Goll took up the telling of war stories. Unfortunately, he lacked the bardic gift. "That day when I took a spear through my body and walked away, it was lashing rain, and . . . och, I'm wrong, the sun was shining to split the stones. It was summer, and we were in . . . the spring, it was the spring. A fine, bright season, my third as Rígfénnid Fíanna. Or was it my fourth? Let me think . . ."

The younger men yawned, stretched. One by one they rose and began constructing beds for themselves of moss and bracken, close to the fire. Occasionally one would say "Mmmm" out of politeness, to make Goll think they were listening to him.

Finn went to urinate down the side of the mountain. Red Ridge followed him. "Is it so wonderful, being in the Fíanna?"

"The best life in the world. Why? Are you interested?"

"I might be. And then again, I might not." A second stream of urine hissed into the cold air.

"It's not easy to join the Fíanna. You have to pass a number of hard tests."

"I'm sure I'm able for anything the rest of you can do."

Unseen, Finn's eyes sparkled mischievously. "Make water for longer than I can, then. And send it farther."

Red Ridge quickly tightened his muscles to control his flow, without stopping to realize that Finn must have done the same before issuing the challenge.

One stream soon dwindled and died. The other did not.

Embarrassed, Red Ridge tried to change the subject. "Why is that one-eyed man with you? He's much older than the rest of you, a generation at least."

"This is my first command, actually. It's customary to send an experienced officer like Goll in such a situation."

"Och, you don't need him. I'd say you'll do well enough without having an old one to carry."

"That old one," said Finn, spacing out his words slowly for emphasis, "is more of a man than any of the young ones. There's no one I'd rather have guarding my back."

Twice embarrassed, Red Ridge returned to the fire and cocooned himself inside his cloak.

Meanwhile, Iruis was remarking to Goll, "Your young rígfénnid is most unusual."

"Because of his youth? Or his claim to magic?"

"Because he disavows revenge. That goes against custom."

"Finn is the son," Goll said sourly, "of a man who defied custom. Cuhal desired a woman who was far above his social rank. Her people were appalled. He'd made a reputation for himself and for many of the Fíanna as outlaws. Supported by the king of Tara, Cuhal and those like him took what they wanted without fear of reprisals. Eventually, Cuhal simply stole the woman against her will, ignoring her rights under the law as a free person. He stole not only the woman, but her jewelry. It was a great scandal. Her father, Tadg, a man of prestige and property, was so outraged that he cursed the Fíanna from a height."

Iruis whistled. "The most serious of curses! Did Cuhal not pay the father the woman's honour price?"

"Cuhal? He laughed at the very idea. He was too greedy, he wanted everything for himself. But what would you expect from a man of Clan Baiscne?"

"You sound bitter, Goll."

"As a fénnid, I didn't have much in those days, but I had my honour. Cuhal stole that from me by disgracing the Fíanna."

"I'm surprised you're willing to serve under his son, then."

Goll gave Iruis a veiled look from his one eye. "He's my rígfénnid. I respect the discipline of the army."

The man they were discussing stood alone in the night. A blanket of cloud had enveloped the mountain. Finn savoured its taste on his lips: damp, chill, almost metallic. The wind had dropped, he noticed. The Burren seemed to be holding its breath. Skin prickled on the back of his neck.

He turned abruptly and went in search of Blamec. "Have you seen or heard anything?" he demanded of the sentry.

"Not a thing, Finn. The only thing that's moving is my hair growing. Why do we have to take sentry duty up here anyway?"

"Huamor requested the Fíanna because outlaws are overrunning the Burren, or so he said. Suppose some of them saw Iruis coming onto Black Head with only one companion?"

"What if they did? They wouldn't follow him all the way up here."

"Why not? We came up here."

"We were chasing game."

"Outlaws might consider Iruis as game. The chieftain's son, alone. He'd be a prize worth taking."

"I still don't think—"

"Go back to the fire and send me a sentry who won't argue with me, Blamec."

"I wasn't arguing. I never argue."

"Send Lugaid. He's the sort of man I want."

"And what's wrong with me?" Blamec bristled. "I'm here and I'm well armed and I'm as fresh as a new-laid egg!"

Finn said one word: "Lugaid." But something in the way he pronounced the two syllables sent Blamec trotting back to the campfire to rouse his replacement.

Waiting for Lugaid to join him, Finn felt intensely alive. His hearing was preternaturally keen. His eyes stabbed through the darkness. As if his body were covered with cat's whiskers, he could feel the tangible weight of danger.

That sound halfway down the mountain—was it a stone dislodged by a careless foot?

That shadow a spear's throw away—had it shifted ever so slightly?

He drew his shortsword from his belt. A spear was no good at night. If they were attacked, it would be hand-to-hand combat.

Finn's heart began to pound at the base of his throat.

"Come on," he whispered into the night. His grip tightened on his sword. *"Come on."*

3

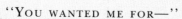"You wanted me for—"

Finn rounded on Lugaid. "Not so loud!"

"Sorry. What is it?" Lugaid asked softly as he came to stand beside Finn.

"There's someone below us on the mountain."

Whisper-footed, Lugaid drifted to the edge of the slope and peered down. Ridges of pale limestone glimmered up at him, but he saw nothing that could be construed as human.

"Where, Finn? I don't see anybody."

"I don't see them either, but they're there."

"No one could sneak up on us up here."

"One of our own men could do it," Finn reminded Lugaid. "Every fénnid has proved he can run through a forest without snapping a single twig beneath his feet. If we can be that stealthy, so can others."

Lugaid took another, longer look down the mountain. "I still don't see anybody. But if you think there's an attack coming, shouldn't we alert the men?"

Finn skinned his lips back from his teeth in an expression that might have been a grin. "Have you forgotten the oath you took when joining the Fíanna?"

"What about it?"

"Part of that oath included swearing never to run from less than nine men. That means one of us is expected to be able to outfight nine men. There are two of us here right now, Lugaid, so between us, we should be able to handle two nines without calling on our comrades for help. Do you not agree?"

Lugaid swallowed hard. "I suppose so, I never quite looked at it that way. But—"

"No buts. Be ready now. Ease off in that direction so we'll have them between us when they come up. They'll follow the same path we did, it's the only way in the dark. Careful now, go handy, Lugaid. The stones are treacherous. Farther. Farther still. About there. And wait for my signal." Finn's voice sounded faint and far away.

Shortsword in hand, Lugaid edged along the shoulder of the mountain, feeling fierce and foolish and frightened. He had been dozing with his belly full of food and his lungs full of mountain air, and wisps of sleep still clung to him like fog.

He shook his head to clear it. The shortsword—a larger version of the dagger, with a leaf-shaped iron blade—was a comforting weight in his hand. He gave it a couple of practice brandishes.

This is a waste of effort, he thought. There's no one else up here.

Then he heard what might be a stealthy footfall behind him. He whirled, dropping into a crouch.

Nothing.

"Stupid," Lugaid said aloud. The sound of his own voice was welcome company.

He tried to make out Finn, but his leader was a shadow among shadows in the distance, no longer discernible.

Lugaid might have been alone on the mountain.

Courage came as easily as breathing when you were boasting with your companions beside a warm campfire. When you were alone in the cold night, with your companions hidden from you by the curve of the mountain, it was different.

I don't much like this, Lugaid told himself.

He was young and untried and he knew it. He belonged to the youngest band of nines in the Fíanna, which was why it had been assigned to Finn Mac Cool, the youngest officer. They were all considered expendable.

Although he claimed the title, Finn still had to earn his official designation as a rígfénnid by acquitting himself well on this venture. If Goll took back a favourable report to the king of Tara, Finn would be given command of a second and third nine, currently being held at Slieve Bloom. If he did not earn the right to command a company, however, he would be demoted to common fénnid and his men would go to some other leader.

So, Lugaid realized, the son of the famous Cuhal would undoubtedly be willing to take considerable risks to prove himself. One of those risks could be Lugaid's life.

I don't want to die, Lugaid thought vehemently, to confirm Finn Mac Cool as a rígfénnid!

But I don't want to dishonour my oath as a member of the Fíanna, either. Disobeying orders could get me expelled from the Fíanna, a shame beyond surviving. The poets would disremember my name and lineage. I would become nothing. No woman would look at me. The dogs in the road would lift their legs on me.

Lugaid drew a deep breath and shifted his sword from one hand to the other, taking a small comfort from the solid feel of the hilt slapping into his palm.

I could have been a stonemason, he thought. My uncle's a woodworker, I could have gone into business with him. I'm good with my hands, and I like building things. I didn't have to—

Then he heard the yell, and all the blood in his body seemed to drain to his feet and congeal there.

Too late, Finn Mac Cool had realized his error. The outlaws knew the Burren as he did not, and were familiar with alternate routes up Black Head in the darkness. They had angled across the mountain and come around behind him.

He heard them a heartbeat before they closed with him; heard them just as Bran streaked past him with a savage growl to hurl a hound's full weight against the leader.

The man yelled as Bran knocked him flat. Two others rushed past while the dog seized him by the throat. They ran to attack Finn, who met them with legs braced and shortsword weaving patterns in the dark air.

"I'm coming!" Lugaid shouted. He ran in the direction of Finn, but one of his feet slipped into a crevice between two cakes of limestone and was trapped. Lugaid fell forward with a crash. It seemed to him that the stars had come out after all; he could see them whirling around his head as he lay dazed.

Meanwhile, Finn was fighting for his life. One man hacked at him with something that was not a sword; the other jabbed at him with a different form of weapon. Neither of the pair was observing the stylized rules of formal combat in which the Fíanna were trained.

They merely wanted to kill. Quickly if possible, brutally if necessary.

Finn did not call for help. Even if he had wanted to, he could not spare the breath. He was ducking, dodging, trying to land blows of his own, feeling backward with one foot for a patch of level ground to make a stand on, feinting with his sword at first one man and then the other, keeping his attackers at arm's length.

One got close enough to slash his hand with something that burned like icy fire. Finn swore and tried to grab the weapon, but the man jerked it back out of reach.

The man Bran had attacked was still on the ground, making horrible noises as the hound tore at his throat.

Finn expected more outlaws. He tried to face in every direction at once. But no more arrived. The two with him were bad enough. If they had been able to coordinate their efforts, they might have proved deadly, but in the darkness and on the steep slope, they kept getting in each other's way.

The one with the hacking weapon struck the one with the jabbing weapon by mistake and there was a new shriek of pain.

Finn seized the opportunity to jump backward and gather himself. Then in one smooth movement, he shifted weight and came forward again, levelling his sword in front of him with a stiff wrist.

Lunging, he felt the sword enter flesh.

His opponent's diaphragm muscles resisted momentarily, but Finn had momentum. Flesh yielded to iron. A man grunted, then doubled over, clutching at his midsection. With a powerful yank, Finn pulled his sword free as his opponent collapsed.

The other outlaw swung his weapon in a wide arc. Finn crouched. Something *whooshed* through the air above his head with killing force. He sprang up from his crouch with his sword at the ready and caught the man off balance at the end of his swing. The flat of Finn's blade took him solidly between the legs.

The outlaw's howl of agony was hardly human.

Running feet, confused shouts.

"What was that? What's happening?"

"Over here!"

"Not that way, this way!"

"Where's the sentry?"

"Are we attacked?"

"Finn! Finn Mac Cool! Are you dead?"

"I'm not dead," Finn gasped. "At least I don't think I am. I'm here, over here!"

He was wildly exhilarated. No measurable time had passed, three enemies were down, and he was still alive and on his feet. An exultant thunder rippled through him in waves.

He did not want the fight to end. He wanted to brace his feet wide on the stony soil of Black Head and let enemies come to him in endless procession, with himself cutting them down, cutting them down, letting the cleansing anger pour out of him at last, hewing and hacking and cutting them down . . .

"Finn!" Goll Mac Morna was shaking him. "Don't you know me? Answer me, are you all right? What happened?"

A great shudder passed through Finn. Exhilaration fell away, leaving him giddy with reaction.

"Your dog's tearing someone apart over here," Blamec reported in a slightly queasy voice.

"Bran!" Finn shouted. The hound ran to him. When he reached down, he felt something wet and sticky on Bran's muzzle.

Suddenly he remembered Lugaid. Where was he? "Lugaid!"

"Over here," came a faint reply.

By the time Lugaid joined the others, Donn and Iruis were giving the men on the ground as thorough an examination as they could in the dark. The others stood around them, talking in excited bursts.

"Where were you?" Finn asked Lugaid.

"I was coming to help you, but I had trouble."

"Were you attacked? How many were there? And where are they?"

Lugaid longed to announce that he had killed nine outlaws all by himself. Instead, after a pause, he said, "I caught my foot between two stones and fell flat. Stunned myself."

Conan sniggered.

Finn did not laugh. "I'm glad you're all right," he said simply.

His voice sounded hollow in his ears. His head felt hollow, come to that, and there were bells ringing someplace. His breathing was shallow and rapid.

Goll Mac Morna recognized the signs. He remembered his own early combats. Briskly, he ordered the fénnidi, "Drag these men over by the fire so we can get a good look at them."

"Any that are alive, go easy with," Finn added. He swayed on his feet. Goll's iron grip clamped his arm, steadying him. "It passes," said the older man. "Breathe deep."

Two of the outlaws were still alive, while the man Bran had savaged was unarguably dead. They dragged him by his heels with his head bumping along the ground and Bran prancing proudly alongside. Sceolaun trotted after them, trying to look as if she had helped make the kill.

Firelight revealed one man dying from Finn's sword thrust, but the other was suffering only from crushed testicles. He kept up a continuous moaning until Conan growled, "Stop that noise or we'll hit you in the same place again."

Finn asked Iruis, "Do you know these men?"

"I do know them. The one the dog killed has been the head and tail of trouble here for years. The others are his clansmen. They raid our cattle and corn and anything else they fancy. Nothing's safe with them around. But with their leader dead, they won't be so bold, I'd say."

Coughing up a great gob of blood, the man with the sword wound died as Finn and Goll were interrogating the third outlaw.

He gave his name as Ceth the Clever—"Obviously misnamed," Conan sneered—and justified his actions by accusing Huamor's people of having taken all the good grassland, leaving his clan with no subsistence but for the fish they caught. The two clans had been warring sporadically for a long time. "We had a plan," Ceth said, "an excellent plan that would have worked but for you interfering. We were going to take Huamor's oldest son hostage and demand a great ransom for him."

"Just the three of you?"

"Three is enough to handle any number of Huamor's kind!" was the scornful rejoinder.

Iruis muttered something and doubled his fists. Fergus Honey-Tongue said, "That's as may be, but apparently one Finn Mac Cool is quite enough to handle three of your kind."

"Two," Finn corrected. "Bran did for one."

They bound their prisoner with strips of leather and raised a cairn of stone over the dead men. "Your people can come up here if they like and carry the bodies home," Iruis told Ceth, "but it's the last time any of you are to set foot on this mountain. As you see, we have the Fíanna here to punish outlaws."

Ceth swept his gaze from face to face. "I don't see any fénnidi. All I see are pimpled boys."

"It takes this one a while to learn, doesn't it?" Conan asked no one in particular. Drawing back his foot, he kicked Ceth between the legs.

This time the man's scream was totally inhuman.

The night was ruined for sleeping. As they waited for dawn, they sat and told and retold versions of Finn's battle; Cael's descriptions were the most effusive. Scraps of meat were flung to the hounds, and dry brush was found to feed the fire with.

By the time an angry red flush appeared in the east, the fénnidi had begun singing triumphant marching songs and teaching the words to Red Ridge.

Finn and Goll sat a little apart from the others. "Not a bad beginning for you," Goll was saying. "A bit nasty, a bit crude, that part with the dog. There's no style in a killing like that, no art. But I'd say you've made an impression."

"If you were in charge, would you track down the rest of the clan?"

"Why? To batter them into submission unnecessarily? Let me tell you something, Finn. The best commanding officer isn't the one who breaks the most battles on his enemies. He's the one who wins the most victories with the least effort.

"You won such a victory tonight. The leader of the outlaws is dead, and Ceth will tell a tale that grows in the telling until his people think the entire Fíanna was on Black Head tonight. They'll be considerably discouraged from their predations for some time to come. You can report to Huamor that his troubles with them are over, at least for this season."

"And you'll report to the king of Tara."

"I'll report to Feircus Black-Tooth," Goll agreed. "Favourably, if you're wondering."

Finn's eyes sparkled with gratitude, though he said nothing. For a while they listened together to the singing. Then Finn said in a low voice, "I'm sorry about Luachra."

Goll shrugged one shoulder. "He probably deserved it. That sounds like him, killing a widow's only son and leaving her to cut her own wood and fetch her own water. Even if he was my brother, I have to say it. Luachra loved killing for its own sake."

"And you don't?"

Goll evaded by asking, "Did you enjoy killing Luachra the Large?"

With a burst of candour, Finn replied, "I didn't mean to kill him. It was an accident."

"Are you serious? What about the widow and her son?"

"Och, that was true enough. She cried on me for vengeance and I promised it to her to comfort her. But as I rambled on my way, I forgot about her. Then one night as I lay on the ground asleep, a twig snapped near my head. I thought it was an outlaw hoping to rob me. I grabbed my spear and lunged upward. By a lucky chance, I took Luachra in a vital spot and he was dead before I was fully awake."

"Then how did you know he was Luachra?"

"I didn't, not then. I only knew he answered the widow's description of her son's killer. But when I finally found my uncle Crimall and told him the story—and showed him the bag I'd taken from the man's body—" Finn remembered to add, "he identified the dead man as Luachra and the bag as having belonged to my father. He told me its history."

In a husky whisper, Goll said, "If you took that bag off a dead man, you'd done no more than Luachra did to Cuhal. But I don't think my brother was trying to rob you the night you killed him. He was probably just trying to get close enough to you to identify you.

"The members of Clan Morna had been watching for you for a long time, Finn. For years we'd heard rumours of a lad who looked like the very reflection of Cuhal Mac Trenmor in a still pond.

"Luachra probably caught sight of that freakish silver hair of yours and followed you, hoping to get a good look at your face to be sure. Cuhal had the same hair, you know. No other man in Erin possessed such a mane. But it was Luachra's misfortune to be clumsy as well as large. If he hadn't snapped that twig, you'd be . . ."

"I'd be what?"

"Dead," Goll replied succinctly. "We assumed you had sworn to avenge your father's death. Killing you before you could kill us would have been a matter of self-preservation."

"But when you finally did meet me, you didn't kill me."

In spite of himself, Goll chuckled. "I did not. Imagine my surprise when an overgrown lad dressed in untanned skins came swaggering into Tara one day, crying 'I am Fionn son of Cuhal!' "

"Was I too presumptuous?" Finn asked innocently.

"Presumptuous!" Goll laughed again. "You should have been killed on the spot. My hand was on my sword hilt to do the deed, but then I had a rush of common sense and waited to see how Feircus would react to you.

"Feircus Black-Tooth was very new to the kingship, having just overthrown and killed the Son of the Wolf. My star had fallen with the old king. I was lucky to still be alive and I knew it. I was trying very hard to stay that way by not getting crosswise of Feircus.

"He was impressed with your audacity, anyone could see that. You amused him. You were bold and different and had the smell of the wild on you and he liked wild things. I had no choice but to let you live."

"A good chance missed," Finn remarked. "If you'd killed me that day at Tara, you wouldn't be second in command to me now."

"Second." Goll spat the word. All warmth was gone from his voice. "I'll never be second to you. Just because I didn't kill you then, don't assume I never will."

Perversely, the surfacing enmity enabled Finn to relax. "I'm glad to know where we stand, Goll. Make no assumptions about me either." He bared his teeth very slightly, signaling intent. "None."

He would kill me! Goll thought. All that talk about never seeking to avenge his father, that was just talk. Lies. He's playing a game with me, trying to lure me into a trap. When I least expect it, he means to kill me. I know it. I know it!

But I can't prove it. What can I . . .

Just then Finn's expression changed and he gave Goll a smile of such radiant affability that the older man doubted his own intuition.

At sunrise Iruis paced solemnly across his mountain, waiting for some ancient instinct to tell him, *This is the place. Build here.* He went by himself, though the others watched from a respectful distance.

"Imagine building your own fort!" Lugaid sighed wistfully. "Your own stones, your own place . . ."

At last Iruis found his site, and he and Red Ridge marked out its perimeter with piles of rocks.

Iruis bubbled with plans. "The walls will be higher than two spear shafts," he enthused, "and from the top you'll be able to see the western isles. Finn, you'll come back here as my guest and I'll serve you such a feast, you'll have to let out your belt."

"Never," Finn laughed. "I'll come, but I won't let out my belt. Once a man does that, it means he's lost the run of himself and he loses status in the Fíanna. Goll over there has had to let out his belt just since I've known him."

Goll, watching, said nothing.

Iruis went over to him, eager to share his own good mood. "That Finn Mac Cool has the makings of a good officer," he said. "He had courage in the dark before dawn, when most men lose theirs. And that story about his origins is very colourful. It's the sort of tale men like to tell about their leaders. Is any of it true, Goll?"

In a carefully neutral tone, Goll replied, "I would say at least some of it is true."

"You've known Finn for some time, I take it?"

"Know Finn? I don't know him at all. I've merely been exposed to him."

They marched the captive Ceth down the mountain and turned him loose, hurrying him on his way with threats and a growl from Bran. Iruis then guided them toward his father's stronghold. "It's not easy to find," he said. "Huamor prefers to avoid visitors who need to be fed."

Along their way, Finn paused once to soak his hurt hand in the waters of an ancient well snuggled into a brambled hillside. Finn overheard Iruis saying that the well was famed for its healing powers, sacred to the Tuatha Dé Danann.

He dropped back a few paces to let the others go on. Then he slipped through an opening in the well-kerb and made his careful way down moss-slick stone steps until he could thrust his hand into the water. The shock of icy cold made his whole arm tingle.

The wound he had received the night before was a deep, ugly gash running from the base to the ball of his thumb. It was sore and inflamed. He had not mentioned it to anyone, however. Compared to Goll's many wounds, a lacerated thumb would have seemed ludicrous.

The damage had been done by a bronze reaping hook that had slashed to the bone. Finn's other assailant had been armed with a fishing trident. Only the man Bran killed had had a sword, and daylight had revealed it to be pitted with rust, the edge nicked, the point broken. Weapons of desperation.

When the cold water had numbed his hand, Finn ran to catch up with the others.

The day was dull and dark. From time to time, sheets of grey rain swept across the Burren. "When we get to my father's fort, you can dry your clothes and fill your bellies," Iruis promised. "Huamor's not the most generous man in Erin, but he'll see you right."

"We can't stay," Finn said. "It's almost Samhain. That means the Samhain assembly at Tara, then we're off to winter quarters."

"You could spend the winter here with us."

Finn shook his head. "Some other time perhaps. After we report to the king of Tara, I go straight to Slieve Bloom."

The smell of Huamor's fires reached them long before they reached his stronghold: rich, thick smoke from flames fed by dead bracken and gorse; billowing sweet smoke that cushioned the sharp air and made a man's guts ache with nostalgia for hearth and home.

Finn's companions began to walk faster.

Rounding a shoulder of hillside, they saw the ring fort ahead of them. A water-filled ditch that reflected the leaden sky ringed a high, circular bank of earthwork and rubble, faced with limestone. Rain spattering into the ditch shattered the reflections, drumming like fingers on a war drum. Set in the earthwork wall was a gateway, two timber doors half open, hanging on iron hinges. Through the gate, flashes of colour were visible as men and women inside the wall went about their chores.

Women.

Finn's companions gathered speed.

"Let me go first," Iruis cautioned. Cupping his mouth with his hands, he shouted, "I am Iruis returned, and I bring the Fíanna with me!"

A kilted man with a spear in one hand peered down from the top of the wall, yelled a greeting, and disappeared. A moment later he was at the gate. "Come in, come in!"

He escorted them to a round stone building in the centre of the enclosure, an impressive house with a conical roof of thatch. A grizzled, jowly man stood waiting in the doorway. He embraced Iruis, but over his son's shoulder, Huamor said to Goll Mac Morna, "Thank you for bringing my son home."

Goll's good eye blinked. "Thank our rígfénnid," he said, indicating Finn. "In single combat he destroyed three men who'd climbed Black Head to take your son hostage."

"The maggots! I hope you fed them to the ravens. Come in out of the weather and tell me about it. You . . . what's your name?"

"Finn Mac Cool."

"You'll sit in the place of honour, Finn Mac Cool."

Inside the lodge there was brief confusion as the fénnidi arranged themselves on the flagstones around the central firepit. Huamor barked a constant stream of orders to various women who moved in and out of the building. He did not, Goll observed sourly, bother to introduce any of these women to the fénnidi.

"Bring cups!" Huamor demanded. "Here to me now!"

"And food," Iruis suggested.

Finn quickly protested, "We eat only once a day, and that after sundown. We travel faster on empty bellies."

"Nonsense. You saved me, my father will feed you." Iruis looked hopefully toward Huamor, who at last snapped his fingers and issued an order for hot food.

He did not, however, order water for washing—a serious breach of hospitality. Finn had to suggest it. "My men and I need to cleanse ourselves and supple our muscles before we eat."

Huamor raised his eyebrows. "You do? Och, of course you do. Good idea, that. Watch them and see what they do, Iruis. You might learn something from these lads. Young as they are, I'd say they're men, every one of them."

The interior of the lodge was blackened by smoke, but an attempt had been made to brighten it by hanging rugs of dyed wool on the walls. Beyond the hearth, piles of seal and otter skins waited to provide luxurious bedding. Honey mead and barley ale gurgled from stone jugs into elaborately chased cups of heavy silver.

A young woman offered mead to Finn. As his hand closed on the cup, his thumb throbbed and he winced in spite of himself.

"Have you a thorn?" the woman asked solicitously. "We keep a jar of foxes' tongues, they're the best for drawing thorns."

Her eyebrows had been artificially blackened for beauty, and her hair was gleaming. Unbound hair, signifying an unmarried woman. Finn gave her a dazzling smile. "I've not a wound on me anywhere," he boasted. "I'm perfect entirely, like a king." He did not show her his thumb.

"You're talking to my wife-to-be," Iruis remarked.

Finn's smile shrivelled like a tender leaf on a hot rock.

Iruis laughed. "She's called Lannat. Her father's a Connachta clan chief with four more daughters as arm-filling as this one. I could have had any of them. I might take another one yet as a second wife."

Lannat turned toward him. "*If* I let you take a second wife," she said with unruffled composure. "Under Brehon Law, the first wife has to give her permission, and I might not. I might not even marry you myself, come to that. We're to spend this winter together to see if we're suited."

Huamor rescued his son from an awkward moment. "A second wife is a grand labour-saving device," the chieftain interjected. "I got one for my first wife when she was heavy with my sons. Then my second wife complained of doing all the work of the first one plus her own, so I got a third wife to share the labours. Now they're all happy."

"Even the third wife?" Conan asked innocently.

Huamor belched a laugh. "Och, doesn't she have the best of me in bed? She's still new enough to make my pole rise!"

His guests joined in his laughter, a hearty rumble that earthquaked around the lodge. The women laughed too, secure in their status. The warriors rolled their eyes at the women, who smiled back as they passed wooden platters heaped with meat and fish. When a male hand happened to fall caressingly on a female flank, no one objected.

As they ate, the men took turns recounting the events of the previous day. They described the weather, the climb up Black Head, the meeting with Iruis and Red Ridge, the cooking of the deer, the battle against the outlaws.

Finn said nothing, content to let the others extol his victory. From time to time he managed a modest little smile.

I wish my mother could see me now, he thought. The smile faded, became briefly sad.

Lannat had settled herself between Iruis's legs and was leaning back against his chest. From time to time he fed her bits of his own food. She asked Finn, "Are you really in charge of these men? You, and not the old one over there?"

"I am in charge. I'm a rígfénnid." He inflated his chest.

"Hmmmm . . ." Lannat's fingers began describing elaborate designs on Iruis's kneecap. Her nails were neatly trimmed and dyed with a berry stain.

Finn tried to capture her eyes. She evaded him by lowering her chin and looking down. Her eyelids had the sheen of rubbed silk. Turning her head slightly, she allowed Finn to admire the plump curve of her cheek. Then she glanced at him sidelong.

Finn squirmed, deliciously uncomfortable.

Lannat looked pointedly at his tented lap. When she smiled, he could see that she had all her teeth.

Oblivious, Iruis sat with one hand ruffling Lannat's hair while he listened to the conversation around him.

Finn's mouth was dry. He wondered what her armpits smelled like. Was the hair in them soft and moist? Was it dark like her brows, or fair? How would it feel to bury his face there?

Something scratched and whined outside the lodge. "My hounds!" Finn cried with a start, guilty for having forgotten them.

"Call them in," Huamor invited. "We appreciate good hounds here." He twisted around to have a look at the dogs. Bran entered first. "What an immense creature!" Huamor said in surprise.

"And not yet full-grown," Finn replied. "Wait until next year. This next one is a litter mate of the first. I call her Sceolaun the Survivor. She was the runt, but she'll be a fine hunting dog with a little more growth on her. I give her extra fat," he confided.

Huamor reached out to touch Sceolaun as she passed him but she curved her body delicately, just enough to avoid his fingers without being insulting, and sidled away. She and Bran threaded their way through the people seated on the floor until they came to Finn, then crowded in on either side of him. When the hounds sat on their haunches, their heads were as high as his.

"How did you come by them?" asked Red Ridge.

Before Finn could answer, Iruis said, "I'm more interested in hearing how our friend here became an officer of the Fíanna at such a young age. He started to tell us last night, but never finished."

"I'd like to hear that myself," said Huamor.

Finn knew that Goll was watching him. "We need to leave soon," he said. "We have a long way to go . . ."

"I want to hear!" Huamor roared so commandingly that Sceolaun snarled.

Iruis leaned toward Finn. "I'd tell him if I were you. My father has a temper, he's famous for it."

"And if I don't tell him?"

"You're expecting payment for your services, aren't you? Some form of tribute to take back to the king of Tara? If you anger Huamor, that payment could be slow in coming. Very, very slow."

Goll Mac Morna was looking fixedly at Finn.

He might be waiting to see what Finn's decision would be, the better to judge the quality of his leadership.

Or he might be waiting to hear what sort of story Finn might tell in response to the question.

4

To give himself time to think, Finn slowly fin- ished the last of his food, savouring every bite, pausing to lick his lips and murmur appreciatively, thus flattering his host. When he could stall no longer, he cleared his throat.

Be careful, he warned himself.

The fénnidi were waiting expectantly for another tale spangled with magic. But Huamor was older, less credulous. His eyes lurked beneath puffy lids like predators in their holes, waiting to pounce on the unwary. He would require a story he could believe.

And what of Goll Mac Morna? What would he accept?

"Your son has heard of my early days," Finn began to Huamor. "He can tell you about them later." And if you find the tale too fantastic, you can blame him, he thought to himself. "As for my joining the Fíanna, I'm a son of Cuhal Mac Trenmor. When I was old enough, it was inevitable I should go to the king of Tara and apply to serve him as my father had done. We are fénnidi. What other course was open to me?"

Goll gave a miniscule nod of approval, Finn noticed.

"The king was surprised to see me. I think everyone was surprised to see me," Finn added, glancing at Goll, who kept a straight face but had one twinkling eye. "Most men weren't aware Cuhal had a living son in Erin until I walked into the Assembly Hall at Tara."

Testing him, Huamor enquired, "Through which of its doorways?"

"The Door of Beginnings, of course. So the king would know my intentions."

"You made certain to learn proper protocol before you went to Tara?"

"I did of course. I was very thorough. I had already apprenticed myself to a poet and learned the twelve epics, so I could prove I was a person of education and wouldn't be an embarrassment to the army of the king. I still remember every word," he added mischievously, "unlike some, who forgot their poems as soon as they were initiated into the Fíanna."

Conan glowered and studied his fingernails.

"Who was the poet?" Huamor asked. "Do we know of him?"

Finn's thumb was throbbing again. Without thinking, he thrust it into his mouth to suck on it.

Lannat noticed. "You do have a thorn!"

Finn guiltily jerked his thumb from his mouth. He was embarrassed to have a woman catch him in a lie. "Not at all. I was just . . . ah . . . remembering . . ."

"You remember by sucking your thumb like a baby?" Huamor sounded contemptuous. "You're younger than I thought."

Hot blood rushed to Finn's cheeks. Searching for a reply, he ran his tongue around the inside of his teeth until it found a tiny fishbone wedged between two of them, relic of the salmon he had just eaten.

Finn's eyes lit up. "The poet who taught me was called Finegas," he announced. "Finegas lived beside the Boyne River, where for seven years he had been trying to catch the Salmon of Wisdom."

"The Salmon of Wisdom?" Huamor looked blank.

"You've heard of it, of course," Finn assured him, "just as you know of the fame of Finegas."

"I do, I do surely, but—"

"Finegas thought he could catch the Salmon of Wisdom because an old prophecy foretold the fish would be caught by someone with his name. Possession of the fish was his dearest desire. Eating its flesh would give a man access to every form of knowledge . . . as you know, Huamor," Finn added deferentially.

The chieftain beamed. "I know that. Everyone knows that." He looked around the lodge, daring anyone to disagree.

"I spent my time with the poet, and he was a fine teacher. But he could never catch that fish. Then one leafsummer day when my studies were done and we were relaxing on the bank of the Boyne, we saw the salmon leap. Finegas ran for his net. But he was an old man, and easily exhausted. He finally caught the fish but the effort left him too weak to do more.

"As he lay gasping on the bank, he asked me to build a fire and cook the salmon for him. I was happy to think he would have his dearest desire, for he had been generous with me."

Finn allowed himself a quick glance around the room. They were caught up in the story now, netted and held. Even Goll was listening with half-parted lips.

Satisfied, Finn continued. "I roasted that fish for Finegas. When a blister came up on its skin, ruining its perfection, I pressed the blister down with my thumb. But the roasting fish was very hot, and touching it burned my thumb. I put it into my mouth just for a moment, to ease the pain. Then I took the fish to my teacher.

"When I set it before him, he asked if I had eaten any of it. I said I had not, which was true, because I knew he wanted it for himself. But I did tell him I'd burned my hand on the fish and sucked my thumb.

" 'Could you taste the salmon on your thumb?' he asked me. When I admitted I could, he looked as if he would cry. 'You had first taste of it then,' he said, 'so the prophecy was meant for Finn and not Finegas.'

"I protested but he would not listen. Sad though he was for himself, he made me eat the whole of the salmon and digest the wisdom it contained—and it a fish that had lived since before the before, swum everywhere, seen everything."

"A mighty amount of wisdom, that," said Lugaid.

"Indeed."

"And now you have all that wisdom yourself, do you?" asked Huamor. He did not sound convinced. He was on the verge of disbelieving the entire episode.

"Not at all! I only have access. When I need to know something—like the name of the poet, which had momentarily slipped my mind in the enjoyment of your hospitality—I can put my thumb into my mouth again and the answer comes to me. Without my thumb in my mouth, I am no more wise than any other man."

"Astonishing," murmured Red Ridge. There was no doubt in his voice.

Finn sneaked a quick look at Goll Mac Morna, but the older man's face was a careful blank.

"That's how I knew we were about to be attacked last night," Finn claimed. "I put my thumb in my mouth and at once knew there were dangerous men creeping up on me in the dark."

Blamec cried, "That's no word of a lie! I was the sentry and I couldn't see or hear anyone, yet Finn insisted they were there. He knew, when there was no way of knowing."

Huamor peered at Finn through a veil of fire smoke. "If that's true—and your man here seems to back it up—then you're valuable indeed, Finn Mac Cool. Too valuable for me to let you go back to Tara. Spend the winter with us in the Burren. You did good work last night, but for all we know, Ceth and his clan will regain their nerve when their bellies are empty enough and try to raid us for our cattle and corn. I'll need you then. You can break battle on them and destroy the whole wretched brood for me."

"I've already invited Finn to stay," Iruis said.

"And I've refused," Finn explained. "We don't fight in the winter. Summer's battle season, Beltaine to Samhain. The winter is cold and wet and it's impossible to fight when you're floundering in mud up to your apples. I thank you for your invitation, Huamor, but we have to go now. I mean to be out of the Burren by nightfall."

Huamor's bushy eyebrows rushed together like stags attacking one another. "And I mean you to stay. I need you."

Finn tried to be polite. "You must understand, it's impossible." With an apologetic smile, he held out his hands palm upward.

"You have to," Huamor snarled, all semblance of politeness abandoned. "I insist. You have to be here with me now that—" He checked himself abruptly. Cleared his throat. Essayed an unconvincing smile. "I mean, with the winter coming and the nights drawing in, we need a good storyteller to entertain us. We have none. I want to hear more of your tales, Finn. As for you . . ." he turned toward Goll ". . . what did you say you're called?"

"Goll."

"One-Eye. I can see that for myself. How are you known?"

"As Goll Mac Morna."

"Indeed! That's who I thought you were. I know about you, you were Rígfénnid Fíanna for the Son of the Wolf. Now here you are, trotting along behind this young one. What happened? Did your apples fall off?" Huamor laughed at his own witticism.

Goll went pale with anger.

Taking pity on him, Finn said, "We haven't time for this, we must leave right now. We have a long way to travel and the king expects us at Tara for Samhain."

Like a trout in a muddy pool, something moved in the depths of Huamor's eyes. "The king?"

"Feircus Black-Tooth. Whom you asked for some of the Fíanna."

"Feircus Black-Tooth," Huamor echoed. "Not a Connachta, or even one of the Laigin, but a northerner. A Ulidian. I swore loyalty to him, though. I thought he could do more good for me than anyone else could, and I suppose he was a good enough king."

Finn felt a sudden tightening in his scrotum. "What do you mean, he was?"

Huamor smiled with secret knowledge. "He's dead. Killed by a usurper in a battle at Crinna on the river Boyne."

In a choked voice, Goll asked, "Who's in control of Tara now?" The puckered skin around his ruined eye began to twitch spasmodically. "Who seized the kingship this time?"

"I couldn't tell you. A runner just brought me the news this very morning. He didn't even know. All he could say was that the survivors of the battle were sending word to Feircus's loyal chieftains to prepare for a retaliatory attack in the spring.

"That's why I want you to stay here," Huamor went on, speaking into a shocked silence. "If the Ulaid have a good chance of regaining Tara, we'll join with them of course. But if this usurper, whoever he is, looks strong enough to keep the kingship, we'll support him. I'll be in a grand position myself, bringing in a band of the Fíanna."

Finn's men were exchanging looks of astonishment. Even Goll was uncertain, caught off balance. "Feircus," he murmured, shaking his head as if the world was moving too fast for him.

Then one decisive voice spoke up. "This band of Fíanna is on its way to Tara right now," said Finn Mac Cool.

Moving swiftly, Huamor blocked the doorway with his body and outstretched arms. "I think not, you're staying here. I have a clanful of good fighting men to hold you by force if you try to refuse my generous offer of winter quarters."

"If he has as many men as all that," Conan said behind his hand to Finn, "why did he need to send for us?"

"I think you exaggerate," Finn told Huamor. "Your numbers of fighting men must be low or you wouldn't have requested help from Feircus. But even if you had nine nines outside your door right now, you couldn't hold us." His hand was a blur across his chest. Then the point of his shortsword was pressed into Huamor's throat while the air still hissed with the sound of the blade being drawn from its scabbard.

Huamor's eyes bulged.

Several of the women gave soft little shrieks, and they all moved back against the walls. Red Ridge and the fénnid were quickly on their feet, looking from one to the other, wondering if Huamor would fight, wondering if Finn would kill him.

Only Iruis remained seated. He helped himself to Cael's abandoned cup and sat watching with relish as someone at last stood up to his father.

Huamor thought of the knife in his own belt.

Finn read the thought on his face. "Don't," he said softly, pressing his sword point deeper.

The two men locked eyes with the blade between them.

"We're leaving," said Finn Mac Cool.

Huamor was no coward. But whatever he saw in Finn's level gaze was profoundly discouraging.

"Go, then," he said at last. "If you feel that way, it would be wrong to hold you."

"Not wrong, impossible." When Huamor's shoulders slumped, Finn slid his sword back into its sheath. The hilt guard met the metal rim of the scabbard with an audible click, the loudest sound in the room except for the crackling of the fire.

"Before we go," Finn told Huamor, "put what you owe in my hand."

"What I owe?"

"For our services. You requested the Fíanna and we came. Now I must carry your payment back to the king. The king of Tara doesn't supply warriors for free."

"What king of Tara, you young fool? You don't even know who he is now. You've missed a tremendous opportunity to be on the winning side by waiting with me until—"

"The payment," Finn said with no inflection.

Iruis spoke up. "Give it to him, Father. Give him what he earned by protecting me. I would be a hostage, or perhaps even dead, but for him and his band."

Huamor glowered at his son, but he said over his shoulder to the nearest woman, "Give Finn Mac Cool a silver cup, then."

"Not enough," responded Finn in that flat voice Huamor was beginning to know.

"Two, then," the chieftain said irritably, switching his scowl from Iruis to Finn.

"Not enough."

Iruis laughed. "At last! Someone who appreciates my worth!"

Huamor rounded on his son. "You stay out of this! If you hadn't gone up on Black Head on your own like a careless cowherd . . ." In exasperation he began grabbing cups and thrusting them at Finn until the other announced, "That's enough, Huamor. Don't impoverish yourself. Just give us a sack to carry this lot in, and we're gone."

"Listen here to me, Finn," Iruis said. "If you ever return to the Burren, remember my promise of hospitality."

"Have nothing to do with these people," a bitter Huamor advised his son. "They're little better than robbers themselves."

"It's an honest debt, Father. If we weren't so tightfisted with Ceth and his people, perhaps they—"

"That's enough!" Huamor snapped.

Leaving the lodge, Finn and his men stepped into clamping cold. Spiteful clouds lurked above the Barren. A clatter of sleet mixed with rain passed over them, dwindled, promised to come again.

Red Ridge ran after them. "Wait, Finn!"

Finn paused just inside the gate. "What is it?"

"I can't leave here until after Lannat's wedding in the spring, but then I want to join the Fíanna. If I come to you, will you train me?"

"I don't know where I'll be. If Feircus is dead, everything's changed."

"Wherever you are, I'll find you. There may be another king at Tara, but whoever he is, he'll want an army, and you'll be with them. Will you take me?"

Finn's eyes warmed. "If I'm alive and if I'm still in the Fíanna, I will."

Satisfied, Red Ridge turned and trotted back to the lodge. Finn and his men set off eastward. Lugaid carried a woollen bag clanking with silver cups. Occasionally he opened the neck of the bag and peered inside, just to assure himself they were still there.

Wind beat against their backs, which were protected by the shields slung over their shoulders. They marched stolidly, ignoring cold and discomfort.

Goll moved closer to Finn. "Would you really have used your sword on Huamor?" he wondered aloud.

"I had no intention of letting him hold us."

"But he's a chieftain, Finn."

"A chieftain pledged to Feircus, who is reputedly dead. Where does that leave Huamor? If I killed him, who'd punish me? The more important question is, who killed Feircus?"

Goll rubbed the scarred skin of his forehead, massaging the numbed, puckered flesh between thumb and forefinger. After all these years he still could not accept the lack of sensation, but must pinch and pull at his face, trying to force life to return to nerves long dead. "I don't know, Finn. It could have been anyone. There was bad feeling over the Ulaid taking control of Tara. And Feircus's men made matters worse, swanning around the place and insisting that Ulidia was so much better than any other part of Erin. Feircus did the same. He made a lot of enemies in a short time."

"Including you?"

"I wouldn't call myself his enemy."

"Though he stripped you of command of the Fíanna?"

"It was inevitable he'd want one of his own to lead the army."

"If Feircus really is dead, Goll, that could mean there'll be another commander needed."

Goll almost smiled. "Perhaps Feircus was killed by some of my old friends who were loyal to the Son of the Wolf. If that's the situation, I could be Rígfénnid Fíanna again myself." But he said it without real hope.

He trudged along in silence for a time, feeling his age. Then he spoke again. "Tell me something, Finn. When we get to Tara, will you give those silver cups to the king no matter who he may be?"

He's testing me, Finn thought. Goll likes to play games. Any answer might be the wrong answer.

Making sure Goll noticed, Finn put his thumb in his mouth. Wearing an intent expression, he chewed on it for a while. When he withdrew it, he promptly asked Goll, as if the question had been suggested to him, "What would you do?"

Goll started to answer, hesitated, inhaled, drawing back his reply for rethinking.

Finn Mac Cool was a riddle Goll had yet to solve, a game whose rules he did not yet understand.

There was no doubt he was an exceptional athlete. He'd proved it once to join the Fíanna, and again to qualify as an officer. He was intelligent as well—and surprisingly adept at poetry. He could not only recite the twelve basic poems required for initiation into the Fíanna, he could also compose poetry, which none of the others attempted to do.

Finn Mac Cool was suspended between two contradictory aspects. Warrior and poet. Could a man be both?

And what sort of man would he be?

In the time Goll had been observing Finn with more than casual interest, he had seen him go from merry youth to cold, hard man and back again in the flick of an eye. Finn was deadly with his weapons, but would stop in the middle of a march to stare in delight at a cloud formation. What did that mean?

This latest ploy of his with the thumb might be just a gambit to lay claim to more wisdom than he possessed.

Or it might—just might—be a demonstration of magic.

Goll did not want to believe it was magic. He did not want to believe in anything other than himself and his weapons. But he had lived his life in Erin and had seen magic before.

"What would I do?" he repeated, stalling for time. It would be dangerous to lie if Finn had access to the truth. "Let me tell you something, Finn. Do you know why I'm still alive? When Feircus overthrew the Son of the Wolf, he could have had me killed. As your father was killed."

Finn nodded expressionlessly.

"In Erin," Goll went on, "loyalty has always gone to the man. I broke the pattern. When Feircus seized the kingship, I went to him straightaway, hard though it was for me, and declared my loyalty to the kingship itself. No matter who held it."

"Did he believe you?" Finn asked with a slight smile.

"He must have done, he let me live. He demoted me, but at least I can still hunt and lie with women and play chess. If I'd been a bold lad your age, I might have done something rash. But I kept my head, in more ways than one.

"That's why I complimented you for having an old head on young shoulders. You're being equally wise, breaking the cycle of vengeance. Any other man would have sought the blood of Clan Morna to pay for Cuhal's blood, but . . . ." Goll stopped talking. There had been no change of expression on Finn's face, yet something had altered. Perhaps the set of his shoulders. Perhaps the air that surrounded him. Something had changed. Dangerously.

Goll swiftly moved the conversation back to the original point. "To answer your question, Finn, I would hand over that silver to whoever holds Tara now and pledge loyalty to the kingship. In just those words."

Finn put his thumb back in his mouth and assumed a listening expression. After a while, he said, "Let's see who the king is first, shall we?"

They travelled by alternately walking and running. Fénnidi walked by swinging their legs from the hip with minimal bending of the knee, and when they ran, they used a ground-eating trot they could maintain for half a day at a time. Their ability to cover distances was legendary.

Ordinarily they would have sung while walking. People thrilled to the sound of the male music of passing companies of the Fíanna chanting paeans to heroism and freedom. Such lusty songs played no small part in encouraging new recruits. But today no one felt like singing. They were edgy, uncertain. Conversation was desultory.

"Finn," Goll mused, "did it ever occur to you that Huamor might have known in advance someone would try to overthrow Feircus? His problem with the outlaws could have been just an excuse he used to get some of the Fíanna in his possession. Pawns to enhance his prestige with whoever won Tara. A clever move, that."

Finn was taken aback. The possibility had not occurred to him. "Could be," he said noncommittally.

He began subtly edging away from Goll. The older man's experienced cynicism made him feel raw, unfinished, his youth and bravado no match for years of successful games-playing on the twin battlefields of war and politics. Finn knew he needed Goll Mac Morna. But he was not comfortable with him. Goll had once been Rígfénnid Fíanna and would, in Finn's mind, forever wear an invisible but disquieting mantle of authority.

Shadowed by his hounds, Finn drifted across the line of march until he fell into step beside Lugaid instead. "Run now," he ordered.

The fían sped across an Erin divided into countless clan holdings occupied by extended families. The clan chieftains paid tribute in the form of goods and services to a *ríg tuatha*, or tribal king, who was responsible for a confederation of several clans. Such responsibility was based partly on blood and kinship, but largely on territory. There were almost two hundred tribal kings. Some tribes were subordinate to others, but all owed tribute to their provincial kings. The west was ruled by a Connachta overlord; the Erainn held Muma in the south; the king of the Ulaid dominated the north; the east was under the control of the Laigin.

The central province of Míd was ruled from Tara ever since Conn of the Hundred Battles, originally a Connachta prince, had established himself there and attempted to claim sovereignty over and tribute from all other kings. Such a claim was, of course, frequently disputed down the years.

Warriors of the Fíanna were drawn from subjugated tribes. Both Clan Baiscne and Clan Morna had long since been conquered and forced into submission, and were now a source of spear carriers for dominant warlords. The most that men of such clans could hope for was to rise to positions of importance within the army, as they were shut out of the ruling class.

When a man was initiated into the Fíanna, his clan loyalties were transferred to his rígfénnid, and through him to the Rígfénnid Fíanna and the king. This placed the Fíanna beyond the bounds of structured society. Many considered them outcasts; they preferred to think of themselves as possessing a unique freedom. No longer subject to familial obligations, they ranged Erin as nomads, answerable only to their officers and king.

To reach Tara, Finn and his men would climb hills rounded like the backs of crouching beasts, force their way through almost impenetrable forests, traverse fertile valleys jealously guarded from sprawling hill forts, squelch through sodden emerald moss, wade glittering, peaty streams, subsist on their own hunting and foraging, and endure whatever weather they met.

"It's stopped raining!" Cael rejoiced.

"That only means it will begin again," Conan grumbled.

When they camped for the night, Finn slept a little apart from the others. If he cried in his sleep—as he sometimes did—he wanted no one to know.

The next day, a reluctant ferryman was forcibly reminded that it was a privilege to pole members of the Fíanna across the Shannon. Donn's knife pressed gently against his throat proved quite persuasive.

Once across the great river, they set off northward along its bank, meaning to intersect the Tara-bound road that ran close by the Hill of Uisneach. They had been following the river for some time when Finn halted abruptly. "What's that sound?"

The others paused to listen to a muffled, repetitive thud up ahead. "It's as rhythmic as a drumbeat," murmured Lugaid, intrigued. "Something man-made, I'd say."

"Whoever it is," Cailte remarked, "I hope they have some food on them!"

Weapons at the ready, they advanced. The path had grown wider and was now deeply rutted with cart tracks that made walking difficult. At a signal from Finn, his men fanned out to advance on either side of the trackway itself, shouldering their way through encroaching under-growth, their eyes constantly darting.

Lugaid found himself bobbing his head in rhythm with the strange beat they were following.

The riverbank led them around a forested spur of land, and an unexpected vista opened before them. Tucked into the bend of the river like an infant in the curve of its mother's arm was a man-made structure of unfamiliar design, but obviously the source of the sound. It was a timber building, almost square, erected upon a foundation of boulders fitted against timber pilings sunk deep into the mud of the riverbed.

The thudding sound was not so muffled now. Accompanied by a curious hiss and slap, it echoed along the waterway.

"Did you ever hear anything like that before?" Finn asked Goll.

"Never. Be ready; it could be danger."

Finn grinned. "Is that a promise?"

When they were but a few paces from the building, a door opened and a man stepped out. He was dressed in the simplest long tunic and woven mantle, but around his waist was a swath of cloth in the pattern favoured by the inhabitants of Alba. As soon as he spoke, his accent confirmed his foreign origins.

"What do you want here? Are we attacked?" he cried with some alarm, his eyes on the weapons Finn's band carried.

Cailte, nose wrinkling, replied, "Is that bread I smell baking?"

"It is. This is a mill, and my wife in the dwelling beyond is—"

"A mill?" Lugaid interrupted incredulously. "You mean like a quern, where women grind corn?"

Finn realized there was no danger in this encounter and sheathed his shortsword. His fían did the same. The man from Alba relaxed some-what. "Shall I show you?"

With the fénnidi at his heels, he conducted a tour of his mill, pointing with pardonable pride to the wooden paddles—"Two of them!"—that churned the water diverted from the Shannon. Set horizontally to make full use of the river's force, they turned the vertical shafts that operated the millstones set at their top.

Most of the warriors were quickly bored, but Lugaid was fascinated by the moving parts and insisted on being shown exactly how everything was constructed and what made it work.

Meanwhile, the others found their way to the miller's house nearby and relieved his wife of her day's baking. It was she who told Finn that her family had fled Alba after incurring the wrath of one king or another, and brought with them their craft of milling, setting up a business for themselves in the most peaceful place they could find. "We want nothing to do with kings and their wars," she said repeatedly. "So we've come west, where it's wild."

"All Erin is wild," Finn assured her.

Fergus snorted. "Only the Erin we know," he said under his breath. "Our kings live as richly as anyone's."

As the fían marched away, carrying with them a large sack of flour, Lugaid said to Donn, "What a wonderful life that must be! His own business, his own snug house, a wife, and an oven for baking and children playing underfoot. He has everything a man could want, I'd say.

"When I have to let out my belt, I'd like to have a mill like that. I could ask my uncle to help me build it, he's good at building things. I might even let him work it with me. We're very close, you know. All my family are very close. Were very close," he suddenly amended, remembering that the Fíanna comprised his family now.

Walking just ahead of them, Finn overheard Lugaid's words.

All my family are very close.

The words scalded him.

Father, he thought.

Mother.

Their names lay heavy on his tongue.

Muirinn of the White Throat.

He envisioned a woman's soft hand laid on his arm, and a woman's huge liquid eyes, pleading. Eyes like a deer's eyes, mournful and beautiful. "My beloved son," said the woman in his mind, "my cherished child. My pride. Do this for me. Do the deed that cries out to be done. Uphold the honour of our family. Avenge Cuhal's murder.

"Do it for me, my son.

"My beloved son.

"My cherished son."

That was what she would have said, surely; binding him with the ties of family and clan obligation that gave a child his sense of place in the world. His place with those who would never reject him. *Mother.* Finn's eyes were opaque, reflecting dark clouds.

The countryside had changed since they left the Burren. The stony western rim of Erin gave way to dense oak forests packed with holly and hazel, then to a lush central plain. The wind no longer smelled of the sea, but of earth and grass. The sun began a struggle against the clouds, forcing its way until the sky was a coldly triumphant blue.

Yet winter remained. The leaves clinging to the oaks were brittle, and little live things snuggled deep in their burrows. Even before Samhain, summer was dead.

Finn had driven his band at an unprecedented pace. They did not speak of it to each other, but they were proud. It was done and they had done it together. They were the better for it. They had excelled themselves, following Finn Mac Cool.

Less than half a morning's march from Tara, he signalled a halt. "We'll be there by midday, and you lot look as if you'd been dragged backward through a gorse patch. Go over to that stream and bathe yourselves."

Blamec objected. "The legs are run off me with hurrying, yet now you want me to stop and bathe?"

Finn's eyes danced. "Don't, then. Make no effort to improve your appearance. Go to Tara just as you are, filthy, your hair a bush on your head, looking like the lowest sort of servant, some refugee from the leather-curing pits."

The unfortunate Blamec was forced to stand watching as his companions scrubbed dried mud from their clothes with twists of dry grass. Leaving their garments to air on the bank, they leaped into the icy stream and bathed themselves. Afterward they ran a footrace, naked—Cailte won—to warm and dry themselves, then redressed and took turns braiding one another's hair, each in the pattern specific to his own clan and tribe.

Finn took the longest to prepare.

A few days earlier, he had believed he had the world by the ears.

But now Feircus was dead and someone else occupied Tara, a stranger who probably knew nothing of Finn Mac Cool and would care less. He might be demoted to a common warrior. He might even be expelled from the Fíanna if the new king's clan or tribe were enemies of his own.

He realized he had no control over his future. The only thing he could control on this day, it seemed, was his appearance.

He insisted that Cailte, who possessed the most nimble fingers, braid his hair. Then he tore it apart and had it done again. He scrubbed his teeth with a frayed willow twig and burnished his leather belt on the oily skin of his young forehead. He noticed without surprise that the thumb he had thrust into the well of the Tuatha Dé Danann was completely healed.

He even groomed the shaggy coats of Bran and Sceolaun, who wriggled resentfully as he dragged his bone comb through their coarse hair.

When nothing remained to be done and his band—with the exception of the bedraggled Blamec—gleamed like new metal, Finn led the way back to the road. There he arranged his men in a unit three across and three deep, facing east toward the green ridge on the horizon.

"Carry your shields on your arms and your spears in your hands," he ordered. "We're going to Tara."

5

Almost at once they began encountering armed sentries spaced at intervals along the roadway.

Five roads led to Tara from the distant reaches of Erin. In attempting to establish his superiority to all other kings, Conn of the Hundred Battles had insolently built roads across land claimed by the Ulaid, the Connachta, the Erainn, and the Laigin. Paved in boggy places with peeled logs, the royal roads allowed trading vehicles to reach Tara in all weathers.

But there was no commercial traffic now. Only the widely spaced sentries, who eyed the approaching fían with deep suspicion. "Name yourself and state your purpose!" demanded the foremost, lowering his spear to the ready position.

"Finn Mac Cool. I bring a band of Fíanna to the king."

No flicker of expression crossed the sentry's face. His eyes were dull, almost glassy, and there was a growth of stubble on his jaw, though warriors usually kept their jaws shaved to give more prominence to the mustaches that were their pride. The guard looked decidedly seedy—but his spear was lethal, and he held it pointed straight at Finn for several heartbeats before he waved it aside and indicated the band might pass.

They made it only as far as the next sentry before they were challenged again and the ritual repeated. And with the next. And the next.

"This is humiliating," Finn snarled under his breath to Goll, who was walking just behind him. "They're trying to make us feel small."

"That's the idea," said Goll. "Don't react, don't give them the satisfaction."

"I wish I knew who's up there."

"So do I, but don't ask. Act as if we already know and are assured of a welcome."

As they drew closer to the ridge, they could make out its details more clearly.

Once Tara had been the royal seat of the Tuatha Dé Danann. Known as the Magic People, the *Sídhe,* they were the race the invading Gael had defeated by pitting Iron Age blades against Bronze Age sorcery. According to the poets, the Sídhe had used their mysterious skills to retreat into the physical fabric of Erin rather than be driven out.

And they were still there.

After countless generations, the Gael could still feel the weight of Danann eyes watching them. From earthen mounds of unimaginable antiquity, from thorn trees blooming like perfumed clouds, from dark caves and sombre forests and solitary peaks, the Tuatha Dé Danann watched. And waited for their time to come again.

Their royal palace had long since been replaced by a timber-and-wattle fortress in the Celtic style. A series of kingly strongholds had been built on Tara, each defiantly erected on the ruins of its predecessor. By now the complex included an Assembly Hall, which was also known as the Banquetting Hall on occasion, the House of the King, the Fort of the Synods, various revered graves and monuments, official and private chambers, kitchens, stables, storehouses and sheds, surrounded by ditches and a timber palisade.

As the fían approached, they saw scorch marks on the timber palisade. Attempts had recently been made to breach the walls with fire. The largest burned area had been carelessly patched with bits of planking.

Goll squinted at it with his good eye. "It appears that Huamor was telling the truth."

The road led upward. Tara was not, strictly speaking, a hill, but a long ridge that appeared to be low until one reached the top. Only then was it possible to appreciate Tara as a royal site. The ridge commanded a kingly view of the surrounding plain.

Finn's band passed more guards, weary-looking men with red eyes and set, stony faces. Every guard issued a challenge. None offered a greeting.

They reached the gateway named for the road they had travelled, the Slige Mor. Two massive oaken gates were closed, and a pair of spearmen stood in front of them.

Now, thought Finn. The future is now. He strode forward with Bran on one side and Sceolaun on the other.

Goll Mac Morna followed almost on his heels. The others advanced as a unit.

"I am Fionn son of Cuhal!" Finn called in a forceful voice. "I bring my fían for the Samhain Assembly and ask permission to report to the king!"

The guards eyed him unresponsively. A man came to the edge of the palisade, peered down, then vanished from sight.

"It's too quiet," Goll muttered to Finn's back.

He was right, Finn realized. Usually Tara was a noisy place, bustling with servants and visitors, brehon judges coming and going, children running and shrieking with laughter, traders arriving and departing, musicians playing from dawn till dark.

Now there was no sound but the wind.

Goll moved close to Finn's shoulder. "Don't repeat that bit about being Cuhal's son until you know who's in charge here," he advised.

Finn started to retort that he was proud of Cuhal no matter what, but he caught himself in time. "Good advice," he agreed.

A small door opened in one of the gates just enough to allow a man to poke his head through and speak to the guards. The door slammed shut again. One of the guards said gruffly, "Go in. They're waiting for you."

He and his companion put their shoulders against the gates and pushed them open; the iron hinges, red with rust, creaked.

Conan was looking at the guards. None of them, he decided, were taller than Finn or stronger than Goll or heavier than himself. If he had to, he could kill several of them before they killed him. Or he could run. He would rather run.

Lugaid confided to Madan, "I'm ready this time. I'm not going to stumble over any rocks today."

Fergus Honey-Tongue said, without conviction, "Tara in her glory. Isn't it grand to be here."

Finn and his nine marched through the gates, which promptly creaked closed behind them. Finn had to fight down an urge to look back. He led his men across sheep-cropped grass toward the great Assembly Hall. Banners flew over each of its fourteen doorways. Finn looked from one of them to the next.

"Not that one," Goll advised. "That's the Door of Confrontations. Go around to the other side and enter by the Door of Fidelity."

They circled the rectangular building, which had originally served as a mead-hall for entertaining visiting chieftains. It was, Finn noticed, as quiet within as without. Even more ominous, no guards stood at the doorways. It was like a house of the dead.

He entered through the Door of Fidelity. It took several moments for his eyes to adjust to the gloom inside. No torches burned there. Then he recognized the familiar central aisle, the side aisles, the twelve timber compartments to separate subtle strata of society.

Someone was occupying a bench on the raised dais that dominated the centre aisle. Someone who slumped, as if unconscious.

Finn said over his shoulder to Goll, "Could the king be asleep?"

"He wouldn't dare. It's one of his obligations. The king of Tara has to be awake before dawn and be the last man to sleep at night."

"Maybe that isn't the king, then."

"I am the king," contradicted a groggy voice. "The new king of Tara. And I'm not asleep. Not quite. Come forward, where I can see you."

Neither Finn nor Goll recognized the voice. Leaving his men behind, Finn started forward.

He went up the aisle alone. Only Bran and Sceolaun dared follow.

The figure on the dais remained in shadow. As he drew nearer, Finn felt the weight of its eyes on him. Hair rose on the back of his neck. "Who are you?" he asked in a hoarse croak.

"I am he who returns," the voice replied hollowly.

Goll gasped. "Cormac!"

Finn turned toward him. "Who?"

"Cormac Mac Airt! By the wind and rain, it can be no other. When he was just a boy, he swore he'd return to Tara, and now he has."

"Cormac son of Airt, son of Conn of the Hundred Battles," affirmed the figure on the dais. "Now come forward, young man, so I can identify you."

Finn approached the dais until he and the speaker could see one another clearly.

Cormac gazed at a tall youth with a frame that would be awesome in maturity. Wide, savage cheekbones provided a startling contradiction to the tenderness of the mouth. Cormac was reminded of a face he had known in his childhood, a face that had also been framed by silvery hair. "Who was your father, lad?" he wanted to know.

"I am Fionn son of Cuhal."

Cormac smiled. Though he had survived thirty winters, his eyes glowed with undiminished vigour. A long, strongly modelled nose, long eyelids, and a tapering jaw identified him as a Milesian Gael. His ancestors belonged to a tribe of iron-forging Celts who had invaded Erin from northwestern Spain and conquered the tribes they found there—some of whom were also Celtic—so long ago that history had become legend.

The king's hair and neatly trimmed beard were corn-coloured, just beginning to fade with the years. His large hands lay quietly in his lap like a pair of docile animals, but Finn took note of the exaggerated development of thumb and forefinger that betokened a seasoned sword warrior.

"I didn't know Airt had a surviving son," he said.

"I didn't know Cuhal had a surviving son," Cormac replied.

"My mother was my father's last wife. I was born after his . . . death."

"I was born at the end of my father's life," the king said softly. "Such sons are the rebirth of their fathers."

A lump rose in Finn's throat. He forced words around it. "I was fostered by two remarkable women."

"I was fostered by two men," countered Cormac. "One was a chieftain, the other was the Son of the Wolf. He was trying to win support for his kingship of Tara by fostering every orphan in Míd. But when he finally discovered I was Airt's son, he sent me away into exile. As you can see, however, I have returned." He spoke with quiet satisfaction.

Edging past the hounds, Goll came forward. "So it was you who killed Feircus. I should have known."

"I defeated him in fair battle." Cormac's voice turned cold. "It was no assassination. I know you, One-Eye. You swung your sword for the Son of the Wolf."

"He made me Rígfénnid Fíanna!"

"Indeed." Cormac sound unimpressed. To Finn he said, "Is that a warrior's neck bag you're wearing under that mantle?"

"It is. I belong to the Fíanna," Finn said proudly.

"Fir Bolg," Cormac replied, his tone indicating the vast difference in their social status. "You come from a conquered people, like your one-eyed companion here."

"My father was Rígfénnid Fíanna!" Finn protested.

"Him too? And am I right in assuming you want to be one yourself?"

Finn dropped his eyes. "I, ah, I aspire to whatever position the king of Tara wants for me."

"Look up. Say that again."

Finn looked up. He could see nothing but Cormac's commanding gaze. He fumbled through his knowledge of the tangled loyalties that must surround this man, slipping his thumb into his mouth to buy time. Someone else could tell the king about the Salmon of Wisdom.

Cormac, Finn reminded himself, was Airt's son. But he'd been fostered by Airt's killer. Finn tried to imagine how he would feel if he'd been fostered by Goll Mac Morna. Children frequently invested their loyalty in their foster parents. Fosterage was an institution designed to build clan and tribal alliances, and it was not uncommon for fostered children to become more devoted to their second parents than to their first.

Would Cormac have killed Feircus to avenge the death of his foster father? Or to regain his real father's position as king of Tara? Which paternal relationship mattered to him?

Finn took his thumb from his mouth. "Cuhal my father served Airt your father devotedly," he said. "I aspire to serve you in the same way."

It was the right answer. The king's eyes warmed, though he said, "What a father does cannot be counted to his son's credit. Sons must earn their own reputations.

"It's true I'll want my own commander. The man Feircus had is still out there somewhere, hoping to recapture Tara with his followers. My new Rígfénnid Fíanna will have to face him."

"How much of the Fíanna will give their loyalty to you?" Finn wanted to know.

"Aside from you? I think fénnidi from Connacht and Muma will support me, but I'm not so certain of the easterners. The Laigin influence renders a man untrustworthy in my opinion."

Finn stiffened. He had been born in Laigin territory. "Nor would I trust a Connachta chieftain called Huamor," he warned Cormac. "He'll throw in his lot with whoever wins."

To Finn's surprise, the king laughed. "He will of course. Most of them will, come to that."

"You expect it?"

"I know people, Finn. You can't hope to succeed at anything unless you know something of human nature."

"You haven't succeeded yet," Goll pointed out. "Tara won't be truly yours until the Ulaid withdraw their claim."

"I'm aware of that. You saw the fire damage on the palisade? Feircus's followers sneak up on us and try to burn us out."

Finn enquired, "How secure are your defenses?"

The king studied him thoughtfully for a time, stroking his beard, before answering. "They could be better. In the battle against Feircus we took a lot of casualties. My men who survived are exhausted, and even worse, they're sick. They've been vomiting a lot and it's weakened them. Those who are able to stand guard can do so for only short periods before they have to be relieved. We're stretched very thin."

"That's why it's so quiet here," Goll remarked.

Cormac leaned forward and pinned him with his eyes. "Are you here to spy on me? You served the Son of the Wolf. Have you given your allegiance to my enemies?"

"He's given his allegiance to me," Finn said. "I was made an officer of the Fíanna by the ki . . . by the last king, Feircus, who assigned Goll to travel with me under my command and give me the benefit of his experience."

Cormac said to Goll, "Playing on both sides of the board, are you? I'm surprised Feircus didn't have you killed when he seized Tara."

Finn interjected, "Goll Mac Morna has more lives than a yew tree. But I vouch for him as an honest man, and no spy."

"I don't need you to defend me," Goll snapped.

"It's to this lad's credit," said Cormac, "that he's willing to say a kind word for the man who killed his father. If Cuhal was his father. We can't call it proven."

Finn's cheeks reddened. But he would not be baited. This Cormac is a blunt-spoken man, he thought to himself. Perhaps he appreciates that quality in others. He cleared his throat.

"What about command of the Fíanna?" he asked.

Cormac leaned farther forward on his bench. A beam of wintry light pierced the thatch overhead where it was broken, lighting his face. His flesh sagged with weariness. "What makes a lad like you think he can lead the Fíanna?"

"What makes you think I can't?" Finn shot back boldly.

Cormac stared at him in silence. At last he said, "I'll strike a bargain with you. If you can hold off our enemies until more help arrives, or at least until my men are rested, you'll get a reward. Not the command of the Fíanna, I can't give that to a mere lad. But something appropriate. And you'll have future consideration, of course. Will that satisfy you?"

"It will not. But I'll do it."

Cormac's lips twitched. "Done. You'll guard Tara. How many did you say you brought with you?"

"One band of nine."

Cormac sat up abruptly. "One band? Ten counting yourself? That's all?"

"That's enough," said Finn Mac Cool.

Cormac laughed again, but this time it was a hollow, despairing sound. "Ten of you. Ten. Wonderful entirely." He shook his head. "Step forward, then, and let me at least have a look at each of you before I send you out to die."

One by one the fénnidi approached. Cailte bowed nimbly. Fergus offered a few words of praise. Madan held his neck as straight as he could. Donn and Cael were obviously awestruck. Lugaid saluted the king with grave dignity. Conan tried without success to appear good-natured and affable.

At last only Blamec was left, cloaked in embarrassment and grime.

"Who's that?" Cormac asked. "A servant?"

"I'm a warrior," Blamec sputtered. "The best of the lot."

Cael suddenly found his tongue. "I'm the best!" he cried. "I've killed a hundred men!"

Even Conan laughed.

Cormac made a weary gesture. "Just do what you can. Finn, a man called Fiachaid is captain of my guard. Find him and tell him you'll relieve ten of his men. You can draw any additional weapons you need from him as well."

Finn tapped three fingers to the centre of his forehead in the salute of the Fíanna. Turning, he beckoned to his band to follow as he left by the Door of Confrontations. When he passed Goll, he murmured something.

"You, One-Eye!" Cormac called. "Wait here a moment!" When the others had gone, the king asked, "What did Finn say to you?"

"He said he'd relieve all of them, not just ten."

"Did he now?" Cormac was amused. "I seem to recall that Cuhal Mac Trenmor made incredible claims for himself."

"Cuhal was the worst sort of braggart. He fooled a lot of people, but he never fooled me."

"You didn't like him."

"I hated him. My father hated his father."

"And would you also hate Cuhal's son?"

Finn had just credited Goll with honesty, thus forcing it upon him. "I should," he admitted. "I should hate Finn."

"But you don't." It was a statement, not a question.

"I don't hate him all the time," Goll reluctantly agreed. "I can't. He has a way about him."

"Then go and stand with him, One-Eye, and serve him well."

"My name," said the other frostily, "is Goll Mac Morna."

Cormac yawned. "I know who you are."

Rigid with affront, Goll strode from the hall.

Near the Slige Mor gate, a disbelieving Fiachaid was facing Finn Mac Cool. "Who are you to dismiss me?" he demanded to know.

"Cormac's sent us to relieve you and your men."

"Us? I don't see any relief force. I just see some hulking boys."

"We aren't boys, we're warriors. The king said we could draw additional weapons from you if we wanted."

Fiachaid, a grizzled veteran with clear-cut Milesian features, said condescendingly, "You don't require additional weapons, lad. I see you're all carrying toys already."

Something flickered behind Finn's eyes. "What's that spear you carry?"

"This?" Fiachaid brandished the weapon. It was a javelin with a trifurcated head, reminding Finn of the fishing trident that had been used against him on Black Head. "This," Fiachaid boasted, "is the most deadly spear in Erin. It's modelled on the famous *Gae Bulga* that belonged to Cuchulain. You do know who Cuchulain was, don't you, lad? The greatest warrior Erin ever produced? The invincible champion of the Red Branch? This spear I have is exactly like his."

"That will do nicely," said Finn Mac Cool.

As he emerged from the Assembly Hall, Goll heard a startled cry. He began to run. He found Finn's band gathered near the Slige Mor gate and shouldered his way in among them. They were watching a warrior of Goll's generation who was lying flat on the ground. Finn stood over him, holding up an unusual spear. Bran and Sceolaun crouched nearby, ready if needed.

The man on the ground groaned and tried to sit up. Finn extended a hand to help him. The man flinched back violently.

"Finn hit him," Cailte explained to Goll.

"Hit him so hard he flew like a bird," Fergus elaborated.

Bran barked sharply twice, adding a dog's point of view.

Finn grinned. "Just a small demonstration. I shan't need to repeat it, I trust?" He held out his hand again. This time the man on the ground accepted it, very warily.

Fiachaid got to his feet and stood waggling his jaw between thumb and forefinger, testing for breakage. "What did you hit me with, and you so fast I never saw it coming?"

"Only my fist."

"Only? With a fist like that, you need no other weapon!" Fiachaid winced and spat out two bloody teeth.

Finn turned to Lugaid. "You still have the silver cups?"

"I do of course. You didn't say anything inside about giving them to the king, so I didn't."

"Let me have one of them now, then. Here, Fiachaid, take this and fill it to the brim with the best ale in Tara's stores. You'll feel better after a long drink."

The dazed man looked down at the silver cup Finn thrust into his hands. "Empty it several times," Finn insisted, "and when you've had enough to make you forget the pain, keep the cup."

Several haggard warriors wearing Connacht plaits had by this time joined the watching fían. "Are those your men?" Finn asked Fiachaid.

"They are."

"Where are the rest?"

"Guarding the roads."

"And that's all the men you have?"

"That's all," Fiachaid admitted ruefully. "We took a lot of casualties getting here. And inflicted a lot on the other side!" he added with surfacing pride.

"How about servants? Are there servants at Tara who could be pressed into defending it?"

"Cormac dismissed the servants straightaway. He didn't want anyone at Tara who'd served the Ulaid."

"Wise move," commented Goll Mac Morna.

"Tell me about the enemy," Finn said to Fiachaid.

"They hide at a distance, but somehow they know when we're falling asleep on our feet. Then they rush in and try to breach the walls with fire. If they can't control Tara, they don't want Cormac to have it.

"At first I thought you were Ulaid, in fact," he added. "Until I saw how combed and polished you were, like friends."

Finn shot a meaningful glance at Blamec, whose round cheeks burned scarlet.

"We're not the enemy, Fiachaid. We've come to serve as your replacements. My men and I will guard the approaches to Tara while you sleep."

"Your men?" Fiachaid pivoted slowly, counting. "You have only nine here." He did not repeat the mistake of calling them boys.

"That's all I'll need."

"What's he getting us into?" Donn whispered to Conan.

"Trouble," was the answer.

Fiachaid protested, "You can't guard the royal roads with only nine men!"

"There are ten of us altogether and five roads. It works out perfectly. Lugaid, you and Cael take the Slige Dala from the south. Conan and Fergus, the Slige Mor. Blamec and Donn, the Slige Asal. I want Goll and Madan on the Slige Cualann that runs to the Great Bay on the east. Cailte and I shall guard the Slige Midluachra, since it's most likely any attack will come from the north."

Fiachaid was staring at Finn as if he could not believe his ears.

Goll caught Finn by the arm. "See here, you're going too far this time. No matter how good we are, we can't hold off an entire army."

Finn gestured to Goll to turn his back to the others so they would not be overheard. Then he said in a low, earnest voice, "We won't have to hold off an army, Goll. Fiachaid just told us the other side took heavy losses. They must have done, or they wouldn't wait until Cormac's men are on the point of collapse before they dare attack. And then they sneak up and try to burn Tara rather than attempting face-to-face battle. I'd say there are very few of them left. Fiachaid and the king are so exhausted they don't realize that. And we aren't going to point it out to them."

"You're learning," said Goll Mac Morna.

Fiachaid called irritably, "What are you two mumbling about? I don't much like this. I'm tired, if you must know."

"Of course you're tired," Finn agreed. He beckoned to Fergus Honey-Tongue. "Take care of this good man, will you? Assure him that everything will be all right. Help him get his ale."

Fergus put an arm around Fiachaid's shoulders. "Come with me," he said in a creamy voice that flowed into Fiachaid's ear and bathed his aching brain. "Come with me and put yourself at ease. There's nothing to worry about now, you'll see. We'll take care of things while you rest. Everything will be fine, just fine."

Almost without realizing it, Fiachaid let Fergus lead him away. Donn trailed after them, curious to see the stores.

"Fergus can talk a badger out of its sett," Finn remarked to Goll.

"I still think you're taking a dangerous risk."

"That's my decision," Finn reminded him briskly. "I'm going to have the least-exhausted of Fiachaid's men start beating things together, banging metal, shouting, making noise. We'll build fires outside so it looks as if people are already here preparing the Samhain feasts. The Ulidians who're watching Tara will think a crowd has arrived for the Assembly. That should discourage them from further attack.

"Then in a few days the lie will be truth and the people will arrive in earnest. It's a great piece of luck that we were the first here. When the others come, they'll find Cormac in firm possession of the kingship and—Och, Donn, there you are. Where did you go off to just now?"

"While Fergus and Fiachaid were getting the ale, I checked the food supplies, such as they are. Look at this." He held out a lump of dark bread. "This is what they've been eating."

"It looks all right to me."

"It isn't. I know food, and this is spoiled in some way. It doesn't smell right and it doesn't crumble right. No wonder Cormac's men are sick. We'd do better to go hungry."

"We can live off the land as always," Finn said cheerfully. "It's only for a few days, until the cartloads of tributes start to arrive. People send the best of their harvest to the king at Samhain, you know. Prepare yourselves now, and go to your posts. We have an interesting few days ahead of us."

"What does he mean by that?" Blamec wondered aloud.

"*Serious* trouble," prophecied Conan.

6

 HE AWOKE DISORIENTED, IN COLD AND DARK. FRAG-
ments of bad dreams fluttered through his mind like birds of
ill omen.

"Mother?"

He reached out blindly, groping.

Finn's fingers touched the coarse coat of the hound that lay stretched
beside him. Bran responded with an almost feline mewling deep in the
throat. The man clutched the loose skin of the dog's neck and held on
tightly.

I'm not alone, he assured himself gratefully. Bran's here.

I'm not alone.

But did I cry out?

He could almost hear an echo.

What did I say? Did anyone hear me?

He sat up in the dark. Straw rustled, and there was the pungent odour
of dried horse dung. Someone snored nearby.

Memory began to return in shards and slivers.

Gathering his men and leading them to . . . to the almost empty
stables. Making careless beds for themselves, straw flung down in heaps.
Flinging themselves on top of the straw, uncaring, too weary for any
ritual washing.

Someone—Conan?—saying, "You look like death in a bowl, Finn.
And that blood on you stinks."

The hounds crowding close, sharing their warmth.

Sleep. Sinking into oblivion for an indeterminate time. And the
dreams coming . . .

Were they fantasies? Or memories? In Finn's mind, the distinction
was becoming blurred. When he told a tale, he convinced himself of its
reality so his listeners would believe. In his imagination, he envisioned

events so vividly he lived them, with the result that now his brain could hardly differentiate between fact and fiction. Both had the ring of truth for him.

Muirinn of the White Throat was my mother, he reminded himself sternly, holding on to what he knew to be reality. And Cuhal Mac Trenmor was my father. There's no doubt of that much. Clan Morna killed him before I was born, and then Muirinn . . .

. . . then my mother . . .

What did she do? What did she *really* do?

He shook his head savagely, trying to isolate the facts. But they eluded him. In his heart, he wanted the fictions. They shielded him from the truth.

Nearby, someone sighed. Someone else farted. As Finn focussed his eyes, he recognized huddled shapes on the straw.

He got to his feet quietly. Bran rose with him. Sceolaun came from his other side. The three picked their way among the sleeping men and left the stable. They emerged into an icy wind. The winter that had begun unseasonably early was chilling Tara.

But the royal seat was bustling with activity. Fiachaid's men were very much in evidence, as were nobles and tradesmen and numerous servants. Wicker-sided carts piled high with goods were entering by the open gateways, often accompanied by chieftains astride shaggy horses.

Finn noticed a small cluster of men by the Fort of the Synods, talking with someone in a crimson cloak. He blinked uncomfortably. His eyes were crusted with matter, the lashes sticking together.

He rubbed them and took a second look. The knot of men wore tunics dyed with saffron, and woollen cloaks speckled or striped in blue, red, green, purple, and white. Taken with the yellow of the tunics, these made up the six colours that a judge, a noble brehon, was entitled to wear. For further identification once they removed their cloaks, the brehons wore conical leather caps fitted close to the skull.

But the man to whom they were talking needed no identification. Cormac Mac Airt would always look like a king.

He stood erect, no longer exhausted. Beneath a short, fitted coat of leather he wore a linen shirt embroidered with gold thread. Tight-fitting trews showed the shape of his legs, his feet were shod in soft leather. Slung around his shoulders was a heavy fringed cloak, fastened with a huge gold brooch set with gemstones. On one arm he carried a small, round shield, painted bright red, with stars on its face and gold and silver animals pursuing one another around the rim—a ceremonial extravagance rather than a protection in battle.

In Finn's eyes, Cormac shone like a red stag seen against grey limestone.

Cormac looked up, noticed Finn, and beckoned to him.

Finn approached with uncharacteristic diffidence. He was rumpled and filthy. He hated having brehons see him like that, but even more, he wished he had bathed before the king saw him.

The king's smile was uncritical, however. "Finn Mac Cool!" he called warmly. "We were talking about you. I was just telling the judges of your great and astonishing deed in defense of Tara. I wanted their opinion as to the rights and prerogatives such valour deserves."

"Rights?" Finn's forehead crinkled. "Prerogatives?" Suddenly he realized he could smell dried blood on himself. His clothing was stiff with it. "Valour?"

"Don't concern yourself now, we'll talk about it later. I'm sure you'd like some heated water and a chance to bathe. And food and drink. Fortunately, tributes have begun arriving, so I can offer you something better than that dangerous bread your man warned us about. Go and clean yourself, and I'll have a meal brought to you. We're still somewhat short of people to fetch and carry, but once I'm properly established here, nothing will be too good for Finn Mac Cool."

Obviously something extraordinary had happened. Something Finn's tired brain did not yet remember.

Mumbling thanks, he escaped the king as quickly as he could and returned to the stable. Searching among the sleeping men, he found Goll first, but he did not want to question Goll.

He almost stumbled over Cael.

Finn bent down and shook him by the shoulder. "Cael! Wake up at once and come outside with me. I have to talk to you."

"Hunh? Wha?" Straw rustled.

"Outside, I said. And be quiet about it."

Cael dragged himself to his feet and stumbled out of the stable in Finn's wake. They turned a corner and paused beneath the thatched overhang, which was so low Finn had to duck his head.

"What happened, Cael? The king claims I performed some great and astonishing deed. He's been talking to the brehons about special rewards. But what did I do? Do you know? When I try to remember, my brain fills with fog. I must be very tired."

"We're all tired," Cael replied, stifling a yawn. "But I know what you did. I didn't see it, of course. None of us did. I wish we had. But you told us. It was magic, what you did. No one else could have done it."

"Done what?" Finn almost screamed at him.

"Killed the monster, of course."

Finn gaped. "Killed the what?"

"The fire-breathing monster Cormac's enemies sent to burn Tara,"

Cael said patiently. "You killed it, thanks to your very special talents, and brought back one of its three heads to show the king."

Finn almost laughed. He had one hand half-raised to punch Cael on the arm in appreciation of the joke.

Then a memory surfaced, rising through the layers of his mind, distorted as an image glimpsed through water.

He saw himself approaching a lodge. Cormac was inside. He saw himself strutting toward the king, displaying something.

Memory returned with a rush.

Finn and his band had guarded the approaches to Tara while Fiachaid's men recovered. As Finn had expected, there was no further attack. There was only wintry wind and silvery silence and time passing. The remaining Ulidians, if they were watching from a distance, had been deceived by Finn's ruse. Or, more likely, they had simply pulled out and gone home as the weather worsened. And Huamor and those like him would not challenge Cormac until the spring—if at all.

But the king would need Finn's band for only a few days. Then they would lose their particular value.

As they relieved Fiachaid's men, Donn had passed a warning. "Rest and recover, but don't eat any of the bread. It's what made you sick, it's spoiled."

The fían had taken up their watch, which proved exhaustingly uneventful. They regretted there was not at least a token attack. Until the third morning they had nothing to do but stand leaning on their spears, watching the horizon, talking desultorily to each other, and shifting legs as they snatched moments of rest without ever lying down.

When Finn felt certain that Fiachaid's men must be recovered, he sent Cailte back to Tara to request a change of guard.

Then destiny came toward him in the form of a solitary figure slouching down the road from the north.

"Not a pretty sight," Finn commented to his hounds as the figure approached. Sceolaun whined agreement.

The stranger's head was huge, grossly malformed, and bore the vacant expression of a congenital idiot. His face was painted with chevrons of blue and ochre in an archaic style only a few Ulidian warriors still affected. With his bandy legs and lurching gait, the man looked more like an afterthought than a human being.

But he was approaching Tara with a blazing torch in his hand.

Finn hefted his spear threateningly. His other hand dropped to his sword hilt. "What do you want?" he challenged.

The idiot kept coming. A drool of spittle hung from his sagging lower lip. He was an obvious expendable, a last gesture of contempt on the part of Feircus's men when they pulled out. They expected him to be killed. Although he probably could not understand, his was a suicide mission.

Finn felt a pang of pity. "Turn around and go back. There's nothing but death for you here."

The man grinned senselessly and lifted his torch. He swung it in a wide circle above his misshapen head. Greasy smoke stained the clear air.

Sitting on their haunches beside Finn, Bran and Sceolaun watched this performance with interest.

"Turn back I said!" Finn's voice rose.

The idiot paid no attention. He walked toward Finn, whirling the torch faster and faster. He might do anything, Finn realized. There was no reasoning with a head that held no mind.

In the instant Finn's hand tightened on his sword hilt, both dogs were on their feet, hackles lifted, fangs bared.

Mimicking them, the idiot stretched his foolish grin wide enough to reveal the broken stumps of rotted teeth. Then he hurled the torch straight at Sceolaun.

In one bound, Finn interposed his body between the torch and his hound. As he leaped, he hurled the spear. His sword was drawn before his feet touched ground again.

Both weapons found their target.

The torch glanced harmlessly off Finn's shoulder.

Bran had leaped when he did. Finn had to grapple the dog aside to get to his victim. When he pulled sword and spear from the idiot's body, life left with them.

Finn stared down at the paint-bedaubed corpse. He felt contempt for those who had used the creature so callously.

"Back, Bran! Leave him in peace now. And you, Sceolaun—are you burned? Och, that's good, it never touched you."

Finn busied himself stamping out the circle of flames that was spreading from the fallen torch. Then after extinguishing it as well, he went back to the dead man, moved by pity to cover the corpse with a cairn of stones.

Poor sad monster, he thought, looking down. What sort of a life did you have, with your head twice as big as a . . .

. . . poor sad *monster?*

A slow smile spread across the face of Finn Mac Cool.

He returned to Tara covered with soot and blood. In a net fashioned of weeds, he carried a bulky object. He met Fiachaid's men coming to relieve him and they stared curiously, but he did not explain.

"Where's Cormac Mac Airt?" he asked.

"In the House of the King. But what's that you've got there? Is it—"

Finn strode past them.

He found Cormac in a rather dilapidated wattle-and-timber structure substantially unchanged since the reign of Conn of the Hundred
Battles. Built like a clan chieftain's lodge, it was circular, with a conical
thatched roof extending almost to the ground, and the customary central firepit.

The pit had not been cleaned out since Feircus, and the fire was
smoking badly. As he ducked through the low doorway, Finn could just
make out Cormac on the other side of the fire, trying to mend a shoe by
the light of the flames.

"That's no task for a king," Finn said by way of greeting. "My Madan
can do that for you. He can repair anything."

"You have a useful collection of men," Cormac replied, squinting at
him. "The one called Donn was here a while ago, offering to cook me a
meal when he'd had some sleep."

"You'll never eat better. Donn can make a tasty meal out of hares'
ears and hazelnut shells."

"Is that what you've brought me?" Smiling, Cormac pointed with his
shoe. "A bundle of hares' ears and hazelnut shells?"

"This?" Finn said with elaborate casualness. "Och, this is just the
head of a fire-breathing monster that's been trying to destroy Tara."

Cormac dropped the shoe. "What did you say?"

"Monster." Finn held it up, being careful to keep the smoke of the
fire between himself and the king. He peeled back just enough of the
weedy netting to reveal a smear of vivid blue and two glaring eyes beneath a bulbous forehead of unnatural proportions. "I destroyed this
thing with magic," he claimed, "after a ferocious battle. I cut off one of
its three heads to show you. The other heads were ruined. That spear that
Fiachaid gave me does considerable damage. I couldn't bring you trophies so mutilated, it would be an insult. And now that you've seen this
one, I can dispose of it too. It's leaking all over me."

Before Cormac could stop him, he flung the head in its net of very
dry weeds into the heart of the flames.

An horrific stench filled the lodge.

"By the sun and stars!" cried an appalled Cormac. "Did you have to
do that? I'm trying to live here!"

"I'm sorry." Finn contrived to look abashed. "I didn't stop to think.
I've carried that disgusting thing so far I just wanted to be rid of it.
Perhaps we should go outside, where we can breathe?" He turned and
led the way, confident the gasping king would follow.

In the firepit, the burning head had swiftly become a grotesque and
blackened ruin.

"Now I remember!" Finn said to Cael. "The fire-breathing monster.
I do remember!"

"I should think you would. Three heads, you said."

"Three heads," Finn echoed.

"I wish I'd seen it myself. But I did see the king after you showed him one of the heads, and he looked quite shaken. Can you describe the monster for me, Finn? How big was it, exactly?"

"Och . . . immense." Finn framed vague shapes with his hands. "As big as three oxen."

"That big?" Cael raised his eyebrows.

"Or maybe only two oxen," Finn amended quickly, calculating the actual size of the head and its relative scale to a body. "Two small oxen. But it was a monster right enough."

"I believe you," Cael assured him, "and so does the king, obviously. Perhaps he'll give you woven clothes! Just think, Finn; warriors are allowed to wear only one colour and officers two, but you might even be allowed to wear three!"

Finn snorted. "That may excite you, but my ambition doesn't end with being given the right to wear three colours."

Meanwhile, the rest of his band awoke, yawned, scratched, cursed straw and fleas and each other, and emerged from the stable. Donn appropriated the sack of flour the miller had given them and went off in search of the ovens. Finn gathered the others and took them to Cormac, offering them as temporary staff.

"As soon as I deem it appropriate, I'll send for my family and household servants," Cormac told them, "but until then, I'll appreciate whatever help you're able to give us."

Behind his hand, Lugaid whispered to Goll, "Should we give him those silver cups now?"

"Not until Finn says so," the one-eyed man replied sternly.

Because his lodge still stank of the burned head, Cormac sent Cailte to ask Fiachaid to meet him outside. They spoke together beside the mound known as the Grave of Taya, a Milesian ancestress who had made the long-ago voyage from Galicia, in northwestern Spain.

In the crisp wintry air, Fiachaid's emotions ran from cold astonishment to hot anger. The astonishment resulted from hearing Cormac relate the details of Finn's destruction of the giant.

"That's absolutely preposterous!" Fiachaid exploded. "You can't seriously believe that . . . that big lad killed a fire-breathing monster!"

"I didn't say I believed it," Cormac replied. "But hundreds will. He's remarkably convincing."

"I never heard of a fire-breathing monster in Erin, not with three heads or one head or no heads. He made it up."

"Very likely," the king agreed. "But that's how reputations are made. According to those who hated him, Cuhal Mac Trenmor was a swaggering braggart—but most men loved him. He talked big and he made his followers feel big. He must have had in some small measure the quality young Finn has by the armful. The ability to excite."

"But I always expected—"

"I know what you expected, Fiachaid. You're obedient and trustworthy, and of my own race. All admirable qualities. But Finn Mac Cool is incredibly audacious. He'll be like a vivid banner proclaiming the kingship of Cormac Mac Airt. People will notice him, and talk about him, and his lustre will reflect favourably on me. I need him, Fiachaid. I need him . . . for a while."

At nightfall Finn and his band were summoned to the Assembly Hall. Under Madan's direction, the broken roof had already been patched. Fresh rushes carpeted the approaches. The light of hundreds of beeswax candles glowed from the open doorways.

"This time," Goll Mac Morna suggested, "I think we should enter by the Door of Heroes."

"I already planned to," replied a scrubbed and burnished Finn Mac Cool.

"What about those silver cups? Lugaid still has them."

"I know. Bring them with us, but say nothing about them."

They marched into the hall, a column of nine with Finn a few steps in front. His hounds followed at his heels, putting a space between himself and his men.

Cormac was waiting on the dais. Brehons stood to either side of him. Finn felt the scrutiny of judicial eyes. These were the men who interpreted the law, the agreement of an entire population as to what controls they would accept. The mightiest king was not as powerful as Brehon Law.

The faces of the judges were professionally stern. Finn felt misgivings. Even if Cormac had believed his story, would brehons be taken in? Seeing him up close like this, would they in their wisdom look through the impressive exterior and find the boy hiding beneath?

He knew only one way to shield himself. Throwing back his head and squaring his shoulders, he cried in his loudest voice, "I am Fionn son of Cuhal, slayer of monsters!"

His eyes dared anyone to contradict him.

A thundering silence descended on the hall. In that silence, Finn thought he could hear beetles busy in the thatch overhead.

Bran pressed close to him and pushed a cold, comforting nose into his palm.

Cormac folded his arms across his chest and leaned back on his bench. "Do you know how the Son of the Wolf discovered I was Airt's son?" he asked with apparent irrelevance. "I'll tell you. I gave myself away."

Finn thought, I don't like the sound of this.

Cormac continued. "At the Great Assembly when I was just a boy, I made a judgment too wise for my years, settling a dispute that had baffled the brehons. Those who heard me claimed they heard the echo of my father's voice. Airt was famed for wise judgments—a talent the Son of the Wolf lacked, I might add."

Finn nodded, wondering where this was leading.

"You have given yourself away," said Cormac Mac Airt.

Finn's stomach turned over, sickeningly.

"If there was any doubt before, I have none now. You are the son of Cuhal Mac Trenmor. Only Cuhal's son would toss a severed head into my firepit and announce he'd slain a monster.

"I've found my Rígfénnid Fíanna."

Stunned, Finn could only stare at the king.

After a moment's silence, his men burst into cheers. Goll was the first to pound the new commander of the Fíanna on the back, so heartily he almost knocked him down. The others clustered around, shouting congratulations and punching whatever parts of Finn's body they could reach.

From his bench, Cormac watched.

The brehons watched with him.

When the excitement died down, the king raised one finger. A brehon immediately began to recite, "As commander of the army of Tara, you are entitled to three fringed woollen mantles, three linen tunics, three pairs of leather boots, a bronze helmet with a flange to guard the nape of your neck . . ."

Finn stopped listening.

It seemed to him that he stood bathed in a shaft of golden light.

This is a dream. This is a tale I've told myself.

But Bran's cold nose was pressing against his hand again, and the ground was reassuringly solid beneath his feet.

The brehon droned into silence. Cormac took over in a crisp voice. "Once I've consolidated my kingship, we'll improve your situation," he said to Finn. "My Rígfennid Fíanna must have great prestige; it reflects on me. You'll be the most honoured man among your people, Finn Mac Cool . . . so long as you serve me to my satisfaction."

If there was a warning implicit in that final phrase, Finn did not notice. Goll Mac Morna did. He tensed, his mind racing as he considered what this might mean for him.

A new game was beginning.

Finn's own mind was beginning to function again. He turned to

Lugaid. "Give me that sack now." Carrying the sack to Cormac, he took out Huamor's silver cups one at a time, holding them up so the light of the king's beeswax candles would reveal the craftsmanship of their design.

"My men and I earned these for you. There was one more of them, but I gave it to Fiachaid as a token of respect."

Cormac's lips twitched. "That was clever of you."

"I wasn't trying to be clever. The gesture was sincere," Finn insisted.

"I'm sure it was. But I'd thank you not to give away any more of my property without asking me first."

Finn tapped his fingers on his forehead.

A rough banquet was served to the warriors of Tara, old and new, in honour of the occasion. Donn oversaw the cooking. Fiachaid and his men took part with stiff formality at first, though as the evening wore on and the ale flowed, they became jollier.

"There sits a disappointed man," Goll told Finn, indicating Fiachaid with a nod of his head. "I know the signs. He thought he'd be given command of the Fíanna, even though he's not one of us. Watch your back with that one."

"Are you saying I should watch my back every time someone else is disappointed?"

Goll shrugged. "Take it any way you will."

Finn got up, collected his new spear from the stack of weapons the warriors had left in a corner of the hall, and carried it to Fiachaid. "This is yours, I believe," he said. "I thank you for the loan of it."

Fiachaid accepted the trifurcated spear. Its iron head was held to its shaft with thirty brass rivets, each gleaming like a star from fresh polishing. "I thought you meant to keep this," he said.

"You were mistaken. It isn't mine, it's yours."

Fiachaid hesitated. Then, like Iruis with the deer's hide, he handed the object in question back to Finn. "It's yours now," he said.

The warriors, old and new, cheered him roundly.

As entertainment for the evening, Finn told again the tale of the killing of the monster, complete with embellishments.

It was a grand night for storytelling. The ubiquitous rains of winter ceased for a time, and Tara blazed with torch and candlelight to rival the stars in the wind-scoured sky. The brilliance of the occasion masked the shabbiness of the old buildings. Everyone who could crowded into the Assembly Hall to listen to Tara's new champion. Persons of rank filled the formal compartments, rectangular timber boxes, while lesser beings stood in the aisles or lounged against the walls or peered in through the doorways.

In spite of nightfall, people kept arriving. Next day was the first of the

Samhain Assembly. Each new arrival hurried to the hall, swelling the throng that soon spilled out over the grassy lawns. People who were close enough to hear Finn repeated his words over their shoulders to others behind them, passing the story out into the night.

By the time he finished speaking, Finn's tale had taken on a life of its own. Each tongue had embellished it in the retelling. Those on the fringes of the crowd were informed that a supernatural force, undoubtedly the Tuatha Dé Danann, had entered into a conspiracy with Cormac's other enemies in an effort to reclaim Tara. A magical monster had been sent to burn down the stronghold while Cormac's men slumbered under a magical spell. It was obvious.

Only the new Rígfénnid Fíanna had stood between Tara and the Magic People.

It was a thrilling story. Everyone enjoyed it. When Finn reached the part where he cut off the monster's head and yelled, "My dogs and I were bathed in its foul blood!" Bran and Sceolaun testified with a volley of barking that echoed across the ridge.

If the Tuatha Dé Danann were slumbering in the mounds and mountains beyond, they surely heard the triumphant roar of Finn Mac Cool.

7

EVERYONE WAS TALKING ABOUT HIM. AT FIRST FINN gloried in being the cynosure of all eyes, the centre of excitement. Then it began to embarrass him. He was uncomfortable with such excess.

A shy, wild boy who lived at the back of his skull wanted to run off into the forest and bathe himself in silence.

But Cormac commanded, "Meet each rígfénnid as he brings in his men. Impress them. Show the officers that you're worthy to command them."

So Finn strode forward with his silver hair gleaming and his face set in savage, triumphant lines. He recounted his victories and gesticulated with his shortsword and dared anyone to challenge him.

He told the tale of the fire-breathing monster so many times he forgot he had ever mistaken it for a human idiot sent by the Ulaid.

Unlike the triennial Great Assemblies that were held at Uisneach and Tara and attracted attendance from throughout Erin, Samhain Assemblies were regional, annual events. Local people came together to celebrate the end of the Celtic year and the beginning of the next with games and rituals and feasting.

At the Samhain Assembly, a provincial king's share of the harvest was delivered to him as part of the tributes due him from the tribes in his territory. Resplendent in the Mantle of Assembly that had belonged to his father, and wearing his grandfather's gold thumb ring, Cormac Mac Airt redistributed some of this wealth in return for oaths of loyalty. Gifts were set aside to be sent to important chieftains outside of Míd to win their support as well—a custom originating with Conn of the Hundred Battles.

Meanwhile, territorial brehons adjudicated local disputes in the Fort of the Synods. If a problem was sufficiently complex, it might be held over and presented to the Convocation of All Brehons at the next Great Assembly.

As rígfénnidi brought in their men, the atmosphere grew rowdier. Fénnidi were hard to control at the best of times. There was posturing and challenging between bands, and officers were taxed to their utmost to keep brawling to a minimum. Some decorum must be maintained. In spite of its festive air, the Samhain Assembly was essentially a solemn event, culminating in the Feast of the Dead. Therefore every effort was made to channel fénnid aggressions into sporting competitions as well as single combats judged for skill and style rather than for the amount of blood drawn.

Goll Mac Morna made a point of seeking out arriving officers who had once served under him when he commanded the Fíanna. Before they could ask, he told them with seeming nonchalance, "I'm with Finn Mac Cool now. He's a son of Cuhal Mac Trenmor, you know. Confidentially, that's why this new king named him Rígfénnid Fíanna. It's a political move to gain Cuhal's people to his own cause. An astute manouevre, but very likely temporary. This lad's far too young and inexperienced.

"Anything might happen. You understand. In the meantime, I'll give him the benefit of my advice and my own extensive experience, of course. At the end of the day, there's no substitute for experience, is there?" Goll would nudge with his elbow and wink with his good eye.

The hard-bitten warriors to whom he spoke understood. "Your time will come around again," they assured him.

Meanwhile, Finn was determined to make himself and his fían indispensable. "Cailte, you're to be the king's personal messenger for the duration of the assembly. Later he'll appoint someone else, of course—but make certain that person can never be as good as you were, or as fast.

"Donn," Finn commanded, "you're to examine, personally, all the edibles brought into Tara. When food is prepared for the king, make it your business to be in the kitchens or at the ovens. Add any little touches of your own that will enhance the flavour. When we are no longer here, I want Cormac to miss us.

"Madan, your assignment is to organize a work crew and mend everything that needs mending, no matter how small. Have this place in perfect condition if you can. Grease the hinges, replace worn ropes, do whatever wants doing. Let the king see you taking care of Tara."

Finn told Blamec, "Since you're so argumentative, the best place for you is nearest the arguments. Stand guard at the door of the Fort of the Synods. You might overhear the debates of the judges. You might even learn something.

"As for you, Fergus—you're to greet the dignitaries. Flatter even the

most minor chieftain. Smear honey all over them. Win every possible ally
for Cormac. And if the king hears you doing it, so much the better.

"Cael, go get the burned skull out of the king's firepit and set it up
on a pole just inside the Slige Mor gate. Tell everyone who passes about
the fire-breathing monster, and who destroyed it. And make it sound
good," he added with a wink. "You know how, Cael Hundred-Killer."

Cael grinned with delight.

"Lugaid, I have a serious job for a serious man. Oversee the counting
of the tributes. Let no one think they can cheat Cormac Mac Airt of one
hide or one sack of grain.

"As for you, Conan . . . is there anything you do better than anyone
else?"

"I doubt it," Conan growled.

"Indeed! You doubt! So stay as close to the king as the skin on his
elbow and question everyone who tries to get near him. Let no one within
a spear's throw of Cormac unless you're sure they have a legitimate
reason to be there."

Goll was the last to receive an assignment. "You recognize most of
the people who've come for the Assembly, don't you?" Finn asked him.

"The nobles and warriors. And not a few of the common people, for
that matter," Goll agreed.

"Then stay with me and tell me their names when we see them, as well
as anything else you think I should know about them. I want to be
well-informed."

"There's no substitute for experience," said Goll Mac Morna.

Later that same day, Finn whispered behind his hand, "Who's that
young woman over there, Goll? The one beside the dark man in the
leather apron."

"He's Lochan the smith. She must be one of his daughters."

Round of face and ripe of body, the woman in question had unbound
hair that rippled almost to her knees. Unbound hair.

She also had a dimple in her chin. Finn had never seen a woman with
a dimple in her chin before. "Stay here," he told Goll. Putting on his
most winning smile, he sauntered over to Lochan's daughter.

She was looking the other way.

Stopping in front of her, Finn cleared his throat. "My mother has a
dimple in her chin," he began.

She looked at him then, this extremely tall youth, obviously a few
years younger than herself, who was looming over her and grinning like
a famished wolf. "I remind you of your mother?" she asked coolly.

Finn was taken aback. "That isn't what I meant. I meant . . . my
mother is very beautiful."

"And I'm not?"

Finn looked distressed.

Conan was watching from the doorway of a nearby storehouse. The king and Lugaid were inside, counting a gift of hides. Conan beckoned Goll over to him. "What's Finn doing, Goll?"

"Talking to a woman. You can see that for yourself."

Conan gave a snort of derision. "Finn doesn't know how to talk to a woman. His mother was a deer."

Goll chuckled. "I wish he'd raise his voice. It would be interesting to hear what he's saying."

Finn was saying, "You're very beautiful. As my mother is. That's what I meant." They were awkward, blurted statements.

"Does she have hair like yours, your mother?"

Finn hesitated, searching for a mental image. "Her hair was . . . is . . ."

"More beautiful than mine? Longer? Thicker?"

Finn chewed on the inside of his lip.

"I told you he couldn't talk to women," Conan sniggered to Goll. "Look at him scuffing his toe in the dirt."

In an attempt to begin afresh, Finn said, "I'd like to know your name."

"Why?"

"So I can talk with you."

"Are we not talking now?"

Exasperated, he said, "Do you always answer questions with questions?"

Her eyes sparkled. "I'm famous for it. They call me Cruina of the Questions, can you guess why?"

Meanwhile, Lugaid emerged from the storehouse. "Finn's found a woman," Conan informed him, indicating the pair.

"That shouldn't be hard for anyone who looks like him. Maybe he'll even take a wife."

"I don't think he's ready for a wife. He's having enough trouble making conversation."

Goll said, "You don't take a wife for conversation. A wife involves four generations, clans and property, ancestors and descendants. That's what a wife means."

"I wouldn't mind having a wife," said Lugaid wistfully.

"You? You're a fénnid, a spear target, a man of no property. Sleep with any woman who'll have you," Goll advised, "but forget about wives. A soldier's marriage is good enough for you."

When his official duties were over for the day, Cormac left the Assembly Hall and crossed the lawn to the area marked out for the footraces.

He saw Finn among the spectators and joined him. "Are any of your fían in this race?" he asked.

"My best runner is Cailte, but he'll only challenge the final winner."

"I wouldn't rely on that. He's been running messages for me all day without stopping to draw breath."

"Och, that's barely enough to warm him up. You'll see, he'll be rewarded with the ivy wreath at the end of the day. And . . . ah . . . speaking of rewards . . ."

"Mmmm?" Cormac's eyes were following the runners as they sped barefoot across sheep-cropped grass.

"You promised you'd improve my situation," Finn reminded the king. "What will that mean exactly?"

Cormac turned to look at him. "I just made you Rígfénnid Fíanna. Isn't that enough improvement for a while?"

"I thought there might be . . . something more. Some token, some emblem of the position . . ."

"A gold thumb ring, perhaps?" Cormac said, displaying his. "Or a silver chain? Do you want something that would make a pretty gift for a woman, is that it? Has some woman heated your poker for you?"

Cormac's gift for accurate guesses was disconcerting. Finn dropped his eyes.

"Listen here to me," said the king. "Events have moved very quickly for you, you've run where other men walk. I'll give you your share of whatever we win when the time is right, but for now, I have other concerns. There's the condition of Tara—it's a disgrace. It's falling down around our ears. Then there are the Ulaid. Conn fought them, Airt fought them, I'll have to fight them again too. They've had a taste of it, now they'll want to recapture Tara and strut and swan around. As soon as battle season begins, I mean to make a circuit of Erin, aside from Ulidia, and start convincing the other kings of my superiority so they'll stand with me against the Ulaid. We're going to be very busy, you and I, so I suggest you forget this current woman. There'll be plenty more when you have time for them, but for now, go easy."

Go easy. When, Finn asked himself, did I ever go easy?

Women remained very much in the thoughts of the fían during the Samhain Assembly. Wives and daughters of clan chieftains in attendance had brought numerous female servants with them. The rounded female form was everywhere, distracting the young males to the point of madness.

With one exception, Finn's band made the most of every opportunity.

The exception was Conan Maol. He remarked to Cael, who was now introducing himself as Cael Hundred-Killer, "Chasing women is more trouble than it's worth."

"Only you would think so. You're shockingly lazy. Just look at you, slumped on a bench when you should be standing tall outside the king's doorway."

"I'm not lazy. I'm just resting before I get tired."

"And what would Finn say if he saw you?"

"I'll be on my feet soon enough if he comes this way."

"You'd better be, or . . . och, Finn, we were just talking about you," said Cael to the air above Conan's head.

Conan leaped to his feet and whirled around.

There was no one behind him.

Chortling, Cael sauntered away.

A good place for meeting women was the Grave of the Dwarf, a stone cist set in a damp hollow. According to the historians, it was the burial site of a dwarf who had been a great favourite of Conn of the Hundred Battles. The tiny man had been killed while trying to separate two blind beggars who were quarreling over their gifts from the king.

Conn had wept for his dwarf and encouraged the women of his household to mourn with him. Since then, the gravesite had become a pilgrimage for women, a place where they could publicly demonstrate the admired tenderness of the female heart by weeping over the long-dead dwarf.

As soon as they learned this, Finn's companions made a point of passing the grave at every opportunity.

A brehon who discovered Fergus consoling a sobbing servant by slipping his hand down the front of her gown was outraged. "You take advantage!" he cried, rushing at Fergus with upraised ash stick. "You must maintain proper decorum at Samhain!"

That night at the feast, another local brehon ponderously recited the verses describing acceptable public behaviour at gatherings, drawing a distinct line between the Samhain Assembly, the Great Gatherings, and rowdy fairs and festivals.

"Samhain," he intoned somberly, glowering at his audience, "is a sober time."

But the fénnidi now flooding into Tara were hard to restrain. They craved action, a last flare of excitement before they settled into their various winter quarterings to endure the monotony of repairing weapons and glaring at grey skies. They quarrelled constantly and bullied bond-servants.

Cormac told Finn, "I expect you to control them. You're their commander now. See they don't disgrace themselves here."

It was not an easy assignment. The stern orders Finn issued were not always followed; some fénnidi took delight in ignoring them.

"It's because you're so young," Goll said. "They don't believe that anyone of your years has been given so much responsibility . . . or will be able to handle it."

"I can handle it."

"Not if the men don't respect you."

"They'll respect me," vowed Finn Mac Cool.

He prowled Tara until he found a grunting fénnid sprawled atop a giggling servant woman behind the Fort of the Synods. Finn jerked the man upright by his hair and administered a beating with such style that a crowd quickly gathered.

"See that? Kicked him on the point of the chin. That takes agility, that does."

"And style. He has style, the new commander."

"Boom, boom, two blows to the head before your man could raise his fists. Impressive. I wouldn't want him hitting me."

It was an admirable performance. Enjoying it, Finn made his opponent last as long as possible, almost propping him up at the end so he could deliver one final blow.

When at last the man was allowed to fall, he did not move until sundown. People stepped over him.

The woman he had been with pulled her garments around herself and smiled tentatively at Finn, but he did not notice. One of the spectators was Cruina. She also smiled. The dimple in her chin winked at him.

Finn was young and vigorous, and the restrictions he had just upheld so forcibly did not seem to apply to himself, not when Cruina smiled. When she left the scene of the fight, he followed her.

She glanced over her shoulder a time or two, then turned to face him. "Why are you stalking me?"

"I'm not stalking you."

"Then why do you have those hounds with you?"

"They're always with me."

"Will you tell them to go away? I don't like the way they're looking at me, can you understand?"

Finn snapped his fingers and frowned. Bran and Sceolaun obediently trotted from sight. Cruina walked on and he drifted along behind her.

This time when she whirled around, she was angry. "Why do you keep following me when I don't want you to?"

"I don't know that."

"I'm telling you, aren't I? Why would I want a warrior pursuing me?"

"And why not?" he asked innocently.

"My father says the fénnidi want nothing more from a woman than a marriage of the seventh degree. My father's a smith, a skilled craftsman. I shouldn't have to settle for a seventh-degree marriage, should I?"

"Not at all," Finn hastily assured her, wondering what a seventh-degree marriage was.

"Good." She lifted her heavy hair off the back of her neck and swung it to fall becomingly over one shoulder instead. "We're agreed then, are we?" Before Finn could answer, she stepped through the nearest doorway. Finn almost ran his nose into the door she closed behind her.

Cruina had entered the *Grianan,* the many-windowed chamber set aside for the exclusive use of the women. No man could enter unless expressly invited.

He gazed hard at the door, muttered under his breath, then turned on his heel and made his way back to the Fort of the Synods.

Blamec was on duty outside the door.

"Och, Blamec, how are you keeping?"

"I have a headache and my feet hurt."

"Interesting work though, is it?"

"Guarding a door? Not particularly. And I'm getting hungry. I've been here all day and no one's asked me where my mouth is."

"You're getting as bad as Cailte, thinking about your belly."

"There's not much else to think about. That fight you had over there a while ago was a diversion, but it didn't last long enough. Are you planning another one soon?"

"There shouldn't need to be another, not like that one. But listen here to me, Blamec. Since you've been standing here, have you overheard much of what's going on inside?" Finn nodded his head to indicate the judges' official chamber, a circular, fortlike structure of timber and wattle.

"Sometimes I can hear them, when they raise their voices."

"Have you heard them discussing marriage? Degrees of marriage? Something called marriage of the seventh degree, say?"

Blamec looked blank. "I don't know, I haven't paid much attention. They talk in fancy language, the brehons. They use words a warrior doesn't even know. They do it so no one else can understand them, I suppose. It works with me, I don't listen."

Finn was disgusted. "I put you here to listen and learn. Don't you remember?"

"That isn't the way you said it at the time. Besides, how can I learn from brehons? They're another class entirely. They spend up to twenty years memorizing all those laws. That's not for me, I'm a Man of the Bag."

"You're a waste of time," Finn snarled at him.

Blamec refused to be insulted. "If you want to know what the brehons are saying, go in there yourself, Finn. I'll pass you through. I'm not about to refuse the Rígfénnid Fíanna."

For a second time that day, Finn hesitated before a closed door. The Fort of the Synods was as forbidden to one of his class as the Grianan was to his sex. He took out his bad humour on the hapless Blamec. "How dare you offer to pass me through! Is that what you call being a good guard? Do your duty and don't disgrace me." Finn stalked away.

That night in the hall, Finn stood opposite the Door of Heroes, watching the assemblage. Everyone was seated according to rank. Bards, druids, and brehons were closest to the king. Beyond them were the most powerful chieftains. When the feast of the day was served, the best meats would go to these. By their proximity to the king, one could tell at a glance the status of everyone in the hall. Two of the druids in attendance were women, as was one of the physicians. Wives and daughters, however, feasted in chambers of their own, where they could speak of things that interested women without having to shout over male voices.

Finn's eye fell on a brehon called Fithel, whom Cormac had that day named to serve as chief brehon at Tara. Short, slim, given to nervous gestures, Fithel had a high forehead atop a long Milesian skull, and thinning fair hair. He looked brittle, almost fragile, but his mind was said to be the keenest in Erin.

Finn eyed him speculatively. Would he be willing to speak to one of the Fir Bolg? His face, Finn decided, was aloof but not unkind.

When the feasting was over, Finn waylaid Fithel outside the hall. "I would speak with you, if it is permitted."

The night was golden with torchlight. Fithel squinted at Cormac's new commander. The request surprised him. Brehons usually had little to do with warriors, though there was no specific prohibition.

"You may speak with me," he decided. "I am not averse to a brief social intercourse with one of your station."

"Can you teach me the law?"

Primly, Fithel replied, "Members of subjugated tribes are not eligible for an education in Brehon Law. Whatever you may require to know, we shall recite for you."

"That's what I meant," Finn said, conscious he had made an error. "I require to know the laws of marriage."

"You do not know them?" The judge's pale eyebrows crawled like worms up his bald dome. "Even subordinate peoples are at least nominally conversant with those aspects of law which govern their lives. Where have you been that you did not absorb such rudimentary information with that most salubrious of beverages, your mother's milk?"

Finn reddened. "I grew up on my own," he said in a low, angry voice.

Fithel's eyebrows climbed higher. He was so startled that his customary speech pattern deserted him. "You did? How could you?"

Be careful, Finn warned himself. Brehons aren't easily deceived.

Don't reveal anything to this man, and don't try to play any games with him either.

Because it was a habit by now, Finn put his thumb into his mouth as he mentally constructed a reply. An earnest smile spread across his face. He made certain it warmed his eyes. There was something in his eyes, he knew from experience, that could unnerve people.

He took his thumb from his mouth and said, "On some long night I'd be happy to tell you my history, but I know you're much too busy during the Assembly. A man as important as yourself has every breath accounted for. All I ask is the merest scrap of knowledge. You have so much, and I have none."

A most diplomatic rejoinder, Fithel thought approvingly. He gazed up into Finn's deliberately ingenuous face. "I should like to hear your history," he said. "But you are correct in your surmise, I am too much occupied with professional obligations during the Assembly to listen to protracted narratives. However, if you will step into my private chamber, we will be out of the wind and I can instruct you in a summary form on matters of law pertaining to marriage."

Fithel led the way to a timber-and-wattle sleeping chamber at some remove from the Fort of Synods. Ducking through the low doorway, Finn found himself in a small single room dominated by a bed piled with furs, protected from draughts by a screen of painted leather. Fithel indicated two wooden benches against the wall and they sat down.

What would my mother think, Finn wondered, if she could see me now, here at Tara, in a brehon's private chamber?

"Tell me the law," he said abruptly.

"You exhibit an eagerness that borders on agitation. Is there a reason?"

"None aside from the fact that I'm now Rígfénnid Fíanna, and I'm thinking of marrying."

"Indeed. You have been remarkably elevated for one of your years. And you are old enough to marry. There are various laws pertaining to marriage, designed to provide equity according to rank and need. Men and women alike tend to act in their own self-interest. For any law to be obeyed, it must be perceived to be in the interest of the person involved. Brehon Law was not designed for the best of all possible worlds, where everyone is kind and trustworthy, but for the world as it actually is, which is rather different. Do you understand?"

"I think so."

"Any relationship that results in the birth of a child is considered to be a marriage, thus assuring the child's rights under law," Fithel explained with sweeping gestures. He often waved his hands as he spoke, as if opening his mouth pulled them into the air like fluttering birds.

"Marriages of the first three degrees require a contract to be agreed upon by both parties beforehand," he went on, "and women married under contract become official wives." He paused, peering narrowly at Finn. "Are you certain you do not know this? Surely you have some learning. You had to become conversant with poetry to qualify for the Fíanna."

"I learn what I need when I need it," Finn responded. "Until recently, I didn't need to know about marriage."

"Ah." Fithel nodded to himself, enlightened as to at least one aspect of the new commander's character.

"A marriage of the first degree," he resumed, "takes place between partners of equal rank and property.

"A marriage of the second degree is one where the man has more property, and supports the woman.

"A marriage of the third degree is the reverse, with the added stipulation that the man must agree to till his wife's fields or manage her cattle, in order to keep a man's dignity and his wife's respect.

"Fourth-degree marriage is different. No property is taken into consideration, and no contract between partners is agreed upon in advance. This particular type of arrangement is described as 'the marriage of a loved one.' The rights of the children are described by law and safeguarded, but the woman is in effect a concubine. She is not an official wife, so if her husband dies, she may not continue to reside beneath his roof but must return to her own people.

"Marriage of the fifth degree is one in which a man and woman share their bodies by mutual agreement, but continue to inhabit separate dwellings.

"When a man forcibly abducts a woman—as a chieftain will sometimes seize his defeated enemy's wife after a battle—that is a marriage of the sixth degree for as long as he can keep her with him."

Finn leaned forward tensely. "What about marriage of the seventh degree?"

Fithel gave a dismissive waggle of his fingers. "That is referred to as 'a soldier's marriage.' Such casual unions often last no more than one night.

"A marriage of the eighth degree takes place when a man obtains use of a woman's body through deception, such as seducing her with lies about his status or his amount of property, or taking advantage of her intoxication."

Through a change in Finn's posture, Fithel became aware that the young man's interest had waned. He sketchily listed the last two degrees. "An act of rape constitutes ninth-degree marriage," he said, "and tenth-degree marriage is a coupling that involves feebleminded persons."

"Would a woman be insulted by a seventh-degree marriage?"

"That would depend upon her status, Finn. If she were a person of low rank herself, such as a bondservant, and the man belonged to the Fíanna, which is higher, she might be flattered. Women are very conscious of rank. A woman aspires to produce children of higher status than her own, if possible."

"Suppose she was a smith's daughter?"

"Ah. A smith is a skilled craftsman, a valuable man who possesses considerable prestige. His daughter would be highly unlikely to accede to a seventh-degree union."

Finn muttered something unintelligible. Fithel, in full spate now, was explaining, "Prestige is the control system of our society, as surely you appreciate. For example, in marriages of the first or second degree, the man must be able to pay a dowry, a *coibche*, each year for the first twenty-one years, in order to maintain prestige within his tribe. In the first year, it goes to the bride's father, who shares it with her kinsmen. In the second year, however, a third portion of the coibche is given directly to the wife. In each subsequent year, providing there is no divorce, she receives an increasingly larger portion of the coibche, until twenty-one years have passed. By then she has enough property of her own to be independent if her husband has tired of her, or she of him. If one has divorced the other in the meantime, she of course retains what she has already received. That is the law."

"What sort of property, Fithel?"

"The coibche would not include the man's fort or lodge, of course, but it would be made up of cattle, or female servants. Or failing that, carts, sheep, grain, timber—"

"What if all a man had were his weapons and hunting hounds? Good hounds!" Finn added emphatically. "But no cattle. And no lodge."

Fithel pursed his lips. "Then I would say to you that the first *five* degrees of marriage are beyond that man.

"If he would take a concubine, he must have a household to install her in, for the law states that such a woman must be well fed and well sheltered. Like every member of society, she does have certain rights. Also, if he would lie with a woman but maintain a separate dwelling for himself, as in fifth-degree marriage, then he must have that dwelling. A housed woman would not accept a nomad, it would damage her prestige." Fithel's hands chopped the air decisively.

A crestfallen Finn left Fithel's chamber to find Goll waiting. "What were you doing in there, Finn?"

"Consulting the brehon."

"In his private chamber?"

"Why not?" Finn bristled.

"What did you want to know?"

Goll was pushing too hard. Recalling Cruina's trick of asking questions, Finn responded, "You've married, have you not?"

"I've had a lot of marriages. And two contract wives," Goll said proudly.

"So you had property."

"Loot from war, and a fine, strong fort. My first wife died, but my second still lives there."

"How did you get the fort, Goll?"

"I acquired it after I became commander. But I was considerably older than you are now, Finn. A lad your age has no more need for a fort than a fish has for ear rings."

"If I had a wife, I'd need a household."

"You don't have a wife, that's something else you don't need." But no sooner had Goll spoken than he saw an opportunity to be taken. Finn was impulsive. If encouraged, he might make excessive demands and annoy Cormac, who would then look around for a different commander for his army. Someone more experienced and temperate.

Goll said smoothly, "But if you are thinking of taking a wife, I would be the last to discourage you. How pleasant it is, after Samhain, to retire to your own fort with your own woman. Someone to heat your bed and your food and mend your cloaks and listen to your stories as if she's never heard them before. A woman who can never reject you—"

"Never reject you?" Finn echoed in astonishment.

"If she does, under the law you can divorce her. Of course, if you reject her, she might divorce you. The marriage contract gives both of you rights and obligations. Neither of you can criticize or satirize the other in public. That, too, would be sufficient for divorce. You can say whatever you want to each other in private, but publicly you must support one another completely. Such a marriage is a strong alliance, Finn. For men like us, I would say it's almost a necessity."

"Like ear rings on a fish?"

"Och, it's late, and I lost the run of myself when I said that. I approve of your taking a wife. That's what this is about, isn't it? I think you should go to the king and demand a fine, strong fort appropriate to the Rígfénnid Fíanna, and adequate property to supply a rich coibche."

"I already suggested some sort of . . . property. Cormac told me to go easy."

"He was testing you. He simply wants to see how aggressive you are. Don't be passive, Finn. Don't just stand around with one arm as long as the other. Go to Cormac first thing in the morning and demand the entitlements due you."

"That's your advice, is it?"

"My most emphatic advice."

Finn studied the older man's face. The evening was dark and bitterly cold and Tara blazed with torchlight. The flickering light made Goll's scar seem to writhe across his features with sinister purpose in spite of his efforts to look sincere.

Putting his thumb in his mouth, Finn chewed on it thoughtfully. Goll watched him. At last Finn withdrew the thumb and said, "I think I'll wait a while before I make demands of the king. But I thank you for your advice, Goll. I'm always interested to hear what you have to say."

He sauntered away.

His thumb warned him! thought Goll, furious. The Thumb of Wisdom!

Stop that, said a cooler voice inside his head. You don't believe that nonsense and you know it. Finn's a great teller of tales, a bold chancer who'll try anything. When you were his age, you were the same; you'd seize any chance that came your way, Goll Mac Morna. If you'd thought you could get away with it, you'd have claimed magic yourself.

Finn does seem to be getting away with it.

But how far can his audacity take him?

When will he make a crucial mistake?

Goll's one eye followed Finn until the younger man stepped from a pool of light into the surrounding darkness and disappeared as totally as if he had fallen off the world.

Still Goll stared after him.

Goll Mac Morna had sired a number of sons. Some had not lived to reach manhood. Others were scattered through various bands of the Fíanna, and at least two had fled Erin to fight in the service of a king in Alba. He had been proud of all his sons, however, until he met Finn Mac Cool.

Compared to Finn, they seemed no great achievement.

Finn was Cuhal's victory over Goll Mac Morna.

I wish he were my son, Goll thought.

I wish I had a good excuse to take my sword and kill him.

8

As THE Samhain Assembly drew to a climax, the Celtic year was dying. Samhain meant the end of the second half of the year, the warm half. The torches on Tara were never extinguished but burned defiantly night and day, as if to hold back the cold.

It had already been cold, however, for a moon's cycle. Druids said the early cold signalled change and danger. Change was obvious. Tara had a new king.

Samhain had another meaning. The death of the old year and the birth of the new was the time when barriers were lowest between the world of the dead and the world of the living. Spirits could freely penetrate those barriers at Samhain, and visit the people and places they had left behind.

The climax of the Samhain Assembly was always its final feast, a splendid and sombre event to which only the dead were invited. The feast served both to placate any malevolent intent on their part, and to reassure them as to the ongoing success and prosperity of their descendants. The best meats and fowl and fishes were served in abundance, together with cheeses and bread and buttermilk and dried fruits and honeycombs and hazelnuts and cups brimming with fragrant ale. The banquet was laid out in trestle tables in the hall. While the dead invisibly entered through the fourteen doorways and feasted, the living stood watch outside, keeping the Samhain vigil.

Finn Mac Cool stood with them, close to the king. He wondered if Cuhal Mac Trenmor's spirit was inside the hall. Closing his eyes, he tried to reach out and sense some flavour of his father, but nothing came.

He wondered what the other people gathered outside the hall were thinking about. Parents? Kin? Loved ones?

Who was inside? And what were *they* thinking?

With the appearance of the first light in the east, the living, numbed with awe, dispersed. When they next entered the hall, all traces of the feast would be gone.

No one spoke of it afterward. That was the custom.

After the Feast of the Dead, the Celtic year began anew, as life follows death, as light springs from darkness.

Cormac's final act of the Assembly was the deliverance of a royal proclamation. In addition to naming Fithel as chief brehon, he appointed a royal bard, druid, historian, physician, musician, and three stewards, who were to accompany the king wherever he went. "This I proclaim for all the kings of Tara who follow me," he announced, setting his stamp firmly on the kingship.

"I shall also name an official companion to be my confidante, my soul-friend; to be the one set of ears I can trust implicitly. Such a man must, of course, have much in common with myself."

At this point Finn drew in a deep breath and held it. A famous father, he thought. Fostered by two women . . .

"I have not yet selected this royal companion," the king went on. "When I do, he will of course be a prince of my own blood."

Finn exhaled. What did you expect? he asked himself bitterly. You're only a Fir Bolg. Cormac belongs to the nobility.

But I'm as good as any Milesian, whispered a tiny voice deep inside Finn Mac Cool.

". . . and the last of my appointments, for now, will be to name Lochan as royal smith. He will be given a workshop for himself and a dwelling for his family within the precincts of Tara," the king concluded.

His words cut through Finn's thoughts and swept them away. The new Rígfénnid Fíanna straighted imperceptibly; a tiny muscle jumped in his jaw.

I'm not going to winter at Slieve Bloom after all, he decided. I'm going to stay right here at Tara.

When the assembly had been formally dismissed and people began leaving for their homes, Cormac returned to the House of the King. He found Madan there ahead of him, clearing out detritus while Lugaid made measurements, using the shaft of his spear.

"What's this in aid of?" the king enquired.

"Finn assigned us to dredge out the firepit, get rid of the smell, then examine your lodge with a view toward tearing it down and building a new one."

Cormac was nonplussed. *"Finn* ordered that?"

"He did," Lugaid said, continuing his measurements.

Cormac went in search of Finn, whom he finally found in discussion with Donn about the provisioning of the king's kitchens.

"Finn! When did I put you in charge at Tara?" Cormac demanded to know. He sounded angry. Donn prudently took himself off to the spring-house to examine the cheeses.

"I'm not in charge," said Finn innocently. "You are, you're the king." He smiled pleasantly. His eyes were as guileless as a child's.

"You know what I mean, Finn. Your men are all over the hill, doing this and that very busily. Tearing my house down, for one thing."

"Och, that. You said you planned to rebuild Tara. I thought we'd better begin with your lodge, since your family's joining you soon."

"You're a warrior, not a builder."

"My Madan's an excellent builder," Finn said cheerfully. "So is Lu-gaid. Each of my men has some valuable talent."

Cormac was losing his temper. "Isn't it time you and your talented men went into winter quarters?"

Finn pretended to be surprised. "And leave you and your family unprotected here?"

"We'll have Fiachaid and his men. They've done a good job so far."

"I noticed," Finn retorted dryly. "When we first got here, I noticed how well protected you were."

"I won't have you say a word against Fiachaid!"

"I didn't. He's a good man and a fine warrior. When you were just Cormac Mac Airt, he was all the guard you needed. But things are different now."

"Not that different. And not so different that a band of fénnidi can fulfill the functions of carpenters and cooks, either!"

"That's what they've been doing," Finn pointed out, "and you didn't object."

"That was a temporary expedient and you know it. I have regular servants now, part of the tributes sent to me by—"

"None of them are as good as we are."

Cormac laughed in spite of himself. "You're an arrogant whelp."

Finn shrugged. "I know how good I am, that's not arrogance. And you know how good I am. You wouldn't have made me commander if you didn't need me. So keep me here at Tara this winter; keep me and my men. You won't regret it."

Cormac gazed at him thoughtfully. Finn stood with his feet planted and his chin high, letting the king see how big he was, how strong, how brimming with energy. How valuable.

Don't reject me, Cormac, he willed silently. Don't you reject me.

Cormac shifted weight from one foot to the other. "What about the two bands waiting for you at Slieve Bloom?"

"I'll send for them to join me here. I can command the army and them too. And we might need them here."

"In addition to Fiachaid's company? I doubt that."

Finn relaxed inwardly, realizing the battle was won. "Anything could happen this winter, even if it isn't battle season. This is your first year as king of Tara. Remember that Feircus Black-Tooth didn't survive his."

Fergus Honey-Tongue was at the Slige Dala gate, bidding mellifluous farewells to departing dignitaries, when Cailte ran up to him. "Fergus! We're to spend the winter at Tara!"

"Are you joking? Did that prankster Cael put you up to this?"

"He did not! Finn is sending me to tell everyone. It's official. We're to spend the season right here, helping ready the place for Cormac's family whenever they arrive."

Fergus broke into a delighted grin. Cormac's family! A king's wife would surely travel with plenty of female attendants, perfumed women with soft hands. As Cailte sped off to pass the word, Fergus almost failed to say good-bye to a departing chieftain of the Deisi, so lost was he in a vision. Himself cavorting through Tara, grappling with scented women.

Lugaid was less enthusiastic about the change in plans. When Cailte found him, he was just walking back toward the House of the King after saying good-bye to a wide-hipped girl with a bush of flaming red hair. The daughter of a carter from Slieve Bloom, she had thrown her arms around Lugaid's neck and sobbed before following her father out the gate.

"You mean we aren't going to winter at Slieve Bloom?" Lugaid asked Cailte, unwilling to believe his ears.

"Don't take it so hard. Your face is as long as a wet winter."

"It will be a very long winter . . . now," Lugaid replied disconsolately.

As the fían were preparing their beds that night, Madan said to Blamec, "Did you happen to see Lugaid's redhead? I had no idea our serious friend was so attractive to women."

Goll Mac Morna spoke up. "It's the serious ones who always have the most success with women."

"I have plenty of success with women!" Cael claimed.

"You succeed at teasing them and pulling their hair. It isn't the same thing."

Cael looked puzzled. "I had seven sisters and that was how I always treated them. They loved it."

The others roared with laughter.

"What women like best," declared Fergus, "is a beautiful voice. They can hear your voice in the dark even when they can't see your face, remember. Use poetry and sweet words on a woman and she'll come to you like a bird to your hand."

As usual, Finn was lying a little apart from the others, with Bran and

Sceolaun on either side of him. He was not asleep. He was listening as intently as he had listened to Fithel explaining Brehon Law.

For the next several days, as he busied himself around Tara, he wore the serious face of a man involved in weighty matters. When he chanced to see Cruina the smith's daughter, he looked particularly serious; abstracted. He no longer stalked her as if he meant to pounce upon her. He appeared unaware of her, so much did he have on his mind.

The less Finn noticed Cruina, the more often she arrived in his pathway.

The majority of the Fíanna had departed for winter quarters, leaving Finn Mac Cool, his original band now augmented by the two nines from Slieve Bloom, at Tara. Together with Fiachaid's men, they guarded the royal stronghold and lent their strength to whatever needed doing.

Finn had just been issuing the day's orders when he saw Cruina out of the corner of his eye. As his men departed to their tasks, she approached him. She wore a bright social smile. "Are you well?" she asked pleasantly.

"I'm always well." He started to add some boastful remark about his health, then caught himself in time. "I have to be well," he said soberly. "Much is expected of me." He began to walk away . . . slowly.

As he had hoped, she fell into step beside him. "Is it so very difficult, being Rígfénnid Fíanna?"

"Very difficult." He dropped his voice lower, until he could feel it resonating throughout his chest. "It's a most serious business."

"Ah. You have no time for pleasures, then?"

Finn's heart gave a jump. "This is not the season for pleasures, Cruina."

"When is, then?"

He stopped and turned toward her. In the deepest voice he could summon—so deep it almost made him cough and ruin the effect—he intoned, "Beltaine. Summer is the season for pleasures. I once composed a poem about summer."

"You did? A warrior composed a poem?"

"I did. I'm not just a warrior. I was trained in poetry by Finegas himself, who demanded not only that I memorize and recite, but also that I compose, so I would truly understand the art."

Cruina's eyes were shining. "I should like to hear one of your poems. The one about summer."

Thank you, Fergus, Finn thought silently.

He noticed a couple of Fiachaid's men walking in his direction. Quickly taking hold of Cruina's arm, he guided her behind one of the private chambers. "It's better here, out of the wind," he said. "You mustn't be chilled."

"Are warriors usually so considerate?"

"I told you, I'm not just a warrior."

Smiling down at Cruina, Finn let his mind flood with memories of summer, with sights and sounds and fragrances, with languor and desire. Softly, he recited,

> *Beltaine! Pleasing season of glowing colour.*
> *Blackbirds sing their sweetest lays,*
> *Strong and constant is the cuckoo.*
> *Welcome to you, sunlit days.*
>
> *Men grow mighty in the heat,*
> *Proud and gay the maidens grow.*
> *Fair is every mountain height,*
> *Fair and bright the plain below.*
>
> *Swallows skim the sparkling streams.*
> *Golden gleams the water-flag,*
> *Leaps the salmon; on the hills,*
> *Ardour thrills the leaping stag.*
>
> *Brilliant weather! Warm wind rushes*
> *Through the wild harp of the wood.*
> *Sings the foaming waterfall,*
> *White and tall, her one sweet word.*
>
> *Long-haired heather spreads bright tresses,*
> *White and fragile bog-down stands.*
> *Passion sets the stars to trembling,*
> *Seas are calmed; flowered the lands.*

A sigh escaped Cruina's parted lips. "You capture all summer in your words," she murmured. She seemed about to sway toward him.

Finn could see the first faint lines creasing the delicate skin around her eyes. That sign of maturity moved him more than her full breasts or her rippling hair. It was hard not to reach out and clutch her to him. He ached to lie with her; there was no mistaking his rising heat. But he wanted more, something he could not articulate even to himself. He was swept by desire to envelop her womanhood and simultaneously be enveloped by it, to wrap her around him and lose himself in her. Flesh of my flesh, he thought.

Finn had never had a woman. Looking up at him, Cruina saw it in his eyes.

She was intrigued.

Experimentally, she thrust her hips forward until they touched his body. She felt an answering surge of heat even through the layers of clothing. Then the shaft of Finn's penis was pressing against her, huge, urgent.

He groaned.

Cruina drew back, more startled than frightened by the size and hunger of him.

Blindly, he followed her. His body was no longer his to control. In some small, dark corner of his mind he realized this, but he could not stop himself. He grabbed her by the shoulders and pulled her against him again, grinding himself into her. The pleasure was beyond anything he had imagined but it was not enough, he only wanted more.

Cruina was trying to back away from him. He pinned her against the wall of the building. "Let me," he said hoarsely. "Let me . . ."

She twisted skillfully, interposing the curve of her hip between his body and hers. "Don't, Finn!" she commanded.

I can't stop, he thought. Don't try to make me stop. But even as the thought formed in his mind, the tone of her voice reached that portion of Finn's brain that was inculcated with Fíanna discipline. He hesitated, shuddered, stepped back.

Sweat was pouring down his face.

They stared at each other.

Cruina whispered, "I didn't think you'd stop."

"I didn't think I could."

"But you did."

"I did. You wanted me to."

"I did?" She gazed up at him, shaken by her own emotions. Now she was not sure she had wanted him to stop. Her body was throbbing with awareness of him. "We could go somewhere," she heard herself suggest.

"What are you saying?"

"I mean . . . if you want to . . ."

Finn's mouth was so dry he could hardly form words. "I thought you didn't want a seventh-degree marriage."

"I don't. But." She put one hand on his chest. "But." Her fingers closed on the fabric of his tunic, pulled him toward her. "But," she said again, helplessly. He seemed to be taking up all the air. She could not draw a deep breath. "I want . . . we could go somewhere, Finn."

"Where? We're quartered in the old stables, I can't take a woman there."

"What about this?" Cruina indicated the wall beside them. "It's a sleeping chamber. Surely no one's in it now."

"Let's see." Taking her hand, Finn led her around to the front of the one-room chamber. The oaken door was ajar. When he peered inside, he saw no one.

He pulled Cruina in after him and shut the door. While the woman watched, he drew his shortsword and with both hands plunged it into the earth before the door. He was so strong he buried the blade in the hard-packed ground almost up to its hilt. No one would be able to force the door inward.

He turned to her. "Now," he said.

She gave a breathless little laugh. "Have you ever had a woman, Finn Mac Cool?"

"I've had hun . . . I've never had a woman before," he said in a low voice, as if speaking was an effort.

"I'm glad!" In the dusk of the windowless chamber, Cruina's voice was very bright. "Shall I show you what to do, then?"

He nodded mutely.

Finn stood like a child while Cruina unpinned his mantle and dropped it on the ground to make a bed for them. Then she unfastened his belt. It fell, with the empty scabbard. Her hands reached under his tunic.

Finn groaned again.

Cruina gasped. "Is all of that *you?*"

He could not answer.

Seizing his trembling hands, she guided them to her clothing. But he did not undress her, nor she him. It disintegrated into a confusion of pulling and tearing, getting obstacles out of the way however they could.

They tumbled together onto Finn's cloak. Cruina opened her legs for him and tried to guide him, but he was out of control again and at her first touch, his body seemed to convulse.

Now she was genuinely frightened. He was immense. She feared he would tear her. She tried to fight him off, but her squirming only excited him more. He was lost in a frenzied need to immerse himself in that hot, sweet core of being from which he had once been expelled, the security he had lost and never regained, the darkness and mystery at the centre of womanhood. Now, now, now! Must do it now! Waves of sensation rolled over him. He plunged wildly, too desperate for any restraint. He ground his penis into her flesh just as a knot of anguish gathered at the base of his spine and exploded upward, shattering Finn Mac Cool into a million fragments.

He screamed through clenched teeth and spent himself on Cruina's warm belly.

For a long time he could do nothing but lie there, panting, letting the waves of pleasure slowly recede. He was afraid he would break into pieces if he moved. Surely the bonds that held flesh to bone had been dissolved.

Gradually the ability to think returned, and with it came realization. I've done it wrong.

He was mortified.

Does she know?

Of course she knows. She's a woman, they know everything, they're full of secrets.

She'll laugh at me. She'll tell others about my failure.

Finn lay with his face buried in the curve of her neck and the thicket of her hair, breathing in the smell of her, a mingled fragrance of damp skin and hair and linen and wool and woodsmoke and dried flower petals steeped in oil of white briony. His nose could not separate the scents; it was just the smell of Woman.

He knew that the moment they separated, his humiliation would begin.

Pinioned beneath him, Cruina was aware of his premature ejaculation. She was not thinking of it as his failure, however, but as her own. There would be no child from this coupling. It could not be considered a marriage.

From the first moment she saw Finn, she had wanted him. He was a fénnid, a Fir Bolg, and she was the royal smith's daughter, but the disparity in their rank had not discouraged her. His elevation to Rígfénnid Fíanna gave him more status, and his spectacular singularity would in time give him still more prestige, Cruina felt certain. She would not be lowering herself if she married him—particularly if he took her as a contract wife.

That had been the thrust of her campaign. Seem disinterested, offer him a challenge, fan the flames of desire until he offered what she wanted. It was a dance women knew well. Then she had thrown it away in a moment when his proximity had overcome her self-control. She had given that which she meant to withhold. And she had not given it well, she had not made the experience one he would wish to repeat again and again with a wife.

Lying underneath Finn, Cruina ached with regret. What can I say to him? What can I do?

When she felt him gather himself, she tightened her arms around him and tried to hold him, but he was far too strong for her. He pushed free and was on his feet in one lithe movement, turning his face from her as he rose.

He could not bear to have her look at him. He could not bear to see contempt in her eyes.

"You were wonderful!" she said too brightly.

He despised her for lying. "I'm always wonderful," he said coldly. He kept his back to her as he adjusted his clothing.

He could hear her breathing behind him. Suddenly he wanted to throw himself on her again. The first frantic scramble had scarcely blunted his passion. Youth and energy reasserted themselves, but he dare not try a second time. Two failures would crush him.

"I have work to do," he muttered because he must say something. He sidled toward the door, still keeping his face turned from her.

"Don't go now!" Cruina pleaded. She got to her knees and held out her arms toward him.

He thought she was mocking him. "That's enough of that," he said harshly. Stooping, he caught the hilt of his shortsword and wrenched it out of the packed earth.

Too late, he realized he might have broken the blade. But it was intact.

My father's sword, he thought. Crimall entrusted me with it and I used it for this . . .

He left the chamber feeling like a small boy who had done something unspeakable in the company of adults.

Sitting on Finn's cloak, Cruina gazed after him. He had forgotten the garment. When he was gone, she gathered it around herself and began rocking slowly back and forth.

9

 UNTIL THE COLD WIND HAD BEEN BLOWING OVER HIM for quite some time, Finn did not realize he was without his mantle.

Cruina must have it. Surely she would not have left it lying in the chamber, for anyone to find.

But he could not face her and ask for it. Instead, he went to the king. "My entitlements as commander include three fringed woollen cloaks, I believe?"

"They do. And linen tunics and—"

"I'd like the cloaks now, if I may have them."

"I'd say you need one," Cormac replied dryly. "What's happened to that massive thing you usually wear?"

With a casual shrug, Finn said, "I left it someplace, and no harm. It's hardly appropriate for Tara."

"You mean you can walk around in this weather without a cloak and not be bothered?"

"Not bothered at all!" insisted Finn. "I never feel the cold."

Cormac shook his head. "You're a wonder. But you should have a cloak." Snapping his fingers, he summoned one of his newly appointed stewards. "Take Finn to the storehouses and let him pick out three of the best woollen cloaks sent to me with my tributes. And if there's nothing there he likes, let him look through my own."

Surprised and flattered, Finn protested, "That isn't necessary."

"I have plenty, just take whatever pleases you."

The comradely gesture almost prompted Finn to mention the unfilled position of king's companion and confidante. But he said nothing. He had suffered enough embarrassment; he did not want Cormac to remind him that he came from a subordinate people.

Someday, he thought. The word was a talisman encapsulating an inchoate longing. Someday these things won't matter. Someday the fact that my mother . . .

None of it will matter. I shall be so famous none of it can hurt me anymore.

But that was someday and this was today. Even his status as commander of the Fíanna did not cushion Finn from the memory of his failure with Cruina. His dawning manhood was blemished.

He examined every cloak the steward showed him, finding none splendid enough to hide his shame. "You'd better show me the king's cloaks," he said at last, though with a sense of effrontery in spite of having Cormac's permission. On this day he did not feel like a man who could wear a king's cloak.

Cormac's clothing was kept in huge oak chests carved with curvilinear Celtic designs. While the king's new residence was under construction, his belongings were somewhat carelessly stored in a nearby shed. One of Fiachaid's men stood guard, however.

"I've brought Finn Mac Cool to make selections from the king's wardrobe," the steward told the guard.

Fiachaid's man gave Finn a cold look expressing the rivalry simmering between Fiachaid's warriors of noble birth and Finn's fénnidi. Fiachaid's men felt they were being supplanted by inferiors, and they were not happy.

"Nothing was said to me about this," the guard growled, continuing to block the doorway with his body.

On any other day Finn would have pushed him aside and strode past him. Today he hesitated. "The king said I could have one of his cloaks." His voice did not sound as convincing as it should have done, he realized.

The guard realized it too. "Did he now?" the man drawled insolently. "Do I have anything other than your word for that?"

The steward was horrified. "I heard . . ." he started to say, but he was too late.

Finn had recovered himself.

Lights shifted deep in his eyes. A slight movement of his lips might have been interpreted as a smile—or a preliminary baring of fangs.

"You want something other than words?" asked Finn Mac Cool.

The scream rang across Tara Hill.

People came running from every direction to find the horrified steward dancing in ineffectual circles around an enraged colossus who was holding a fully grown man at arm's length above his head. Spinning around and around, Finn gained enough momentum to hurl the unfortunate guard for the distance of an ordinary spear's throw.

The man sailed through the air, shrieking.

He fell in a heap at the feet of Cormac Mac Airt.

The king stared down at the guard, then raised his eyes to meet those of Finn's. His new commander's face was transfigured by a wild rapture. For a moment Cormac feared he would seize the next nearest man and throw him too, for the joy of it.

"What's the meaning of this?" the king cried to forestall further damage.

With an effort, Finn dragged himself back from a fine, free place where action—crisp, decisive, uncomplicated—took precedence over confusing emotion. He forced his eyes to focus on Cormac.

But the feral light was still in them. For the first time, the king saw what others had seen in Finn Mac Cool. In spite of his warm cloak, Cormac shivered.

Finn said harshly, "He wouldn't give me access to your cloaks."

"Is that all? You may have killed him!"

Finn's blood still raced through his body. He did not want to think about consequences. For a while longer he wanted to enjoy the elation that came from the unfettered use of his total strength. Tossing his hair out of his eyes, he continued to dance on the balls of his feet, hoping someone else would challenge him.

"Finn!" Cormac cried in a voice of command. "Follow!" He turned and went to the fallen man.

Somehow Finn obeyed, feeling the joy drain out of him. A crowd had gathered. He heard someone say, "It's not possible! Did you see where the commander was standing? No one could throw a grown man that far!" Finn smiled.

The man who had been thrown grunted, coughed, opened his eyes. When he saw Cormac and Finn, he closed them again. "Please," he tried to say.

"Would you rather I speak to you?" Finn asked softly, "or lay hands on you?"

"Speak to me," said the man, gasping for the breath that had been knocked out of him, "but don't touch me again!"

"My words are good enough for you now, are they?"

"I'd not question them," was the heartfelt reply.

A few remained to help him to his feet and check for injuries, but the majority of the spectators followed Finn to the shed. They waited outside, talking in excited voices about this latest of his feats, while he, Cormac, and the steward went in.

The king stood to one side, watching with folded arms and an air of quiet amusement as his steward lifted piles of clothing out of the chests. Finn's face was a study in astonishment that Cormac enjoyed.

The new king of Tara possessed stacks of tight-fitting linen shirts with voluminous bell-shaped sleeves sewn into countless tiny pleats. He had finely woven linen undergarments made in one piece to serve as stockings and trews, tight to the leg to show off its shape, and held in place with ribbons passing under the arch of the foot. His tunics were elaborately embroidered, with folds and plaits using excessive amounts of material. There were short, tight coats of wool or leather, to be worn over the shirts and fastened at the throat with jewelled brooches. He also had short capes, with or without cowls, made of unbleached black wool from the common sheep of Erin. But even this simple fabric was enriched with linings of brilliantly dyed silk obtained from the sea traders who frequented the coasts.

It was the first time Finn had been intimate enough with any member of the ruling aristocracy to see a royal wardrobe thus displayed. He was speechless with realization of the wealth of Erin.

The steward held up a selection of knee-length hooded mantles composed of stripes or chevrons of bleached and dyed wool sewn together. But most splendid of all were the full-length cloaks. These great mantles were either lined with fur or finished with row upon row of thick fringe as long as a man's forearm, sewn along the outer edges of the garment to keep the wearer's throat and wrists and ankles warm.

Like a dazzled child, Finn reached for the nearest, a vivid polychrome-striped cloak fringed with crimson.

The steward laid a timorous hand on his arm. "Not this," he said, half expecting a blow. "If you please, that contains seven colours, which only a king may wear." When Finn did not hit him, the man was encouraged to continue, "Six colours are allowed bards and brehons and a king's senior wife. Noble princes may wear five according to Brehon Law; four colours are permitted to teachers and hostellers; clan leaders wear three—"

"And the Rígfénnid Fíanna?" Finn interrupted, looking not at the steward, but at Cormac.

The king's lips silently shaped the word. Four.

Finn turned back to the steward. "I'll have this, then," he decided, taking a cloak composed of squares of wool in black, white, and brilliant blue, with a yellow fringe. He swirled it dramatically around his shoulders.

Cormac's amusement deepened. "You do that as if you'd always worn fringed cloaks."

"I've never worn anything," Finn told him, "but what I made with my own two hands. Not since I was weaned."

Cormac gave him a long look. "You could wear a saffron tunic under that cloak," he said at last, "and still be wearing but four colours, as the fringe is yellow too."

When Finn left the shed, he wore the chequered cloak and carried an armload of other garments. He stepped into an icy rain. Beyond the doorway stood the guard who had challenged him, on his feet again but shivering with cold and reaction.

Finn walked over to him. From the armload he carried, he extracted a black woollen mantle lined with fox fur and handed it to the guard.

The man gaped at it. "What's this in aid of?"

"It's for you."

"I can't—"

"You can. The king gave it to me, and I give it to you."

"But—"

"It's only the one colour," said Finn with the air of the newly knowledgeable, having questioned the steward closely when he made this selection. "Fur isn't considered a colour."

When the man seemed too stunned to respond, Finn draped the mantle around his shoulders with his own hands and walked away.

That night in the stable, Fergus Honey-Tongue said, "If the leaves falling from the trees were gold, or the foam on the waves silver, Fionn son of Cuhal would give them away. None can match him for generosity."

Finn smiled, almost shyly.

Goll was moved by curiosity to ask, "Just why did you give that cloak to Aed?"

"Is that his name?"

"Aed son of Aebinn. I knew his father, a fine warrior."

"I gave it to him because he was frightened of me, Goll."

"That's no reason to give away a king's cloak!"

"Och, but it is. You may know a lot of things, but no one knows more about hunting than I do. An animal who is afraid of you may well turn on you and do you a mortal injury. I don't want men like Aed, whom I must work with, to be afraid of me."

Goll shook his head. "You're the strangest mixture of wisdom and ignorance I've ever seen, Finn Mac Cool."

Finn shrugged. "I'm what my life has made me."

Goll looked at him in anticipation of something more, but Finn clamped his lips together.

The incident with Cruina continued to haunt him. He did everything he could to avoid her, and to avoid being reminded of it, but this was not easy in an enclosed stronghold such as Tara. If he saw her coming, he ducked behind the nearest building or pretended to be so occupied that he passed her unaware.

He was, of course, agonizingly aware of her.

He had lain with her, after a fashion. As he understood the law, a marriage had taken place. But it was no more than a seventh-degree marriage, an embarrassment to her and to him.

She must hate him.

For his part, Finn felt diminished. He was Finn Mac Cool, Rígfénnid Fíanna. He had gloried in his strength and what he expected would be his virility. His marriage should have been something more than a shameful fumbling in a deserted chamber.

In the privacy of the night, lying a little apart from the other men, Finn considered the situation. Marriages with contracts were prestigious enough for a commander but they involved property he did not yet possess. Besides, he and Cruina had made no contract. She would probably never agree to one now, not with him. Not after the way he had humiliated himself.

But what if she had a child? Was there a child, growing? How was he to know?

Ask Cruina.

But for that he must face her, and he could not face her.

Meanwhile, he was thankful for the rebuilding of Tara. His days were filled with work. Every morning found Cormac up long before dawn, striding across the hill, looking for things that needed to be done. He and Finn entered into an unspoken contest to see who could discover more possible improvements.

"I think I shall wait until spring before I send for my family," the king decided. "I want this place to be perfect before they see it for the first time."

"That will give us time to improve the Grianan," Finn replied. "More windows, so the women have even better light for their sewing."

"I've been thinking about the Assembly Hall myself. There isn't enough room. I should like to be able to serve five hundred men mead there, or to at least give a banquet for a hundred."

"We can extend it that way . . ." Finn pointed.

"And have wider doorways. A higher roof, too, newly thatched every year so it shines like gold and can be seen from far away," Cormac enthused.

"Would not the brehons feel slighted if you build a new hall for your guests while they must continue to meet in their old one?"

"You're right of course, Finn. They should have a new, nobler Fort of the Synods. Didn't I mention that? I'd already decided on it myself."

"And if it is to be called a fort, and the royal residence is to be called a fort, should not both have earthen banks and ditches and their own wooden palisades, to call attention to their importance?"

"Perhaps there should be two royal forts," Cormac mused. "A ceremonial House of the King and another that will serve as my private residence and home to my family. I don't want people coming into my private dwelling at any time of the day or night and throwing heads into my hearthfire!" he added with a laugh.

From first light to last, Tara rang with the sounds of construction. On the day Finn's other bands of nine arrived, they were promptly given not warriors' weapons, but adzes and mallets and stripping knives, and sledges for dragging heavy materials, and pointed toward the nearest building-in-progress . . . much to their astonishment.

Cormac's brain overflowed with lavish plans. Finn interpreted them as best he could, with a growing sense of excitement. It was intoxicating, being part of an explosion of energy and optimism. He began to imagine a Tara that would stand unchallenged through all the centuries to come, a kingly centre for Erin.

And he was helping build it.

His ambitions began to expand with Tara. He had already attained what he once considered the zenith of achievement, but he was still very young. There must be more.

He would make more of Finn Mac Cool, warrior and poet and dreamer. Fionn Mac Cuhal, Rígfénnid Fíanna.

But the problem of Cruina cast a blight on his dreams and on his vision of himself. He had behaved badly with her, he had been less than he should have been. His inability to face her and resolve the situation only compounded his misery, making him accuse himself of cowardice, the worst dishonour he knew.

He longed to talk with someone older and wiser than he, but there was no one he would entrust with such secrets. Finn Mac Cool had no soul-friend. The one man with whom he had the most in common was probably Goll Mac Morna. But the last person to whom Finn would reveal any vulnerability was Goll.

He managed once to allude to his problem without indicating its specifics, or that it involved himself. "Goll," he said very casually as they were eating their meal at the end of the day, "did you ever do anything you were sorry for afterward?"

"Every man's done things he regretted, Finn. And every woman too, I suspect. Hand me that bowl of cheese, will you?"

Finn passed the wooden bowl brimming with soft white cheese. Goll scooped out a large portion with three fingers.

"I mean," Finn persisted, "have you ever done anything that, uh, that you felt dishonoured you?"

Goll's eye flashed. "What are you trying to say? Are you accusing me of something? If you are, you can forget about it. I've never done any-thing in my life that I considered to be dishonourable, nor shall I. I'll tell you something for nothing, Finn Mac Cool. A man lives after his life, but not after his honour!"

Jumping to his feet, Goll stalked off to finish his meal elsewhere.

For several days afterward, Finn was very quiet. "What's wrong with him?" Donn asked Blamec. "Does he have a sour belly? Perhaps I should examine the foodstuffs again."

Brooding, Finn watched Cruina covertly. He looked for some indication of pregnancy, while avoiding coming too close to her or meeting her eyes. From the glimpses he stole, he could not decide if she was expanding or not. In winter, women wore voluminous mantles over loose-flowing tunics. Only in the warmth of their houses did they undress to the gowns beneath, which were usually of linen fitted more closely to the body.

Finn, of course, was never invited into the smith's house.

He had lived a solitary life, but he could no longer bear this alone. He must talk to someone. Cailte was his choice, after considerable thought. The thin man tended to keep to himself as Finn did; he did not talk about his fellows.

And he was the only one of the fían from whom Bran would accept food, other than Finn himself.

"I hope you're right in your judgment," Finn told his dog.

He approached Cailte one misty morning as the two were working together on the ditch and bank for the new structure to be known as Cormac's House. "Cailte," he began casually, "have you had much experience of women?"

"Some."

Finn applied his tools in silence for a time. Then, "Did you ever, ah, fall short of your own expectations? With a woman?"

Cailte, working beside him, did not look up. "Once or twice, in the beginning. Like everything else, women take practice."

Finn put down his tools. "But you got better after a time?"

"I did of course. You will too."

How did he know? Finn wondered.

Cailte was smiling. "It's all right, Finn. I won't tell. I suspect we've all had similar experiences."

Finn gave a sigh of relief. "I thought something was wrong with me."

"You were probably overeager. I was myself, the first time I had a woman under me."

"Was there a child?"

"Not that I know of. I've neither son nor daughter, so far as I know. Not yet anyway."

"Have you had many women?" Finn was beginning to suspect Cailte's experience was more extensive than he had thought.

"Not enough. The ones I want rarely look at me. I'm built for speed and not for comfort," he said ruefully.

Finn began to relax. This was the sort of conversation other men had about women; he had overheard them. He felt he had just entered into a new fellowship, a rite of passage.

"I haven't had time for women until now," he confided. "But . . ."

"But once you start, it's hard to stop," Cailte finished for him. "You keep thinking about them."

"You do."

"One in particular?"

"One in particular. I . . . did not make a very good start with her."

Cailte smiled. His eyes were a warm grey, the expression level, easy. "Try again," he advised. "Is this by any chance the woman you've been avoiding?"

"You noticed?"

"We've all noticed. It's the most obvious thing about you these days, the way you duck and dodge when the smith's youngest daughter is near."

"What would you do, Cailte? If you'd made a bad beginning, I mean."

"I told you, try again. If she accepted you once, she probably will a second time. Who knows? Perhaps she feels the fault was hers and would welcome a chance to make up for it."

Finn asked eagerly, "Do you think so?"

"I don't know. But it's worth a try. Anything would be better than to see you skulking around Tara while at the same time trying to look like you're running the place all by yourself."

Finn flinched. "Am I that ridiculous?"

"Not at all. Just awkward."

Heartened by his conversation with Cailte, Finn made one more try. When he saw Cruina emerging from the Grianan, he strode purposefully toward her, rehearsing a little speech in his head. But just before he reached her, she looked up, saw him . . . and turned away deliberately, twitching her lips in an expression of disgust.

Finn sagged where he stood.

He went back to Cailte. "It's no use. She wants nothing to do with me."

"Do you want me to speak to her?" the thin man asked.

"Would you?"

"If you think it would do any good."

"Have you a gift for talking with women? I thought Fergus was—"

"I'm not like Fergus. But I can talk to women. They trust me."

Looking into Cailte's grey eyes, Finn understood. He felt that same trust. "Do what you can for me, then," he said gratefully.

Cailte approached the smith's daughter as she sat on a stone kerbing, combing her hair with a comb of polished yew wood. The living strands crackled with energy as the wooden teeth moved through them.

The thin man sat down beside her on the kerbing, nodded to her pleasantly, then busied himself massaging the balls of his feet.

"You're the runner, aren't you?" said Cruina.

"I am that."

"And your feet bother you, do they?"

"My feet ache sometimes. The arch . . . right here. I'm only human. We're all human, we fénnidi."

"Who are you including?"

"My companions. And Finn himself, of course."

"Oh. Him."

"You know him?"

"Slightly," Cruina said with a delicate lifting of her upper lip.

"He seems to feel there's a problem between the two of you."

"There's nothing between us. Nothing!" Cruina stressed.

"Nothing ever?"

She hesitated. "Nothing now."

Cailte studied his feet. "Was there a time when you wanted something to be between you?"

"What woman wouldn't at least look at the Rígfénnid Fíanna? There was a time when I thought he was grand. And brave. But I know better now."

"He is grand and brave."

"He's a craven coward!"

Cailte was taken aback by her vehemence. "What has he done to make you think so?"

"He avoids me. He all but runs from me. When I discovered he was a coward, I wanted nothing more to do with him!"

Cailte reported the conversation to Finn. "So you see, it wasn't your, ah, performance that upset her, Finn. It was your failure to face her afterward. Whatever went wrong between you, if only you'd talked to her about it, she wouldn't be so angry."

Finn's worst fears were confirmed. Cowardice was the ultimate dishonour. To have a woman think of him as a coward was agonizing. "I meant to take her as a wife in the second degree," he said miserably. "I was going to do everything as the Rígfénnid Fíanna should. But . . ."

"But?"

"But I lost the run of myself entirely, Cailte. I lay with her before I got around to arranging a contract. And then I did it . . . badly. All we had was a soldier's marriage, and an experience I shouldn't think she'd be eager to repeat."

"Och, Finn, the flowers will bloom in the spring anyway. But if this is bothering you so, go and face her. Prove she's wrong about you. Tell her you want a contract marriage with her, she'll be flattered. She'll probably say all sorts of admiring things about you after that."

Finn's whole being yearned to hear a woman say flattering things about him. "I'll do it!" he vowed. "But . . . you'll help me, Cailte?"

To prepare for his confrontation with Cruina, Finn dressed with extra care. Cailte plaited his hair precisely, scraped his jaw with a blade, and peered at the pale sprouting of a warrior's moustache on Finn's upper lip. "You're so fair, it hardly shows," the thin man said.

Finn tried a weak joke. "If I was a king, I'd be expected to grow a beard as well as a moustache, and that probably wouldn't show either, so it's just as well I'm a warrior."

When at last he was ready, Finn hung the great checkered mantle from his broad shoulders. "How do I look?"

"Splendid," Cailte told him, regretting the comment about the moustache.

"Will you stay nearby?"

Cailte was strangely moved. This magnificent youth, this dazzling man, needed him; needed thin, unprepossessing Cailte, a man with but one talent.

Or perhaps two.

Cailte had a gift for loyalty.

"I'll be within shouting distance," he promised.

Together they walked to the smith's dwelling, which was just outside the palisade of Tara. Beside the smith's door hung a blackthorn cudgel on a thong. Finn used the cudgel to pound on the oak door. He wanted to sound powerful, male, aggressive.

The door boomed.

It was opened at once by Lochan's wife, a wizened woman with no chin. She peered up at her visitors. "You want the smith?" she asked, squinting.

"I want his daughter, the one called Cruina. To speak to," Finn added hurriedly.

The woman turned back inside the house. There was a low-voiced dialogue, broken with an emphatic negative.

Finn looked over his shoulder. Cailte made shoving motions with his hands.

Finn gritted his teeth and pushed the door open, then strode into the house with grim determination.

At the far side of the dwelling, Cruina was sitting behind her mother's loom. When Finn burst in, she jumped to her feet angrily. "You have no right here!"

"Mind yourself, girl!" the mother cried. "This is the Rígfénnid Fíanna."

"Is that what he is? It's an honour he doesn't deserve, isn't it?"

The mother gasped. Eyes wide with fright, she stared at Finn. This was a man to be feared, the slayer of monsters.

"I came to discuss a contract of marriage," Finn blurted out. "Second-degree marriage."

The mother gasped again. "Did you hear that, girl?"

"Am I deaf? I heard it," Cruina responded. "I know nothing about a contract of marriage. I didn't ask him to come here, did I?"

But she was looking at Finn with something other than contempt in her eyes. He suddenly wished he knew more about women, so he could interpret her expression. For a moment he was tempted to shout for Cailte.

But this was something he must do for himself. He must demonstrate courage.

Unconsciously, he doubled his fists into huge balls. The mother was dismayed and shrank away from him. He quickly opened his hands, but by then he had lost her. She fled from the house, abandoning her daughter to her suitor.

Cruina faced Finn across the shadowy room. "Go away," she said. "And take your cloak with you—it's over there."

"A contract of marriage," he repeated doggedly. "Between yourself and myself. I'll ask the king to give me enough property to support you well."

Instead of looking at him, Cruina began fiddling with the loom. "I don't have to marry you," she said coyly. "I'm a free person, I can marry as I choose. I have rights."

"But we've already married. I just want to arrange—"

To Finn's astonishment, she laughed. "We are not married! There's no child coming."

"But we lay together."

Cruina left the loom and walked over to him with the laugh still on her lips. In a uniquely female gesture—which Finn interpreted as pity—she put the palm of her hand on his chest. "You don't know very much, do you?" she asked, looking up at him. "Och, Finn, are you really as young as all that?"

Embarrassment washed over him like scalding water. "I'm not so young," he grated. "And I won't have you laughing at me."

Cruina tried to swallow the offending smile. "I'm not laughing at you. I'm just telling you there's no child, there couldn't be. We lay together, but we didn't . . . I mean, you weren't able to . . ." Now she was the one fumbling for words.

Her hand, forgotten, still lay on his chest.

Her words beat at him. *You weren't able to.*

Finn felt an almost overpowering urge to throw her to the floor and complete what had not been completed. He could do it now. He could do it a hundred times over. He could seize her and savage her like a wolf in the forest, he could . . .

He shuddered back from the brink, panting and trembling. He would not put himself in a position to risk any further humiliation with this woman.

Taking hold of her wrist, he lifted her hand from his chest. When he spoke, his voice was hard, tightly controlled. "I made the offer. You did not accept. And there is no child, so there is no marriage of any kind. Are we agreed?"

Cruina sought conciliatory phrases that would not come. This was not the ending she wanted. She had been deeply angry, and hurt by his obvious avoidance of her—until the moment he came bursting into her father's house with his silver hair gleaming and the smell of the outdoors on him.

"Are we agreed?" he demanded to know.

She licked her dry lips. "I kept your cloak," she managed to whisper, hoping that would tell him what she could not.

"I don't need it now," he said coldly. He took a step backward, away from her, building invisible barriers.

She knew then how much she had hurt him. He was not a coward; he had come to offer her a contract marriage. Cruina's eyes stung; her vision blurred. Finn was brave and honourable, he was . . .

. . . gone. While she dashed tears from her eyes, he had turned and left the house.

Cailte joined him outside and had to trot to keep up with him. "Your face is a thunderstorm, Finn. What happened?"

"We agree there is no marriage."

"You agree? Both of you?"

"Both of us."

"What will you do now?"

Finn considered. "Repair my honour," he said at last. "I'm Rígfénnid Fíanna. People have to know . . . what that means. To me."

They entered the gateway in the palisade. The sentry acknowledged Finn with a salute.

"Respect," said Finn softly as if to himself, cherishing the gesture.

Their trot slowed to a walk as they approached the Assembly Hall, which was in the process of being demolished. Finn drew a deep breath and confided to Cailte, "The next time I have anything to do with a woman, I mean to be in complete control."

"Easy to say. Not easy to do. They're very different from us, you know. Slippery as fish, some of them."

"I'll control mine," vowed Finn Mac Cool.

10

Finn regretted having committed himself and his men to spending the winter at Tara. The last thing he wanted to do was to keep seeing Cruina. But he took it as a test, a test of himself and his control.

He no longer tried to avoid her. Whenever he saw her, he gave her the same polite nod of recognition he gave everyone, with not one degree more or less of warmth.

Once she came to him with the great mantle of wild-animal skins draped over her arm. "I meant to return this to you," she began tentatively.

"You want nothing of mine?"

Now she was flustered. "That isn't what I meant—"

"How kind of you to return it," Finn interrupted in an even tone. He took the cloak from her without actually touching her. While she stood watching, unable to decide what to say or do next, he folded it as well as the bulky material would allow.

Then he turned and walked away, leaving her standing there.

That night he wrapped himself in the old cloak, his nose pressed against the skins, seeking some trace of her remembered scent. His body burned and throbbed, but no one knew.

No one except Cailte, who was aware of the commander's restlessness as he tossed and turned throughout the night. But Cailte never mentioned it. Whatever he knew of Finn Mac Cool he kept in trust.

Afterward, Finn would think of that winter as the best and worst of his life. He endured a constant, aching awareness of Cruina, of embarrassment and frustration and baffled longing that surfaced when he was least prepared and washed over him in waves.

Most of the time, however, he was able to submerge himself not in regrets, but in joy. Tara was growing and he was helping build it. Tara was growing and so was Finn Mac Cool.

For centuries, the green ridge that dominated the plain of Míd had been but one of several royal provincial strongholds. Five generations earlier, Tuathal Teachmar had built himself a sprawling timber fort atop the Hill of Uisneach, from which the stronghold of his rivals, the kings of Connacht, could be seen on a clear day. The hilltop complex of Emain Macha in Ulidia was even older, and famed for its associations with the legendary Cuchulain and the Red Branch warriors.

Now Cormac decreed that Tara was to outshine them all. He was a man who dreamed in superlatives—a quality he subconsciously recognized in young Finn.

"I mean to be more famous than Conn of the Hundred Battles or die in the attempt," Cormac had confided to his wife Ethni before he departed to challenge Feircus Black-Tooth.

"Come back carrying your shield or on it," Ethni the Proud replied in the time-honoured way of Celtic women.

Tara—rebuilt, enlarged, extended—was to be emblematic of Cormac's success. As was Finn Mac Cool. For the son of Airt, only the most spectacular would do.

"Nothing less will be sufficient to impress the other kings and force them to bow to the superiority of Tara," he told Finn. "What my grandfather began, I mean to complete. I shall make Tara the royal hub of Erin, home of the king of the kings."

Every ablebodied person was pressed into construction work. The fresh, clean smell of adzed wood was everywhere. Old wattle-and-daub walls were being pulled down by one work crew even as another arrived with new timbers for a longer, stronger, higher wall.

Everything was to be bigger and better.

Blamec, of course, complained.

"I don't see why we have to work like labourers," he muttered to Cailte as the two were securing a roof beam for one of the lesser chambers. "I thought we were supposed to be warriors."

"We are warriors." Cailte sighed. One had to be patient with Blamec.

"But this isn't fighting."

"Neither is hunting. The Fíanna does a lot more hunting than fighting, Blamec. Battles break from time to time, but we have to eat every day," the thin man said.

Just then Madan arrived. He squinted up at the beam. "Should that not be higher?"

"Why?" Blamec challenged. "I can stand up in here."

"That's not the point. The king wants the buildings to be seen at a distance, so their roofs must be visible above the palisade. You're going to have to add some courses to that wall and raise it a bit."

Blamec ground his teeth audibly.

"How much is a bit?" Cailte enquired.

"Half a spear length should do it." Madan turned and hurried off to his next inspection.

Blamec was dismayed. "That will take us another day at the least!"

Cailte shrugged. "Have we anything better to do?"

"We could find Finn Mac Cool and break his neck for him. That would be pleasant."

But in spite of his constant moaning, Blamec worked. They all worked. Tara rose against the sky, golden-thatched and gracious, more regal than any stronghold in Erin.

One evening Finn noticed Cormac ambling all alone toward the Slige Asal gate. With a muttered imprecation against Conan for neglecting his duty, Finn followed him.

Cormac nodded to the guard, who opened for him. Finn slipped through the gate behind him. Lost in thought, the king did not notice. He strolled along the outside of the palisade for a short distance, then turned to stare toward the west, toward the mountains huddled there in cloaking darkness.

The night was drawing down. The last rays of the sun were gone.

A guard peered down from the sentry platform atop the gate, satisfied himself that Finn was with the king, and relaxed.

Cormac stood wrapped in his thoughts. Wondering what they might be, Finn watched patiently. At last he stepped closer.

"It's very quiet out here tonight," he remarked.

Cormac gave a start. "It is," he said, regaining composure.

"And growing very dark."

"It is."

"What do you see, then?"

"Nothing."

"Nothing?"

"I'm listening."

"Listening?"

"For the sound of breathing in the dark."

"But we're alone out here."

"Are we?" Cormac turned toward the younger man. "Are we ever alone? They're always watching us, you know."

"They?" Finn thought he meant the Ulidians. "They've gone, they won't come back until spring."

"They never go," Cormac said grimly. "Not the Tuatha Dé Danann. They're always out there, night or day. The Milesians defeated them once and drove them out of their Tara, but they couldn't kill them. Not really. They tried; with sword and spear they tried. But the Dananns just melted away into the land and the mist. We'll have to fight them again one day, Finn. The Tuatha Dé Danann haven't surrendered Erin. They never will."

A chill ran up Finn's spine.

"I've overthrown Feircus Black-Tooth," Cormac continued, "and I'll force submission on the other kings. I can do that, I have swords and spears. I have the Fíanna and you.

"But when the Tuatha Dé Danann appear and demand to take Tara back again, can I hold it against *them?*" Cormac's voice rasped with a doubt Finn found disturbing.

Cormac was his future. He could not allow the king to doubt his own prospects. "Together you and I can hold Tara against anyone!" Finn proclaimed ringingly. "I killed that monster, didn't I? The one the Dananns sent?"

"I thought the Ulidians sent it."

"Och, the Ulaid could never have controlled such a creature. It obviously came from the Sídhe and their sorcery."

By daylight Cormac found amusement in Finn's tales without having to believe all of them. Now, however, in the night . . . in the dark . . . when an old fear rose in him, a fear implanted in the dawn of his life, he was less inclined to scepticism.

"Do you ever suffer from nightmares, Finn?"

"Never! What could frighten me?"

"Some things," Cormac admitted, "terrify even the bravest. When I was a child, I used to listen to the poems of history our bard recited. The ones I heard most often were about the coming of the Milesians to Erin. The poems brought it to life for me. I could see Éber, and Éremón of the Iron Sword, and that greatest of all bards, Amergin, whose poetic vision led his brothers here.

"And I could see the Tuatha Dé Danann raising a shining mist to terrify them, and stirring up a great storm to sink their ships. How frightened the Milesians must have been, facing powers beyond the abilities of even their most knowledgeable druids! Wherever they looked there was something they could not understand but must find a way to fight. All of the Sídhe had magic, you know, even the weakest. A dangerous and subtle people. There were stories told of them . . ." He broke off as if he did not dare remember.

Finn waited. At last Cormac went on. "It ended with the vanquished Sídhe disappearing, but the historian always added that they were still here, waiting. Waiting to take back from us what we had taken from them. I'd lie on my bed at night with my robes over my head and imagine the Sídhe dissolving the walls of our lodge and walking through as if through water, with a shining upon them, with shining bronze weapons and shining silver eyes.

"They could shift shape, Finn. Did you know that? They could weave time. We never understood them and we never made peace with them. The stronger I become, the more I think about that unresolved conflict. I suspect they're too jealous to let me succeed in my plans. They're the ancient enemy of my people, and they'll fight me. That's my nightmare. War with the Sídhe."

He is confiding the secrets of his soul to me, Finn thought with a thrill of pride. I *am* his soul-friend. But he won't acknowledge me publicly, because I'm not a prince of his blood.

Standing beside Cormac, Finn stared into the haunted night. The wind crooned over Tara Hill, singing songs of a Bronze Age past . . .

What if I were a prince of an older race? Finn asked himself. And no one had told me? That's possible, isn't it? Who was there to tell me? Crimall spoke to me only about my father, never about the other side of my family.

"You needn't fear the Sídhe," he said aloud. "Not while you have me. I know how to fight magic with magic, that's how I killed the monster. Who better than Finn Mac Cool for your ally, Finn who has magic blood himself?"

Cormac turned toward Finn. "What are you talking about?"

"My own ancestors. Everyone knows about yours. Erin was conquered with Amergin's dream and Éremón's iron sword. The Milesians subjugated the Fir Bolg tribes and defeated the Tuatha Dé Danann . . . more or less.

"But I have extraordinary ancestors myself. My mother," he said offhandedly, "was a shapechanger. She could assume the form of a deer." He was aware that Cormac was staring at him through the darkness. "My mother was the daughter of Tadg and Evleen, and Tadg was a son of Nuadath, chief druid to King Cathaer Mor of the Laigin. Evleen herself was kinswoman to Manannán Mac Lir."

In an incredulous voice, the king said, "Are you trying to tell me that your mother's mother was . . ."

"One of the Sídhe. The Tuatha Dé Danann. Indeed. You said it yourself, they're still here. Sometimes they come out of their mounds and caves. Evleen mated with a druid's son because magic calls to magic. Furthermore, I myself was taught magic by one of the women who fostered me. Lia, she was; a kinswoman of Nuadath."

How brilliantly it ties together! Finn congratulated himself silently. Almost as if I were not making it up.

Is that possible?

Am I remembering facts I did not know I knew?

Finn Mac Cool did not know what reality was.

In the atmosphere of the moment and the grip of his own private fears, neither did Cormac Mac Airt. Unable to disbelieve, he stood beside Finn outside the walls of Tara and wondered just what sort of a Rígfénnid Fíanna he had acquired.

Later, as the king lay courting a sleep that would not come, another question occurred to him. If Finn really did have Danann blood, might he be a spy for them?

It was an unsettling thought.

Any man who sought power soon learned that his enemies multiplied in step with his success. The last thing Cormac wanted to believe was that Finn, his spectacular Finn Mac Cool, might be duplicitous. The youth had brought only credit to him so far. Yet . . . when the king was tired and drank too much mead, was there not a silvery shimmer to be seen around Finn?

Surely not, he told himself. It was just the effect of the light on Finn's strange hair. Surely.

As each new building was begun, the royal druid, a ruddy man called Maelgenn, sacrificed an appropriate animal to be buried beneath the walls. The animal was to serve as guardian for the structure, and its sacrifice was to propitiate the gods of the Gael, who, with the passage of centuries, had become inextricably confused with the ancient leaders of the Tuatha Dé Danann.

When the debris of the old Assembly Hall had been cleared away, Maelgenn announced that he required the heads of fourteen wild boars to be buried under the fourteen doorways of the new hall.

"Fourteen boars? Easily done!" said Finn. All in his company clamoured for the hunt, but he insisted on taking only the original band of nine with him. "Ten of us can take down any number of savage animals," he claimed. "More men would just get in our way. With nine fénnidi and a pack of hounds, I could strip Míd of game in nine days if I chose to."

"I was just getting into the rhythm of this building business," Blamec complained, more out of habit than conviction. Like the others, he was thrilled by the prospect of a boar hunt. Only Goll seemed preoccupied, his thoughts elsewhere, a faraway look in his eyes from time to time.

As they were preparing to depart, Lochan the smith approached Finn carrying three swords. "I haven't had time to forge more of these," he said, "but if these prove successful, I'll make one for each of you."

Finn examined one of the weapons curiously. Unlike a shortsword, it had a blade as long as his arm, and honed edges meant to cut and hack rather than to thrust and stab.

"It's an old-fashioned sword, actually," Lochan explained, "but if you're going after boar, this is what you want. There was a time when all warriors carried them. It's a Milesian design, a greatsword like this."

Finn frowned, hefting the weapon. "Too heavy," he decided. "We travel, we don't want to be weighted down."

Lochan was offended. "If it was good enough for the Milesian princess, it's good enough for you!"

"Take it, Finn," said Goll in his hoarse whisper.

Finn took the sword.

He gave the second one to Goll, then hesitated over the third. His men watched him tensely, each aware that it would be prestigious to receive the last weapon. Finn looked from face to face, searchingly.

Cael grinned at him. Conan scowled. Lugaid folded his arms and looked thoughtful.

Finn considered each in turn.

"Cailte," he said at last.

To carry the heavier swords, Lochan had fashioned sheaths fitted with bronze chapes. "You wear these scabbards like this," he demonstrated, fastening Finn's in place at his belt. "When a man—or a boar—comes at you, bend your leg like this . . ." he caught Finn's leg at the knee and bent it at an angle ". . . so you can hold the scabbard behind your knee. Then you can draw the sword with one hand and keep your shield in front of you with the other."

The shortswords were now worn by fastening their scabbards across the chest. In addition, the fían were armed with hunting javelins and an assortment of light birding spears for small game. A leather holder for the spears was worn hanging down each man's back.

"I clank when I walk," Blamec muttered.

Lugaid asked Finn, "Are you bringing that special spear with you?"

"Cuchulain's spear?" It sounded much more impressive than saying "Fiachaid's spear." "I am of course. I go nowhere without it, anymore than I would travel without my hounds."

Next morning, in a dawn as crisp as a green apple, the hunting party left Tara. A number of people gathered at the Slige Asal gateway to see them go. There was a festive air. Hounds danced and yapped, men laughed and boasted about the number of animals that would be killed, their size and ferocity.

A sharp wind sprang up before the hunters were out of sight of Tara. Following Finn, they broke into a trot to keep themselves warm. Because of the severe cold of recent days, the mud of winter was frozen solid, so Finn turned off the road and headed for the nearest expanse of trees.

Entering the forest, he had an immediate sense of homecoming.

Even leafless, the great oaks seemed alive and aware. Together with the ash, yew, and hazel, they comprised the nobility of the forest. Commoners, according to the druids, were such plants as birch and alder and willow. There was a still lower order, the so-called "slave" species, such as gorse, bog myrtle, and the bracken that was used in soapmaking and to provide potash for bleaching linen.

"In childhood I used to think of myself as a silver birch tree," Finn confided to Cailte as they slowed to a walk. "But I don't anymore."

"You don't?"

"I am an ash tree," said Finn Mac Cool.

Cailte raised one quizzical eyebrow but made no comment.

Ten men walked through the forest with the total silence of long training. But for one of them, it was impossible to walk for very long without saying something. Fergus Honey-Tongue softly recited, "The full property of each clan includes the kindling from their woodlands, the cooking material from their woodlands, the nutgathering of their woodlands, wood to supply the frame for every cart they require, spear shafts and yokes and horse goads and timber for the carriage of corpses."

Finn turned to him. "What's that?"

"Brehon Law, of course. Every member of a clan is entitled to an equal share of their woodlands. But it must be exactly equal. I grew up on the edge of a forest of yew and holly, so we learned the law as soon as we were old enough to start gathering kindling. Surely you did too, Finn."

"I did of course," Finn said firmly.

As they walked on, he recited Fergus's words silently to himself until they were memorized, adding to his store of knowledge.

Goll said, almost wistfully, "There are apple trees beyond my fort."

Suddenly Finn recalled Goll's words: "How pleasant it is, after Samhain, to retire to your own fort with your own woman!"

But when the Samhain Assembly had ended, and Finn had decided to keep his men at Tara, Goll had never complained, never said a word. However much he might have longed to go home, his Fíanna discipline had overridden the desire.

Finn moved closer to Goll Mac Morna. "Once the new Assembly Hall is up," he said softly to the one-eyed man, "the heaviest construction will be done. I think you could go then, and winter in your own place."

Goll's head snapped around. He gave Finn a piercing look. "Why do you want to be rid of me?"

"I don't! I just thought—"

"I'm one of the nine," Goll said abruptly. "They stay, I stay."

"Ssshhh," hissed Donn, raising one hand.

They froze.

The grunting was distant but unmistakable. Wild boar. Ten men grinned as one.

Finn cast an anxious glance at Bran and Sceolaun. The hunting party had brought a small pack of hounds with them in addition to Finn's pair, but the others were experienced dogs accustomed to wild boar, which were notoriously unpredictable. Bran and Sceolaun were very young. Finn did not want them to get excited and rush in with eager abandon, getting killed before they could learn the game.

He made a short, sharp signal with his hand, bidding his hounds stay close beside him no matter what happened.

The other hounds had now got wind of the boar and were beginning to fan out through the woods. Finn and his men advanced cautiously. He beckoned to Goll and Cailte to join him in the lead.

Hush-footed, they drifted like snow through the forest. Behind them, Cael whispered mischievously to Blamec, "I can hear you clanking," and was rewarded with an angry glare.

Suddenly one of the hounds gave voice in the forest. At once there was the sound of something crashing through underbrush, then a wild, insane squealing followed by an agonized yelp.

Finn ran forward, the others hot on his heels. He carried his javelin upright to clear the closely packed trees, the joint of his wrist flexing so he could alter the angle of the spear at any moment and throw it.

There was a noise like thunder coming toward him, a roaring in the forest like a great gale approaching.

Another cry of pain from a hound.

Beside Finn, Sceolaun answered with an eager whining. "Stay!" he commanded.

A massive boar burst from the undergrowth, running at an angle to Finn. Its rounded back was covered with coarse bristles; its curving yellow tusks were smeared with blood.

Finn hurled his javelin at one tiny, malevolent eye, but the boar was astonishingly agile. It skittered sideways. The spear flew past its head to embed itself, shaft vibrating, in the earth.

Bringing his left arm forward to cover his lower torso with his shield, Finn hooked his scabbard with his leg as Lochan had demonstrated and drew his new sword one-handed. He did not think even this sword could sever the spinal column of a boar, protected as it was by layers of hide and tendon and muscle. But when the boar bolted past him, he could deliver a powerful hacking blow that would begin the process of weakening the creature for the kill.

But the boar did not run past him. With an adroit change of direction, it charged straight at him, squealing with manic fury. Finn gave a desperate swing of his sword, but with the animal coming toward him head-on, it did little damage.

The boar struck Finn's shield with such force the hard yew wood split down the middle and one half fell away. Another leap and the boar would tear Finn's belly open. Finn staggered backward, lost his balance, fell.

The boar was on top of him.

Bran hurtled forward. The hound did not make the mistake of trying for the spine at the base of the skull. Instead, the agile dog slid along the beast's side, dived, and ripped its genitals from its body.

The boar screamed like a human. Finn twisted and managed to wriggle out from under as a geyser of blood erupted from the severed femoral artery.

As he was getting to his feet, Bran leaped forward to clamp relentless jaws behind the boar's ear, grinding down, down, seeking the kill. The huge hound shook its head and growled as if worrying a giant rat. The boar swayed, made a strangled, choking sound. Blood began to stream from its nostrils. Its forelegs buckled.

The fénnidi attacked from every side.

Goll and Cailte were already swinging their swords so wildly Finn could not get in a blow, and he swore at them both impartially. The other fénnidi were hurling their spears into the boar with shouts of glee.

Slowly, almost decorously, the great beast toppled onto its side. Unseen organs gurgled. Slender legs thrashed convulsively.

Panting, the men ceased their attack and stepped back to allow a noble adversary to die with dignity.

At last the boar lay still, a monstrous mountain of cooling meat.

Monster . . .

Finn remembered the idiot with the torch. Bran had fought for him that day too—and had surely saved his life on Black Head.

He crouched down beside his dog. Bran was pungent with the rank smell of wild blood. It dripped from the hound's coarse coat. Finn ran his hands along muscular flanks and across the white belly to assure himself his dog was uninjured; then he threw his arms around Bran's neck, blood and all. "Was there ever such a deed or such a dog?" he murmured.

Whining softly, Sceolaun crowded close for her share of the affection.

Cailte was examining the dead boar. "Look at all this meat!" His belly rumbled; his companions laughed.

"It's heads we came for," said Blamec.

"But we have to take the meat back too. We can't leave it here for the wolves. The haunch is the champion's portion!"

"I can stay here," Conan volunteered, "and guard this carcass while you hunt for the others. Cailte's right, we can't let the wolves get it, and we can't carry it with us and hunt too." As he spoke he was already seating himself on the ground beside the dead boar and making himself comfortable with the energy a lazy man brings to such a task.

"That's not a bad idea," Finn admitted. "We'll bring the others here as we kill them and you can guard the lot."

"I'm glad this one didn't kill you," Goll told Finn. "It would have been a great nuisance having to carry your body back to Tara slung on a pole, along with fourteen wild boars."

Finn laughed. "I'm glad you won't have that inconvenience!"

The forest was teeming with wild game. By the time the dim forest light faded, they had slain more animals than they needed. Fifteen carcasses were piled beside the reclining Conan Maol.

"We'll camp here tonight," Finn decided, "and go back to Tara in the morning."

It was partly a selfish decision. He wanted to stay in the forest.

Finn's body still tingled with the elation of being one with the forest again. The fragrance of earth and leaf mould was in his nostrils. He wanted to sleep pillowed on a tree root and feel the night alive around him.

As they gathered their bedding materials, he remarked to Cailte, "My favourite sleep music is the cackling of wild ducks on the Lake of the Three Narrows, the scolding of the blackbird of Derrycairn, and the lowing of cows in the Valley of Thrushes."

"Is that poetry?"

"It sounds a bit like poetry," Finn conceded. "Perhaps it is—or will be. Poetry comes to me when I'm out under the sky. In the silences, I hear it."

"I'm not always sure when you're talking poetry," Cailte told him. "Sometimes you sound like a bard and sometimes you sound like the rest of us. Which voice is the real Finn's?" he asked teasingly.

But Finn did not answer.

Finn did not know the answer.

They caught small game for their meal and roasted it over a cheery fire. Wild boar was royal food; they would return it to Tara unsampled.

When they finished eating and settled back to watch the fire shimmer into embers, Finn cleared his throat.

Putting one hand on the head of Bran, who lay stretched beside him, he asked his companions, "Shall I tell you how I came to have my two fine hounds?"

"No better time than now!" cried Blamec eagerly.

Recalling the story he had told Cormac about his magical heritage, Finn began. "Muirinn my mother had a sister a full generation younger than herself, but equally gifted. This sister was called Tuirna, and like my mother, she was wife to a rígénnid, a man called Iollan.

"But this Iollan had a marriage with another woman as well, and this woman was jealous by nature. When she learned about Tuirna, she went to see her, pretending to offer her friendship and approval. She took Tuirna walking among the hills, and when they got where no one could see them, the jealous woman took a weapon from under her cloak and tried to strike Tuirna a fatal blow. Tuirna saw it coming, fortunately, and changed herself magically into a hound. She ran away and thus saved her life.

"But the jealous woman would not let her be. She set a trap for her rival and caught her in it. She was too afraid of Tuirna's magic to try to kill her again, so she contented herself with taking the hound a far distance away and giving her into the care of a man known to hate hounds.

"Tuirna began hunting game and bringing it back to this man. Eventually he came to appreciate her, and through her, to love all animals. He was so devoted to Tuirna and cared for her so well that she never wanted to change back into human shape.

"In time she gave birth to a pair of whelps, one great fine strong puppy and a little weak one. I had joined the Fíanna at this stage and was looking for a young hound I could train to hunt, and I heard of this wonderful animal and her two whelps. So I went to the man to ask for one of them.

"When I saw the bitch Tuirna, there was the same look in her eyes as my mother had. I begged the man to let me take her out for one day's hunting, to try her so I should know if I wanted her offspring. He agreed, though reluctantly. I could tell he did not like to be parted from her. He made me promise to be good to her and bring her back promptly.

"I took her into the forest and persuaded her to reveal her true form to me, which at last she did. She showed herself as a woman and told me her story, including the fact that she was the youngest sister of my mother.

"I offered to help her find Iollan and to restore her to him, but she refused. She said she had for many years lived the wild, free life of a huntress and she would not give it up now, not to be any man's wife. I took her back in her hound shape and told the man I wanted both her whelps, promising to cherish them as he cherished her.

"They lie at my feet this night, dearer to me than any," Finn concluded, stroking Bran and Sceolaun.

They gazed back at him with absolute devotion.

The fían relished the tale. More than one fénnid got up and came to rumple Bran's ears or smooth his hand down Sceolaun's back admiringly.

Only Goll stayed where he was, watching Finn with an inscrutable expression on his scarred face.

As they set off for Tara in the morning, Goll took Finn aside, leaving the others to tie their trophies to poles for carrying suspended between them. In a low voice, Goll said, "That's your most preposterous tale yet, Finn. I wouldn't tell that where anyone else can hear if I were you."

"Why not? They enjoyed it."

"Those ignorant lads? They'd believe anything you told them. But if you trot that tale past a more knowledgeable audience, you'll be humiliated."

Finn balled his fists. "How?" he challenged.

"You'll be called a liar. You've given yourself away at the beginning. No woman of your mother's clan would have been wife to a rígfénnid."

"My own mother was!"

"She wasn't Cuhal's contract wife, Finn. In fact, she wanted nothing to do with him. Her father was a *bo-aire,* a cattle lord; her family had wealth and prestige. They thought of Cuhal and those like him as social outcasts. Cuhal's attentions were an embarrassment to Muirinn and she complained to her father, who demanded Cuhal's word of honour he'd leave the woman alone. But he didn't. He kidnapped her against her will and stole her jewelry with her, then refused to pay her father the honour price for her."

Aghast, Finn cried, "I don't believe a word of it!"

Goll shrugged. "That doesn't alter the facts. There are still men in the Fíanna who remember; ask them. Cuhal broke his word, defiled a woman of superior rank against her will, and then wouldn't compensate her family as he was obliged to under the law. It was a great scandal, and it all rebounded very badly on the Fíanna. I wasn't surprised when Muirinn ran away from Cuhal as soon as she could."

"She didn't!"

"She did—before the Battle of Cnucha. Clan Morna fought to overthrow Cuhal, who'd disgraced us, and Muirinn ran away and abandoned Cuhal's baby on the Bog of Almhain. Then she found some Kerry chieftain who didn't know the story, and married him."

Finn was livid. His eyes were terrible. Goll began to regret having said anything. True though it was, it seemed a petty revenge to have taken against the long-dead Cuhal.

He extended his hand. "Finn, I—"

Finn knocked it aside. "Leave me alone."

On the way back to Tara, the fían carried their trophies triumphantly and sang as they marched. Only Goll and Finn were silent. Goll kept his eye on Finn, who walked rigidly, indifferent to the weight of the pole he shouldered, his gaze fixed on the ground in front of him.

Goll wondered what he was thinking.

The exuberant singing heralded their arrival, and people came running out to meet them and exclaim over their success. In the forefront was Lochan the smith, who went straight to Finn. "How were those new swords?" he wanted to know.

Finn shook his head as if shaking off a dream. "They served us well enough. You see we killed fifteen."

"Fifteen!" Lochan's eyes shone. "There'll be some feasting surely!"

"Indeed." Finn stopped walking. At the other end of his pole, Cailte stopped too. The rest of the men followed suit. Finn gave Lochan a concentrated look. "Fifteen," he said again. "More than we need. Have you ever had a whole boar for yourself, smith?"

"I? Never. A boar is the feast of chieftains and kings."

"You would consider a boar a noble gift, then?"

"Sumptuous!" exclaimed Lochan, wondering where this was leading.

"Would a whole boar every year be sufficient for a coibche?" Finn asked him.

Lochan the smith was not easily disconcerted. With hardly a hesitation, he said, "Which of my daughters do you want? I have several, any of them a fine armful for a man. And can I assume it's a contract marriage, since there's to be coibche? First degree, is it? How much property will she have to bring with her to equal yours?" He was eyeing Finn's checkered cloak.

The young man's sexual pride had suffered a painful blow, but another sort of pride was rising in him to redress the damage, to redress a great amount of damage. From the corner of his eye, Finn noticed that his men were listening avidly to the conversation.

He raised his voice. "From now on, no member of the Fíanna will take any property with a woman. We're hunters and warriors, we can support our women entirely with battle loot and the spoils of the chase."

"I see. Second degree, then?" Lochan had still not asked the name of the lucky woman.

Finn told him, "I shall pay you one whole boar each year for twenty-one years, beginning today, if you agree." With one hand he signalled for his men to untie a boar from the pole.

Lochan was already reaching to help them. "I do of course!" he said enthusiastically. "And as for your wedding gift—"

"No wedding gift."

Lochan turned to face Finn as the heavy boar crashed to the ground. "No gift? But I have to give you a wedding gift! The father always gives a gift to the man who's taking over responsibility for his daughter."

A muscle jumped in Finn's jaw. "Didn't you understand me? A member of the Fíanna takes nothing with a woman but herself. Nothing. No property of any sort. No gift. Nothing."

His men exchanged puzzled glances. "Is this some new rule he's making?" Cael asked Donn.

"Sounds like it."

"I don't understand."

Neither did Lochan. He scratched his head, his permanently blackened fingernails making furrows in his thick grey hair. "You'll pay the coibche but you reject the wedding gift? A strange way to . . . if you're sure that's what you want . . . you'll marry at Beltaine, I suppose? And take my daughter to your . . . which daughter did you say?" he suddenly thought to ask.

Finn's face was impassive, a block of granite behind which the real Finn Mac Cool hid. "I'll pay the coibche but I reject the wedding gift. And I won't take your daughter with me. I have no home to shelter her in. We live a free life. She will be better off staying with you."

Lochan was dumbfounded. "But you're marrying her!"

"I didn't say that. I said I'm giving you coibche for one of your daughters."

"Which one?"

"I didn't say that, either. Just accept that I am doing what I believe to be honourable. No man can ever accuse Finn Mac Cool of dishonour."

Consternation reigned. Talk of Finn's unprecedented behaviour spread like fire through Tara.

Cormac summoned his commander. "What's this about you paying coibche to Lochan? Are you marrying his daughter or not?"

"One of the smith's daughters may feel she has a grievance against me," Finn said guardedly. "She is now compensated. That's not a marriage."

"Is Lochan satisfied with this peculiar arrangement?"

"He seems to be. He took the boar."

Cormac was baffled. "Do I also understand you've made a new rule for the Fíanna, something about taking no property with their women?"

"I have."

"Why?"

Finn met Cormac's eyes squarely, the gaze of equals. "You're making new rules for the kingship. Why should I not make new rules for the army?"

"That roil of rowdies? They're barely under control at the best of times. Any new rule you make is just one more for them to break, Finn. They're fénnidi, you can't expect too much of them."

The skin at the corner of Finn's eyes tightened. "I am a fénnid," he said quietly. "I am also Rígfénnid Fíanna, which means I share in the reputation of my warriors. I intend that reputation to be above reproach."

"In your dealings with women?"

"Particularly in our dealings with women."

Cormac was forced to laugh. "What are you trying to do, turn the fénnidi into nobility?"

He meant the question as a joke.

Finn took it seriously. "We're as good as anybody," said Finn Mac Cool.

I I

WHEN HE FOUND TIME TO BE ALONE WITH HIS THOUGHTS, Finn was bitter. *Crimall should have told me. If what Goll says is true, Crimall should have told me.*

But when he had drunk the cup of bitterness to the dregs and taken no pleasure from it, he enlarged the horizon of his thought. *Why would Crimall have told me? He loved Cuhal, and the story reflects badly on Cuhal Mac Trenmor. My uncle would not have wanted me to know something that would, perhaps, make me think less of my father. Instead, he told me the stories of battles fought and won, of great hunts, and of men singing my father's praises.*

Still, someone should have told me.

But who?

The two old women? What could they have known?

And how did it happen that they took me in?

Did my mother give me into their care, as they let me believe? Or is it as Goll said . . . abandoned her Fir Bolg baby on the Bog of Almhain.

The words hurt like knives and he flinched from them, yet he could not help repeating them to himself.

I don't believe it. Abandoned her baby.

I won't believe it. Abandoned.

He tried to remember something, anything, that one of the old women might have said that could reinforce the story he wanted to believe. At the same time, he kept pushing away the one memory that did surface, the clarifying memory of his only meeting with the woman called Muirinn of the White Throat.

Any fiction was preferable to remembering the words Muirinn had said to him when he appeared, young and excited and eager, flushed with his success at finding her, expecting to be welcomed by his long-lost mother.

With all his strength, Finn slammed doors in his mind.

I remember what she said. Of course I do. I remember clearly. She said, My beloved son, my cherished child. Do this for me. Avenge your father's murder. My dearly beloved son.

That was what she said. My loving mother, that was what she said, it was! It was!

Without realizing it, Finn was pounding one fist into the palm of his other hand with such force that Cailte thought a fight was taking place. He trotted into the gloom of the stable only to find Finn there quite alone, in the middle of the day, with his features contorted by some emotion.

"Are you all right?" Cailte asked anxiously.

Finn looked at him through a red haze. "All right?"

"Hurt? Sick? Finn, what's wrong with you?"

"I . . . nothing's wrong with me. I'm grand entirely."

"But you're standing in here all by yourself beating your fist against your hand!"

"So? Is there a law against it?"

"It just seems a strange thing to be doing."

"I was . . . pounding home a resolution I just made."

Cailte continued to watch Finn with a worried expression. "What resolution?"

"To put every member of the Fíanna beyond reproach. To make fénnidi the most admired and respected of men."

Cailte said loyally, "We are now."

But there were some fictions even Finn could not accept. "We aren't. A roil of rowdies, that's what the king called us. We're outcasts, we're all expendables. Tools to be used by the nobles and chieftains and thrown away when the blades are broken. A cattle lord wouldn't give his daughter to a fénnid any more than he would marry her to the blade of a plough. But things are going to change, Cailte.

"Didn't you tell me you had difficulties getting the women you wanted? I promise you the day will come when women will swarm around you like bees. Not just servant women, but cattle lords' daughters and chieftains' sisters!" Finn flung out both arms wildly. His voice rang, his eyes flashed fire.

Suddenly aware that his vehemence bordered on irrationality, he turned away from Cailte and shook himself all over, like a hound. When he turned back, his eyes were calm, his voice soft. His whole appearance was changed. "You'd like that, wouldn't you?" he asked with a boyish grin. "To have the pick of the women? To have the best of them begging to bear the children of Cailte Mac Ronan because it would be a great honour to marry any one of the Fíanna?"

"Sounds grand," Cailte replied dubiously. "But I shan't hold my breath until it happens."

"It will happen," Finn promised. The boyish look was gone. Once more he pounded his fist into his palm. "It will happen."

Like a woodcarver whittling pegs, winter had whittled down the days until only a splinter of light remained between one night and the next. Ceaseless construction took place on Tara Hill during the brief period of daylight, but when light faded, fénnidi—their strength unspent—were forced by darkness to set aside their tools and find other ways to occupy themselves during the long nights. Young men, overtrained and underexerted, simmered on the verge of exploding. During the day they were tractable. At night they were a challenge beyond the skills of the most experienced officer.

Fiachaid approached Finn about the problem. "Your Fíanna are picking fights with my guard every night," he complained. "Stupid fights about nothing. I won't have it, Finn. My men are the younger sons of chieftains of the Milesian blood, the noble guard of a noble prince, chosen from his own people. I can't allow them to be mauled by . . ." He hesitated.

Finn had a dangerous glint in his eye. "Mauled by what, Fiachaid?" he asked with deceptive softness.

"You . . . ah, you know what I mean."

"Mauled by their inferiors? Is that what you mean?"

"I didn't say that."

"You didn't have to. But I appreciate your not using the term. I'll . . . control them."

"Can you?" Fiachaid asked doubtfully.

"I can," said Finn Mac Cool.

That very evening he announced a new series of tests that every member of the Fíanna would be expected to pass. Blamec was the first to protest. "But we passed the initiation tests when we joined the army! We ran, we demonstrated with sword and spear, we even recited. We proved we have good heads on strong bodies. What more do you want?"

Finn smiled slightly. "Everything," he said.

He knew these men. The same fires were smouldering in them as in himself. Even the most civilized of the fénnidi were half-wild, raised in relative poverty in a land fat with cattle and gleaming with gold. Oppressed, denigrated, subservient, they seethed. Given the slightest provocation, they would throw off all restraint, fighting and pillaging, not for spoils or glory, but merely to ride the cresting wave of their own uncontrolled passions. And the officers were little better than the men.

The Fíanna Finn now commanded were controlled by the most tenuous of bonds. Fíanna discipline, such as it was, was instilled in them by such rituals as bathing and suppling before meals, or memorizing epic poems of barbaric battle, which only succeeded in encouraging their basic natures.

Finn, however, determined to go much farther in dominating and shaping them into models of himself as he wished to be. A cold, hard resolve to this end had been born in him, and would last all his life. He would re-create the Fíanna in his enhanced image, replete with unquestioned honour.

He began by giving his men physical challenges that seemed beyond human capability. When they protested, he performed the feats himself, every one, with an ease that embarrassed the fénnidi.

If they were to hold up their heads in his presence, they must emulate him or die in the attempt.

One cold evening Cormac came down to the training ground Finn had prepared. There an exercise was being undertaken beneath whipping torchlight in a bitter north wind.

"You're going to kill those men," Cormac observed mildly.

"I doubt it. They can do this, they just don't know they can," said Finn.

He had ordered a trench dug deep enough to shelter a standing man to his waist. In turn, each of his warriors was sent to stand in the trench, armed only with his small round shield and a staff of hazel wood the length of his arm. Nine more warriors armed with javelins were commanded to face him from a good throwing distance. At Finn's signal, they were to cast their spears simultaneously at the man in the trench.

"If you receive a single wound," Finn said sternly to the current victim, Lugaid, "you are not fit to be in my Fíanna."

Staunch, grim-eyed, Lugaid stood in the trench with his shield raised and the hazel staff in his hand. Finn whistled. The spears sang through the flickering torchlight. Some thudded against the shield and fell. Two distinct cracking sounds told of the skill with which Lugaid deflected two more of the spears with his wooden staff.

He emerged from the trench unscathed.

"See?" Finn said to Cormac. "It can be done."

"What if he'd been killed?"

"He wasn't. I knew he wouldn't be. He's too good."

"But what if he wasn't as good as you think?" Cormac insisted.

"Then I'd need to know that, would I not?"

"You're a hard man."

"I am Rígfénnid Fíanna."

The king shook his head.

Finn would not give him the satisfaction of the answer he wanted, though it was a question Finn had asked of himself. Though he knew very little about the emotion of love, he realized he had come to love these men. He wanted no harm to touch any of them, ever. To that end, he would protect them by making them invincible. And by making the Fíanna invincible, he would make them more noble than any fénnidi had ever been.

On a level he could not articulate to himself, he understood that this was how kings were made from common clay.

Winter was passing. Buildings were nearing completion. The light was gaining strength, pushing back the night—and Cormac's wife Ethni, with her retinue, at last arrived on the Hill of Tara.

She had taken her time about making the journey. Born a princess, she let no one dictate to her. On a day of her own choosing she set out with an accompaniment of servants, her two young daughters and infant son, and a picked bodyguard of the best of Fiachaid's men, sent to her by Cormac for the occasion.

Finn Mac Cool accepted without comment that men of the Fíanna were not chosen for this purpose, were not deemed a proper escort for a king's wife.

Someday, he promised himself. Someday.

Ethni the Proud was tall and broad-shouldered and strode like a man. When Cormac went to meet her, she advanced toward him with dignity and an impassive face, deliberately slowing her pace so he must come to her.

If she had been worried about him at any time since he left her to fight Feircus Black-Tooth, no sign of that worry was on her face now or in her eyes. As calmly as if they had parted from each other the day before, she greeted Cormac by saying, "How kind of you to welcome me, husband."

Without instructions from the king, Finn had arranged his men into two lines, forming a corridor of honour from the gates toward the new fort known as Cormac's House. Every fénnid was polished until he shone, brushed and burnished and gleaming. The warriors stood at rigid attention, sternly forbidden by Finn to do more than flicker an eyelash.

"Don't look like a roil of rowdies," he warned them, "or you'll suffer for it. I want you to look like an avenue of oak trees."

He stationed himself at the head of the row, standing tall in his checkered cloak, with his silvery hair catching the light of the strengthening sun.

In spite of herself, Ethni glanced at him.

"Who is that?" she asked Cormac as the royal couple passed Finn and made their way up the human avenue, between two rows of vertical spears.

"Finn Mac Cool. My Rígfénnid Fíanna."

Ethni walked on a pace or two, then slowed her step and glanced back. Finn felt her eyes on him. She examined him with the same degree of detachment she would have shown to a horse or a servant.

"He's very tall for a Fir Bolg, is he not?" she asked her husband as if Finn were deaf and could not hear her. "I thought they were short, dark people."

"Some are." Cormac was aware that Finn was listening, must be listening. He took his wife by the elbow and tried to guide her into walking on again. But Ethni planted her feet and stood where she was. "Then why is this one tall and fair?"

"His father was tall and fair. They aren't all identical, Ethni, any more than we are."

"Oh?" She raised one carefully soot-blackened eyebrow and looked at Finn again. "How interesting." She sounded as if she did not find it interesting at all.

Ethni walked on then, with Cormac beside her. Finn's eyes remained fixedly staring straight ahead rather than following them. But Cailte, who was standing next to him, was aware that the spear Finn held upright was trembling.

Cormac took his wife on a tour of Tara, proudly showing her the royal magnificence he had created. Always they were accompanied by Fiachaid's men, almost like a human wall between Ethni the Proud and the Fíanna. This was so much a matter of routine that none but Finn gave any thought to it.

"This is the Assembly Hall," Cormac said, showing his wife the centrepiece of the new Tara. "It used to be just a rectangular wattle-and-daub structure capable of holding at most a hundred men. Now it is capable of containing the largest banquets ever served in Erin. The length is three hundred cubits, the width fifty, the height thirty. A bronze lamp is always kept burning inside. It can hold one hundred and fifty benches for feasting, plus one hundred and fifty warriors to attend me, and a cupbearer for every man I entertain here."

"Do you need so many doorways?" asked Ethni. "Doesn't that create a chilling draught?"

"The doorways are traditional. Even when this was a much cruder structure, there were fourteen of them, one for each of the reasons a visitor might approach the king here."

Ethni swept a coolly appraising eye over the new structure, which ran north and south along the slope of the hill. Its woodwork was carefully joined and finely planed. All the doorways were elaborately carved. The new thatch gleamed like a roof of gold, with layered patterns along the ridgeline of the roof where the thatch had been worked into swags and scallops. Turning slightly, she surveyed the other buildings now crowding the interior of the palisade until Tara resembled a town rather than a fort; a brand-new town, perfect and prosperous and impregnable.

"You are king of all this?" she asked her husband.

Cormac nodded gravely.

"And our eldest son Cairbri will be king here after you?"

"If I can hold it until he is old enough to succeed me, and I am ready to give up my kingship to him."

Ethni gave her husband a hard look. "Do you mean to hold on to it selfishly all your life?"

"I can be king," Cormac reminded her, "as long as I am unblemished and strong enough to wield a sword. That's the law."

"Sons often grow tired waiting for their fathers to relinquish the sword to them."

Cormac dropped his voice so no one else could hear as he said, "Are you threatening me, Ethni? Are you so ambitious for an infant still at the breast?"

"All mothers are ambitious for their sons," said Ethni the Proud with the faintest shrug of one strong shoulder.

That night the king held a great banquet in his new hall, in honour of his wife's arrival. It was the first true banquet ever to be held in Cormac's Banquetting Hall, and would set the pattern for innumerable events to follow.

Cormac and his retinue reclined on fur-draped couches on the west side of the hall. The king was attired in his best: his crimson cloak, his gold torc around his neck, a white linen shirt threaded with crimson at the throat and wrists, a multicoloured tunic belted with a girdle of gilded leather inlaid with precious stones. Even his leather shoes were banded with gold.

For this occasion Ethni feasted beside her husband, in the company of bards and brehons. Beyond them were the members of the king's court in order of descending rank, and as this was no Assembly and so no other nobles were present to fill the hall, the rest of the vast space was occupied by Fiachaid and Finn and their men.

"Watch the king as a hawk watches a sparrow," Finn had warned his fían before they entered. "Do whatever he does, the way he does it. Eat as he eats, drink as he drinks. Don't root at your food like hogs in acorn mast, but follow Cormac's example in manners at all times. I want it to look as if the Banquetting Hall is filled with nobles, not rabble."

"I know how to eat," growled Conan. "I've been doing it for years."

Cailte added, "There's only one way to eat, and that's right- and left-handed and as quickly as you can, before someone takes it away from you."

Finn glared at him. "No one's going to take anything away from us.

Eat as if you expect there will be more whenever you want it, because there will be. Eat like a king."

That night, among the fragrant cedar pillars that upheld the roof soaring high above them, Finn's fénnidi watched Cormac covertly and tried to eat like kings.

Sometimes, as Finn continually tested his men and devised new challenges for them, Cruina the smith's daughter came to watch. The practice sessions of the Fíanna were drawing spectators from throughout Tara by now. Ethni's servant women came every evening to stand on the sidelines, pointing out with a stabbing finger or a darting eye this or that man, commenting on his prowess, or possible prowess, giggling behind their hands.

"Ignore them," Finn commanded his men.

He was aware of Cruina, but he paid no heed to her. Then on one exceptionally cold evening, when the wind was howling through Tara like a mad thing, he saw from the corner of his eye that she was shivering. She stood apart from the other women, watching silently, her arms wrapped around herself, shivering. Finn abruptly turned and went to his own quarters. When he came back, he had the great animal-skin cloak over his arm. Without saying a word, he put it over Cruina's shoulders and went back to his men.

Lochan, when he heard of it, was overjoyed. He took the gesture as a public sign of commitment and began referring to his daughter Cruina as being "married to the Rígfénnid Fíanna, you know," with great pride. He did not quite dare say "wife," however. He was very aware there had been no contract.

He was also aware, as was Cruina, that Finn made no other gesture toward her.

There was a time in the not-too-distant past when Lochan would have been horrified to learn of any relationship between one of his daughters and a fénnid. Already that time was over.

Finn Mac Cool was proving himself a force to be reckoned with, a hero and champion whose embrace would honour a woman. Several of the noblewomen who had accompanied their cousin Ethni to Tara turned to look at him as he strode by.

One or two of them also cast speculative glances toward his band; his always-burnished, always-gleaming band, whose unfailing courtesy toward women was being rigidly enforced by their Rígfénnid Fíanna.

Finn found himself lecturing Fergus Honey-Tongue almost daily. The man seemed constitutionally unable to avoid passing remarks with women, and for him, oral conversation was just a prelude to physical communication.

Finally an exasperated Finn dragged him into the stable and threatened, "If I see you put your paws on one more woman, I'm going to break both your arms, Fergus!"

The warrior was perplexed. "But she smiled at me, Finn. She likes me. Are you trying to say I can't ever enjoy another woman? That's madness!"

"I didn't say that at all. I'm just telling you not to gobble them right- and left-handed. See how the king treats his wife? As if she's valuable, not digestible."

"But she is valuable. If someone harmed her, they'd have to pay her family three white cows as an honour price."

"Then," ordered Finn, "treat every woman as if she were worth three white cows."

Fergus looked at him aghast. "I don't understand Finn anymore," he subsequently lamented to Goll Mac Morna.

"Did you ever?"

"I thought so. He was just one of us."

"Is that what you thought?"

"And why not? When we joined the Fíanna, he was simply another fénnid. Better with weapons, maybe, but aside from that, no different. Quieter, sometimes. And . . ." Fergus paused, slowly enumerating in his mind those things that after all, he now realized had made Finn different from the beginning. "And bolder sometimes. And that poetry . . . he goes off somewhere inside his head when he's composing or reciting poetry, someplace we aren't allowed to follow him.

"He does that out in the country, too. Once we're in a forest, or on a hilltop, have you ever noticed what happens to Finn, Goll? He sort of . . . glows. It's like he's come home again. He gets a look about him I never see on his face when he's under a roof."

Goll said, "Finn's wilder than the rest of us. He has a quality in himself you and I don't have."

Fergus, thinking he understood, nodded. "The magic, you mean. His mother being of the blood of the Tuatha Dé Danann and all that."

"That's not true, Fergus."

"What are you talking about? Of course it's true. Finn told us himself."

"And that makes it true?"

"Is he not always talking to us about honour? Insisting that we be honourable no matter what? It's practically the only song he sings. Do you really believe a man like that would lie?"

Goll's lips twisted cynically. "In my experience, it's a man like that who's most likely to lie . . . if only to himself."

"Then you don't understand Finn at all."

"And you do? You just said you didn't."

Fergus snapped, "Obviously I understand him better than you do, Goll Mac Morna!"

Goll's patience with Finn was running thin. Even though he was older than the others and had once commanded the Fíanna himself, Finn insisted he perform the same feats and pass the same tests as everyone else. Goll considered this insulting. And almost impossible, physically. Years of battle and hard travel had ground him down more than he wanted to admit.

He began to suspect Finn not only knew this, but was deliberately taking advantage of it to undercut his position with the other men. That meant Finn must still see him as a rival; an obscure compliment.

Goll began trying harder than any of the others during the almost nightly competitions at Tara.

The days were growing longer, however; more work was being done, leaving less time for Finn's incessant drilling. As Lochan frequently remarked to his daughter, "Beltaine's approaching faster than you think, Cruina. Has Finn said nothing to you yet? No mention of a contract, or of a marriage at the dawn of summer?"

"How could he, when he doesn't speak to me at all?" she replied sadly.

"Then that's your fault, isn't it? Make an effort, girl!"

Cruina began dyeing her fingertips bright red and curling her hair into ringlets that looked like frizzed hemp whenever it rained, which was often as spring descended on Tara. She stationed herself where Finn could not fail to see her a dozen times a day.

He always nodded formally and walked past without a word.

Finally she could wait no longer. The promise of spring was thick in the throat of the day, reminding men that battle season would soon begin. Last details of construction were being completed by the fénnid, even as professional carpenters were being recruited from the nearby populace to replace them when the Fíanna took to the hills again.

On a misty morning with vapour rising in silver waves from sodden earth, Cruina stepped directly into Finn's path and stood there, daring him with her eyes to dodge around her.

He stopped. "Can I do something for you?" he enquired politely.

"You can talk to me."

"What have we to talk about?"

"Our marriage!" she burst out.

"You said there was no marriage. Is there anything else, or can I go?"

"You said you wanted a contract marriage!"

"That was then and this is now."

"You don't want to marry me?" She met his eyes squarely. "Answer me, Finn. They are saying of you that you tell the truth, that you insist upon it for all the Fíanna. Tell me the truth now. Do you not want me?"

To his dismay, Finn realized his heart was pounding. She was standing a little too close to him. The day was a little too warm. Blood was running in his veins like a river.

"I want to lie with you," he said in a voice from which he withheld any trace of emotion. "I want to lie with many women. I want to eat all the fat meat in Tara and drink all the ale. But I don't do it; I have other things to do."

"Are you going to take me as your wife at Beltaine?" Cruina demanded to know.

He smiled then. "Cruina of the Questions." He almost reached out. He almost touched her. But he could not risk another humiliation with this woman. The next time he touched a woman, he had promised himself, it would be one who did not know about his initial failure. "I shall soon be away for a long time. If I wed you at Beltaine, you would not see me until Samhain, and perhaps not then, depending on what happens in the coming year," he told her. "Better for you if things continue as they are."

Giving her a smile that she could interpret any way she chose, Finn left her standing there.

Cruina stood for a long time, head down, listening to his words in her mind. Analyzing the tone of his voice. Trying to believe what she wanted to believe.

Then she drew in a slow, deep breath, lifted her head, and retraced her steps to her father's house.

As Beltaine approached, the Fíanna began to assemble from their various winter quarters. Runners came almost daily to Tara, advising of the readiness of this company or that and their expected arrival to be given their summer's orders. Meanwhile, other runners were arriving from chieftains who had sworn loyalty to the new king and now requested some of his Fíanna to patrol their borders or fight their enemies or intimidate doubtful friends.

"You realize we won't actually leave Tara until quite some time after Beltaine," Goll told Finn. "You'll have to personally issue orders to each rígfénnid, and that means waiting here until the last one comes in. And you'll have to plan your own season, of course."

Finn nodded. "Whatever we do, it will be the thing Cormac most needs done."

As the bands of Fíanna arrived, Finn met them personally. Each rígfénnid was informed, to his astonishment, that there would be additional testing of his men before they were allowed to go back out into Erin in the king's name. Some of the older officers were amused. "That youngster takes a lot on himself," one commented to Goll Mac Morna.

"He does, but it isn't a bad idea. Sharpening them up before battle season can only benefit them if there is any serious fighting to be done."

"Och, there's always serious fighting to be done!" the other said heartily.

The sun steadily grew hotter, brighter, closer. Finn began to dream of rustling silken summer, of being adrift loose-footed in the honeyed season, all juice and joy. He chafed at the need to remain within the walls of Tara, making assignments, listening to complaints, balancing needs and demands.

He wanted to run free again.

12

RED RIDGE ARRIVED AT TARA AS FINN AND HIS MEN were making the last preparations for their departure. He appeared at the Slige Mor gates with his shield on his arm and Finn Mac Cool's name on his lips.

The sentry was suspicious. "Where did you meet him?"

"I knew him in the Burren."

"The Rígfénnid Fíanna doesn't come from the Burren."

Red Ridge hesitated. Rígfénnid Fíanna? "I don't need to see him yet, I just want Finn Mac Cool. He's a rígfénnid with one company and he—"

"I knew you didn't know him," said the sentry. Raising his voice, he called over his shoulder, "Ronan! There's an imposter here who claims to know the Rígfénnid Fíanna! Come separate his joints, will you?"

A large redheaded man approached, grinning like a bear scenting honey. As he walked toward Red Ridge, he began bending his fingers and cracking his knuckles with a sound like bones breaking.

Red Ridge hefted his spear and stood his ground. "Finn Mac Cool will vouch for me. Send for him."

The sentry watched him with an appraising eye. "Doesn't bluff," he remarked aloud. "Come inside then, and we'll send for Finn. If he knows you, you might live until sundown. If not . . ." The sentry shrugged.

The large redheaded man cracked his knuckles again and looked as disappointed as a child deprived of its ball of mutton fat smeared with honey and studded with pine nuts.

As they waited for Finn, Red Ridge stared through the open gateway. What he saw dazzled him. Numerous structures, all of them big, all of them new, walls gleaming white with limewash, every exposed timber elaborately carved with the finest craftsmanship, brilliant banners fluttering from every ridgepole, splashes of green and blue and crimson vivid against golden thatch. Tara was colour and light, opulence and power.

Finn, the Finn I know, would never be in such a place as this, Red Ridge told himself. The wisest thing to do would be to saunter off down the road as casually as possible, right now, hoping not to feel the thud of a spear between the shoulder blades.

But before he could put action to thought, Red Ridge saw an apparition striding toward him and stayed where he was, rooted by astonishment.

The face was that of Finn Mac Cool. So was the strangely silver hair, now divided into many partings and tightly plaited, each plait fastened with a twist of dyed leather. The figure was as tall as Finn, the shoulders as improbably wide, but there the resemblance ended.

This man wore a great woollen cloak striped and speckled with yellow and green and black, and deeply fringed in red. Beneath this he appeared to have a linen tunic bleached snowy and embroidered with green knotwork. Such garments would require the weaving and sewing of many women, and Finn Mac Cool—the Finn that Red Ridge remembered—surely had no such women.

The man in the striped-and-speckled cloak hurried forward, calling warmly, "Red Ridge! I was beginning to think you forgot us."

Red Ridge struggled for words. "I never forgot. I had to stay with Iruis until the wedding, but when the wine still stood in the cups, I left him and hurried here. I ran most of the way, I think, hoping you'd still be here, or at least they'd know where you were, but . . . I never expected . . ." He paused and made a single gesture that included Finn and Tara and a setting beyond his powers of description. "I never expected this."

Finn threw back his head and laughed. It was the same laugh, boyish and merry; the same Finn Mac Cool.

Even the sentry smiled, and Ronan the redheaded man.

Red Ridge began to relax.

Finn took him by the arm. "Come inside and say hello to the others, Goll and Cailte and the fían. They're all here with me. In a couple of days we'll be leaving; you got here just in time."

He led Red Ridge through the gateway and into the gleaming, golden fortress. Out of the corner of his eye, Finn watched the newcomer's face and took delight in his obvious amazement.

Finn's original band gave Red Ridge a warm welcome and introduced him to the second and third nine, plus an assortment of other warriors and rígfénnidi who would serve the king that summer. Finn said the same to each of them. "This is a good man, this Red Ridge."

Red Ridge glowed.

But that night as they sat by the feasting fire, he made a mistake.

Looking around expansively at his fellow fénnidi, his belly full of fat meat and his cup brimming with barley ale, he said with satisfaction, "So this is what it's like to be in the Fíanna."

Bald Conan growled, "You aren't in the Fíanna. This is what it's like, but not for you—except as our guest."

Red Ridge straightened up. "But I thought—"

"You thought Finn would just take you in and say 'Well done'? Hardly. You'll have to pass tests, the same as the rest of us."

"I can learn poetry," Red Ridge said. "It may take me a little while, but I've a good head."

"You'll need more than that," Donn informed him.

"I'm good with sword and spear, too."

Cael sniggered. "Insufficient. To join the Fíanna now, you have to be able to walk on the water, fly through the air, sing through your eyes, and breathe through your eyes."

The others burst into raucous laughter.

Reassured by it, Red Ridge said, "You're joking, of course."

Finn, who had been listening without comment, spoke up. "He's not joking. Och, we don't have the requirements he describes, but others equally severe now. And if you want to march with us, you'll have to meet them all before we leave here. All except the poetry, I suppose; we might wait on that until you find someone to teach you—if you assure me you can learn."

Red Ridge nodded emphatically. "I can learn."

Finn's eyes bored into his. "On your honour?"

Before Red Ridge could answer, Fergus Honey-Tongue warned him, "Say it only if you mean it. The honour of a fénnid these days is pledged with his life."

The underlying grimness in Fergus's voice was a warning. Red Ridge paused, then said, "Just what does that mean?"

"What it says," Finn told him. "A member of the Fíanna will pay for dishonour on the point of a sword. My sword. That's the rule now. If you can't accept it, don't apply."

Red Ridge licked grease from his fingers and gazed at the others through slitted eyes. Their faces glowed in the firelight; their eyes glittered with the promise of adventures to come.

More than anything in his life, he wanted to be one of them.

Meeting Finn's eyes, he said, "On my honour I will learn and do whatever is required of me. My honour rests on the point of your sword."

Finn smiled.

That night Red Ridge slept on the cold earth outside the walls of the stable that had been rebuilt to garrison Finn's company. No more than two spear lengths separated him from them. Two spear lengths, and the most demanding challenge of his young life.

It began at sunrise, with Blamec shaking him by the shoulder and complaining, "I don't see why I have to be the one to make you show a leg. I'd as soon be sleeping myself. Wake up and throw off your cloak, you're wanted down below."

Down below was the training ground, which was already lined, Red Ridge noticed to his discomfiture, with spectators. The testing of prospective members of Finn's Fíanna was considered an event not to be missed.

Finn, dressed in a checkered cloak this time and looking more imposing than ever, as if his youth was already slipping from him, met Red Ridge at the head of the training ground. In a ringing voice, he said, "If you would join the Fíanna, you must accept four injunctions.

"The first: you will never receive property with or through a wife, but choose her solely for her qualities.

"The second: you will never offer violence to any woman.

"The third: you will never refuse to give anyone anything you possess if they are in need of it.

"The fourth: you will never flee from less than nine armed warriors."

Red Ridge had listened carefully, and he nodded as each prohibition was given. They did not seem too hard to accept. But then Finn continued.

"Before you can be counted as one of the Fíanna, your nearest kinfolk must guarantee that they will never seek revenge should you be killed in battle. If someone does you an injury, you may avenge yourself while you live, but no one else can do it for you if you die." As he spoke these words, Finn covertly watched Goll Mac Morna. By now, Goll had heard this same speech quite a few times and accepted it. His features were relaxed, his one good eye calm, unsuspecting.

Finn went on. "No man shall be counted as one of the Fíanna until he can recite twelve epics to prove he knows the history of this land. As these conditions require time to fulfill, and as we have discussed before, we plan to march soon. So I shall give you until Samhain to fulfill them. But if at that time you have not done so, you will be expelled from our number and may not try to enter the Fíanna again."

Red Ridge nodded respectfully, though he was finding it hard to reconcile this stern authoritarian with the spellbinding storyteller he had met atop Black Head. This Finn was a warrior to his spine; dominant, demanding. The dreamy boy who had captured Red Ridge with words and magic seemed someone else entirely.

But whoever he was, the Connacht man longed with all his being to be numbered among Finn's Fíanna.

When he was shown the trench and its purpose explained, however, he had momentary doubts.

Finn ordered Red Ridge into the trench and then the original nine attacked him as if he were a mortal enemy, running toward him yelling, hurling their spears, making every effort to kill him. He defended himself as best he could with shield and staff, moving faster than he had ever done in his life. When the attack ended abruptly and he found himself still alive, he expected to be congratulated.

Instead, he was plunged headlong into the next test. "Plait your hair tightly," Finn ordered. "Then we take you to the wood beyond Tara. We give you a standing start of the distance of one tree. Run as fast as you can, for we will be pursuing you. If we catch you, we wound you. If you are wounded, you fail the test."

"If one plait of your hair is loosened by being snagged on a branch, you fail," said Cailte.

Goll added, "You fail if your hands tremble."

And from Lugaid, "You fail if you break a single fallen branch with your foot as you run your course."

"You must avoid your pursuers with visible courage and pass through the wood without disturbing a twig in your flight," Fergus Honey-Tongue concluded.

Aghast, Red Ridge stared at the fían. "You've all done this?"

"We have," Madan said smugly. "Now it's your turn. Of course you could leave right now and go back to Connacht . . . and never know if you could have done it or not."

But Red Ridge's fingers were already busily plaiting his hair.

They took him to the edge of the forest, gave him the briefest of head starts, and set off after him. What followed was the most harrowing experience of Red Ridge's life so far. Once again they seemed determined to kill him, hurling spears and hewing the air with swords. In addition to avoiding them, he had to duck and dodge, break no dead branches on the ground, be touched by no twigs on the trees. He had to run with all his strength and concentrate with all his mind, run and run and . . .

He burst from the woods to find himself on the grassy plain of Míd, still running, his heart pounding under his ribs. He reached up to feel his hair.

The plaits were not disturbed.

He slowed to a trot, turned, and went back. They waited for him at the edge of the wood. But there were still no congratulations.

"Do you see this tree?" Finn enquired, indicating a gnarled oak twisted by centuries into a series of grotesque gestures. "Now you must leap over this branch that's as high as your head, then turn at once and duck beneath this branch that's as low as your knees. Touch neither with your body."

Wearing a look of grim, slightly wild-eyed determination, Red Ridge took a running jump at the first branch, hurtled over it, then turned and ducked under the second. He thought it might just have grazed his shoulders, but he could not be sure. As he straightened up, he looked at Finn.

Finn looked impassively back. "Now drive this into the heel of your bare foot without flinching," he said, holding out his hand. On his extended palm was a single gleaming thorn, long and dark and sharp.

"You protested that, I recall," Madan muttered to Blamec.

"He protested everything," Conan reminded them. "But he did it anyway."

Red Ridge drew a deep breath, bent his right leg at the knee, reached down and drove the thorn into his heel. With all the willpower he possessed, he refrained from flinching.

No one congratulated him. Instead, Finn said, "Now run at your top speed from here back to the gates of Tara, and on the way, pluck the thorn from your foot without missing a stride."

Blamec muttered with some satisfaction, "Everyone protested that."

"But we did it," said Fergus Honey-Tongue, "and the sun shone and the wind blew and we shouted our triumph."

Red Ridge ached to shout his triumph.

Trying to ignore the pain in his foot, he set off at the run, back toward Tara. The gates yawned open, waiting to receive him, but they seemed very far away. Every step was an agony as his weight drove the thorn deeper and deeper into his foot. He was aware of Finn and the others running behind him, watching him.

He bent at the waist and made a swipe at his foot. Missed. Ran on and tried again. Missed again. Swore. Heard someone laugh behind him. "Is there some trick to this?" he panted over his shoulder.

"Run," called Cailte. "Bend your knees."

He ran. The gates were getting closer. Soon he would be there.

The others could do this. Why couldn't he?

I can, Red Ridge told himself, not believing. He grabbed at his foot again and felt the rounded head of the thorn, but his fingers were clumsy and he only drove it farther in. He knew the distance now though, and the moment in his stride when the foot was in the best position.

Just short of the gates, he made one last try. His fingernails, pincer-like, seized the head of the thorn precisely as the foot thrust forward . . . leaving the thorn in Red Ridge's hand.

As he ran through the gates, he threw up both arms with a great shout of triumph.

And they all shouted with him, Finn loudest of all.

People crowded around him then, and he expected the longed-for congratulations. But there was one more requirement.

Finn led Red Ridge to a post mounted in a place of honour within the palisade, a post topped by a grotesque and blackened skull. Without explaining either the object or its significance, he told Red Ridge to stand with his back against the post. "Now," he said, "this is the final requirement. You must swear your loyalty, on your honour."

Red Ridge had expected this. He began, "I swear my loyalty to the Fíanna and the king of Tara, as—"

Finn's face tightened. "Swear your honour to the Rígfénnid Fíanna," he said in a low, intense voice. "That's the only loyalty you need. But remember: you swear on the point of my sword, and if you fail in honour, your life is forfeit to me."

Red Ridge gazed at Finn Mac Cool; at the piercing, commanding eyes; the wide and savage cheekbones; the tender, brooding mouth. Why, he wondered, all this emphasis on honour? How important could such a thing be to a simple fénnid? But if it was what Finn demanded . . . he shrugged and repeated the vow.

And even as he spoke, something seemed to clamp around his spirit like a hand.

His startled eyes flared wide. He stared at Finn Mac Cool . . . and felt the touch of magic.

Finn's first nine danced around him, punching his biceps and the air and each other, jubilant. "That's it!" cried Cael. "You're in the Fíanna now!"

"But the poems and the guarantee from my people . . ."

"Later," said Finn. "We leave Tara tomorrow, and you with us."

Trying to hold on to the moment, Red Ridge stood beside the skull-topped post and was swept by a strange euphoria. I am part of the Fianna, he told himself; I actually *am!*

Until he arrived at Tara, joining the Fíanna had not seemed such a dazzling accomplishment. For a man of his birth, it was probably the best he could do, but he realized that being part of the king of Tara's band of sometime-warriors was no immense distinction for anyone but a fénnid.

Or had not been.

Until Finn Mac Cool.

Already, Finn was making the Fíanna something very special. Those who followed him were being driven by their commander to heights beyond themselves, beyond their perceived abilities. Finn was making his men better than they ever thought they could be and they adored him for it. Looking around at them, Red Ridge saw their adoration in their eyes—except for the single eye of Goll Mac Morna.

He recognized the same quality of adoration in himself. He was part of the Fíanna now, part of Finn Mac Cool. His feet were firmly fixed in legend.

Throughout the winter, Cormac had been making plans. As he had told Finn, his first move would be to make a circuit of Erin and wrest as much support, or submission, as he could from its various kings, before he had to face the challenge of the Ulaid. If he had the kings of the Connachta, the Erainn, and the Laigin behind him, he felt sure he could force the Ulaid to accept him as overlord.

But he could not afford to make any mistakes.

Dominance in Erin was always shifting; today's king was tomorrow's corpse; war was the game everyone played.

Cormac Mac Airt intended to play to win.

Long before Beltaine, he had commanded Finn, "Send runners to every fían in winter quarters, giving them exact orders as to where they are to be by the first day of battle season. Spread the Fíanna across Erin like a fisherman's net, so that wherever I go, I have fénnidi already there, armed, rested, and ready to fight for me if need be. Tell them to be obvious; let the people see them."

Finn had ordered a large contingent of the Fíanna, under the most seasoned rígfénnidi, to patrol the territory between Míd and Ulidia. When battle broke, it would begin there.

But as Goll had advised him, "The Ulaid won't be here spoiling for war on the first day of battle season. I know those northerners, they're a foxy lot. They'll hold back for a while to see what Cormac does before they make their move. I expect them to march on Tara late in the summer, after they've fully assessed his strength."

"That's not what I would do," replied Finn. "I'd hit him right now, before he has his allies gathered."

"Would you?" Goll looked at Finn unblinkingly. "If you have an enemy and you break into his stronghold and batter him while he's trying to put on his clothes in the dawn, what have you accomplished if you win? There's little glory in that."

"But an easier victory," said Finn Mac Cool.

Goll managed, even with one eye, to look disdainful. "I've referred to your lack of style before, Finn. There is a certain way of doing things that we've always—"

"There is a new way now," Finn said coldly. "My way."

"You think you know so much about war, do you?"

"I know about winning, and I'm not talking about chess. You get what you have the strength to take. You keep what you have the power to defend."

With the rest of the Fíanna assumed to be in place, Cormac left Tara on a high, clear, wind-scoured day with all his banners flying. He rode a powerfully muscled grey horse, a stallion whose hide was still dappled with youth. For the first time in many seasons, his kinsman Fiachaid did not ride a few paces behind him. By the king's order, Fiachaid and his men were to stay to guard Tara, reinforced by a detachment of the Fíanna.

Cormac was surprised that Fiachaid did not protest the arrangement. Indeed, his response upon receiving the order was, "Take good care of the new Rígfénnid Fíanna, will you?"

Cormac raised an eyebrow. "I thought he was supposed to take care of me."

"I have no doubt he will. But I should not like for anything to happen to him either. He is . . . special."

"You actually like him."

"I do," Fiachaid agreed. "I actually do. Which is more than I can say for Goll Mac Morna. Keep an eye on that one, Cormac. I think his feelings toward Finn Mac Cool are at best ambivalent."

Finn had never been on a horse. No Fir Bolg rode horses; the equestrian skills were above their station. The back of a horse was meant for the seat of a king, so he could survey his territory from a regal perch and his people would be forced to look up to him. Fir Bolg were expected to keep their eyes on the ground in front of them.

Finn—who chose to disregard this—often gazed at the stars.

On this morning of departure he trotted at the shoulder of the king's horse, running with the easy grace of a warrior. He was fully armed, carrying both his swords and an assortment of spears. His plaited hair gleamed silver in the sun. Behind him flowed his Fíanna like a small river, carrying spears upright. Light glanced off the polished spearheads like stars.

With their bodies, the populace of Tara formed a channel for that river, so that it flowed between two banks of people, star-crested.

Behind the Fíanna were the king's official attendants, a small army themselves. But there was no appointed companion for the king, no confidante and soul-friend. There was only Finn Mac Cool.

As they reached the Slige Cualann gate, Cormac reined in his horse and twisted around, looking back. His eyes found Ethni standing proudly. He raised a hand to her. She raised a hand to him. Whatever was said between them passed through their eyes.

Watching, Finn felt a thud of envy like a fist in the belly. But he did not look around in search of some woman's eyes for himself. He knew Cruina was watching. There was nothing to communicate to her.

Cormac Mac Airt and the Fíanna swept through the gates of Tara. Ahead of them lay history.

13

BATTLE SEASON. SWEATING AND SHOVING AND YELLING. Bared teeth and clenched fists, faces white with fear and red with rage. Shoulder into belly, elbow into throat, hurl slash thrust, dance away dance away and come back roaring.

Immortality gushing out of a body suddenly emptied of its future.

Sport and war knotted together, and the only thing a man could be sure of was the certainty that he was alive right now, this moment, this heartbeat. In battle, he was so alive!

Cormac Mac Airt travelled the roads of Erin, excluding only Ulidia, that summer, meeting friendship with friendship and hostility with hostility. Some were willing to accept his sovereignty. Others resented him, or hated him, or fought him simply because fighting was what they did.

The provincial kings were ostensibly amenable to persuasion, willing to hear him out and bide their time to see how strong he truly was. But some of the tribal kings and chieftains saw the advance of Tara's dominion as just another tribute to be added to the load they already carried. They would not listen.

For them, Cormac had the Fíanna.

While he and his retinue were being entertained in some princely stronghold, Finn and his men were stationed outside the walls. To their astonishment, Finn would not allow the Fíanna the usual petty thievery and pillage that was the traditional pleasure of armies on the march. "When we leave one of Cormac's allies," he said sternly, "we shall drag branches behind us to smooth away our footprints, so nothing has been disturbed by us in the land of a friend."

But when they entered a region where armed warriors met them with spears raised, they were happier. After battle there was permissible plundering. Half of what they took belonged to the king. The other half went to Finn Mac Cool, to be divided among his men.

"I bitterly resent the fact," Blamec commented on one occasion, "that Cormac's friends are the wealthy ones, who would have good plunder if we were allowed it, and his enemies always seem to be poor, so that what we take from them is shabby and mean."

"If you don't want your share, you can give it to me," replied Conan Maol.

"You always seem to get your own share and half of everyone else's too," Donn interjected. "You're greedy, Conan."

"I'm not greedy. I just have big hands."

Fergus Honey-Tongue said, "Conan the Hairless has a mighty reach."

When they were in amicable regions, the Fíanna devoted most of their time to hunting. They built hunting booths in the glens and on the hillsides to screen themselves from the weather and the eyes of their prey, and ceaselessly trained their hounds to hunt the deer and the wolf. Along their way, many of them had acquired hounds, so that Bran and Sceolaun now led a pack of huge, shaggy animals as eager as they. Finn had added Lomair and Brod and Lomluath to his personal pack, and rejoiced in watching Bran lay down the law to them. No dog questioned Bran's leadership, ever.

Deep in Erainn territory, a man called Robartach brought a huge dog to Finn, extolling its virtues above all the hounds of the Fíanna. The creature was as tall as Bran, though not as shaggy, heavier through the jaw, with pricked ears and a crescent of white showing at the edges of the eyes.

"I don't like the look of that animal," Finn said behind his hand to Cailte. "There's a nasty glint in the eye."

"You don't like the look of any dog that doesn't resemble Bran."

"True. Would you say this one's any good at all?"

Overhearing, the owner replied eagerly, "The only way to know is to match them at fighting! As for a wager, if my dog overcomes yours, he will replace Bran as leader of the pack of the Rígfénnid Fíanna and his whelps will command great prices. I have a few of them available," he added.

"Bags full, I'd say," remarked Conan. "And you can't get rid of them."

Robartach, who was red-faced and balding, glared at the totally hairless Conan before turning back to Finn. "Is it a wager?"

Confident of Bran, Finn replied, "It is. But when Bran defeats your dog, I pledge you to tell every person you meet that Finn Mac Cool's Bran is the mightiest hound in Erin."

Robartach smirked. "I won't have to. My dog will win."

The warriors formed a circle. Finn and Robartach crouched beside their dogs, rubbing them and whispering to them. Then they stood back. The dogs knew what was expected of them. After circling one another stiff-legged and snarling, they attacked simultaneously.

Finn's assessment of the other dog proved correct. The animal was not only savage, but devious. Its hide was very loose so that every time Bran took a hold, the other dog twisted away, leaving Bran with a mouthful of flesh but no real damage done. In that moment, Robartach's dog would double back with a dropped shoulder and try to seize Bran's foreleg in its jaws to snap the bone.

Bran fought cleanly and fiercely and bravely, but was not experienced in fighting other dogs, while it soon became obvious that Robartach's animal had been bred and trained for that express purpose.

The sounds of the dogs growling and the spectators yelling soon brought Cormac and his host outside to watch. They had to shoulder into the crowd, which was more respectful of the fighting dogs at the moment than of princes.

The battle went on and on, progressively bloodier, with Bran refusing to surrender even when it became obvious the other dog must win. At last Finn could bear it no longer. "Call off your dog!" he cried to Robartach.

"I will not."

"Then give me his name and I'll call him off myself!"

Robartach clamped his jaws shut and stood with arms folded.

Without the dog's name, Finn could not command him. He yelled inarticulately and waded into the melee, hoping to pull the combatants apart by brute force, but the dogs were too fast even for him. He shouted at the prick-eared dog, but it ignored him and continued to rend and tear Bran's flesh.

Robartach only laughed. "Admit it, Finn. Mine is the better animal."

Heedless of the danger to himself, Finn continued to try to separate the fighting dogs. As he struggled, he could hear the comments of the spectators, some of whom had come with Robartach. A youth spent in the wilds of Erin had given Finn almost preternatural hearing. Even over the growling of the animals, he heard one man mutter the name of Robartach's dog to a companion.

Finn froze. He stood erect, jammed his thumb into his mouth, and appeared to listen intently. Then he yelled, *"Coinn Iotair!* Hound of Rage! Stop fighting and come to me!"

When he heard his name, Coinn Iotair hesitated. In that fatal instant, Bran sank deadly fangs into his throat and ripped it open.

Robartach was dismayed. "How did you know the name?" he asked, watching his dog in its death throes.

Finn gave a nonchalant shrug. "I listened to my thumb."

"What?"

"One of my men will explain it to you, ask any of them. You should never underestimate Finn Mac Cool." He sank to his knees beside Bran, who was bleeding profusely. Bran tried to lick his hands.

Finn lifted the hound in his arms and approached Cormac Mac Airt. "I request your physician to heal Bran's wounds," he said to the king.

Cormac was taken aback, and his Erainn host was appalled. "A king's physician tending an animal? You must be joking."

"Not about this," said Finn Mac Cool, his eyes locking with those of the king.

For the first time, Cormac felt the full force of his will. Suddenly feeling it was necessary, the king told his Rígfénnid Fíanna, "You can't always have what you want, Finn."

Finn's posture did not change, nor did he move a muscle in his face. Nothing changed. Yet a Thing looked out of his eyes that had not been there before, a creature more feral than a wolf, more terrible than a storm. A creature wild beyond imagining, an elemental force, a power capable of destroying everything in its path if opposed.

"Your physician will heal my dog," said the Thing in Finn's eyes.

Cormac recalled that Finn claimed kinship with the Tuatha Dé Danann. Shapechangers.

I must face him down now, the king told himself. I must face him down surely, I dare not allow him any advantage over me.

He drew in breath to speak. The words of royal refusal were already on his tongue when his talent for reading the thoughts of others rose in him, and he knew beyond doubt that Finn would kill him where he stood if he did not help Bran.

Would kill him where he stood as a wolf would kill a king, caring nothing for his titles or ancestry.

And Finn Mac Cool was so fast that the deed would be done before any human could stop him.

With a great effort, as if his features were carved of stone that he must first soften, Cormac made himself smile. "As a favour to the Rígfénnid Fíanna," he said loudly, "I accede to his request. This is a splendid hound whose death would be a loss. My own physician will tend the wounds."

The Thing that had looked at the king from Finn's eyes was gone in a blink. "I thank you for your generosity," said Finn.

With trembling hands, Cormac's own physician bathed and dressed Bran's wounds and pulled the flaps of skin together, poulticing them and binding them with strips of linen as precisely as he would have done had the wounds been on the body of Cormac Mac Airt. The whole time he was working, Finn stood over him, saying nothing, merely watching.

The whole time he was working, Bran's eyes were fixed on Finn with absolute devotion. The dog neither flinched nor whined, just watched Finn.

When it was over, the physician got himself a big cup of mead and went off with it for a while.

That night as they sat by their feasting fire under the stars, breathing fresh, clean air while Cormac had to breathe the stifling atmosphere of his host's banquetting hall, Cailte remarked to Finn, "You love that dog."

Finn smiled. "I love the clamour of the hunt on the mountainside, the belling of stags in the glen, the screaming of gulls on the shore, the sound of the waterfall in the forest, the song of the blackbird in the morning.

"And I love Bran."

Lying beside him as always, Bran pricked one badly torn ear and thumped the ground with a feathery tail.

"Poetry again?" enquired Cailte.

"I had to be a warrior today. I can be a poet tonight."

"Is it hard to be both?"

Finn Mac Cool did not answer.

Those were indeed the days of high summer. Cormac's circuit carried his name to remote clanholds where no king of Tara had ever visited before, and wherever he went, Finn and his companions accompanied him. The legends grew around them, acquiring a life of their own. After the king's entourage had moved on, those who had met them told tales to those who had not, tales that grew in the telling like ripples spreading on a pond.

The stories of Finn's hounds, particularly of Bran and Sceolaun, multiplied in the same way. At a feast held in Cormac's honour by a king of the Deisi, Fithel the royal brehon enumerated a number of the laws pertaining to hounds, who had an extensive category of their own.

"Brehon Law," he explained, "grades dogs into fully lawful, half-lawful, and quarter-lawful animals. Lawful dogs enjoy full recognition under the law, and for any damage done them, there must be compensation. Lawful dogs include hunting hounds, dogs kept as watchdogs, and the lapdog of a king's woman. The value of the whelp of a lawful dog is one ninth the value of its mother.

"In dogfights, every type of bite and action must be considered. If the inciter of the fight is a sensible man, his dog is free of liability. If he is a foolish man, the dog has more liability, it being considered that the animal's brain exceeds the owner's."

Finn, who had offered no compensation to Robartach, spoke up. "When the dog of an inciter is killed, should there be an honour price paid for it?"

Fithel happily launched into a long explanation of the different grades of distress and compensation as applied to every sort of injury, including those of dogs in fights. He would as gladly have spent the night listing the laws applying to beekeeping, which were even more detailed and extensive.

But Finn did not keep bees. He did not need that information.

In the high, golden days of summer, there were women. In the royal forts of provincial kings, there were women. In the wattle huts of cattle herders, there were women. When a woman's eyes met the eyes of one of the Fíanna, sometimes a look passed between them. Sometimes a word, a touch on the arm . . .

Finn did not deny his men the pleasure of women. He did, however, hedge them with rules, so they would do nothing to dishonour themselves or the Fíanna. When he saw a glance pass between man and woman, he invariably took that man aside and spoke to him in a strong, urgent voice, reminding him of his vows and obligations, demanding that he treat the woman in a way that would leave no regrets.

For himself, there were no women. Sometimes at night he lay on his back and stared at the stars and thought of Cruina.

Sometimes he clenched his fists in the darkness.

More than once he sent Cailte with a string of runners to Tara to learn if the Ulaid had made any move. The reply was always the same. "No sign of them," Cailte would report as he sat on the ground, thinner than ever, his legs scarred with briers, gulping ale as if he had drunk nothing the whole journey to Tara and back.

Cormac wondered, "When will they make their move?"

No one could tell him. Even Goll could not guess.

As the summer passed, the lack of activity on the part of the Ulaid preyed increasingly on Cormac's mind. He began, almost without conscious thought, to wend his way toward Tara again, leaving behind a network of self-proclaimed allies and supporters, all of whom had been promised rewards for their allegiance or threatened with dire punishments for their defection.

"How many of them will we still hold at this time next year?" Finn wondered aloud to Goll Mac Morna.

The one-eyed man squinted and stared up at the sky; a hot sky, that summer, of a blue so strong as to be opaque, filled with the sun in his blazing chariot. "About half," Goll hazarded. "Of course that depends on what happens between now and then. If the Ulidians attack Tara and we hold them off and pursue them back north, and loot them as they deserve, we'll find ourselves with a lot more allies from the south clamouring for admission to Tara."

"And for their share."

"To be sure."

"Are all men greedy?" Finn asked unexpectedly.

"The best way to answer that," Goll told him, "is to look inside yourself. Honestly. Know how you are, and that will give you some idea of what other men are like. What do you know of yourself?"

Finn waited a time before answering. When he spoke, his voice was low, the words measured and somehow very sad. "I know that I am quiet in peace and angry in battle," he said. "And that is all I know."

As they made their way through the territory of the Laigin, Finn recognized the landmarks of his childhood, though not with fond nostalgia. He seemed to retire within himself, brooding. Earlier in the summer he had entertained his companions with vivid tales by the campfire, but now he sat silently, apart from them, staring into the flames and saying little.

Late one day found them camped in a valley not far from the Bog of Almhain. All day Finn had been silent, only issuing an occasional order in a distracted tone when absolutely necessary. Cormac and his retinue were spending the night in the stronghold of a tribal leader some distance up the valley. At the other end of the valley, the land gave way to a meandering stream, then rose to form a hill studded with ancient ruins.

"Once," Goll told the others, "a mighty fortress was on that hill, but it's a long time gone. Legends still haunt it, though. Some say it was a seat of the Tuatha Dé Danann. Whether that's true or not, no one builds a fort there now, though it's the most defensible site within half a day's walk."

Once the Fíanna had set up camp, Finn and some of his men went hunting. Sceolaun pranced at her master's side. Bran followed more sedately, still sore from the wounds of battle but refusing to be left behind. For a long time Finn had made his men carry the injured hound on a litter as they would a wounded warrior, but that was no longer necessary, and both man and hound were thankful.

Summer days in Erin were as long as winter nights, with only a sliver of darkness between. The hunt lasted late. Enough game was soon taken, but the joy of the chase was not exhausted and Finn and his men went on and on, occasionally sending a runner back for porters to carry the meat to camp.

At last even the most ardent hunter had to admit it would be wasteful to kill any more game. They reluctantly turned toward camp, boasting among themselves of this spear throw or that rack of antlers.

Finn walked with them but not among them. Slowly the distance between himself and the others widened, though he was not aware of it. He was alone with his thoughts.

Nearby, just on the other side of a strip of woodland, was the Bog of Almhain.

Sometimes he could not resist sinking into melancholy. His was the nature of the poet who understands intuitively that pain is the balance of pleasure.

Abandoned her Fir Bolg baby on the Bog of Almhain.

Lost in the darkness inside his head, Finn at first did not see the deer. Then a flash of colour just at the periphery of his vision caught his attention and he turned his head.

A young doe stood at the edge of the woods, sun-dappled by the light of the setting sun as it streamed between the leaves. The pale patches on her back and flanks might have been the last remnants of a fawn's spots. She stood with her head high, her eyes fixed on Finn.

He stopped in mid-stride; stopped slowly, not abruptly, and gently lowered his raised foot back to the earth. Then he stood like a tree, returning the deer's gaze.

She did not run. Her large ears swivelled back and forth in search of threatening sounds. Finn made himself breathe slowly, so he would not sound like a predator panting. With one hand, out of sight of the deer, he signalled to Bran and Sceolaun to be still and was thankful that the rest of the hounds had gone on with his men.

The deer took half a hesitant step forward, toward him.

"Do I know you?" he breathed. Perhaps he said the words aloud. Perhaps he said them only in his mind.

But she heard. Her mouth opened slightly, as if to speak, and she took another step forward.

In that moment, the final line of demarcation between fantasy and reality was forever destroyed for Finn Mac Cool. There was no going back.

The deer walked toward him with incredible grace, each delicate lifting of leg a miracle of beauty.

Finn could not breathe. I made this up, he thought. Now it happens. Here is the deer . . . but not Muirinn. Not my mother. Someone else . . .

He and the doe gazed at one another across the gulf that is supposed to separate man from the animal kingdom, and as they gazed, the gulf vanished.

Finn saw a woman standing in dappling, golden sunlight.

What the deer saw, he did not know.

But she continued to approach him until she was only a few paces away. Then she paused. He thought she smiled.

The deer . . . the woman . . . lay down . . . seated herself . . . on the grass.

Ignoring Finn's command for the first time, Bran and Sceolaun ran up to her then and fawned at her feet, licking her, wriggling with joy as she caressed them.

Her brown eyes never left Finn's eyes.

He did not know if she was beautiful. His standards of beauty had until this moment been those of other men, but what he was seeing now, other men would not see. He could only stare and wonder that he had thought himself alive before this day.

Now I am alive, he thought. Because she is alive.

He knew she would not run from him. She waited calmly, watching him. But he did not take the final few steps to her. He dared not reach out and touch her for fear his fingers would deny the evidence of his eyes. He could only stand and envy the hounds she was caressing so tenderly, and it was as if he felt her touch on his skin too.

How long he stood, he did not know. He only knew that her eyes never left his face.

From far away came the sound of a hunting horn. Bran and Sceolaun lifted their heads. Finn's men had reached the campsite and were calling him.

At the sound of the horn, fear leaped into the brown eyes.

"Don't . . ." Finn said, reaching toward her then, but in one bound she was on her feet. Trembling.

"They won't hurt you. I'll never let them hurt you."

She took half a step backward.

Bran and Sceolaun looked from her to Finn, uncertain what was required of them. The horn sounded again, insistently.

She took a full step backward.

"Don't leave me!" he implored, holding out both hands.

She tried to obey, but could not. The trembling became great shudders that ran through her body.

Before he could say anything more, she turned and was gone, vanishing among the trees without disturbing a leaf.

His trance broke, and he ran after her faster than he had ever pursued a quarry before. His feet did not seem to touch the ground. No twig snapped under them, no branch brushed his face. He ran frantically, desperately, longing to call her name but not knowing the name to call.

His hounds ran with him, but Bran, still suffering from the fearful injuries of the dogfight, soon fell back. Finn glanced over his shoulder. The gallant dog was making every effort to keep up, and suffering for it. No matter how far or fast Finn ran, Bran would try to stay with him, to the death if necessary.

Finn groaned.

Slowing his pace, he peered ahead. She was out of sight. She could be anywhere, the deer, the woman. She had vanished as if she never existed. Yet his hounds had seen her. She had to be real.

And if she was real, he could find her again.

He stopped running and crouched on his heels. Bran and Sceolaun came to him, pressed against him. Bran was gasping for breath. "Remember her," he commanded them. "Know her when you see her again. Let no harm come to her."

He lifted Bran into his arms and stood up.

With frequent glances over his shoulder, he retraced his steps until he came to the small patch of flattened grass where she had rested. Setting Bran down, he knelt and felt the earth with his hand.

Under his palm, there was heat.

14

When Cormac returned to Tara, bronze trumpets blared a welcome from every gateway and sentry platform.

Resplendent in a pleated linen gown girdled with gold, Ethni the Proud paced with stately tread to her husband's side, gave him a dignified smile, then turned to face his people with him.

His greeting to her was equally calm, Finn noticed.

If I were coming home to my woman, thought the Rígfénnid Fíanna, I would seize her in my arms and lift her into the sky and shout for joy.

People swirled around him, welcoming the returnees. Officials and servants alike were questioning, gesticulating, importuning, offering ale and cakes and wreaths of flowers. The other fénnidi pushed past Finn, eager to enter the precincts of Tara and accept the accolades that were their due. Voices competed until they rose into one great yammering clamour that had no meaning at all for Finn . . .

. . . but in the heart of the clamour was a stillness.

And in the heart of the stillness was a deer in a sun-dappled meadow, watching him across time and space.

Finn stood alone in his bubble of wonder. People glanced at him, but no one spoke to him. There was a wall around him that they could not see or touch, but sensed. Finn was alone in the crowd, and the crowd could not intrude.

This is Tara, he said to her in his head. I helped build this place.

He invited her to look through his eyes at limewashed walls and golden thatch. I am part of this, my sweat and effort were spent here, he told her.

He looked at the craftsmanship of pillar and post so she could see them too. Running his fingers across the deep carving, he gave her access to the touch of the polished wood. He cocked his head to listen to the first strains of music as the musicians prepared to play in honour of the returned king, and he thought of her inside his head, listening with him.

None of this seemed strange to him. She had always been there. He simply had not known.

Companioned by her nameless presence, he sat that night in a place of honour in the new Assembly Hall and took his turn at reporting the events of the summer. For once, he did not exaggerate. She was in his head, listening. He could tell her only the truth. She would know the difference.

"What's wrong with Finn?" Madan asked Cailte. "He doesn't sound like himself at all. You'd think he'd be overflowing with tales of our victories. Instead, we get a few terse words, then down he sits as if his jaws were locked."

Leaning across to them, Conan suggested, "Perhaps he has that girl on his mind, the smith's daughter. Has he seen her since we've been back?"

"She was in the crowd down at the gate," Cailte replied, "but as far as I could tell, Finn never looked at her. He walked right past her. If I didn't know better, I'd say he's taken a blow to the head."

The three turned as one and looked up the hall to their Rígfénnid Fíanna. He did not notice.

Cailte frowned, beginning to worry. "Perhaps he did take a blow to the head in some battle and said nothing about it. That would be like him."

That evening Cormac reported to the assemblage in the hall, "We have the sworn support of the most powerful king in Muma, Oilioll Olum, who is married to Sabia, daughter of Conn of the Hundred Battles. We have the sworn support of several powerful kings of the Laigin, and of many Connachta chieftains."

"The king of the Erainn stands with you because he's married to your aunt," one of the local brehons spoke up, "but Oilioll Olum is not a young man. When he dies, the king who follows him may not have such a connection with your line. Conn and the king of the Erainn were once great enemies who divided Erin between them. What makes you think you can always hold the south, never mind the Connachta and the Laigin?"

"Because I am careful and clever," Cormac replied candidly, with no trace of arrogance. "I did not rely on ties of blood or fosterage, but on those things that appeal to men on a different level entirely."

"What?"

Cormac's lips twitched. "I took gifts from one king and gave them to the next. Although none knew this, I kept hardly anything for myself. I bought them, if you like, these allies of mine. And I paid a high price for them in cattle and gold and servants."

The brehon pulled his lower lip and looked disapproving. "I would not," he said ponderously, "trust any man who could be bought."

Cormac threw back his head and laughed. "And I would not trust any man who claimed he could not be bought! You know the law. I know men."

"They succumbed to your bribery, then?"

"Not all of them. But for those who at first resisted, I had Finn and the Fíanna. They gave in soon enough."

Finn's men grinned and elbowed one another. As fénnedi, they were not allowed seats in the king's presence, but as the companions of Finn Mac Cool, they would not be kept out of any place they wished to go. They stood shoulder to shoulder around the walls of the hall, a circle of strength.

The others in the hall were very aware that the status of members of the Fíanna had improved, though nothing was said. The mere fact of their unchallenged presence at an official occasion was enough.

When everyone else had been served the king's wine, cups were passed to Finn's men. Cups of gold and precious woods.

In spite of the summer's successes, Cormac knew the matter of Ulidia was unresolved and festering. The provinces had enjoyed a long and honourable tradition of warring on one another, the legacy of a warrior aristocracy dating back to the Milesians. It was unrealistic to suppose that tradition had ended just because Cormac Mac Airt held Tara . . .

. . . and had the Fíanna.

They, the king admitted to himself but to no one else, were the real reason for his success during the summer. Finn Mac Cool had exceeded his fondest expectations. Not only was Finn endowed with exceptional strength and reflexes, he also had the nebulous quality known as leadership, and an innate organizational ability uncommon among his kind. In one battle season, he had made a loose confederation of semi-outlaws— devoted to roving and pillaging when they were not fighting—into a disciplined army by challenging them beyond their abilities and compelling their obedience.

It was as if Finn had envisioned an army in his mind and deliberately imposed its pattern on the chaos of fénnidecht.

Day by day and step by step, he had made more demands of and for the Fíanna, tightening his control as he enhanced their lustre. As the army grew, so did the respect in which people held it. Men began flocking to join in ever greater numbers. Every young man with hot blood in him yearned to have his name called in the pantheon of Finn's warriors who were cutting a memorable swathe across Erin.

They were not once defeated, that battle summer.

By the time Cormac returned to Tara, he knew he had such an army as no king in Erin had ever possessed.

That, he told himself, is why the Ulaid are holding off. They've heard tales that make them wary.

The tales were growing faster than the Fíanna, taking on lives of their own. Finn Mac Cool could now tell any sort of story about his own prowess or that of his men and have it accepted.

Yet he was growing strangely disinclined to outrageous tales. At the end of the day he preferred to sit quietly by the fire, staring into space, while others enhanced the growing legends of Bran and Sceolaun and Cailte and Goll and the rest.

As they settled into Tara and began anticipating the Samhain Assembly, Cormac grew increasingly worried.

"Finn's too quiet," he told Ethni the Proud on their pillow.

"I shouldn't say so," his wife replied. "I heard him yelling orders on the training ground today and the blast from his lungs would blow you away."

"That isn't what I mean. He has usually been . . . exuberant. I am used to him that way. Aggressive, vivid, giving off sparks. This Finn who sits and thinks makes me . . ."

"What?"

"Nervous," admitted Cormac Mac Airt. He did not go further, however. He was the king, the glory and the problems were his. He did not confide to his wife that Finn was possibly of the Tuatha Dé Danann, and an enemy spy.

But he had not forgotten the possibility.

Goll Mac Morna was also puzzled by the change in Finn's behaviour, and disturbed. Any shift in strategy on the part of an opponent always disturbed him. Finn was his opponent, he had no doubt of it, and the only way he could prepare himself for whatever Finn might do was to stay close to him, study him, understand him, anticipate him.

He was finding Finn a difficult man to understand.

One evening he deliberately sat down next to the Rígfénnid Fíanna and stared into the fire with him. Bran, who lay between them, pressed closer to Finn.

Goll remarked, "Your dog doesn't like me."

"It isn't that. Bran only likes me, it's nothing personal against you."

"Your dog, your cousin. If that story of yours was true. Which it isn't."

Finn said nothing.

Realizing he was not rising to the bait, Goll changed strategies. "I hate to see the end of battle season."

"Even though it means you will soon be free to go to your home and your wife?"

"Even though. The wife and I have been together too long, we're too used to each other. I can tell you exactly what she'll say when she sees me next. 'How much was your share of the loot?' Those will be the first words out of her mouth."

"You should go to her though," said Finn. "We'll make our winter quarters here in Tara again this year, I think, but there's no need for you to stay."

"You're always trying to get rid of me. Do you doubt my loyalty to you?"

Finn turned and looked straight into Goll's one eye. "Should I?"

Perhaps, thought Goll, honesty was best. Honesty was disarming. "I want to be commander of the Fíanna."

"Of course you do. And so do I. But remember what you told me? You get what you have the strength to take, you keep what you have the power to defend. I've learned a lot from you, Goll."

Goll—almost—smiled. "You may yet learn a lot more from me," he said. "But while we wait, tell me something. Tell me why you sit here staring into the fire night after night."

Finn's body tensed by an infinitesimal degree. He saw the question for what it was: an attempt to gain access to his innermost thoughts. But there was no way he would allow Goll Mac Morna into his mind.

Someone else was already there.

His features reformed in a radiant, boyish smile. "I've been composing a poem," he said.

Goll's one eye blinked. He felt the earth shift under him while he tried to adjust his thinking, but Finn had already begun to recite,

> Many were the battles we broke in the summer
> Against the warriors of Loch Luig,
> The inhospitality of Lios of the Wells.
> Where we went was red blood and white heat
> And our enemies ran from us.
> Ran like the blood red and hot in us,
> The wind to our backs, the sun on our heads,
> The trumpet calling, its voice
> Bronze and mighty, summoning, but one
> Did not run, in the summer.

Finn felt silent. Goll waited. At last he enquired, "Is that all?"

"It is."

"There's no more?"

"There's not."

"What does it mean, then?"

"It's a poem. If you have to ask what it means, you cannot understand it."

"Oh, I understand battles well enough, and red blood and white heat—I remember them well. But who did not run when the trumpet blew?"

"Did not run . . . at first," Finn said softly.

This, Goll realized, was a mystery Finn was keeping to himself. No explanation would be forthcoming.

One of Goll's strongest traits was a gift for fortitude and endurance. He had endured much since he was first assigned to Finn's company, always in the hope that someday he would gain his own back at the younger man's expense . . . if Finn did not succeed in killing him first, which he fully anticipated. But his patience was wearing thin. Every new honour heaped on Finn Mac Cool seemed taken from Goll's own shoulders. Having to sit by the fire listening to this pretentious, dreamy youngster recite overblown poetry that he could not understand was quite unbearable.

Goll got to his feet and brushed himself off. "I think I will go home," he said. "You can send Cailte for me when you need me again. I'll winter with the wife."

Finn looked up at him. "I'm grateful for all you did for me this past year," he said truthfully.

Goll did not want gratitude, not from Finn. It made him even more angry. His lips narrowed to a thin line. "I only did my duty. I always do my duty." He stalked away.

From the other side of the fire, Finn's original companions watched him go. "That's one less knife to shield your back against," commented Conan.

Finn replied airily, "Goll Mac Morna's not going to hurt me." He put his thumb in his mouth, chewed on it for a while, then winked at his men with a sudden, sunny smile. "I'll outlive him!" he announced.

They laughed. But Cailte's eyes followed Goll until the darkness swallowed him, and there remained a thin line of worry etched between Cailte's eyebrows.

One day after Goll Mac Morna left Tara, the Ulaid made their move.

Battle season was over, but the autumn had proved unusually warm and golden and the earth was still dry and firm enough for marching when the army of the north came howling down the Slige Midluachra.

Cormac was in the House of the King, conferring with Maelgenn his druid, when the sentries on the gate shouted the first news. Dubdrenn, Cormac's chief steward, ran white-faced into the House of the King to be first to tell of the bad tidings. "The Ulaid! They're coming this way! An army!"

Cormac got to his feet. "Maelgenn, did you not foresee this?"

The royal druid licked his lips nervously. "I did of course. I told you nights ago of the signs I had read in the entrails of the red squirrel." He did not dare suggest the king had forgotten; nor did he dare remind the king of how ambiguous the prophecy had been. But it was always safe to prophesy some sort of attack, sometime. This was Erin.

By the time Cormac reached the northern gateway, Finn and his men were already there, armed and preparing for battle.

"Why do you think they waited until now?" the king wondered aloud.

Finn was adjusting the scabbard of his great hacking sword. Without looking up, he replied, "I'm sorry Goll isn't here, that's the sort of question he could answer."

"Isn't here? Where is he?"

"I told him he could go home."

"Without my permission?"

Finn raised his eyes to Cormac's then. "The Fíanna is mine to command," he said.

Once again Cormac had the profound conviction that Finn was deliberately going too far, testing the limits. But this was not the time for a confrontation with him, not with an enemy marching toward the gates of Tara.

"You anticipated my suggestion," Cormac said smoothly. "I meant to have Goll sent to his fort this winter. He's not exactly in the same situation as the rest of you and there's no harm in showing him a little extra courtesy."

"I thought so too," said Finn.

He was almost disappointed that the king had not challenged him on the issue. He had expected Cormac to make a point of stating his own supreme authority, perhaps by countermanding Finn's orders and sending someone to bring back Goll Mac Morna.

But the king had accepted Finn's authority without protest.

Finn knew a moment of elation.

I am stronger than the king, he dared whisper in the inmost recesses of his mind.

I am not only as good as he is, but my will is stronger and he knows it.

I could be a king.

A sudden superstitious twinge raised prickles on his arms and he braced himself, half-expecting lightning to strike him from the heavens, or the earth to open and swallow him.

Neither happened.

Cormac turned and said over his shoulder, "I'll go back to the House of the King and give orders for its defense."

"That won't be necessary," Finn called after him. "No Ulidian will enter Tara."

Cormac kept on walking, however.

The army of the Ulaid, descendants of the once-invincible Red Branch, did not march all the way to the walls of Tara. They prudently halted a long walk away and regrouped, drawing themselves into their own approximation of a battle formation, which meant a broad line stretching almost from horizon to horizon but only one man deep. Seen thus, they believed they appeared more numerous than they were. Through chants and exhortations, the druids who marched with them raised their battle lust to fever pitch, until many of the painted Ulidians were in a state of full erection, the swords of their manhood as stiff as the iron swords in their hands.

Then, howling, they charged toward Tara.

They had intended a glorious battle.

They met Finn Mac Cool.

Finn had waited in front of the northern gateway until he could see their formation clearly as it ran forward. Then with a few swift words, he ordered his own men into a triangular shape like the head of a spear, with himself at the point. They marched stolidly forward to let the broad line of the Ulaid break itself on this spear.

The advancing Ulidians found it difficult to determine just how many tightly packed warriors were in the solid mass behind the silver-haired leader of the Fíanna. But they did not flinch or slow their pace; they thundered their feet on the earth of Míd beneath a golden autumn sun and tried to keep thinking about the epic poem their bards would compose to celebrate this victory against the full strength of Cormac Mac Airt.

An earlier attack would not have been as prestigious.

As the two armies came together, the air sang with spears.

Men shrieked; men fell. There was a great thudding of bodies hurling themselves against each other, a ringing of iron swords, and a roaring of battle cries as each man shouted the motto of his clan and tribe.

It might be the last chance he would have in life to identify himself as an individual.

Finn Mac Cool did not cry out the name of his clan and tribe. Nor did he call the name of Cormac Mac Airt. He gave one piercing scream that blew like the wind into the faces of the Ulidians, and the sound of the wind was the name:

"FÍANNA!"

The battle that followed was hard and bloody.

In the forefront, Finn was the target of every Ulidian spear. Yet they all sailed harmlessly past him. He ducked and swerved and spun like a

blown leaf, and was as hard to hit. Then, sword in hand, he closed with
the Ulidian leader, easily identifiable because like most of his tribe, he
smeared himself with paint, which in his case included a sun symbol on
his forehead to proclaim himself superior.

In battle skills he was not superior, nor even equal, to Finn, who
hacked through his knees with an angled blow of his sword, then thrust
Fiachaid's spear through the man's throat and left him dying, pinned to
the earth he'd tried to win.

The Ulidian was dead before he knew he'd been wounded.

Finn's followers included not only his original fían and the additional
bands of nine, but also a number of other fíans that had not yet left for
winter quarters. Numerically the Ulidians were superior, but they were
facing men who had been fighting and travelling and fighting again all
summer, men who were rock-hard and supremely confident. Men who
had passed the most strenuous tests Finn Mac Cool could devise for
them, and were not about to be beaten by painted northerners.

The battle did not last very long. The sun was still high in the sky
when the surviving Ulidians turned and fled.

Wiping his bloody hands on his arms, Finn watched them go. "I
thought you wanted to fight!" he called derisively.

No one turned to answer him.

The next morning Cormac waited in the Assembly Hall with his
officials and the Rígfénnid Fíanna, and in time an emissary from the
Ulaid arrived. He was a big-nosed, big-eared man, with a voice like
chains dragging over stone, dressed in a cloak striped black and cream
and fastened with a brooch of iron. He was obviously unhappy.

"You have done great damage to our fighting men," he lamented to
the king of Tara.

Cormac nodded gravely but said nothing.

"Our warrior force is depleted. If an enemy attacks our homes, who
will defend them?"

Cormac nodded again.

The Ulidian made a third attempt. "We offered you honourable
battle but you showed us no mercy."

Cormac smiled. "You came here looking for mercy?"

"We came here to take back what was rightfully ours."

"Tara was never rightfully yours. It was built by a people older than
yours or mine, and made into a kingly seat by men of my blood."

"And fairly won by men of mine," the emissary pointed out.

"And fairly lost as well. Tell your kings for me to give over now, and
submit to me as their High King. They will find me merciful then."

"Submit." The emissary tasted the word, working it around in his
mouth. "I have no orders to offer submission."

"Then why did you come?"

"To offer . . . a truce."

Cormac glanced meaningfully toward Nede, his chief poet. A truce was traditionally arranged through bards.

Nede was a handsome, broad-headed man with thick yellow hair belying his age, and a presence that commanded attention. Dressed in the six colours allowed a bard and standing tall beside his king, he intoned, "As you ran from us, we shall dictate the terms of truce."

The big-nosed man growled, "Agreed."

"Your leaders are to send to Tara three hundred cattle, three hundred sheep with the wool unshorn, and three hundred servants."

The emissary shook his head violently. "That is not acceptable! You would rob us!"

"If three hundred is not acceptable," Nede replied with composure, "then I change the number to six hundred."

The emissary drew a swift breath. "Three hundred is acceptable. Three hundred cattle, that is."

"And sheep. And servants."

"Sheep, three hundred," the emissary agreed, looking more unhappy than ever. "But it is not possible to deliver three hundred servants, we simply don't have them."

Cormac spoke up. "I doubt that. It is well known that marauders from Ulidia routinely plunder the coasts of Alba. Surely you bring back slaves?"

"Some few, I suppose, but—"

"Quality slaves?" the king went on.

"Some few, but—"

Cormac silenced him with a hand and turned toward Nede again. "An adjustment," he said softly.

The bard told the emissary, "We will accept one hundred quality slaves, strong men, and women of accomplishment."

"And if we cannot deliver them?"

Cormac looked in the other direction, toward Finn Mac Cool, who had been standing all this time immobile and with his arms folded. At the king's signal, he unfolded his arms and took one step forward, standing as tall as he knew how. The emissary looked into his face.

Something looked back at the Ulidian out of Finn's eyes.

The man swallowed, hard. "I think we can deliver one hundred quality slaves," he said.

That night there was feasting at Tara.

In due course, herders arrived with three hundred small black cattle and three hundred woolly black sheep. It was a very small price to pay for a truce, but as Cormac explained to his court, "Showing them generosity now will help avoid animosity later. I could have demanded much more, but the Ulidians would have simmered with resentment and boiled over sooner rather than later."

Finn said, "You expect them to boil over again?"

"Ah, they never give up, the northerners. Once they think something is theirs, they fight for it as a hound fights for its bone, past all reason, even if it means the bone itself is destroyed in the fighting. They'll attack again, Finn. But not, I trust, in the immediate future."

Finn was satisfied with the reply. As long as Cormac expected on-going trouble, his Rígfénnid Fíanna was invaluable to him.

The one hundred quality servants arrived a day after the livestock, though under almost identical circumstances. They too were herded down the Slige Midluachra by men with wooden staffs to prod them into a pack and keep them there. Reaching the gates of Tara, they stood in a wordless huddle, eyes on the ground, awaiting their fate with equanimity, though one or two looked coldly angry.

When they were brought inside, Dubdrenn the steward was put in charge of examining the men and assigning them work, and the chief attendant of Ethni the Proud examined the women. Cormac's wife took no part in this operation. She considered herself above dealing with raw material. "If any of them seem suitable to attend me," she commanded, "train them properly before you bring them to me. I would not object to finding a better hairdresser, if there is one among them with that skill."

Finn's men watched the parade of new women with interest. They were looking for other skills, and as the captives from the north were led through Tara to their assigned quarters, the fénnidi commented on this one and that one, not always quietly.

"Hair like a raven's wings!" Fergus Honey-Tongue said admiringly of a tall woman with a sumptuous bosom.

"She could not drown, that one," added Blamec with a snigger.

Finn overheard. Before Blamec knew what hit him, he found himself sitting on the ground with a sore jaw. "Speak respectfully of women!" Finn commanded.

"I thought I was."

"Then think again."

Blamec looked up at Fergus. "What did I do this time?"

"Opened your mouth," replied Fergus. "Never a good idea for you."

One of the women was exceptionally beautiful by any man's standards. That night in the hall, Dubdrenn remarked to Cormac, "There is one female servant you might want to take a look at—privately."

A light came into the king's eyes. "Something special?"

"Something very special. You've been talking about a reward for the

Rígfénnid Fíanna for his defeat of the Ulidians. This might be the very thing.''

"Bring her to me—privately—in the morning. If she's good enough, I think it would do no harm to make Finn a gift of her. I'd say he's ready for a woman; he certainly pays no attention to the one we thought he'd chosen.''

But when Dubdrenn brought the woman in question to Cormac's chamber the next morning, Finn Mac Cool went out of the king's mind.

She was bronze-haired and red-lipped and her eyes were smoky. She did not bow her head in the king's presence, but gave him a long look and then smiled with pleasure at what she saw. "Am I to be yours?'' she enquired.

Cormac drew a deep breath. "I have not . . . ah . . . decided. What are you called?''

"I am Carnait of the Cruithni.''

"Have you a husband anywhere?''

"None. But I am strong. I could bear strong children,'' she added proudly. Her cheeks glowed with the red blood coursing through them—and through her lips. Cormac kept looking at her lips. They would be like drinking wine, he thought.

The king remained in his chamber all day with the door closed. When people asked for him, Dubdrenn said he was occupied with important matters.

When night fell, customarily Cormac would have returned from the House of the King, his official and formal residence, to Cormac's House, his new and private home where Ethni waited. But that night he did not leave the House of the King.

In another break with custom, Dubdrenn personally carried food and drink to him, rather than leaving that chore to lower-ranking servants. Only Dubdrenn saw Cormac; only Dubdrenn knew what was so totally occupying his time.

"This is for me,'' the king told his chief steward. "This is something I am doing just for me for a change.''

Built around Cormac Mac Airt, Tara was sensitive to his every mood and undertaking. He had been shut away in the House of the King for less than half a day before people began wondering and speculating. No one spoke openly, but glances were exchanged. Eyes rolled heavenward. Lips smiled or smirked or tightened. A strange sense of playfulness seized the inhabitants of Tara, relieved to discover their king was as human as anyone else.

"I saw that woman,'' Madan Bent-Neck told Cael Hundred-Killer. "When she first arrived, I saw her, and the face on her almost put out the eyes in my head.''

"That ugly, was she?"

"That beautiful."

"Carnait of the Cruithni," Fergus Honey-Tongue pronounced, "is the sun breaking through a bank of clouds."

But other clouds were building. Even in a stronghold as large as Tara, such a secret could not long be kept. When on the second day Cormac was still shut up in the House of the King, Ethni the Proud decided there was some aspect of his life from which she was being excluded. A few judicious questions were asked, and by the time the sun was at midpoint in the heavens, she knew as much as anyone else about Carnait of the Cruithni.

Ethni was furious. "I'm his wife," she complained to Fithel the chief brehon. "He cannot do this."

Fithel contradicted her. "He can of course. There is nothing in the law that forbids him having as many women as he likes."

"Then there should be!"

"But," said the brehon reasonably, "if you legislate to restrict the freedom of the man, you also restrict the freedom of the woman."

"I'm not asking for freedom to take another man."

"You are not, but you cannot speak for every member of your sex, Ethni. It is imperative that society be governed in ways that will avoid creating unnatural situations that force people to act counter to natural law."

A thin, hard line formed between Ethni's black-dyed brows. "What does that mean?"

"It means, simply, that Brehon Law takes into account the desire of men for women and women for men."

"But what about my children? My status as his wife?"

"Neither of which is under threat," Fithel pointed out.

"What about my pride?"

"Ah." The brehon made smoothing gestures with his hands. "Your pride. Pride cannot be legislated, it is in the hands of each individual to govern his own. If I assure you the king has chosen a woman of incomparable beauty, can you not take pride in having such a creature become part of the royal family? She may give him children as finely made as herself who will do honour to the household of Cormac Mac Airt. Do you not seek his honour? Was that not part of your marriage contract?"

"Agreeing to concubines wasn't part of my contract."

"I did not say he wanted her for his concubine."

Ethni's eyes blazed. "I'll never give permission for her to be a wife! Never. My husband has done this without even consulting me once, he who talked with me about everything. He has made a grave mistake."

Fithel did not like the look in Ethni's eyes, and privately resolved to speak to Cormac himself as soon as possible.

But still Dubdrenn denied anyone access to the House of the King. Conan Maol had been stationed outside, spear at the ready, looking decidedly unlazy for once, almost menacing.

Fithel went to Finn Mac Cool. "I need to see the king, you must have your man let me in. There is a matter of urgency of which the king must be informed before the situation becomes untenable."

Finn spoke to Dubdrenn, who spoke to Cormac. The word came back.

Leave things as they are.

All that day Tara brooded under the lowering skies of autumn. In the Grianan, ostensibly sewing with her sewing-women, Ethni the Proud sat in frosty silence and none dared speak to her. Cold rage radiated from her in ever-widening circles.

As the light began to fail, she returned alone to Cormac's House and ordered a huge fire built in the central firepit, beside which she sat brooding and sleepless throughout the night. Her attendants tiptoed around her.

On the morning of the third day, Cormac returned to find a coldly hostile woman whom he hardly knew occupying his house. Ethni barely spoke two consecutive words to him. But she was proud, she did not question him. She simply treated him as if he were a mange-ridden hound who had entered by mistake.

Cormac had been king of Tara long enough to refuse to cower to anyone. "What's wrong with you, woman?" he demanded to know. Better to bring it out into the open than let it fester, he thought. "Are you angry because I have another woman?"

Ethni turned her left side toward him, a deliberate gesture of insult. "I'm surprised you're capable. You've had very little use for your rod with me since I've been here, you're always too busy and preoccupied. I thought it had dried up and fallen off."

"When did you show any particular interest?" he asked, the quarrel escalating. "You're always busy with your women, your sewing and embroidery, the children, your chatter . . ."

"Things I use to fill my time while waiting for you!" she countered.

"You never wait for me. You live your life, as you should. I'm living mine. This has nothing to do with you."

"It has everything to do with me! Why have you kept this, this . . . woman a secret?"

"I haven't kept her a secret. I just didn't run over here to tell you about her because it has nothing to do with you."

"Stop saying that!" Ethni clamped her hands over her ears.

Cormac was baffled. Other kings had more than one woman. Even the most minor chieftain could have as many women as he could afford to feed and house if he chose, their children raised and tended together, their work shared, forming a small community of their own with common interests under the benevolent protection of one man. Life was not easy; it was important to have as many offspring as possible so that some of them would be assured of survival.

His body still burning with memories of Carnait's body, Cormac wondered if a new child had already begun. If so, he would not have its existence blighted by Ethni's egocentric nature. She had always wanted to be at the centre, at the forefront; she had insisted her foster father agree to her marriage with Cormac Mac Airt primarily because she knew he had great ambition and she wanted to climb the heights with him. She had taken the man; she must take the man as a whole, and part of that whole was now Carnait of the Cruithni.

But how to make her see and accept?

He tried arguing his case reasonably only to discover, as had many a man before him, that few angry women are interested in being reasonable.

"Get rid of her," Ethni grated through clenched teeth.

"You cannot demand that of me."

"I am demanding it! I'll never accept her, Cormac. Never!"

Cormac went to his brehon, but Fithel was not able to offer him much comfort. "Without Ethni's permission, you cannot arrange a contract marriage. Unless you first set Ethni aside, of course. Is that your desire?"

Cormac was angry. "What are the acceptable reasons for setting aside a contract mate?"

"There are two types of divorce. The first is blameless, and may take place if illness of either mate makes cohabitation impossible, or disease renders either incapable of sexual intercourse. A serious blemish or disfiguring injury, if one's mate finds it distressing to view, is reason to end the marriage if desired. Prolonged or perpetual absence from the territory is sufficient to allow for divorce. So is loss of sanity. If one of the couple is incapable of producing a child, that may be used as reason for divorce if desired. Death is also reason for divorce, to keep the surviving mate from claiming penalties against the kin of the deceased."

Cormac was shaking his head. "What about the other type? Divorce where someone is at fault."

Fithel waved his hands in small, precise circles as he enumerated, "Couples may separate and end their contract, and the woman take her coibche with her, under the following circumstances: If one mate has circulated a false story about the other. If one mate has satirized the other and made of him or her a figure of fun."

"Ethni has done neither of those things to me," the king admitted, "principally because she would bring disrepute on herself."

"Any woman who has been struck a blow that blemishes her is entitled to divorce," Fithel went on.

"I've never hit her. At least not yet, though the thought crossed my mind today."

"A woman who is repudiated for another is entitled to divorce," the brehon said dispassionately.

"Ah. I haven't repudiated her, I never intended to. She can't claim that. But what can I claim? How can I force her to accept what I want? Tell me the rest of the law."

"A woman who is deprived of sexual intercourse by her husband may divorce him," Fithel said. "If her husband gives her a charm or potion of some kind to induce her to sleep with him when she does not wish to do so, she is also entitled to divorce. Likewise, she may divorce a husband who fails to provide her with the food and clothing she desires insofar as he is able."

Cormac doubled his fist and slammed it against the nearest wall. "All these are to the woman's advantage! What is there for me?"

"You have the right to take other women. As your wife has the right to other men, if you give her permission," the brehon had in honesty to add. "And you must have her permission to make another woman a contract wife."

Cormac sank onto a bench and buried his head in his hands. "She'll never give it. She'll never, never give it."

"Repudiate her, then. Proud as she is, she will divorce you."

"I never intended to repudiate her, I don't see the necessity for it if she'd just be reasonable."

Fithel, who had some experience of women himself, laughed hollowly.

15

ETHNI WAS BEING PERFECTLY REASONABLE. HER HUS-
band, whom she always believed had included her in every
aspect of his life, was now excluding her from something. She
was owed compensation. She would take compensation in the form of
making his new woman miserable.

She informed Cormac, "Since I cannot make you send her away,
Carnait will remain at Tara. But as your wife, I insist that she be made
my servant."

Cormac went at once to Fithel, who was sympathetic but unable to
help. "Carnait came to you as a captive of the Ulaid, not as a free woman.
She is therefore of the servant class and your wife has the right to
demand her services."

"At least," Cormac subsequently consoled Carnait, "you'll be here. I
can see you as often as I like."

"But where will I live?"

He could not keep his wife's servant in the House of the King, nor in
his private residence, where Ethni dwelt in undisputed and angry possession. And he did not have another separate house to offer Carnait. The
recently rebuilt Tara was crowded with buildings, but each was fully
occupied or had an official purpose. For some reason, Cormac Mac Airt
had neglected to order that houses be prepared for concubines.

So Carnait of the Cruithni was forced to live with the rest of Ethni's
attendants, in a rectangular wattle-and-daub chamber with limewashed
walls but no firepit and no privacy.

Ethni did not limit her revenge to this small discomfort. "Servants
must work," she decreed, "and Carnait is to be my grinding-woman. She
will grind all the corn for the royal household and attendants."

The amount of corn to be ground daily was nine pecks, a formidable
amount considering it was to be done on a stone quern, by hand, by one

woman. Before the arrival of Carnait, Ethni had employed several grind-
ing-women for the purpose, but they were now relieved of this taxing
physical duty and rewarded with new clothing and lives of visible ease,
while Carnait was sentenced to spend long days in the small, dark grind-
ing-shed, labouring over the quern.

By nightfall she was exhausted, too exhausted to be enthusiastic
when Cormac urged her to meet him in one place or another.

No one at Tara could fail to be aware of the king's distress. He did
not formally repudiate Ethni—he would not give her that satisfaction, he
would deny her the freedom she was denying him—but he slept every
night in the House of the King and spent his days in simmering anger.

When he learned that Carnait was expecting his child, the anger
exploded.

He unwisely attempted to vent his anger on Finn Mac Cool.

Summoning the Rígfénnid Fíanna, Cormac roared at him, "Your
men lack proper respect for their king! I see them smirking at me, I
overhear them talking behind their hands. Control them, Finn! No
matter what you've tried to make of the Fíanna, they are still little better
than animals and I won't have them laughing at me behind my back."

Finn replied in a tight voice, "The Fíanna are not animals. They're
men, and entitled to as much respect as you are."

Cormac was shocked. "I'm a king!"

"You squat to empty your bowels just as we do, and the result smells
just as bad."

"Don't be insolent with me!"

"Then don't misdirect your spears."

Underneath his anger, Cormac Mac Airt was both intelligent and
fair-minded. He recognized the truth when he heard it. He would not
apologize, but he could redirect the conversation.

They were in the House of the King, a large circular structure with
a soaring roof supported by posts of fragrant cedar. A broad, carefully
laid flagstone hearth surrounded the firepit, which was appointed with
elaborate iron firedogs. Brilliantly dyed woollen hangings all but covered
the walls, and as soon as one set became blackened by smoke, another
was woven. The finest craftsmanship was employed in every detail of the
building; the tiniest hinge and pin were embossed and set with polished
stones.

Slumping uncharacteristically on a couch piled with furs, Cormac
surveyed Finn through bloodshot eyes. "I have a problem," he admitted.

Finn said nothing.

"A problem with women."

Finn said nothing.

"My wife is slowly killing a woman I care about very much, and I seem unable to do anything about it."

Finn, who was as aware as everyone else of the situation, nodded. "You should have spoken to me sooner. I can."

"You what?" Cormac sat up straight. "I don't want either of them hurt, Finn. When I've had too much ale, I tell myself I want to break Ethni's neck, but I don't. I'm still . . . fond of the woman. It's just that—"

"I know. And I wouldn't hurt a woman. The Fíanna are sworn to be gentle always in their dealings with women."

"That's a new one," commented the king. "You've made a lot of changes."

"I can make another. I can relieve Carnait of the chore of grinding corn."

"Assigning one of the Fíanna to the quern is a ridiculous notion."

"I can do away with the quern altogether," said Finn, "and you'll still have all the corn you need for Tara."

Finn approached Lugaid, who understood at once what was wanted. Taking Blamec with him, he searched the countryside surrounding Tara until he found a stream ideally suited for the purpose. There he constructed the mill he had carried in his mind since the day he saw its prototype on the banks of the Shannon.

When the mill was completed, Cormac was invited on a tour of inspection. With due formality, he invited Ethni to join him—the first such invitation he had issued her since the problem arose with Carnait.

"Bring your grinding-woman," he added. "Let her see what is to replace the quern."

When she saw the mill Lugaid had built, Ethni bit her lip. It was sturdy, sizable, and capable of grinding an impressive amount of grain. Compared to the new mill with its two horizontal water wheels, an old-fashioned stone quern—a shallow trough fitted with a grindstone and labouriously hand-operated—was not only slow, but embarrassingly primitive, unsuitable for a royal establishment.

Sullenly, Ethni conceded, "I shan't need a grinding-woman now. But I can find another use for—"

"Not for Cairnait," interrupted Cormac in a loud voice. "She's heavy with my child."

The assortment of officials and dignitaries gathered to observe the new mill heard him. Ethni realized that any response she wanted to make would sound petty. With everyone aware of the situation, she did not dare assign Cairnait to some other demeaning labour.

She gave her husband a long, cold stare and favoured Lugaid with another. Then, gathering her dignity in both hands, she paced with stately tread back to Cormac's House.

The king caught Finn's eye . . . and winked.

"Reward your man well," he told Finn that night. "Give him whatever he desires for building that mill."

Lugaid knew exactly what he wanted. She had a bush of flaming red hair and lived with her family half a day's walk from Tara.

"Go to her," said Finn with a smile. "Spend the winter with her and come back to us for battle season."

But Lugaid had given much thought to the sort of life he would like, if he had his choice. Now he told Finn, "I don't want to return to the Fíanna. I've enjoyed my service with you, but I'd prefer a different future. I want to stay with my woman and build another mill beside swift water and run it myself. I don't want to be a spear target any longer. I want to bounce my children on my knee."

Finn felt a spasm of envy. "Send me your firstborn son and I'll make him an officer of the Fíanna."

"How do you know you'll still be commanding the Fíanna by the time I have a son old enough to take up weapons?"

"I will," said Finn Mac Cool.

Red Ridge was named to Lugaid's place in Finn's original fían. Each of those nine was then appointed a rígfénnid and given three nines of his own.

That winter Fithel the chief brehon fell ill. With the care of Eogan the chief physician, he lingered until nearly Beltaine before dying. The funeral games held in his honour almost overshadowed the Beltaine Festival. The historians recited in poetry the list of his achievements and wise judgments, commanding the next generation of poets to memorize them exactly, "with no word put to it and no word taken from it." One word altered was sufficient to discredit oral record.

In further honour of Fithel, Cormac ordered the next Great Assembly due to be held at Tara postponed until a replacement for Fithel was named and had time to grow into the position.

Death and life were celebrated jointly that Beltaine. The funeral games were followed by marriages, and there was joyful dancing around the ritual Beltaine pole.

Finn Mac Cool was very much in evidence.

He stood, hiding his thoughts behind opaque eyes, as various couples recited their contracts before the regional brehons and made the vows of wedding: to honour one another in public, to respect the other's rights, to guard the other's back.

I would guard you if you were here, he said in his mind to she who was always in his thoughts.

With the other members of the Fíanna, Finn competed in the funeral games. He was unbeatable at javelin-throwing and high-jumping. No one would challenge him with the sword. On the last day he found himself matched against the victor of the earlier footraces—Cailte Mac Ronan—for the championship.

Before the race began, they walked together over the grassy course, looking for sharp stones or hidden holes, their eyes fixed on the ground. "I beat you once," Finn said out of the side of his mouth. "On Black Head."

"I had a bad day." Cailte bent to pick up a stone and toss it clear of the course.

"I hope you have a good day today, then. I only want to beat the best."

"I'll have a good day," Cailte promised, laughing.

When the signal was given, they raced each other across the green sward of Tara, down a lane lined with spectators screaming for their favourite and laying wagers with every stride. Banners snapped and crackled in a warm wind. Cormac Mac Airt waited at the finish line with an ivy wreath in his hands.

Cailte was at the top of his form, inarguably the fastest of the Fíanna. He knew he could beat Finn. He almost did. Then, at the last moment, he deliberately broke the rhythm of his stride just enough . . .

. . . and Finn passed him.

The crowd roared, "Finn Mac Cool!"

Finn stood, eyes closed, in a pool of sunlight and felt the wreath settle onto his brow.

This is the best, said something in him. This is the best it will ever be.

Then he thought of her, waiting in a corner of his mind, and amended, this is the best it has ever been.

Ethni the Proud stood on one side of Cormac, and on his other side stood Carnait of Cruithni. The two women did not look at one another, or speak to one another, but they were not at war. Some subtle shift had taken place, an acceptance and adjustment growing as organically as the child grew within Carnait.

Perhaps it was the fact of the child. Ethni found she could not hate a woman big with child, with life; life the most sacred of forces.

But I am his senior wife, she told herself proudly, standing with her head high.

It was to be another battle summer, of course. Some of the tribal kings who had originally sworn to Cormac had changed their minds. Others were willing to be persuaded. A few old battles must be refought. The Ulaid, discontent as always, hovered on the fringes of Cormac's consciousness, vociferously reiterating their claims to Tara from a safe distance.

They were not eager to face Finn Mac Cool again.

Having allowed Lugaid the reward of his choice, Cormac was aware of an injustice toward Finn. "You've served me brilliantly," he said to his Rígfénnid Fíanna, "and asked nothing for yourself."

"You've given me my share of permissible plunder."

"We had a discussion about your entitlements before, I believe—"

"And you promised to improve my situation," Finn quoted.

"I did. The time has come to deliver on my promise." Cormac was feeling expansive. His new happiness made him desire similar pleasure for the tall, baffling young man who stood before him. "A landholding appropriate to the Rígfénnid Fíanna is certainly required," he said. "Is there a particular territory you would like to hold as your own? Your birthland, perhaps?"

A glow entered Finn's eyes as if a light were burning in deep water. He thrust his thumb into his mouth, waited, then said, "A landholding in Laigin territory?"

"My relationship with the Laigin is amicable, at least for now. I could demand a landholding for you, though I would have to offer them something in return."

Finn seemed to be looking through, and past, Cormac Mac Airt. "There is a place . . . a hill, near the Bog of Almhain. Once it was the home of the Sídhe, they say. It is deserted and avoided now, for that reason. No one dare live there. But I should like to build a fort upon it."

Cormac felt as if a cold wind had unexpectedly blown over him. "You want me to give you an old Danann stronghold?"

"The Laigin certainly won't object," Finn argued reasonably. "None of them wants it."

"Is there not another place that would suit you better?"

Finn pulled his eyes into focus and fixed them squarely on the king's face. "There is not. I want the Hill of Almhain. I have given you great service, I'm entitled to the reward of my choice." His eyelids tightened slightly, a minute change that alerted Cormac in time for the king to avert his gaze so that he did not have to see what looked out of Finn's eyes.

"You are of course," the king said in a voice he was able to keep steady with some effort.

Messengers were sent, arrangements made. At the end of battle season, Finn went to see his new landholding.

He travelled with something of a retinue of his own by now, including not only a number of companies of the Fíanna, but porters, a keeper of hounds, a smith whose only occupation was forging and repairing weapons, and a steward who had charge of the ale supplies.

He left them all behind in camp, however, when he went to examine the new territory carved out for him by Cormac, and including the Hill of Almhain.

"Keep everyone in camp," he told Cailte, who with his own men was a permanent part of Finn's retinue. "See that no one follows me. All the companions I want are my hounds."

"You plan to do some hunting?" Cailte asked, brightening. "For that, you'll want the pack, and I could—"

"Not the pack, Cailte, nor you either. Just myself, and Bran and Sceolaun. While I am gone you and the other rígfénnidi can drill the men, or do a bit of hunting yourselves if you want. Just go in the opposite direction from the one I take, and if you see any deer, keep the hounds away from them. We hunt no deer in this territory."

He did not explain, nor did Cailte ask for an explanation. The thin man had long since learned that Finn rarely told his reasons for anything.

Slowly, almost reluctantly, Finn approached the hill that dominated the surrounding countryside and bogland. He did not know what he expected. Bog to the north and west, tree-covered hills to the south, mountains to the east . . . the hill was remote, and wild.

Finn was remote, and wild.

He wondered if They were watching. They, the Tuatha Dé Danann. By now they had become as palpable a presence in his mind as they were in the mind of Cormac Mac Airt, though for a different reason. Finn had incorporated them into the creation of Finn Mac Cool.

This hill could have belonged to ancestors of mine, he told himself. Those tumbled stones where the hawthorn grows, that could be the ruins of their fort. That dark hole could be the entrance to their underground kingdom, screened now by briers. If I stop, and stand, and listen, I just might hear the strains of their faraway music . . .

He stopped and stood and listened, and his hounds stood with him. Even Finn's preternaturally keen hearing detected only the wind soughing through the grass. But then . . . then there was something else. Something moving toward him. Something coming so slowly, so delicately, he knew of its approach not by sound, but by a sense of space being occupied.

He turned his head.

The woman emerged from the tumble of stones where the hawthorn grew.

Finn's first reaction was a feeling of profound disappointment. He had truly expected magic. But this was not a deer, merely a human woman: a slender human woman with a light step and regal head carriage, walking forward across the grass. Her hair was the colour of a red deer's coat.

Then Bran and Sceolaun raced toward her, wagging their plumed tails.

Suddenly Finn's heart was pounding so hard he could not breathe.

His hounds threw themselves at the woman's feet and wriggled with ecstasy as she stopped to rub their upturned bellies. Still bending over as if on all fours, she lifted her head and looked toward Finn across the intervening space.

There was no intervening space.

She was inside his head.

"I know you," he heard himself say.

She straightened then—a movement of ineffable grace—and smiled. "Have we met before?"

"We have surely. In this very place."

"I don't come here often. I would remember if I'd seen anyone else here, it is rarely visited."

"I know. I was here, though, toward the end of last summer. And I saw you over there, emerging from the woods on the slope just as you emerged from . . . those stones."

"I didn't come out of the stones," she said, laughing.

"Did you not?" The question was serious.

She hesitated before answering. Her large brown eyes searched his face, as if wondering how far she could trust him.

Walk toward me, he pleaded in his mind. Just walk toward me, that's all you have to do. But don't run away. Don't reject me.

Don't reject me, he begged with desperate urgency in the black silence of his mind.

His hounds got to their feet and pressed against the woman's legs, looking up at her as devotedly as they had always looked at Finn. When she started to walk, they walked with her, toward him.

"I was back in there," she said with a nod of her head to indicate the pile of stones, "looking for berries."

Finn was a man of forest and field; he knew at a glance there were no berries in that tangle of hawthorn and ruins. Only the tree sacred to the Sídhe grew there, guarding the entrance to their destroyed stronghold with its thorns and its magic.

His heart leaped and lurched in his breast, threatening to break out through his ribs. "Did you find any?" he asked in a choked voice.

"I did not. Perhaps it's past the season."

"Perhaps," he agreed, wondering why they were speaking inanities. Wondering why they were speaking at all. They did not need to speak.

Or perhaps they did. He had to have a name for her, in case they were separated again, so he could ask after her and find her and bind her to him. "What are you called yourself?" he asked in that same choked voice.

"I am called Sive," she replied. "And yourself?"

Finn's pride suffered a blow. "You don't know who I am?"

"I do not. I trust you will tell me."

He stood his tallest, his shoulders their widest, his silvery hair gleaming in the autumnal sun. "I am called Fionn Mac Cuhal, and I am Rígfénnid Fíanna."

There were trumpets in his voice.

For a moment her eyes widened as if in fear. He thought she might run. With one swift step he covered the unimportant space between them and put his hand on her arm . . . gently, gently but firm enough to hold her. "Don't run," he said in an urgent whisper. "Nothing will harm you, I'll never let anyone or anything harm you. I *can* protect you, I'm the Rígfénnid Fíanna," he repeated.

She was trembling. He could feel the tremors run through her body into her arm, into his hand, up his arm, through his body . . .

"Is the Fíanna nearby?" she asked anxiously.

From no more than the inflection of her voice he understood. She was a noblewoman, her very grace and posture made that plain. The fénnidi had a less than savoury reputation with women—or had done, until Finn Mac Cool.

"No member of the Fíanna will hurt you," he told her. "Not now, not ever. I have sworn them to respect all women and treat them gently." As if I knew about you, he added silently in his head.

She was still trembling. So was Finn.

It did not feel like fear.

Glancing toward the stone ruins, he asked, "Is your family nearby? Can I take you to them?"

He felt her tense beneath his hand. "My people are far away; I've wandered a great distance from them."

"Why?"

She dropped her voice so low he could barely hear her, even with his exceptional hearing. "I refused to marry a man to whom my father owed a debt. I ran away with my father's curse on me. They've been hunting me a weary time."

It took all the strength Finn had to refrain from gathering her protectively into his arms. "No one will harm you now; you're with me. With the Fíanna," he added. "And I promise you the Fíanna will not hurt you. How could your father dare try to force you to marry? Does that not go against the law? You're a free woman surely, you have the right to refuse."

"My father," Sive replied, "obeys only those laws that suit him."

Finn said with a bitter laugh, "He's not alone in that habit. No matter how carefully the law is crafted, there is always someone displeased."

She looked up into his face, and for the first time, he realized just how small she was compared to himself. "You know about law?" she asked wonderingly.

"I know about a lot of things," said Finn Mac Cool.

He took her—cajolingly, step by step—to meet his men. Bran and Sceolaun frisked beside her, choosing her over Finn, which for some reason pleased him inordinately.

When they saw him approaching, Cailte and Fergus trotted out to meet him, slowing their pace when they realized he had a woman with him. They looked from his face to hers and back again, then stared in wonder at the hounds pressing their bodies against Sive's legs.

"This woman is under our protection," was all the explanation Finn offered.

Methodically, he stripped the camp of everything rich and fine. The warmest furs were collected for her bed, the best food, the golden ale cups that had been a gift from the king—Finn gave it all to Sive.

"He's given a new meaning to the word 'protection,' " Conan remarked to Cael.

Finn appropriated Donn to do the cooking for Sive, taking him away from his own company without a moment's hesitation. "Add his men to yours for the time being," he told Red Ridge. "I need the best cook there is, and that's Donn."

To Donn he said, "Prepare anything she likes, but don't offer her deer meat."

Donn lifted his eyebrows. "I can cook deer meat three hundred ways! It's the best thing I do! Why can't I prepare some for her? Even if she claims not to like it, I can make it so delicious that . . ."

His words ran down, overwhelmed by the weight of Finn's scowl.

"Very well, if you insist. I'll cook her anything she wants, but I won't offer her deer meat. Seems a pity, though," Donn could not resist adding.

That winter Finn did not return to Tara. He sent Cailte to explain to the king, an explanation Cormac did not find convincing. "Finn thinks you would be better served by his remaining among the Laigin," the thin man said. "There are rumblings of discontent, some of the tribal kings may rebel against your authority. He says that if the Fíanna are highly visible there during the winter, the kings will probably have second thoughts."

"Companies of the Fíanna have always been quartered in that territory. There's no need for Finn specifically to stay there," Cormac argued.

Cailte replied, "He thinks there is."

The king started to issue an order demanding his Rígfénnid Fíanna return to Tara for the winter, but then he thought better of it. What if

Finn refused? Would that not force a confrontation better avoided? As long as Cormac did not ask something Finn would refuse, he could maintain the illusion of total control, though he knew to the depths of his being that he did not have total control over Finn Mac Cool. No one did, he thought. No one could.

Although Cormac did not give him credit for it, Finn had told the truth. The various Laigin kings were growing restive. When they sent their tributes to Tara after the harvest, they had resented Cormac's demands, and as the winter progressed, they resented them more. The presence of a sizable contingent of the Fíanna in Laigin territory, and under the very visible command of the Rígfénnid Fíanna himself, served to keep their fires smouldering rather than bursting into flame.

Even in the season of shortest days, Finn demanded that the Fíanna drill incessantly. Trumpets summoned them from their various quarterings to gather on a training ground and practice with sword and shield and javelin until their arms ached and their backs knotted with muscle. Fondly they recalled the relative ease of battle season, when fighting was a sport like hunting and the sun shone warmly.

Most of Finn's time, however, was spent overseeing the construction of his new fort on the Hill of Almhain. For this work, he demanded the services of his original fían, who had learned the arts of the builder while working on Tara.

To the surprise of no one, Blamec complained. "I'm a rígfénnid now with men of my own to command, why do I have to go back to being a carpenter? It's demeaning."

"No work well done is demeaning," Finn said sternly. "Besides, I need you. This fort must be completed by Beltaine, and while it won't be as large as Tara, I want it to be as finely made, as dazzling with limewash and golden thatch, as . . . as kingly as Tara. And for that, I need it to be built by the men who made Tara what it is today."

Later, Cael confided to Blamec, "I heard Finn say that if he isn't satisfied with the work we do, he'll cut us into three pieces just for sword practice. Head to heart, heart to knees, knees to toes." Cael made suitably descriptive gestures with his hands as he spoke. "It's a new feat he's developing."

Blamec paled. "Are you serious?"

Madan gave a snort of laughter. "Can't you tell yet when he's joking?"

"I can. I can of course."

"Well, I can't," said Red Ridge. "And I wouldn't be surprised if Finn had made that very threat. He's serious about this fort of his."

Fergus Honey-Tongue commented, "Very serious is Finn Mac Cool, his fine skull filled with wisdom."

"His fine skull filled with thoughts of a woman," growled Conan Maol to himself.

After a diligent search, Finn had found safe shelter for Sive with a family of stonemasons at the edge of the Bog of Almhain. There he visited her almost daily while his fort was being built. Sometimes he had only time to greet her and ask about her health, her warmth, the quality of food she was receiving, before he had to turn and dash off again, his time filled to overflowing with a thousand busynesses. But he never failed to think of her during the day, even when he could not manage to steal a few moments to be with her.

One day she noticed that he was shivering when he arrived. It was a day of unprecedented cold, with a wind like glass knives and a sky like black hatred. Finn had run so hastily to Sive that he had neglected to bring the heavy clothing the weather demanded. Before he left her, she begged a blanket from her hosts and gave it to him. "I sleep with this on my bed at night," she said, handing it shyly to him. "Wrap it around you."

That night Finn slept with the blanket on his own bed. He had not yet touched her in an intimate way. There was a fear in him that he would not express even to himself, a Cruina-shaped shadow that threatened him with failure. So he put off the moment when he would claim Sive's body, though his own ached for hers. But he could lie with her blanket wrapped around him . . . and never think of how Cruina must have lain wrapped in his cloak.

Sometime during the night he awoke with a start. He thought someone called his name, a voice like a bell chiming. The call had cut through his sleep like a blade. He lay immobile, scarcely daring to breathe, waiting to hear it again.

"What?" he murmured softly. "What?"

He pressed his face against his bed, waiting.

Then he knew.

Her scent was in his bed; faint, fading, but as clear as a call to him. He lay with his face pressed down against the blanket, trying to capture the elusive fragrance of her.

He knew he was alone in the bed, but he did not feel alone. He felt like a piece of soft wax worked by a candlemaker, with the imprints of the maker's fingers embedded in its surface. He was not the man he had been. He was reshaped.

She was part of him. Though her body was not in his bed, she was there. She was in him and of him, and wherever he went, he carried her with him.

As he rose and prepared for the day, he talked to her inside his head as if she were an arm's length from him. Some of the things he said were profound; some were the trivia that flickers through a man's mind while he scrubs his teeth with a hazel twig. The content was unimportant. The conversation itself was crucial.

Finn's silent monologue to Sive continued through every aspect of his day. He gathered his officers, issued orders; simultaneously he was talking to Sive. A senior rígfénnid reported a problem and Finn listened gravely, eyes hooded, considering the man's words and making a decision; talking to Sive. Ate, drank, walked, surveyed the lowering weather with a practised eye; talked to Sive. Selected ridgepoles, ordered the edge restored to his blades, sent runners east and south with messages for various fíans, emptied his bladder, had a protracted discussion with Red Ridge and Cailte about the condition of the roads and trackways; talked to Sive.

How strange, he thought, that none of them see her beside me or realize she's breathing the breath I breathe.

Sive had become more real to Finn than he was to himself, though in a rare moment of leisure he discovered he was no longer envisioning her physical face as an arrangement of certain features, or her body as a pleasing design of curves and planes. He was seeing the elemental Sive in his mind as she had looked when she was born, and as she would look if she lived a hundred years. He would never again see her any other way.

The elemental Sive.

16

SUPERSTITION PRECLUDED ANY LOCALS FROM WORKING on Finn's new fort, so all the construction was done by the Fíanna, which meant the building took longer than he would have liked. Still, it would be finished by Beltaine. He had given the order.

He brought Sive to see it when it was nearing completion. "My stronghold will be as fine in its own way as Cormac's at Tara," he boasted. "Tara expresses him. This is me."

Her eyes wandered over stout-timbered palisades erected upon banks of stone, their supports sunk deep. "It looks very strong," she said, because he obviously expected her to say something.

"It is very strong. Impregnable, almost. To keep you safe."

"I see no way in."

Finn grinned with boyish glee. "You don't of course! It's around on the other side where no one would expect it to be, screened with a thicket of hawthorn. There's only one gate, so it's easy to guard."

"Only one gate? What about fire?"

"Och, there's an escape tunnel, a souterrain, under the palisade. We can use it for cold storage as well. It comes out at the base of the hill, well clear of the fort. We can never be trapped here, Sive."

He took her to the surprisingly well-concealed gateway and gave a low whistle, a series of notes like the cry of a nightjar. Oak gates opened fractionally on oiled iron hinges. Conan Maol peered out.

"It's me," said Finn.

"Is it?" Enjoying the moment, Conan favoured Finn with a long, suspicious stare before finally stepping aside and letting him enter. "And who's this with you?"

"The woman I'll marry on Beltaine," said Finn. "I've brought her here to show her the home I'll give her."

"And what's she giving you?"

"She doesn't have to give me anything, Conan. You know my rule."

"So what sort of a marriage is it to be, then?"

"The marriage of equals," said Finn Mac Cool.

Glowing with pride, he led Sive from building to building, starting with the outhouses and storehouses and working his way up to the great round structure, stone-based, fragrant with adzed cedar, which would be their dwelling.

"This is the first roof that's ever been my own," he told her.

Inside, he showed her the numerous small tables, the benches, the couches draped with hides and furs, the carved boxes and chests, the wall hangings, the unlit fire laid on the hearth, waiting the touch of his wife to bring life to the house. "Firedogs," he said, showing her. "Shears, on a rope. A loom, for you. A henbox for fowl, so we can have fresh eggs. New pots and baskets. Platters. Everything we need."

She dutifully examined each item, praising its workmanship or convenience or ingenuity. "You've thought of everything, Finn. I've nothing left to desire."

Light shifted in his eyes. Desire, said a voice in his mind. Desire.

He had sent a request to Tara for the king's own brehon to witness their marriage contract. After Fithel's death, the position had been taken by his oldest son, a man called Flaithri, whose only resemblance to his father was in the extravagance of his gestures. Still, he had been trained by Fithel himself and was now the foremost living expert on the law.

No one else would do for Finn on his wedding day.

The Beltaine pole was raised beside the gate of the new stronghold and painted in vivid colours and explicit symbols of virility and fertility. Finn invited the entire Fíanna to attend his wedding, an event that would therefore see them conveniently assembled in one place at the start of battle season, so orders could be issued to the whole army at one time.

The night before the wedding, Cailte, at Finn's request, sat watch with the Rígfénnid Fíanna. They built a small fire outside the new residence, which would not be occupied until Sive came to live there. She was still sleeping with the mason's family. In the morning Finn would send a guard of honour to bring her to him.

He was so nervous that Cailte had to bite the inside of his cheek to keep from laughing at the spectacle of the feared Rígfénnid Fíanna, pale and tense, a muscle clenching in his jaw, trying to pretend he was not anxious.

"Relax," the thin man advised. "You aren't going into a battle, you're just taking a wife."

"I know what to do in battle," Finn said hoarsely.

"You know what to do with a wife, too."

Finn turned an anguished face toward him.

"Don't you?" Cailte asked.

"I . . . I haven't had any noteworthy success with women so far," admitted Finn.

"None?"

"None."

"In all this time?"

"In all this time."

Cailte was thunderstruck. "Why, Finn? Surely the women are throwing themselves into your path like hailstones, you have only to reach out and take one. You must have—"

"I haven't. And tomorrow—"

"You at least know what to do," Cailte said. "I mean, you've seen animals . . ."

"I'm not an animal."

"And neither is she," Cailte replied, trying to lighten the moment. To his astonishment, Finn groaned as if in pain.

"Is it different?" he asked Cailte. "Between people and animals, I mean. Is it different?"

"What are you talking about?"

"I . . . nothing. Pay no attention to me, I've lost the run of myself tonight. I'll be all right tomorrow."

Cailte said, "You'd better be. This is something you'll have to do yourself, you know. No one can help you."

"No one can help me," Finn echoed in the voice of a man anticipating his doom.

Long before dawn, Finn Mac Cool began preparing for his wedding day. He selected his clothing, changed his mind, made new selections. Cailte had to plait and re-plait his hair, though there was no difference between the precision of the first plait and the second. But Finn was not satisfied.

He sent for Flaithri to discuss the matter of contract and vows yet again, having done so seven times previously. Flaithri was out of patience. "There's no point in continuing to plough the same ground, Finn! The contract you've described is very clear and boringly simple. Your rights, her rights, the rights of any children . . . without arrangements for property, there's hardly anything to contract. But I must say, it's highly irregular. A marriage of the first degree, the most prestigious, with no property even mentioned . . ."

"Each marriage is shaped by its own requirements," Finn said. "Is that not part of Brehon Law?"

"It is," Flaithri agreed, having become aware that the Rígfénnid Fíanna had made a more extensive study of the law than one would have expected of a man of his station. "Tell me, Finn, since I have not spoken with the woman herself. Is she satisfied with this contract? If not, she is free to refuse it, you know."

"She left it up to me," Finn replied.

Flaithri was astonished. In his experience, women were not that passive. The construction of their marriage contracts was of paramount importance to the sex whose biology demanded practicality. Marriages, even of the first degree, lasted only as long as the partners desired, but the futures of children must be safeguarded before they were ever conceived.

But the only time Finn had mentioned the contract to Sive, her reply had been a simple shrug of one shoulder and the words, "What are contracts to me? You have said you will take care of me, that's all I need to know. I have no property of my own, and it's safe to say I have no family either. I am free," she added in a tone that might have been joy or regret.

I made you out of my dream, Finn said to her in his mind. Of course you have no family, no property. And I provided for that eventuality long before I found you!

When the sun was halfway between horizon and midpoint, an honour guard led by Finn's original fían, together with the cream of their companies, marched away from the Hill of Almhain to bring Sive to Finn Mac Cool.

No sooner were they out of sight than another group of warriors approached from the opposite direction.

Finn was the first to see them, having mounted the sentry platform above the gateway so he would have the first glimpse of Sive. Instead, he saw hostile warriors approaching at the trot. He gave a howl of disbelief. "Someone's breaking his pledge to the king of Tara!" He leaped from the platform without bothering with the ladder and ran for his weapons.

The choicest warriors had gone to escort Sive, but Finn swiftly rallied the rest.

"Whoever the warlord is who has broken his peace agreement with Cormac," he vowed grimly, "he made a mistake by doing it on my wedding day. He'll not leave the Hill of Almhain alive."

The attack was led by a disaffected clan chieftain called Ilbrecc, who had chosen to disregard the arrangements made between Cormac and the kings of the Laigin. He had a long-standing quarrel with the king of his tribe anyway, and considered the man a traitor for giving in so easily to the power of Tara. He had chosen his time with great care for expressing his feelings. Like the Ulaid, he attacked just outside the recognized boundaries of battle season to take advantage of the element of surprise.

He received some surprises himself, however.

The first came when his scouts could not find a way into Finn's stronghold. They reported, "There's a wall all the way around but we see no gates."

"There have to be gates! There are always gates!"

"This is the site of an ancient stronghold of the Tuatha Dé Danann," one scout said nervously, showing white all the way around his eyes. "Perhaps they worked their magic, perhaps they're in league with Finn Mac Cool."

"Nonsense. There's a gate, I tell you. Find it and break it down!" Ilbrecc commanded.

They marched uncertainly forward to be met by a rain of spears hurled over the wall.

"If men are inside, they had to have some way to get in," Ilbrecc reasoned. "And if they got in, so can we!"

A second attack was mounted. This time, more by chance than cleverness, they stumbled upon the gates concealed by the hawthorn. Logs were brought up to use as a battering ram.

"Open to them before they damage my new gates," Finn ordered.

The gates swung open. Ilbrecc rushed forward first—to find himself facing a single, startling apparition, a tall, silver-haired man who stood with legs braced wide and a sword in his hand. And clothes on his body fit for a king.

Finn smiled pleasantly. "You are very welcome, stranger," he said in a dangerously quiet voice, "if you come as a guest to my wedding."

Ilbrecc was disconcerted. He skidded to a halt, his men crowding against his back. "I've come to kill you!"

"Have you now?" Finn asked in the same quiet voice. He did something with his sword—a move so swift that witnesses afterward could never agree on what it was—and Ilbrecc's head rolled across the grass.

The body stood on its legs a moment longer, then fell backward into the press of men behind it.

They scattered like sheep to let it fall.

A fountain of blood erupted from the severed jugular, drenching Finn in his wedding clothes, crimson dripping from linen, soaking into wool, as he hurled himself over the still-falling body and flung himself upon Ilbrecc's retreating men, scything his sword.

The deliberate narrowness of his gateway meant that no more than four men could enter the fort abreast at any one time. Added to this was the cluster of hawthorn shielding the gateway, a serious impediment to men trying to get their weapons into the clear for fighting. It seemed in retrospect, when the survivors told of it later, that the hawthorn actually conspired with Finn to block their way and entangle their sword arms, while allowing Finn to move freely. He hacked and hewed and Ilbrecc's men fell, unable to strike him in return.

One of them began to scream. "The Sídhe!" he howled in terror. "The Sídhe!"

His companions in the front line whirled and tried to run, only to find their way blocked by the men behind them. They attacked their own allies in their panic, desperate to escape Finn and the hawthorn and the mindless fear from the past that rose like dark clouds over the Hill of Almhain.

Inside the palisade, Finn's own men were jostling for position and trying to get outside to help him. But the congestion of packed and struggling bodies at the gate stoppered them like a cork stoppering a bottle. They could only rage impotently and call to Finn, who was too busy to answer.

The stopper gave way. The survivors fled the hill, shrieking. Finn Mac Cool clambered over piled bodies to watch them go and shake his sword in the air at their fleeing backs. "It was my wedding day!" he cried in outrage. "It was *my wedding day!*"

By the time Sive and the guard of honour arrived, the little army that had thought to attack Finn had disappeared. At least, those still living were gone. As Sive approached her new home, her horrified eyes were greeted by the sight of a pile of bloodied bodies stacked near the gates.

Cailte was the first to recover from the shock and ran forward, calling Finn's name. The gates opened to him at once, and he and the others poured through.

Fergus Honey-Tongue held back, staying with Sive. He put a hand on her elbow to steady her; she looked as if she might bolt in terror at the sight of the piled bodies and at the stench of their emptied bowels. "Death takes a bit of getting used to," he commented, adding consolingly, "but it's all right, our side obviously won. Those aren't our men feeding the ravens."

Sive made a tiny sound in her throat.

Fergus guided her through the gateway and looked around anxiously for Finn. He would not have recognized him but for his height and his hair.

The Rígfénnid Fíanna was literally bathed in blood. As he strode forward to greet Sive, flakes of dried gore fell from his clothing in a brown rain. For his wedding day he had selected a new shirt and tunic and a woollen cloak with three rows of fringe, but it was impossible to tell what colour any of them had been. All was the colour of blood now.

Sive's nostrils flared.

Accustomed to blood, Finn did not realize, until he saw the look on her face, what a shock his appearance must be to Sive. I should bathe, he thought. But he could not leave her when she had just arrived. He could not leave her at all. If he issued the order to his feet, they would simply refuse to obey.

He held out his hands to her. They too were caked with blood.

"This isn't the way I meant to greet you," he apologized. "It was to be . . . I had planned . . . trumpets . . ." He waved vaguely. A fénnid saw the gesture and tardily put a horn to his lips and blew. He was no musician. The trumpet made a sound like a slaughtered pig.

Finn looked stricken. The woman in Sive recognized his pain. Unflinchingly, she reached out and took his two bloody hands in hers. "I am glad to be here," she said.

Finn held her hands, or she held his, flesh welded to flesh with no seam. "We'll make our vows now," Finn decided, "before anything else happens." He raised his voice. "Flaithri! Here, to me!"

Hurrying forward, the brehon discovered Finn and Sive in the centre of a circle of Fíanna, holding hands like two children at bay. Flaithri scowled disapproval. "You must go and bathe and put on fresh clothing," he told Finn. "And surely your woman would like to refresh herself after her journey. Then you can—"

"We're going to take our vows now," said Finn.

"But—"

"Now," said Finn Mac Cool.

He was gripping Sive's hands so tightly they throbbed with pain, but she made no effort to pull free. She had known fear in her life, and desperation. She recognized the grip of a drowning man.

"We take our vows now," she said to the brehon.

Flaithri rolled his eyes sunward. "This is highly unusual."

"Finn Mac Cool is highly unusual," Fergus interjected, "and he has an awesome temper. I suggest you do as he asks rather than provoke one of his famous demonstrations."

Nine rígfénnidi stepped, as one man, closer to Finn and Sive. Nine pairs of warrior eyes fixed themselves firmly on Flaithri.

The brehon knew a threat when he saw it. "It's your marriage of course," he told Finn. "I shall certainly do as you wish." Meanwhile, he was trying to ignore the blood drying on Finn's clothing and growing increasingly pungent as the day warmed. "Hold hands," he instructed unnecessarily. "Now repeat the vows of first-degree marriage after me, the two of you speaking with one voice."

They nodded, heads bobbing in unison.

As Flaithri recited, they echoed, "You cannot possess me for I belong to myself. But while we both wish it, I give you that which is mine to give. You cannot command me for I am a free person. But I shall serve you in those ways you require and the honeycomb will taste sweeter coming from my hand.

"I pledge to you that yours will be the name I cry aloud in the night, and the eyes into which I smile in the morning. I pledge to you the first bite from my meat and the first drink from my cup. I pledge to you my living and my dying, each equally in your care. I shall be a shield for your back, and you for mine. I shall not slander you, nor you me. I shall honour you above all others, and when we quarrel, we shall do so in private and tell no strangers our grievances.

"This is my wedding vow to you. This is the marriage of equals."

As Finn and Sive repeated the words, the blended voices of man and woman became one voice.

Flaithri raised his extended arms above them toward the sun and solemnly intoned, "These promises you make by the sun and moon, by fire and water, by day and night, by land and sea. With these vows you swear, by the gods your people swear by, to be full partners, each to the other.

"If one drops the load, the other will pick it up. If one is a discredit to the other, his own honour will be forfeit, generation upon generation, until he repairs that which was damaged and finds that which was lost. The vow of first degree supersedes all others. Should you fail to keep the oath you pledge today, the elements themselves will reach out and destroy you."

Surrounded by his Fíanna, bathed in blood, Finn let the words sink into his bones. Then, for the first time anyone could remember, he humbly bowed his head.

There was a wedding feast afterward, with dancing around the Beltaine pole and songs sung and stories told and massive amounts of barley ale consumed. It was an occasion of rampant revelry. No one could equal the Fíanna when it came to revelry.

But Finn did not join them. He led Sive into the house he had built for her and barred the door behind them.

The world went away.

In the house, their house, Sive knelt by the firepit and built a smaller house out of kindling to contain their first fire. Finn struck sparks from his flints, and she encouraged them with her breath. When the fire came to life, the house came to life.

Finn had acquired a copper cauldron for heating water, and working together, they dragged this close to the fire. They did not speak. Words were not necessary. The silent conversation went on as before, a dialogue now, and from time to time, Sive caught Finn's eye and smiled.

He could feel the wounds on his spirit healing.

As the water heated, Finn began to unfasten the bronze brooch that held his blood-stiffened cloak to his shoulders, but Sive reached out and pushed his fingers away, opening the brooch herself. She peeled the sticky woollen cloak from the tunic beneath and dropped it heavily to the ground.

Then she removed his tunic and shirt.

Finn stood unable to move. His eyes never left her face.

With tenderness, she stripped him. She did not appear to notice the tremors running along his thigh muscles. With her cupped hands, she took warmed water from the cauldron and poured it over his body, then wiped away the blood with a dampened cloth. She began with his face and neck and worked her way down, across his shoulders, his chest, his belly. Touching him gently in his private places, lifting and cleansing him with grave reverence.

He had been frightened, terrified of the moment when his manhood would be tested. But Sive was so gentle she encouraged gentleness in Finn, and with it came patience. He was able to control himself and let his desire rise easily, like a flowering.

Sive knelt before him to bathe his legs.

After a few moments he reached down and lifted her to her feet. Taking the cloth from her, he dropped it into the cauldron. Then he removed her garments as she had removed his, fumbling only briefly with the complexities of female dress.

He did everything very slowly, with a sense that time had stopped.

When she was naked, he gazed at her in the firelight and she stood vulnerable to him, her arms hanging at her sides, palms outward.

She was, he thought, the most wonderful being he had ever seen.

He ran his fingers from her collarbone to her nipples, watching in amazement as the pink cones stiffened to his touch. "Like you," she said, looking down. He followed her eyes and saw his erection like a lance between them. One tiny move and it was pressed against her, sinking into the softness of her belly.

They gasped one breath together.

Sive cupped Finn's buttocks with her hands and drew him closer. Then she ran her warm palms up his body, up his rib cage, lifting them to frame his face so she could study his eyes.

He wondered what she saw.

He knew what others had seen, sometimes.

But Sive was not frightened. She looked deep into him, so deep, he thought, she must surely see the forest and the boglands and the wild mountains, must see the secrets of his spirit. "Come into me," he said.

"Come into me," she replied.

He lifted her in his arms. She weighed no more than a thought. A dream. Yet there was a warm, solid weight to her too, a smoothness of flesh and scent of hair that was unique to Sive. With his eyes closed, he would have known her among thousands. This is how Bran and Sceolaun knew her, he thought. She was as instantly familiar to them as she is to me.

He laid her down on his couch of furs. The passion roaring through him was hotter than the fire on the hearth, yet not out of control as it had been with Cruina. When he was with Sive, their every move together was like a dance they both knew, and he made no mistakes. "Let me touch you," he whispered. "Let me look at you."

She parted her legs for him and let him see her secret mouth, like petals in soft moss, moist and open to him. He touched her and she gasped again, spine arching. Reaching for him, she put her hands on his hips and guided him toward her. Slowly, slowly. Savouring.

When he touched her, he was shot through by lightning. But he could contain the lightning. He could hold it within him, waiting, as she waited, while he slid into that soft, warm secret mouth and felt its lips close around him. Then all was silken heat and he did not have to wait any longer.

She had been like a wild creature, living by her wits, running on the hills. Her muscles were firm and strong and very much at her command. She squeezed him deliberately, deep inside herself, wringing a cry of astonishment from him.

Then she did it again. When he looked down at her, her eyes were brimming with mischief. She licked her lips.

She squeezed him a third time and the throbbing thunder overtook them. They cried out with one voice then, sharing an explosion of sensation beyond bearing in its intensity.

Finn Mac Cool was shapechanged by ecstasy.

Later, much later, he was able to draw away from her an infinitesimal distance and study her by firelight as she slept. Her fair skin was caressed by the piled furs on which she lay.

In the glow from the hearth, her skin tones were not pale, however. They were golden . . . they were ruddy . . . like the hide of a red deer burnished by the westering sun.

Dreams, thought Finn. And reality. Which is she? Does it matter? She's here. She's here. He touched her curving flank, he ran his fingertip along the knobs of her spine, between the strong back muscles.

She's here.

Sive opened her eyes.

He continued his exploration of her, pausing when he found the first scar. "What's this?" he asked in a hoarse whisper.

"I was in a forest, and some hunters came. They must have mistaken me for an animal. I ran from them, thinking my father had sent them, but they ran after me and hurled their spears at me. One spear took me . . . there, in the side. It fell out when I kept running, but it left a scar."

The sight of the mended flesh gave Finn a pain more physical than his own injuries had ever caused him. He could have lost her! Some hunter's spear might have ended her life before he ever knew there was a Sive!

He seized her in his arms and pressed her against his chest as if he would fight off all the world for her.

She felt his heart beating against hers, with the same rhythm. Then the rhythm grew faster.

When at last they rested again, he continued his examination, questioning every scratch and scrape. There were pale white marks where briers had torn her legs; he kissed them. He kissed the calused soles of her feet, and discovered to his delight that the curve of her instep fitted the shape of his cheekbone.

Every part of Sive fitted every part of Finn.

Sometime before dawn he got up to feed the fire, and brought back the bathing cloth. He sat naked beside her on the furs and stroked her clean with aching tenderness, while she lay smiling.

"Is this a thing men do for their wives?" she asked him.

"I don't know. I don't know what men do. I only know what I do," said Finn Mac Cool.

17

 "Is he still in there?" Donn asked.

"Still in there," Conan muttered. "And ourselves out here waiting for orders."

"Does he ever come out?"

"He opened the door yesterday and peered out long enough to ask for more food and drink and to glance at the sky, but before I could say anything to him, he closed the door in my face."

"Did you pound on it?"

Conan stared at Donn. "Are you mad?" The hairless man settled himself more comfortably on the fasting bench outside Finn's door. There was no point in standing at attention. Finn was paying no attention to him.

Donn gave the closed door a long look, then walked away.

Before long, Red Ridge took his place. "It's battle season," he informed Conan unnecessarily. "I thought we'd be fighting someplace, or at least hunting."

Conan picked his teeth with a sliver of fishbone. "You can go hunt if you want to. Or fight, come to that, if you can find someone to fight. But don't count on him in there." He indicated the dwelling at his back with a jerk of his thumb.

"What if the king sends for him?"

"Has he done?" Conan asked irritably, suddenly faced with the prospect of action instead of sprawling in the sun.

"Not that I know of, but he might. We're his army, after all, and peace is a sometime thing."

"If and when the king sends for him," Conan drawled, "you can be the one to tell him. I prefer to keep the head down."

Finn was aware of them outside his door. He was aware of the Fíanna as he was aware of sky above and earth below, but he did not think of them. He thought only of Sive.

Once, with a start, he realized he had not thought of his mother in a very long time. He was relieved.

When they were not sharing each other's bodies, he shared his thoughts with Sive. At first, thinking to entertain and impress her, he told her the stories he told his Fianna, the stories of battles fought and triumphs won and relationships that set him apart from other men.

Sive listened. She had the quality of listening, as if her ears could swivel to detect and concentrate upon the slightest sound.

Finn told her of his battle against the Cat-headed men and the Dog-headed men and the White-backed men. He described the taking of Lomna's head, and the rescue of Manannán's daughter. He spun stories from the firelight and wove them around her head like a wreath, and she listened and smiled and murmured appreciatively in all the right places.

He was telling her, with great detail and impeccable timing, the story of Meargach of the Green Spears when he began to hear his words as she was hearing them. With a critical ear, he noted implausibility piled upon impossibility, and events stretched out of all shape in order to make room for more colour.

The spate of words slowed. Sive continued to watch his face, her luminous eyes fixed on his.

If she is inside my head, he thought—and she is—then she can see what is real and what is not.

With great effort, he retraced the threads of his story. "Meargach didn't actually bring seven times seventy men against us," he admitted. "There were . . . seven or eight of them altogether, I suppose. And I didn't kill them all myself. In fact, I don't think I killed any of them, Meargach included. I know that Goll killed one of the man's sons and Conan struck the head from the other one, but now I look back on it, I think Meargach accidentally stepped in the line of one of his own spear throwers and took a fatal wound in the back.

"His wife came to the field of battle afterward. I couldn't tell her how he died, so—"

"So you made it sound heroic," Sive said gently.

"So I made it sound heroic," he echoed. "And that was the truth of it in a way, don't you see? When I told her the tale of his death, I told it as he would have wished it to be, a glorious death in the midst of a mighty battle. What man wants to be remembered by the bards for having gotten in the way of his own spear thrower?"

Sive nodded. "Is there always a seed of truth in the tales you tell?"

He considered the question. She was not being judgmental, merely curious. "There is," he said at last. "I am an honest man, you know."

"I know," Sive replied.

The next time he began to relate the details of some incident, he kept them stripped to the bare essentials, the verities he knew. Halfway through the narration, he saw her smile. "You can tell it better than that," she said. "I love to hear the bard in you."

Delightedly, Finn wove magic and mystery into his words at once, shapechanging a simple anecdote about hunting into a sprawling epic replete with every enhancement.

He knew, without being told, that she knew where the seed of truth lay. His tales were safe with her. And when he was with her, Finn gradually began to be able to tell reality from dreams . . .

. . . except in the case of Sive herself. He never told her about that first meeting with the deer near the Hill of Almhain. He never asked her if she had been that deer.

There were some truths he did not want to know.

For the same reason, he did not query her about her past before they met. She had told him the essentials; he knew she was haunted and hunted, cursed by her father. It gave them a bond.

At last he found enough courage to explain that bond, without alluding to her own history. In Sive's presence, Finn found the courage to examine his history as he had never done before.

They had been together on furs piled beside the hearth, enjoying one another with a passion that never seemed to fade, even when their bodies were temporarily exhausted. As she lay in Finn's arms, he found himself telling her, "I grew up wild, you know. Really wild. Cailte told me that Cormac once called me his 'wolf cub' behind my back, but there is more truth to that than the king knows. When I was born . . ." he paused and drew a deep breath, as if he were about to dive into a bottomless lake . . . "when I was born, my mother abandoned me on the Bog of Almhain."

Abandoned me.

Saying the words aloud did not hurt as much as he had expected. In fact, they hardly hurt at all. They simply dropped into the deep pool that was Sive and were absorbed, the pain drained away. She put her hand on his chest, over his heart.

"Two old women found me," he went on. "I think they were kin to me, probably from my father's tribe. They never told me, though. They never told me anything. I was the result of a disgrace, a shame on my father's head, that his people wanted to forget. They raised me as best they could, though they had little to offer except the secrets of survival that sustained them. I learned well," he added musingly.

"Mostly I ran like a wolf cub, untaught and unfettered. As soon as I could survive on my own, I left the old women altogether. I was tired of the sight of them and the smell of them, tired of chewing their food for them because they had no teeth, tired of threading bone needles for them because their eyesight had failed. To me they were old sticks in bags of wrinkled leather, they even smelled old. They smelled of death. I wanted something else. Something alive.

"I wandered. In time I met a man who recognized my father in my face and told me who he thought I was. He told me of my mother as well, and I set out to find her.

"I thought she would want me, Sive. I thought she would be as overjoyed to meet me as I would be to meet her. I didn't know she'd abandoned me, you see—I learned that only later. So I rushed across Erin to be reunited with a mother I expected to meet me with open arms."

"And she didn't?"

"She didn't. When I finally found her, she . . ."

Under Sive's hand, Finn's heart was racing. "You don't have to tell me if you don't want to," she said gently.

"I do want to tell you. I have to say it sometime, and I can say it only to you." Drawing another deep breath, Finn summoned all his courage and laid it at Sive's feet, like a gift.

"When I found my mother, she had married a chieftain of Kerry. She had jewelry, servants; her eyebrows were dyed and her fingertips were reddened. She looked like a princess. She had come from people of high rank, you see—originally. My father had stolen her, and himself only a Fir Bolg. His touch, unwanted, had defiled her. When I suddenly appeared at her chieftain's gateway, wearing my father's face, my mother was appalled.

"She ran toward me, I remember, and I knew at once who she was. She had brown eyes like yours, and a look that went right through me. I couldn't understand why she was shouting at me. 'Go away!' she kept saying. 'Go away!'

"I protested that I was her son and that I had been looking for her. 'I haven't been looking for you,' she said. 'Go away before my husband returns and finds you here. I don't want you. I don't want you!'

"That was what my mother told me, Sive. "I don't want you.' "

Her eyes filled with tears. "Oh, Finn."

He closed his eyes and saw once more, on the inside of the lids, the chieftainly stronghold in Kerry, with its stone walls, the houses, the sheds, cauldrons of dye boiling over an open fire.

His mother standing glaring at him, demanding he go away.

Truth was ugly.

But with Sive in his arms, he could face it.

That summer no battles broke in Erin; at least, none involving the interests of the king of Tara. As if an enchantment lay on the land, Finn was left undisturbed on the Hill of Almhain with his wife. His men, colossally bored, organized hunting expeditions, sporting competitions, and vigorous faction fights that kept their battle skills polished. Reports on these activities were dutifully submitted to the Rígfénnid Fíanna, but he seemed singularly disinclined to take part. He spent his time with Sive, and few other people even saw him.

There was a rumour that he was dead.

"Finn Mac Cool is not only alive, but immortal!" Fergus Honey-Tongue proclaimed to all who would listen.

The summer passed, the celebration of Lughnasa was held in honour of the sun, autumn began. Samhain lay ahead.

Finn could not spend Samhain at his fort, not if he wanted to remain Rígfénnid Fíanna, and he knew it. With reluctance, he began making preparations to attend the Samhain Assembly at Tara.

Sive asked, "Shall I go with you?"

"I've been having a think about that. Everyone comes to the Assembly—at least everyone who's important in Cormac's territory. If you're there, someone will surely recognize you and word will get back to your people. They might even," he added, aware of the irony, "assume I'd stolen you."

"Are you saying I can't go with you?"

"I want you with me, I want you everywhere I go. But I want you safe; that's more important. I've decided it's best you stay here. I'll leave Donn and Cael and Red Ridge and their companies here to protect you, and I'll come straight back to you when the Assembly disperses."

Sive did not argue. She never argued with Finn. She had weapons more potent than her tongue. Reaching out, she captured one of his hands and pressed it against her belly.

"Come back to us," she said.

His face went blank. "Us?"

"Us. Your child and me."

"My child?" Finn said the words but they had no meaning. He repeated them slowly. "My child."

A bolt of terror went through him.

My child!

How does one have a child? How does one be parent to a child? He had never known a parent. The nearest approximation had been the two old women who raised him, and he had walked away from them without a backward look.

I abandoned them, he realized, suddenly horrified by a thought he had not entertained before.

Will my children abandon me when I am old?

My children.

My child. *A* child. A person. A separate person.

The concept staggered him.

Until Sive, he had lived for no one but himself. The Fíanna were his responsibility, one he sought with all the determination he possessed, but he had taken them on as an adjunct and enhancement to himself, and as a way of mantling himself with his father's heritage. Finn was young, so very young that until this moment he had thought himself the centre of the cosmos. Himself . . . and Sive.

And now a child.

He started to say something, stuttered, lost the thought, stared at Sive.

She laughed.

Like everything else she did, Sive laughed gently, without cruelty. "It's all right, Finn," she said.

"What am I supposed to do?" he asked in bewilderment.

Sive laughed again. "You've already done it, I'd say. It's up to me now."

"When . . . I mean, what . . . I mean . . ."

"Will it be a boy or a girl? I don't know, Finn. You need a druid to tell you those things, and you have no druid here."

"I'll get one!" Finn promised. "By nightfall there will be a druid in residence on the Hill of Almhain! We must have someone close to you to protect you from evil spirits, to foresee difficulties, and—"

Sive laid slender fingers across his mouth to silence him. "You protect me, Finn," she said confidently. "There won't be any difficulties."

But he could not be sure. He must erect palisades of security around his wife and child. Mere stone and timber were not sufficient, not in Erin.

By the time Finn was ready to leave for Tara, he had expanded his household to include a female physician called Bebinn, a bard known as Suanach Mac Senshenn, whose duty it was to keep Sive entertained, and a druid whose name was Cainnelsciath, meaning Shining Shield.

"Where are we going to put these people?" Sive wondered.

Obviously, new dwellings would have to be built for them and other provisions made for them. In a fever, Finn organized construction to take place in his absence and even found a steward, a man called Garvcronan, who would manage the household and relieve Sive of that duty.

None of these appointments were easily achieved. No one seemed anxious to take up residence on the Hill of Almhain. As Cainnelsciath pointed out, "This place has a bad name, Finn. You should have built your stronghold somewhere else."

"If there are evil spirits here, it's your responsibility to protect my family from them," Finn replied.

Like many of his class, the druid was a person of indeterminate age.

He had a youthful face and bright, ruddy hair, glossy with health, but his hands were old, as gnarled as tree roots and speckled with brown. He let people guess his age but neither affirmed nor denied. "I am too old to live and too young to die," was all he would admit.

Sive warmed to the druid immediately. The first time she saw his face, she felt the child move in her womb.

"Your son recognizes a friend," Cainnelsciath told her.

"My son?"

The druid nodded. "You carry a healthy boy in you."

She put her hand lightly on his arm. "Don't tell Finn," she pleaded. "If he knew it was a son, he might not go. And it's important that he go. Being Rígfénnid Fíanna means everything to him."

Cainnelsciath's eyes glinted. "Not quite everything," he said. He had been on the Hill of Almhain for only one day, but he already knew that Sive was its beating heart. Druid sensibilities were attuned to the invisible.

Finn found leave-taking impossible. When the time came to go, he pushed Sive away from him almost roughly. "Go back in our house and close the door," he told her. "Don't stand where I can see you. Don't."

She did as he asked, then stood on the other side of the closed door with her back pressed against it and her hands cradling her swelling belly.

Leaving three companies to guard his stronghold, Finn marched to Tara.

Along the way, he talked.

"Incessantly!" Blamec complained. "I don't recall his being such a talker! Now every other word out of his mouth is Sive this and Sive that. He won't talk about war or weapons or anything interesting, just that woman. You'd think she was the only woman in the world."

"She's not the only woman," remarked Cailte, who had at last found one of his own.

"Not the only woman at all," agreed Madan for a similar reason.

The new respectability of the Fíanna was making its members attractive to a higher level of female society than they had enjoyed before. Finn was not the only warrior who had taken a wife at Beltaine. But mindful of his rule, his men accepted no property with their women, whom they treated with utmost courtesy, as if they were the wives of kings.

Erin was changing.

The gathering of the Fíanna at the Samhain Assembly that year saw warriors loyal to Cormac Mac Airt arrive from almost every part of Erin. Even Ulidia had been a hunting ground for the fénnidi that summer, roistering across its hills and chasing its wild boars. There had, of course, been small wars, but nothing of importance, merely altercations between clans, or even between individuals, the normal explosions of energy to be expected among vigorous people.

But Cormac Mac Airt was too wise to expect peace to be a constant.

He was glad to see Finn. "I was almost afraid you weren't coming," he told his Rígfénnid Fíanna. "There have been stories circulating about you. It is said you've become something of a hermit on that hill of yours. Some even claim the Sídhe have captured you."

Finn grinned the old familiar grin, mischievous and merry. "I am captured," he told the king.

Cormac's voice was suddenly tight. "What do you mean?"

"A woman has me in thrall," Finn admitted cheerfully.

The king gave him an incredulous look. No man would make such an admission—but then, Finn was unlike other men, Cormac reminded himself. "Are you talking about your wife? What's her name . . . Sabia?"

"Sive. Her name is Sive, it means sweet."

"I know what it means, Finn. Is she truly named?"

"Truly."

"When do we see this paragon of yours at Tara? Why didn't you bring her to the Samhain Assembly?"

"She's carrying a child. I thought she'd be safer at home."

Cormac clapped Finn on the back. "Your child! And I having one myself with my new wife!"

"Carnait? I thought she'd already had—"

"She did. This is another new wife."

It was Finn's turn to be incredulous. "And Ethni consented? How in the name of the seven stars did you manage that?"

"Once Ethni got into the habit of agreeing about Carnait, it was just a matter of encouraging her to keep on agreeing. In time she came to see the sense of it. Women are very practical, really. Now they are quite good friends, they chatter together daylong, complain to one another about me since they can't complain to anyone else. They share clothing and discover new ways of dressing their hair and are raising their children together. My women have more in common with each other than they do with me anyway, and having them together keeps them amused when I am busy.

"In time you might think of taking a second wife yourself, Finn. Lochan's daughter is still here, you know. In fact, I gather she considers herself yours already."

Finn tried to recall Cruina's face. But he could see only Sive. "I don't want any other woman," he told the king.

That night in the hall, Cormac repeated their conversation to an amused audience, adding, "Our Finn will change his mind once the new wife becomes old cheese."

Finn's face darkened dangerously. "Don't speak of her," he grated through clenched teeth.

The atmosphere in the hall changed abruptly. In one heartbeat it went from amiable conviviality to crouching tension. Radiating invisibly from Finn, his anger infected the fénnidi standing around the walls. Their eyes narrowed, their lips pressed tightly together. They became an extension of himself.

Cormac recognized the danger. This was what he had long feared, the power held in check not by his own authority, but by Finn Mac Cool. It could be turned against anyone at any moment, according to Finn's whim.

Finn is too dangerous to have at Tara, Cormac thought. And it would be even more dangerous to have him elsewhere.

With a casual remark, the king changed the subject. For the rest of the evening he was an expansive host, urging his poets to entertain, encouraging his musicians to play, calling for more food and drink, laughing at witticisms, taking part wholeheartedly in various conversations—avoiding the eyes of Finn Mac Cool.

The dangerous moment slid by like turbulence in a river and was gone, but the memory lingered with Cormac.

Next morning, Goll Mac Morna arrived at Tara.

While Finn had spent the battle season with Sive, Goll, unsummoned, had remained at his own residence, increasingly curious as to why his services were not being required. He had sent messengers to Tara to enquire, only to be repeatedly informed, "The Fíanna are free this summer."

Goll knew what that meant, or thought he did. The fénnidi were running wild across Erin, hunting, pillaging, getting into mischief in spite of Finn's efforts to force self-discipline upon them. "I am better off out of it," he told his wife.

Still, he worried.

Neither the ground opening nor the sky falling could have prevented his journeying to Tara for the Samhain Assembly to find out what was happening.

Among Goll's survival skills was a highly developed sensitivity to every change in the wind. Even from a distance, he recognized change at Tara. There were more banners flying above the palisade than he remembered, and more roofs showing, too. And fénnidi, rather than Fiachaid's men, were patrolling the approaches.

Tara was thronged with the Fíanna, not just officers but common spear warriors, stalking arrogantly through precincts once reserved for royalty.

Goll felt a stab of alarm.

Before reporting to Finn, he went in search of Fiachaid, whom he found in a hazel grove beside the palisade, sitting in feathery shade and calmly cracking nuts. Wearing no weapons.

"Why aren't you on duty?" Goll demanded to know.

Fiachaid put one hand over his eyes to shade them as he looked up at Goll. "What duty?"

"You're in charge of the king's guard, aren't you?"

"I'm eating nuts, that's what I'm doing. Have some?"

"I didn't come here for nuts! What's going on? Where are your sword and spear?"

Fiachaid paused to pick a bit of shell out of his teeth before replying, "Finn Mac Cool has my spear, remember? He handles it better than I ever did. I suppose you could say I've retired from active service in the military."

"Shame on your beard!" cried Goll. "A warrior's supposed to die in battle!"

"A fénnid perhaps. But I'm Milesian, the king's kinsman, and I'm entitled to certain advantages now that Cormac is securely established here. One of those is the right to enjoy some leisure and let others do the fighting if need be."

"Finn won't fight for you. He'll take over. I know him."

Fiachaid seemed unperturbed. "Take over what? He can't be king, he's Fir Bolg. He already has everything else one of his class could hope to win, so what's left for him to take over?"

Goll could hardly believe his ears. "You've accepted his ascendancy without a fight?"

"I fought in Cormac's service to regain power for our tribe. We have that now. Let the professionals keep it for us, men like you. And Finn. Men born and bred for the work."

"Aren't you even jealous of Finn?"

"How could I be jealous of a Fir Bolg?" Fiachaid asked reasonably.

Goll strode away muttering to himself.

He still did not seek out and report to Finn. Instead, he made his way toward the House of the King, noting how many additions had been made to Tara since he saw it last. The great stronghold was more sprawling than ever, its palisades extended to accommodate a total of seven forts, including both Cormac's official house and his private residence, plus five others of almost equal grandeur for visiting kings. A long, timbered building known as the Hall of a Thousand Warriors now housed members of the Fíanna, and a House of the Hostages had recently been completed to contain prisoners of battle.

In addition to being a kingly centre, Tara, fragrant with cedar and brazen with bronze, was very obviously a military fortification unparalleled in Erin. And construction was continuing on the very eve of the Samhain Assembly.

Goll paused to question a man adzing planking. "Who designed all this?" He waved his hand to indicate the entire complex.

The woodworker looked at him in surprise. "The king, of course. He designs everything."

"But where did he get his ideas? All these walls separating one structure from another . . . it's a maze in here, it isn't broad and gracious anymore at all."

The woodworker shrugged. "That's to make it harder to attack any one building, I think."

"And that was the king's idea?"

"Och, perhaps not. I believe the Rígfénnid Fíanna had something to do with the plan."

"I believe he did," Goll said grimly.

In much of the design of Tara, Goll recognized the patterns of Finn's mind, a mind accustomed to the wild ways of the wilderness, to tangled forests and secretive glens. A mind most comfortable when hiding behind elaborate constructs of the imagination.

Walking through Tara, Goll felt, was like walking through Finn's brain. It made him distinctly uncomfortable.

At the House of the King he found four men from Conan's company guarding the outer wall and surmised there would be a similar guard on the inner wall. Cormac was well shielded. "I want to see the king," Goll announced firmly.

They watched him impassively. "Why?" asked one.

"Because I'm an officer of the Fíanna and I've come here with my three nines to report to the king."

"Where are your three nines?"

"I left my company down at the gate."

"You should have sent them to the Hall of a Thousand Warriors to be fed and—"

"I'll keep them apart for the time being," Goll replied coldly. "Now, about the king . . ."

"I have no orders to let you in." The guard lowered his spear, pointing it at Goll's heart.

The one-eyed man's face flamed. "Don't you know who I am? I'm Goll Mac Morna!"

"I'm Druimderg," said the other, unimpressed, "and my spear is called Croderg, the Red-Socketed. Take another step forward without permission and Croderg will drink your blood."

Goll threw back his head and screamed, "Cormac!"

Fortunately, Cormac was just emerging from the House of the King and heard the familiar voice cry his name. He rescued Goll just as Druimderg's men closed in on him. Cormac took a shaken and outraged Goll Mac Morna into the House of the King and ordered a large measure of wine brought to him at once.

Goll refused to be mollified. "They treated me like a stranger, an intruder. Me. Me!"

"They have orders to treat everyone that way until proven otherwise."

"But this is Tara! You're supposed to welcome all who—"

"Don't lecture me on the duties of kingship, One-Eye. I extend a most gracious welcome indeed to all visitors. But you're a fénnid," Cormac said bluntly. "Any warrior who arrives at our gates is suspect."

"I'm an officer of the Fíanna! I was—"

"I know." Cormac waved a silencing hand.

"Did Finn do this? Did he give orders that I, specifically, was to be insulted and turned away?"

"Why would he do that?" Cormac asked in surprise.

"There's war between us. There's always been war between us."

"I've seen no evidence of it," Cormac said.

"Of course not, why would a king pay any attention to the undercurrents among the warriors? We occupy a different world altogether. But I assure you, Finn hates me."

Cormac pulled thoughtfully at his upper lip. "I've seen no evidence of his hating anyone. On the contrary, he goes out of his way to make friends. Finn is very popular."

"Like his father before him. It's a gift the men of Clan Baiscne have," Goll added bitterly. "They're spectacular and they have charm. They dazzle others. But Clan Morna is their equal, Cormac! We've just been done out of our—"

"Is that why you came here? To complain of Finn to me?"

"I came to find out why I was given no duties in your name this past battle season."

"There was no need. Thanks in no small part to Finn's reputation— whatever you may think of him personally—no battles broke that required the Fíanna. This proved to be a summer of building, not of fighting, and it's glad I am of it." But as he spoke, Cormac was watching Goll intently. Kings should be aware of undercurrents among their warriors, he was telling himself. Mindful of his own misgivings about Finn, he resolved to question the former Rígfénnid Fíanna.

"You still haven't drunk your wine," he pointed out, gesturing toward a carved bench carpeted with furs. "Sit yourself and take your ease, Goll. You remarked on my hospitality, so the least you can do is accept a demonstration."

Goll tensed. "I am a fénnid," he said formally.

Cormac laughed as at a joke. "Ah now, we can forget that here, just between the two of us, can we not? Sit, drink, be a guest of the king of Tara for a change. What harm is there in it?"

Goll sat on the very edge of the bench, keeping his feet firmly on the floor. Every instinct warned him to be wary. Kings did not entertain fénnidi informally.

"Does Finn ever sit like this with you?" he enquired.

"Is there some reason why he should not?" Cormac countered.

"He'll take advantage."

"He can take no advantage I do not allow. What is your specific grievance against Finn, Goll? The matter of Cuhal's death? Finn was wronged, not you, and he's obviously forgiven you long ago for denying him a father. From what I can see, he's treated you with extraordinary forbearing, considering the circumstances."

Goll lifted his upper lip in a sneer. "That's the style of him. Whatever Finn does, he does totally, more than is required. He goes to extremes. That's what he's done here, in fact, making Tara more his than yours."

Cormac's eyes turned into polished, opaque stones. "That is not true."

"You think not? I tell you, Finn's a usurper just as Cuhal Mac Trenmor was. The command of the Fíanna should have gone to my clan, did you know that? But Cuhal dazzled people. Few could resist his extravagant behaviour. They mistook the boasting for the man. I see the same qualities in Finn, and in him they're even more dangerous. Cuhal just wanted things: women, jewels, plunder. He used the Fíanna to get them. He encouraged a company of outlaws to steal for him when they weren't stealing for the king of Tara.

"But Finn Mac Cool's doing something else with the Fíanna. He's trying to make your army into . . . into . . . a band of heroes. A band of noble heroes!" Goll said indignantly.

"What's wrong with that?" Cormac asked.

"You said it yourself, we aren't nobility, we're fénnidi. That should be good enough for him. It was always good enough for my people. But Finn's trying to shapechange us into—"

Cormac leaned forward, his face a study in intensity. "Shapechange? Why did you use that word?"

Goll drew back from the avidity in the other man's gaze. "I didn't really mean—"

"You did mean. That's not a term one would use lightly. Do you think Finn can shapechange? Is it possible that he is what he claims to be—descended from the Tuatha Dé Danann?

"Tell me, One-Eye, on your sword's point: would Finn betray me to the Sídhe?"

18

HAD CORMAC NOT REFERRED TO GOLL AS "ONE-EYE," he might have received a different answer. But Goll took the name in the way he had first heard Cormac use it: as an insult.

With a sullen light burning in his single eye, he replied, "I cannot tell you more about Finn Mac Cool than you already know."

"That's no answer."

"That's all the answer I can give."

Cormac realized ground had been lost. Tardily, he recalled having just said One-Eye instead of giving Goll his true name, and also recalled that Goll was sensitive about the subject. Had I been less preoccupied with other problems, Cormac told himself, I would not have made that mistake.

But it was too late. He could only smile warmly and say, "Goll, I have to trust you. Surely you realize that if Finn fails me in some way, he must be replaced. You are the obvious choice. If there is something about the man that will work against me and my kingship, I need to know and I rely on you to tell me." He spoke in a low, intimate voice, encouraging confidences.

But the effort was wasted. Goll said huffily, "Finn Mac Cool is giving the Fíanna a new reputation for honour. I belong to the Fíanna. You ask me if Finn Mac Cool might betray you, but in asking that, you are requesting that I betray Finn. You want us both lowered, King. You want to reduce us to simple fénnidi again, men of no property, spear targets who will betray one another for a cup of wine.

"You make a mistake, Cormac." Goll rose, turned his left side, the side of insult, very deliberately toward the king.

He left the House of the King seething with anger. Wisely, Cormac did not try to stop him. To do so would have caused an explosion that would further damage their relationship.

The explosion came anyway, however. Goll had no sooner emerged through the outer gateway of the House of the King than he met Finn Mac Cool, on his way to report to Cormac.

Finn stopped short. Noting the direction from which Goll came, he said coolly, "So you're here. And I see you reported to Cormac first, instead of to me."

Goll was taken aback. The accusation was unfortunately true, but he longed to make a satisfactory explanation. He simply could not think of one. As always, when he had his back to the wall, the one-eyed man reacted angrily, "Why shouldn't I call on the king? My rank is not that much less than yours, I'm an officer in his service."

"In his service? When you are first sworn to me?"

Goll stiffened. "Am I? When did I swear to you exclusively, Finn?"

"That's part of the oath all the Fíanna take."

"It is now. But it wasn't when I joined the Fíanna. I never took that oath, it's an innovation of your own."

The two men stood facing one another with only a few paces between them. In the bustling precincts of Tara, other men and women moved past them, going about their own business but instinctively giving them a wide berth. The air was hot and shimmering between them.

"So your first loyalty is not to me," Finn said slowly, keeping any inflection out of his voice. "Did you go to see Cormac to ask him for the position of Rígfénnid Fíanna?"

Goll was infuriated that Finn would make such an assumption about him—especially when he had just been defending Finn to Cormac. He burst out, "I didn't ask him for it, he offered it to me! So there! He said if you failed him, I was the most obvious choice to command the army!"

A muscle jumped in Finn's jaw. "That's what you've been after all along, isn't it? You've watched my back just to be sure you were there when the time came to stick a knife into it."

"And what have you wanted all along?" Goll shouted, too furious for caution, for game-playing. "You've been biding your time too, Finn Mac Cool, waiting for the opportunity to take revenge on me for the death of your father. Do you think I didn't know? You made such a point of renouncing vengeance, you forced it on your men as well, you were excessive about it. That's what gave you away, Finn. You're always excessive! Such a man has no business commanding the Fíanna!"

Goll's one eye was starting from his head with the power of his emotion. He raised his clenched fists and shook them in the air, in the narrowing space that separated him from Finn as both men moved forward, seemingly without awareness or volition, until they were an arm's length apart.

One arm's length.

Finn's hand was on his sword hilt.

With an almost superhuman effort, Goll mastered his temper. "Kill me now," he said. "Take your revenge on me here and now, with all these witnesses around us, so that everyone will know your true heart and not be blinded by the smoke you blow in their eyes."

Something flickered across Finn's face, heralding a subtle change as if the bones beneath the skin shifted ever so slightly. While Goll stared incredulously, they realigned themselves in a new configuration. The face was no longer that of Finn Mac Cool. The hot, bright eyes looking out of it were not even human.

In that moment Goll's life was forfeit. The wild creature in front of him would kill him without conscience and enjoy the hot spurting of his blood. The wild creature in front of him had, indeed, always longed to take revenge for the death of Cuhal Mac Trenmor, and now Goll had foolishly invited its attack.

In the moment before it tore him apart, he had one hysterical thought: it's true, he can shapechange! Finn Mac Cool is one of the Tuatha Dé Danann!

Against such ancient power Goll had only mortal courage. The glowing, intense eyes of the feral spirit facing him were burning that courage away as the sun burns moisture from stone. Goll lost the power to resist. He stood impassively, arms at sides, waiting.

Waiting like a stag for the hunter. But in Finn's head the image was not of a stag. He saw a doe. A red doe.

Sive, he thought. The one cool word sliced through the hot cloud of his passions. Sive.

The cloud lifted. His vision cleared and he saw Goll Mac Morna, who had helped him, taught him, fought beside him. Goll, who had slain his father, perhaps with justification, but never done Finn an injury. Goll, who surely had not betrayed him to Cormac, for what was there to betray?

Finn drew a deep, shaky breath and made himself relax his white-knuckled grip on the sword hilt.

"I desire no vengeance," he said in a choked voice. "You are mistaken, Goll. You do not understand other men as well as you think you do, obviously. For that reason, I should remain as commander of the Fíanna. But I would . . . I would appreciate having you remain one of my trusted rígfénnidi. I want no animosity between us."

Goll looked stunned.

"Is your company with you?" Finn went on, his voice growing stronger. "They can be housed in the new quarters, you know. This summer the Hall of a Thousand Heroes was prepared for us. No army in Erin has ever been so well treated. We've earned it, of course." Incredibly, he reached out and clapped Goll on the bicep. "You and I and the others, we've earned it," he said heartily. "It's over this way, if you want to inspect it first."

Turning his unshielded back on Goll, Finn strode away in the direction of the warriors' hall.

Goll stared after his back. And in that moment loathed Finn and loved Finn and was very, very afraid of him.

The Samhain Assembly in the constantly expanding Tara was spectacular that year. More people attended than ever before. A city of leather tents sprang up beyond the palisades to accommodate those who wanted to establish some connection with the king of Tara. Traders came by the score, by the hundred, following the five royal roads first laid down by Conn of the Hundred Battles.

The warriors of the Fíanna met them all and examined them thoroughly before admitting them to the stronghold of the king.

At the final banquet, Finn Mac Cool himself stood guard at the principal doorway of the great hall while the Feast of the Dead took place inside. He stood immobile, sword in hand, staring off into space. But he was not thinking of Cuhal Mac Trenmor this time. His attention was not focused on the unseen spirits at all. His thoughts were far away on the Hill of Almhain, with Sive and his unborn child, the new life about to come into his world.

From time to time, in the privacy of the darkness, he smiled.

The next morning he left Tara.

"I shall garrison as many of the Fíanna as you require here with you through the winter," he assured Cormac, "but you don't actually need me here. I have things to do elsewhere."

The king did not try to detain him. "Who will you leave in charge of your men here? Goll Mac Morna?"

Finn raised an eyebrow. "Goll? Och, what makes you think of him? He has a home of his own to go to, and a woman as well. I wouldn't think of keeping him from them. I'll leave Cael in charge, he's a good man."

Cormac looked dubious. "He laughs a bit much for a warrior."

"The merry-hearted boys make the best men," Finn assured the king. He grinned. Merrily.

He left Tara at the trot and never looked back, and to those who remained behind, it seemed that some of the shimmer went out of the sunlight. Cruina of the Questions strolled down to the gateway through which he had departed and stood there for a long time, following the road with her eyes.

When he reached the Hill of Almhain, Sive was waiting for him at the gate behind the hawthorn trees. She had needed no herald to announce his coming. Big-bellied and beautiful, she ran into his arms and he lifted her high and cried out with joy.

When her labour began, the women wanted to send Finn away. "This is female work," they told him. "Go and sharpen your swords or drill your men or throw rocks in the bog pools, but leave us to it."

"Is that what other men do?"

"It is," they assured him.

Finn did not leave. He fixed Sive's attendants with a strange stare that made them lick their lips nervously and avert their eyes, and when Sive's baby was born, Finn was crouching beside her as she squatted, panting. The bloody little bundle was delivered into his hands, and he felt his soul expand until it was too large for his body.

"I have a son!" cried Finn Mac Cool.

Cainnelsciath conducted the naming ceremony. The infant, who had his mother's huge eyes, did not cry, though he was held aloft to be presented to the sky and laid on the ground to meet the earth. He was handed through the smoke of a fire, and sweet cold water was touched to his lips, and still he was quiet and trusting. Although Bebinn, the female physician, insisted that babies his age could not really see, he seemed to keep his eyes on either Sive or Finn throughout the ceremony.

They named him Oisin; Little Deer.

An exultant Finn ordered Garvcronan his steward to make his entire store of mead and ale available to the Fíanna. The celebrating roared on for days. Finn made a token appearance, then promptly vanished into his house with his wife and his son and his joy.

As he and Sive lay on their bed with small Oisin between them at his mother's breast, Finn remarked lazily, "It would be good to die now. Nothing will ever be better than this."

Sive was appalled. "I forbid you to speak of dying, ever! I never talk of anything unpleasant and neither should you. Why do you think of it at all?"

"Warriors think of death," he told her. "And I was raised with it as a constant companion. I grew up the hard way, with every day a struggle. Two old women and a small boy, outcasts, hiding out, living rough, do not easily provide for themselves. Death was always at our elbow, waiting. The two who raised me were as tough as boiled leather, there was no gentleness in them, but I'm grateful to them. They taught me to face death without flinching."

"I can't," Sive said. "Not your death." She reached out to cup the back of his head with her hand. Gently, insistently, she drew Finn's face down beside Oisin's and pressed his mouth to her other breast.

"Take my life into you and live always," Sive whispered with infinite tenderness.

There was a glow around the bed where the three of them lay. Finn could feel its magical warmth as he took her small pink nipple into his mouth.

That glow would haunt him the rest of his days.

For love of Sive and in gratitude for their son, Finn began showering his wife with gifts. He gave her amethysts from Kerry and gold ear rings from the craftsmen at the Tailltenn Fair.

But he gave her what would prove to be the most important gift of all quite by accident.

He was sitting on a couch, watching her comb her thick russet hair. The locks were determinedly wild in spite of her best efforts; her little silver comb would not unsnarl the tangles.

Reaching into his neck bag, Finn took out his own comb. It was larger than hers and carved of bone, with wide-set teeth and a design on the spine. "Try this," he offered, handing it to her.

She smilingly accepted. He sat fascinated by the lovely, crisp crackle as the implement moved through her hair. "Let me try," he said.

She gave the comb back to him. Her hair flowed like water across his hands. But the last snarl would not be separated. When he gave a tug too impatient, the comb, brittle from long use, snapped in half.

Finn was stricken. "Did that hurt you?"

Sive laughed up at him. "Not at all. And aren't you clever! Where there was one comb, now there are two. Here, give the smaller one to me and I shall keep it near me always."

"I'll get you a better one."

"I want this one, this part of one. Just because it was yours," she assured him. "You keep the other part. Together they make a whole, as we do."

The peace that Cormac had been enjoying, and claiming credit for among his people, came to an abrupt end. Oisin was only a few nights old when a runner arrived at Almhain to announce, "The king needs you and the Fíanna! A band of foreigners has come from across the sea to pillage and plunder the east coast, and they must be driven away. You are commanded to assemble the Fíanna and march upon them at once."

Such a clarion call would have made Finn's heart leap with joy—had that heart not been given to Sive and his new son. He found leaving them physically painful. Other warriors, he observed, seemed able to step from one aspect of their lives into another without hesitation, closing doors behind them and instantly forgetting, but he was made of different cloth.

He was partly Sive, and she him. Any sort of separation was an amputation.

But he was Rígfénnid Fíanna. He put on his sternest face, had his weapons sharpened, and he and his men prepared to march off to war on a day of driving rain. Usually, Erin's rains were soft; this one was like hurled lances. Carrying Oisin, Sive followed Finn as far as the gateway, though the rain drenched them both within moments.

"Go back," Finn told her. "You might make yourself sick."

Sive merely laughed. "And how could rain hurt me? Water is holy, and sweet. Water on my head will do me no harm—nor Oisin either."

"Go back," Finn repeated, the words strangely thick in his throat. He was suddenly afraid he could not march away at all, not if she persisted in standing there where he could see her.

She read the pain in his eyes and understood without words. Smiling, she stepped back inside the gateway. But her voice floated out to him. "I wish I were one of your hounds so I could go with you," she called.

Finn walked blindly through the rain, and all the moisture on his cheeks did not come from the clouds. Bran and Sceolaun were at his heels, but it was not enough.

I am not as hard as other men, he thought, surprised by this discovery. But no one knows—except Sive.

The plunderers had beached their boats along the rim of the great curving bay below Ben Edair, a prominent headland connected to the mainland by an isthmus. Cormac Mac Airt made the journey from Tara to join Finn and his men on the banks of the river Liffey, a short march from the bay itself. "I have a need to observe just how Finn is conducting his battles these days," he remarked to his attendants.

As Cormac and the royal retinue joined the encamped Fíanna, columns of black smoke were rising into a grey sky all up and down the coast, testifying to plundering and pillage. "I know how a woman must feel when she's raped," the king said grimly, his eyes on the smoke. "That's my land, my people. Destroy the foreigners, Finn. Destroy them utterly."

His servitors pitched the royal tents on a height overlooking the bay, from which vantage point the king watched with mounting excitement as Finn organized various companies of the Fíanna, issuing orders to their rígfénnidi according to some plan in his own brain. It was obvious he meant to separate the raiders from one another, cut them off from their ships, then drive them like panicked sheep straight into a wall of Fíanna spears.

The raiders from across the sea had not come a very great distance—only from as far as Alba. It was a well-travelled route. Men from both sides of the narrow sea frequently crossed the cold and treacherous stretch of water to seize one another's goods and women. Reprisal generally took the form of a raid from the other side next season.

But on this occasion, reprisal was immediate and savage. Commanded by Finn Mac Cool, the Fíanna slaughtered the majority of the invaders with remarkable efficiency. Cormac, on the height, felt the blood of his warrior ancestors pounding with excitement through his veins, and at last was moved to mount his big brown horse and gallop down to join the battle personally. But just as he took up the rein and prepared to move off, a luminous mist blew in from the sea, obscuring everything.

Cormac's horse began to sweat. It danced nervously, arching its neck and blowing through its nostrils as if in fear. He patted its muscular crest, but the stallion would not be calmed. At any moment it threatened to bolt. The king of Tara had all he could do to control the animal with his wooden horse-goad and the single leather rein that passed from the bronze bit in the horse's mouth up its face, between its ears, and down to his hand.

An infuriated Cormac was so occupied with the unreasonable horse that he could not have watched the battle even had the mist lifted. He could hear the shouts and screams, however. He could hear the clash of metal on metal, the thud of metal on wood. At last he slid from his horse, swearing, and gave the rein to a horseboy so he could at least concentrate on what was happening invisibly below.

The sounds of battle were fading. Cormac peered through the mist, straining to see. Then it lifted and the curve of blue water lay before him, with small, dark figures floating quietly on its breast and distant ships pulling away with every dip of eager oars.

The battle was over. Finn and the Fíanna had routed the foreigners quite thoroughly.

And Cormac Mac Airt had seen none of the fighting.

During the long journey back to Tara for the celebratory feasting, Cormac tried, discreetly, to question men who had been in a better position to see what happened. He dared not ask any of them if Finn had won his victory through magic, but he wanted to hear each advance and stratagem described.

To his relief, it all seemed straightforward. One of the rígfénnidi, a gruff, broad-faced man called Dremen, reported, "Finn had divided the Fíanna into bands that encircled the foreigners and separated them into small groups. Once they were broken up, it was easy to kill them, and those we did not kill ran away to their ships."

"What about the mist?" the king could not resist asking.

"The mist? Och, that was good fortune! It blew in just as the battle was beginning, when all our men were in place. We knew where we were but the enemy didn't; they became confused, and it was as easy to close on them and kill them as if they'd been birds on the ground."

Cormac, against his better judgment, enquired, "Where did the mist come from, would you say?"

"Come from? From the sea, of course," replied the puzzled Dremen. "Mists from the sea are very common, as you know yourself. You see them almost every day."

The explanation was simple and natural. Sea mists were indeed common; this was the season for them. Cormac should have been pleased.

Yet part of him kept thinking of the magical mist of the Tuatha Dé Danann, and wondering about Finn.

Finn himself was not thinking of magic, however. He was exultant, drunk with the glory of having won a huge victory in the presence of the king. Never before had the army of Tara defeated so many foreigners at one time. The poets would sing of it for centuries. The participants were reliving it now, telling one another their various stories over and over again, punching their comrades on the arms, beating the innocent air with triumphant fists, shouting and laughing and boasting until every last drop of juice and joy was extracted from the event.

"Did you see how they ran?" Cael demanded of Madan. "Did you see how I slaughtered another hundred?"

"Did you see how I threw my spear so hard it went all the way through that thick yellow-haired man?" Madan countered. "No one survives my spear!"

"Nor mine," growled Conan Maol.

The other two turned toward him. Cael said, "I don't recall seeing you in the thick of the fighting."

"I was there with my three nines, we were right in the worst of it. There was probably so much blood spewing you couldn't see us through it. I hurled my spears and swung my sword until my arm was tired."

Fergus laughed. "The mighty arm of Conan the Hairless grows tired more easily than some."

"That's not true!"

"It is true. Would you deny you're the laziest officer in the Fíanna?"

"Rather I would say I have the least to do because my fíans are the best fighters. I need only lead them to the enemy," Conan boasted.

Cael laughed. "Are you saying your men are too blind to find the enemy for themselves?"

Conan glowered at him.

The army rumbled on toward Tara. Soon the singing began. Long before they reached the tall palisade and the shining white buildings within, their triumphant voices announced to all of Míd that Cormac Mac Airt had won a great victory over the foreigners.

The king ordered a huge feast prepared and served in the Banquetting Hall. Whole oxen were roasted over deep pits where the fires burned as hot and sullen as the desire for revenge.

While they waited for the feast, Finn ordered his men to compete in spear-throwing competitions and footraces to keep themselves sharp as well as to impress the populace of Tara. Even in victory, he would not let them relax.

They had to be special.

They had to be, and remain, the best.

The woman called Cruina of the Questions stood silently at the edge of the racecourse, watching the runners, but Finn did not notice her. He was present too, physically. His mind was elsewhere, however. Even before the feasting he had begun talking to Sive again, telling her about the battle, assuring her of how proud he was of their new son.

Sive, Sive, the elemental Sive.

Once he would have taken inordinate pride in sitting, as he did that night, on a bench at the king's sword hand, a place normally reserved for the chief bard but on this occasion given to the Rígfénnid Fíanna in honour of his victory.

Now he accepted the honour gracefully, but with barely concealed impatience. He sat trying to assess how long the celebrating would last, and how soon he could leave for Almhain.

To his disgust, everyone seemed happy to go on eating and drinking and boasting for days.

Cormac was in an expansive mood. "I'm going to reward you and your officers with an unprecedented gift for rígfénnidi," he told Finn. "When I can acquire them, I'll furnish you with horses to ride. Make everyone look up to you as they look up to chieftains!"

Finn drew his thoughts back from Sive. "Fir Bolg have no experience of riding horses," he said.

"You," Cormac replied with confidence, "can do anything. You needn't start building stables right away, of course. It may take some time, good riding horses are in short supply."

Finn nodded. His thoughts were already racing to Almhain. Building stables . . . seeing Sive. Oisin. Sive.

Toward dawn, when the singing and boasting was at its loudest, he rose from his bench and went to Cailte. "I'm leaving here at sunup," he told the thin man in a low voice. "While I'm away, you're my second in command."

Cailte looked astonished. "I am? What about Goll?"

"You are. With you in command at Tara, I won't have to guard my back. Get some sleep, I suggest—if you can. As for me, I'm going home."

Without sleeping, Finn departed in the dawn light, accompanied by three fíans, the minimum complement for a commander. They were outstanding warriors every one, but he did not have the same feeling for them he still retained for his very first band of nine. As they marched toward Almhain, he realized he was not only eager to see Sive and Oisin again, but also Donn and Red Ridge, whom he had left in charge of guarding his fort with their own fíans.

As they entered the bogland, Finn picked up the pace. His men pounded along behind him, splashing through sodden turf. For much of the year the Bog of Almhain was tapestried with colour. Spring brought bluebells and primroses and violets; summer was heralded by the fragrant orchid with its scent of cloves, and by the waxy white blossoms of Grass of Parnassus; autumn found yellow flags like flecks of sunlight reflected in the bog pools.

Almhain was as treacherous as it was beautiful, however. One careless fénnid put a foot wrong and was nearly swallowed by bog before his companions caught him under the arms and dragged him to safe footing. Finn paused only long enough to warn them all to be more careful, then he ran on again. Toward hill and home.

Rising from its hilltop, the gleaming white walls of his fort made his heart leap at first sight. He had covered all exterior walls with limewash, emulating Tara, so they dazzled in the sun. "Almhain of the White Walls," people called it.

Home, Finn called it. Home. Where Sive is.

He was running his fastest now, leaving the others behind. Only Bran and Sceolaun were able to keep up with him.

"Sive!" he shouted, all decorum forgotten. He had outrun the position of Rígfénnid Fíanna. He was only Finn, going home. "Sive!" He would grab her in his arms, he would swing her high in the air, he would . . .

Red Ridge emerged from the gate behind the hawthorn and stared down at the silver-haired, grinning young man running up the hill toward him. "Finn?" he asked in a puzzled voice.

"Of course it's me. Where's my wife? Go back in and tell her I'm here. Bring her to me! Or better still, I'll go to her myself and—"

"Wait, Finn." Red Ridge put a delaying hand on his commander's arm. "She isn't in there."

Finn paused, wrinkling his forehead. "Not in there?"

"We thought she was with you." Red Ridge looked as baffled as Finn felt.

"How could she be with me and I away fighting?"

"But you came back. Yesterday."

Finn stared at Red Ridge. "I came back just now. Not yesterday."

"Your steward saw you. You and the hounds. He told your wife you had come home, and she ran out to meet you with the baby in her arms."

Finn's jaw dropped. "She *what*? Where were you when this happened? Where was Donn? Why weren't you guarding her?"

"We were, Finn. Of course we were. But at the moment you arrived—"

"I never arrived. Not yesterday," Finn insisted, feeling his heart begin to thunder dangerously.

"At the moment the steward thought he saw you," Red Ridge amended, "Donn had taken his company and gone hunting for meat; we were running low. My men were guarding the hill, of course, standing sentry duty, but somehow none of them noticed your arrival. We weren't aware anything had happened until after Sive went out to you and didn't come back."

"Didn't come back?" Finn's words were hollow with horror.

Red Ridge would have given a year of his life to avoid having to meet Finn's eyes. But he was a brave man. He met them. Whatever he saw in them chilled him to the bone. "She never came back, Finn. We've been searching for her ever since, her and the infant. They've simply vanished."

For a heartbeat Red Ridge thought Finn Mac Cool would kill him where he stood. Faster than the eye could follow, Finn had a sword in his hand. But he did not use it on the other man. He did not use it at all. He simply held it, lifted it to eye level, stared at it blankly.

Put it away.

A sword was no use to him.

"Vanished," he said.

Red Ridge hastened to explain, "We haven't stopped searching, we had parties out all through the night. I'm surprised you didn't meet some of them as you approached."

"I wasn't looking for anyone else, I was just . . . hurrying home." Finn drew a deep breath. He was very pale, his face almost as colourless as his hair. Red Ridge began to think it would be a wise idea to send for Bebinn and have the physician close by in case Finn had some sort of seizure.

"Send my steward to me," Finn ordered.

Garvcronan of the Rough Buzzing had a voice that made men flinch, but he was a good steward. Finn had recruited him personally from a fían from the west, recognizing qualities of organization and responsibility in the man. He had entrusted Garvcronan with running his household in his absence.

He had never expected betrayal.

"I didn't betray you!" the steward protested repeatedly, his rasping voice rising and falling like a storm of locusts. "I would never have let your wife go out to you if I had known it wasn't you! Mind her, you instructed me when you left, and mind her I did. No stray wind chilled her, no drop of rain fell on her. Wherever she went, she was accompanied. But when I saw you and the hounds coming up the hill, of course

I ran inside to tell her. And of course she brushed me aside and hurried out to you. What could be more natural?"

The man's face was so naked in its honesty that Finn could not doubt his words. He wanted to strike someone. He wanted to kill someone to redress the terrible loss he was already feeling. But he could not kill Garvcronan, anymore than he could understand just what had happened.

He sent for Cainnelsciath the druid. Meanwhile, and on his own responsibility, Red Ridge had summoned Bebinn the physician. Druid and healer entered Finn's house together to find the Rígfénnid Fíanna slumped beside his firepit, his eyes burning more hotly than the coals.

He glared at the two of them. "What do you know of my wife's disappearance?"

"Nothing," admitted Bebinn with regret while professionally studying Finn's livid face, his hoarse breathing.

Cainnelsciath said, "I did not see her leave, but I know something of her going."

Finn was on his feet in an eyeblink. "What?"

The druid ran his hands like ploughs through his ruddy hair. "I warned you not to build on this hill, Finn. It belonged to the Tuatha Dé Danann, and they do not welcome intruders."

Finn thrust out his jaw at a belligerent angle. "I have as much right to this hill as anyone, then. Suppose I told you I inherited it from the Dananns themselves, through my mother!" Had he not been so distracted, he would never have dared lie to a druid, but he was in a mood to lash out at anyone, to deny anything, to make any claim. To tear down walls and negate distance and alter the progress of time if need be.

Bebinn saw with her healer's vision that a sharp yellow light was pulsing from Finn, unmistakable aura of a spirit in torment. She slipped from the room to prepare a decoction to soothe him, if possible.

Finn did not see her leave. All his attention was focused on his agony.

"Whether you inherited rights to this hill or not," the druid was saying diplomatically, "you should never have tried to live here. At least, you should never have planted a family here. I cannot be certain, Finn, but the signs indicate that the Sídhe have extracted compensation from you in the form of your wife and child."

It was a safe guess, neither provable nor unprovable, but it was the last thing Finn wanted to hear.

He groaned. "What makes you think so?"

"Because a figure that was the image of you lured Sive away. That sounds like Sídhe magic. It was at least good enough to fool your steward on a misty day."

Finn's breath caught in his throat. "Mist?"

"Indeed, there was a cloud of it obscuring the hill yesterday. You could hardly see your own toes if you took a long step. It came up suddenly, that mist—just before the man Garvcronan mistook for you arrived."

"Mist." Finn gazed thoughtfully into inner space, then put his thumb into his mouth and began to chew on it. After a time he said "mist" again and removed the thumb. He stared at it intently, studying the gleam of saliva on flesh.

"There was a mist when we fought the invaders," he said. "It worked in our favour—then. A sea mist, rising suddenly, swirling around us, hiding us when we needed to be hidden, lifting just enough to reveal the enemy to us when we were ready to fall upon them.

"Now another mist has worked against me. The Tuatha Dé Danann, you suggest." He raised wondering eyes to the druid's face. "Is it possible, Cainnelsciath?"

In spite of his unlined complexion, the druid was not young. During his years he had learned the arts of survival as well as Goll Mac Morna, though his were different arts. He would not dream of denying the existence of magic. "Anything is possible," he replied somberly.

"Compensation," said Finn, as if he had never heard the word. "Everything must balance. Isn't that what the law requires? Ah. So. Cuhal took Muirinn from her father, Muirinn took me from mine. I took the Danann hill, they took . . ."

His throat closed; he could not finish. When he clenched his fists, it was an impotent gesture, there was no reality for him to grasp. With Sive he had begun to appreciate a reality superior to his fantasies, but now that vision had been torn from him, lost in swirls of mist.

He was human, he was Danann, he was Fir Bolg, he was prince. He was warrior and bard. His mother was a deer. His wife was a deer. His son was stolen from him as his mother had stolen him from . . .

Finn groaned again, a tortured sound. "My head aches," he muttered, shoulders slumping.

Bebinn returned, carrying a silver pitcher with a square of bleached linen folded over the top. Beads of moisture ran down the pitcher's sides. Edging past the druid, she took a cup from a table and poured out a fragrant liquid that she offered to Finn. "This will ease you," she promised.

He did not take the cup. "Will it bring Sive back?"

"She'll come back if she can, you know she will," Bebinn said soothingly. She pressed the cup to Finn's lips and tilted it until he was forced to swallow.

Then her eyes met the druid's. Slowly, with infinite regret, Cainnelsciath shook his head. She won't, he mouthed silently.

19

FINN LOST HIS MIND. THERE WAS NO OTHER WAY TO describe what happened to him when he lost Sive. He lay in his house raging with fever, babbling incoherently most of the time, calling on Sive and for Sive and recognizing no one.

"His is a brain sickness," Bebinn informed the others. "A fire in the mind. It may kill him; I've seen it happen before. I shall apply all the cures I know, and Cainnelsciath will sacrifice to the gods, but all we can really do is wait. Finn is strong, he may live.

"But he may not. You should know and be prepared."

The fíans crowded around Almhain of the White Walls, keeping a vigil. Donn and Red Ridge denied themselves sleep to stand guard personally outside Finn's door. They felt so guilty they could not articulate their emotions to one another. But they endlessly discussed the day of Sive's disappearance, as if by going over each detail again and again, they could find some overlooked clue that would take them to her.

Poor Garvcronan was subjected to so much questioning that his rasping voice dwindled to an anguished whisper. He could only keep repeating the same story: "I saw a fair man coming up the Hill of Almhain toward the fort. There were hounds with him. I thought he was Finn. There was a mist, but I thought I was seeing Finn return and I ran to tell Sive."

"Perhaps it was one of her own kinsmen," Donn suggested. "They might have learned where she was and decided to send someone for her, or for her honour price. A man who could be mistaken for Finn on a dull day in a lowering mist. Perhaps it wasn't even an intentional deception, but coincidence."

"Perhaps it was a white-haired man," Red Ridge suggested. "Her father? Could it have been her father, Garvcronan?"

"How would I know?" the steward replied, burying his face in his hands. His next muffled words were almost incomprehensible. "I've never seen her people, I know nothing about them. She never talked about them. I've thought about this so much it's become a muddle in my mind and I don't know anything anymore."

Long days passed, and longer nights. At last a messenger had to be sent to the king of Tara to inform him Finn was ill.

Cormac promptly summoned Goll Mac Morna. "If Finn's going to be incapacitated for any length of time, he'll have to be replaced," he told the one-eyed man. "Cailte's an able second in command, but he's not equipped to lead the Fíanna permanently. Will you accept that responsibility—at least until Finn returns?"

Those last words cut deep. Goll did not flinch, except inwardly, but he added them to the list of grudges he held against the king.

"So I'm second-best?" he said, tight-lipped.

"Of course not. You're the best available."

"The best available. I see." Goll began pinching and rubbing the puckered skin of his facial scar. "Tell me this, Cormac—is it merely a ploy on your part? Do you hope to force Finn to leave a sickbed and come back to your service through jealousy of me?"

"Would I do that?"

"I would in your place. It's a clever move."

"Will you do it?"

"You have a brass neck, asking me that."

"Will you do it?"

"Will I let you use me, you mean?"

"Will you do it?" the king repeated.

Cailte insisted on carrying the news to Almhain personally. When he arrived, a reluctant Garvcronan finally admitted him to the lodge where an emaciated, pallid Finn lay tossing restlessly on a bed of matted furs.

Cailte was appalled at the change in his friend. He bent over him. "Finn? Finn! Wake up! I bring word from Tara."

Finn's eyes opened slowly, pulling apart gummed lashes. "Wha . . . ?" His speech was slurred, his expression vacant. "Who . . . ?"

"I'm Cailte Mac Ronan," the thin man said crisply, "and I've come to inform you that Cormac Mac Airt has appointed another commander for the Fíanna in your absence."

A miniscule animation flickered across Finn's features; faded. "So? Needed to be done, I suppose." His eyelids began to drift shut.

"It didn't need to be Goll Mac Morna," Cailte said in a voice like a whiplash.

For a moment he did not think Finn had heard him—or cared.

Then Finn's breathing deepened. He lay still as if gathering himself.

"Who did you say?"

"Goll Mac Morna."

Finn's eyes met Cailte's. They were clearer now. "Goll is acting as Rígfénnid Fíanna?"

"He is."

"Och. Goll Mac Morna." Finn closed his eyes again and seemed almost asleep. But he was not asleep. The watching Cailte saw his face slowly . . . change.

He stood up in one smooth motion, so unexpectedly that Cailte jumped backward in spite of himself. The man before him was obviously weak, shaky, but on his feet. And recognizably Finn Mac Cool. He cleared his throat. "Garvcronan? Bring me food. A lot of food. Meat. Pots of cheese. Buttermilk. Why are you standing there staring at me, Cailte? Help him fetch it. Run!"

Cailte ran.

With single-minded determination, Finn Mac Cool healed himself in a matter of days. Bebinn watched in disbelief as he did through willpower what all her herbal concoctions could not. Cainnelsciath the druid was equally astounded. "The omens said he would die," the man kept repeating, shaking his head.

Every night found Finn heavier and stronger than the night before. Part of the cure was not to allow himself to think of Sive. Or of Oisin. Relentlessly, he put them in a box at the back of his mind and forced the lid closed while he ate and slept and began practicing his battle skills again to restore his reflexes.

"Finn Mac Cool is back!" a relieved Red Ridge soon reported to the rest of the Fíanna at Almhain.

"We're going to Tara at the next change of the moon," Finn announced to them the very next morning, "so the king can see for himself that I'm able to resume command of the army. And," he added with a sudden, unexpected grin, a flash of white teeth, merry and impish, "we'll go singing."

Of all those who heard him, and cheered him, only Cailte noticed that it was not quite the same old grin.

The youth had gone out of it.

The morning before they were to depart for Tara, Finn left Almhain of the White Walls. He went alone, to the distress of his men, who kept insisting he should take a bodyguard. But Finn was in no mood to take advice from anyone.

He went alone, to track the waveless ocean of the Bog of Almhain and search one more time for Sive.

As always when his spirit was in chaos, he instinctively sensed order in the patterns of nature. He could find no peace under a roof, any more than he could find Sive there. He needed sky over him and earth under him.

A man from a different background might have chosen other, more reliable earth. The bog was a land that quivered and quaked, more water than soil, dotted with countless tiny islands and hillocks that were only nominally more substantial. Stepping-stones through a treacherous morass. Beautiful, humming with reed-song, billowing with bog cotton, glinting with pools that reflected the perfection of the sky, the bog was deadly to all but the feet that knew it best.

Finn walked with the ease of familiarity. The bog's fluid surface was more stable to him than the fluctuating borders of reality.

Perhaps Sive had drowned in one of these pools. Perhaps she had lost her way. He must admit it to himself just once, in total privacy.

Perhaps she and Oisin were dead and gone and he was left in a world without them.

If that were true, he could fight battle after battle until a sword or spear took him, and he would never care when that day came. He would be the greatest warrior Erin ever produced simply because he had nothing left to fear.

Simply because he had nothing left.

Or perhaps Sive had been taken by the Sídhe. As Finn saw it, this was a possibility.

She might reappear.

He might find her.

If that could happen, then life was very precious and every moment, every breath, mattered, because they underpinned the future he would share with Sive.

Which was true?

How could he know?

He walked on across the bog, lost in thought. Accompanying him as always, Bran and Sceolaun had stayed close to him for a while. When they realized he was not hunting, they gradually began wandering away from him, doing a little hunting on their own as was their wont, not out of hunger, but out of love of the sport.

Finn paid no attention. He knew they would come back.

But would Sive?

The land sank beneath his feet. He found himself on the brink of a reedy pond, the reflective residence of a blue heron that stood one-legged on the far side, eyeing the interloper with regal disdain.

Finn sank slowly until he was crouching on his heels at eye level with the heron across the bog pool. The bird did not take fright but continued to regard him, turning its head to look at him first with one fierce yellow eye, then with the other.

The heron's single-eyed stare reminded Finn of Goll Mac Morna.

"I'm not hunting today," he told the bird. "You know that, don't you? That's why you're not flying away."

The bird did not reply, but it appeared to listen.

As Sive listened.

A spasm of anguish gripped Finn's gut.

"I need to talk to someone," he admitted to the heron. "It's a habit I've developed. In my head, mostly," he added with an apologetic little laugh.

The heron raised a thin crest of dark feathers along the top of its skull, then let them sink back.

"If I've really lost her, I'm alone," Finn said miserably. "Alone in my head."

The heron lowered one leg and raised the other without ever ceasing its unblinking scrutiny of Finn.

Finn went on reflectively. "I didn't know that I minded being alone, until Sive. I didn't know how alone I'd always been. I loved the silences of forest and mountain. I loved standing, listening, letting the world fill me with poems. Then Sive filled me with herself. She became all my poems. Sive . . ."

Her name caught in his throat. He swallowed, hard. "I've been trying not to think of her," he confessed to the heron. "When I let myself think of her and my son, it cripples me. I feel as if a mountain has fallen on me. I've dug myself out from under the mountain, you see . . . but I shan't stop looking for her. I'll always be looking for her. I can't accept that she's . . ."

Finn could not say the word. The heron was looking at him very intently, extending its slender neck as if to hear his softest whisper. Suddenly he was convinced the bird understood him and might even *know.*

"Where is she?" he asked hoarsely. "Where is Sive, where is my son? Do they live? *Can I find them?*"

For one agonizing heartbeat he thought the heron would answer. It actually opened its beak while reality spun and spiralled and Finn was willing to believe anything, even a talking heron that would guide him to his wife. He willed it to be with all the fierce intensity of a will forged in iron and loneliness.

"If her people came for her, tell me who they are and where to find them!" he commanded the heron. "She would never tell me; she would never talk of them. I think they had made her very unhappy. But if I knew where they were, I could go and get her, you see? Just tell me. You fly across Erin, surely you know, you've seen her, a woman with soft brown eyes and a child, a little boy with pale hair . . ."

In an excess of longing, Finn stretched out his arms toward the heron.

The bird's beak yawned wider. Finn yearned toward it across the pond. "Just tell me she didn't leave me on purpose," he pleaded. Then he expressed his innermost fear, the one that unmanned him. "Tell me she didn't abandon me of her own will on the Bog of Almhain!"

But before the bird could answer—and Finn would go to his death believing it could have answered—Sceolaun came bounding toward them, bringing Finn some small furred creature she had caught and wagging her tail in anticipation of his praise.

The heron squawked and leaped onto the wind, carrying Finn's answer away on whispering wings.

The man let out a howl that shivered the surface of the bog pool.

Alarmed, Sceolaun dropped her catch and pressed close to him, trying to lick his face in an excess of sympathy. He struck out at her savagely. The astonished bitch shrank back from the blow. Finn had never hit his hounds. She sank to her belly and crawled toward him, pulling herself forward with her elbows, making small conciliatory noises in her throat that were drowned in the terrible sound of his choking sobs.

Next day Finn and his men left Almhain of the White Walls. He marched resolutely away without looking back. He could feel the fortress like a presence behind him, a presence without a heart.

He looked back only when they reached the edge of the bog and the land solidified beneath his feet. He paused then and half turned, so the fénnid behind him thought he was about to issue an order. But he said nothing. Instead, he just gazed back at the Bog of Almhain where yet another woman had rejected him, or so he believed.

Then he turned his face toward the north, and Tara.

Goll Mac Morna was drilling several companies of the Fíanna on the training ground when the storm that was Finn Mac Cool broke over his head. Finn came striding through the gateway, paused only long enough to cock his head and locate the source of the sound he heard, weapons clashing, then rushed toward it. When he saw Goll pacing back and forth, correcting and criticizing, he flung himself at the one-eyed man and hurled him to the ground before Goll knew what hit him.

"Who gave you the right to order my men?" Finn roared.

Goll stared up at him. "The king did. They're my men now. By his order." He could feel his own anger growing. Finn had no right to humiliate him in front of the Fíanna. He got to his feet with alacrity, half-expecting Finn to hit him again and fully prepared to strike back with a blow of equal intensity.

But Finn did not hit him. Instead, he regarded Goll coldly, turning his head as if to look at him first with one eye, then with the other. In a voice as cold as the longest night of winter, he said, "I seem to have lost my wife and son. I'm not going to lose the Fíanna too, if I have to kill you to reclaim it."

Goll, who had not been told the particulars of Finn's recent illness, was taken aback. "Your wife and son? Finn, I didn't know . . ."

"No reason for you to know. It concerns no one but myself," Finn said in that same cold voice. "But the Fíanna's different. That concerns you and me. The command is mine, not yours, and either you surrender it to me right now or I take it from you the way you took it from my father."

Refuse, Finn was thinking. The desire was naked on his face.

He wants me to refuse, Goll realized, so he can kill me. He's more angry than I've ever seen him, but it's not about the Fíanna. This is a different game—one I dare not play.

Goll gave a brief, tight nod. "I never meant to replace you permanently," he said. "You are of course Rígfénnid Fíanna. It will be my pleasure to go to the king this instant and inform him of the happy news of your return to active service."

He took a step backward, still facing Finn. Every line of his posture bespoke the demeanor of subservience. Then he turned and went to find the king. But though Goll kept his face carefully impassive, a passing porter was startled to hear his teeth grinding like boulders rubbed together.

Goll found Cormac at the royal stables, inspecting a score of horses that had just been delivered from the south, tribute of a Laigin prince. Cormac glanced up briefly as Goll entered the long, low shed where the animals were stabled, then turned back to perusing them. But only for a moment. His mind registered something amiss.

Turning back toward Goll, the king said, "Is there a problem?"

"Not for you. Finn's come back."

"Is that a problem for you?"

"He wanted to kill me."

"He *what*?"

"He wants to kill someone, anyone, I think. He says he's lost his wife and child."

Cormac's eyes widened. "I'd better see him at once." He brushed past Goll, headed for the doorway. "Where is he?"

"Here," said a voice.

Finn blocked the doorway with his massive shoulders. In the dimly golden light filtering through the wickerwork walls of the stable, he was little more than a dark silhouette with pale hair. Yet he seemed to fill the entire building.

Cormac went up to him and said, as kindly as he could, "Goll just told me you've lost your wife?"

"Lost?" Finn's voice was strange, distant. "I didn't lose her. She's just . . . gone."

"Kidnapped, you mean? Or sick? Died? What is it, Finn? What's happened? I knew you were ill but I didn't realize that you'd suffered such a—"

"I'm back," said Finn curtly. "The reasons for my illness are unimportant except to myself."

"But what happened to your . . ."

Finn's eyes burned through the dimness. The barely contained fury in them dried Cormac's question on his lips.

"Obviously, you don't want to discuss it," the king said. "If you change your mind, though . . . if there's anything we can do to help . . ."

"If there's anything to do, I'll do it. In the meantime, I shall continue to command the Fíanna," said Finn Mac Cool.

He had not been a day in Tara before everyone knew he was a changed man. He radiated a white heat. If before he had been ambitious for himself and his fénnidi, now he was manic, demanding more than was humanly possible even for them. He fell upon the men Goll had been satisfactorily drilling and forced them to double their exertions, driving them out of some exploding force of his own that eventually communicated itself to them until they were as frantic as he. Javelins were hurled farther that day on the Hill of Tara than any javelin had ever been hurled in Erin.

Thus began the epoch of the Fíanna. During its duration, it would create imperishable legend.

Men who had been born to subjugated tribes and raised in louse-ridden, flea-infested huts stinking of urine and rotting meat would be elevated to a form of nobility, admired and emulated, entertained royally and laden with gifts of the finest craftsmanship. Every child would know their names. Every poet would celebrate their deeds. They would range the length and width of the island as Cormac Mac Airt consolidated his control, bringing all Erin under the overlordship of Tara as even his grandfather had never done.

For the first time in its history, the land became more than a collection of tribes in a constant state of flux between alliance and war. The battles did not cease totally; they were an integral part of society, the means by which men defined themselves. But they became more stylized, a highly developed combination of sport and art, patterned on the specific skills of one man—Finn Mac Cool.

The idealistic ambition of generations of warriors to create a form of battle as elegant as Celtic art had never been achieved, except in the rarest of situations. War had remained barbaric. But with the coming of Finn and his Fíanna, it developed, in Erin, into a complex game rather like chess, though with warriors for the chess pieces and the possibility of a fatal outcome.

Goll Mac Morna approved.

He never told Finn he approved. As one of Finn's rígfénnidi, he watched without comment, obeyed orders without hesitation, accepted his share of the accolades and the rewards without question. Only once in those years did he remark to Fiachaid—on a star-drenched night at Tara when they had both had too much mead—"Before I ever joined the Fíanna, I used to hear the songs sung and the tales told, and I thought it would be the army as it is today. The army Finn's made of it."

"Was it not?" Fiachaid asked in a slurred voice, holding up his cup for yet another refill from a passing servant.

"It was nothing like, not in those days. Och, we all talked about the grand things we would do, and what fine lads we were. But . . . we were none of us very different from Cuhal Mac Trenmor, not really. We joined the army so we could run wild and plunder with the protection of a king. I've always condemned Cuhal for his behaviour, but . . ." Goll's words were interrupted by a violent hiccup. His single eye flared wide. "But I suppose he was just doing what we all wanted to do. That's why so many men were glad to follow him. I should have done, too. I don't know why I didn't. Looking back, I think I was rockheaded."

Fiachaid grinned. "Sometimes you still are," he told Goll Mac Morna. He leaned closer, squinting at Goll in the light of the countless beeswax candles that illumined the halls of Tara at night. "Can I ask you something?" he enquired with drunken politeness.

"Absolutely." Goll drained his cup in one long swallow and held it up above his shoulder, awaiting the unfailing refill. "Absolutely."

"With all the history between you . . . and you know what I mean, Goll—" Fiachaid stabbed Goll's chest with a stiff forefinger "—with all the history between you two, why do you follow Finn Mac Cool? Why don't you simply walk away? You have a home to go to. Why don't you go?"

The cup was refilled. Goll cradled it in his hands and peered down into the amber depths as if seeking an answer there. "Why don't I go." It was not a question. "Indeed." He looked up blearily. "Shall I tell you a secret, Fiachaid? I don't go because I'm waiting around for Finn to try to kill me."

Fiachaid was shocked almost sober. "You're what?"

Goll nodded to himself, having just articulated a condition of which he had not been consciously aware until the mead loosened his tongue.

"You mentioned the history between us. Finn's always wanted to kill me. Aches to do it. As revenge for Cuhal. I know it even if he doesn't. And if I walk away, it's an act of cowardice on my part. Don't you see that, Fiachaid? Don't you see?"

20

DURING THE SEASONS THAT FOLLOWED, NEW NAMES WERE added to the pantheon of Fénian heroes, besung by the bards to eager audiences. There was Cron Crither son of Febal, and the swift-footed Taistellach, and Cuban from Muma, and Fidach the Foreigner, who applied three times before Finn would accept him. There was Dubh the Black and Dun the Brown and Glas the Grey and Aig the Battle and Ilar the Eagle. There was even a former rígfénnid from the army of the Ulaid, who turned his back on his tribe to become an officer in the army of the king of Tara.

Not only Fir Bolg, but sons of chieftains and kings began appearing wherever Finn was and requesting to be tested for membership in the Fíanna. But no matter what their rank, Finn accepted them only if they passed his most stringent requirements.

"It's surprising how many do pass," Cormac commented to Flaithri the brehon.

The other man replied, "Men do what they really want to do, no matter how hard it is. It seems that almost every man in Erin today who hasn't three legs and a squint wants to be numbered with the Fíanna."

"If I were not king of Tara, I would apply to join them myself," Cormac admitted ruefully.

The brehon chuckled. "So would I. Even the women . . ."

Cormac nodded. "Indeed. Even the women."

For the women had, without invitation, made themselves part of the army. When the Fíanna were marching, a sizable contingent of women, not all of them young, followed them, to tend the wounded and do the foraging and free the men to fight. Like Celtic warrior women of the past, a few even took up weapons and fought alongside the men, and not a few became wives and loved ones of members of the Fíanna.

But Cael Hundred-Killer took his wife from a different level of society.

It was late in the summer, and there had been hard campaigning in Muma. Several southern kings had rebelled against Cormac's authority and refused to send their harvest tributes the year before, so this year the Fíanna had come in person to oversee their collection. Battles had ensued. The Fíanna had, to the surprise of no one but a few disappointed kings, triumphed, and were rewarding themselves with a period of hunting and sport on *Fionntulach,* the White Hill.

Even when going to battle, Finn Mac Cool always traveled with his hounds. To Bran and Sceolaun had been added a pack of similar breed, lean-hipped and red-eared, and a man called Caurag to mind them. "Train these hounds to take only stags," Finn had cautioned Caurag sternly. "In the event they flush a doe, always hold back all but Bran and Sceolaun. If those two go up to her but make no effort to bring her down, and seem to know her, send for me at once no matter where I am, and keep that deer safe until I arrive if you value your life!"

Caurag, a thickset, bandy-legged man who loved hunting more than eating or women, was baffled by the order but obedient. "Your hounds will kill no doe unauthorized," he promised.

Every member of the Fíanna was given similar orders. The result was to make stags scarce wherever the army went, including this part of Muma, the region of Kerry. After a long day spent with only a few animals taken, Finn and his men were refreshing themselves with berries and haws while waiting for the evening meal to be prepared. Suddenly they heard a shout.

"I saw a huge stag!" cried Cael, who with his company was at the periphery of the encampment. He raced away with his men pelting after him.

The others resumed their customary conversation, mostly about battles and women. The sun had long since set and the bones of the meal picked clean before someone remarked on Cael's continuing absence.

"He knows his way back," said Goll, unconcerned.

But Finn worried. When two days passed with no sign of Cael, he took a search party and went looking for him.

They did not find him until the fourth dawn, when they met him on a narrow trail through gorse, wearing a glow that had nothing to do with the sunrise. His three nines, following, merely looked weary.

"Where have you been?" Finn wanted to know.

Wearing a foolish grin unbefitting a rígfénnid, Cael waved his hand vaguely in the direction he had come from. "Och . . . there."

There was no sword in the hand.

"Where's your sword?" Finn demanded to know with a growing feeling of alarm. Cael did not look like himself at all.

"The one with the gemstone in the hilt?"

"The one Cormac gave you, indeed. Where is it?"

Cael said blithely, "I gave it away."

"You *what?*"

Under Finn's furious glare, Cael's bravado withered. "I, uh, gave it away. To this woman. I mean . . . it was a token, you might say. She took us in for the night. Hers was a noble household and we had brought no presents worthy, so . . . och, I, uh . . ."

"Gave your sword away." Finn spat the words. "You'd better grow roots where you stand until you explain this to my satisfaction. If it's one of your jokes—"

"It's no joke," Cael assured him hastily. "Her name is Creide and her father's a king in Kerry. She was very . . . uh . . . good to me."

To everyone's astonishment, Cael Hundred-Killer blushed bright red.

When they returned to camp, Finn asked Goll if he knew anything about Creide. "I do know. She's the daughter of a ríg tuatha, all right, but she hasn't lived with her clan for years. She's said to be very fond of possessions. She's accepted no husband, but she's accepted the gifts of many who aspired to take her as wife."

Cael, listening, scuffed his toe in the dirt. "She accepted me," he said softly.

Finn and Goll exchanged glances. "Are you trying to claim," said Finn to Cael, "that this woman's agreed to marry you?"

"Not exactly. I mean, not yet. I think she will, but I . . ."

"But you nothing," Finn interrupted. "We'd better go with you to see this woman. I don't want one of my rígfénnidi tied in knots by any woman." His voice was harsh.

They found Creide presiding over a spacious fort shielded by the mountains called the Paps of Danu. Sentries challenged Finn's approach and only reluctantly admitted him and a select group of his officers into the protective palisade. But Finn noted that all gates and doors were opened without question for Cael, who swept through them as if returning home.

A yellow-haired woman with eyebrows dyed dark in the height of fashion hurried forward to capture Cael's two hands with hers.

The erstwhile Hundred-Killer glanced over his shoulder to be certain his companions were watching. "This is Creide," he said proudly. "She's always like this, she's mad for me. I don't like even one side of her, of course," he added with a laugh.

"Nor I of you," retorted Creide, also laughing. "You're hard on my eyes entirely. So when I see you, I close them." She put deed to word.

Cael promptly kissed her on both closed eyelids.

The watching Fíanna gaped. "Do you suppose," Blamec whispered to Cailte, "we should just go away and leave them alone?"

Cailte looked around the interior of Creide's dwelling. It was sumptuously equipped with fur-strewn couches and dyed wall hangings on rods of copper. Bronze and copper inlaid the vertical timbers supporting the roof. Bustling servants carried laden dishes and cups wrought of precious metal. "They wouldn't be alone if we did leave," he drawled. "Look at all her bondwomen! This woman lives like one of Cormac's wives."

"Better," Cael interjected. He lifted a heavily embossed silver cup bearing a beaded rim and held it for his friends to admire. "Creide actually has three score of these and enough mead and ale to fill them all at once."

Creide positively beamed. "The night Cael arrived, he made himself free of my house and examined my possessions, and him a stranger with no right to do so. Then he wove them all into poetry. An appallingly bad poem," she said, her fond tone belying her words, "but it gave me a record of everything I own, which was more than my steward knew. I never expected such a skill from a warrior."

Finn told her, "Every member of the Fíanna has to learn poetry before joining us. A warrior has to have a proven mind, and poetry is good for strengthening the memory. An officer does not want to have to repeat orders because someone forgot them, or to repeat directions to a meeting place because someone did not remember whether to go east at the ford or west. We can, any of us, recite a battle epic. Any of us with the possible exception of that one," he could not resist adding, glancing with a grin toward Conan.

The hairless man refused to be abashed. "My brain's as good as anyone else's. Better; it gets more exposure to the sun."

Creide left them for a few moments to issue orders to her steward and servants. Cael drifted away in her wake.

"What can a woman with all this possibly want with old Hundred-Killer?" Red Ridge asked Blamec when they were out of earshot.

"It's beyond knowing," the other replied.

But Creide obviously did want Cael, and he her. They could keep neither their eyes nor their hands off one another. Simultaneously they exchanged a constant stream of fond insults totally at variance with the flowery conversations favoured by Fergus Honey-Tongue.

The Fíanna were mystified.

Cael was delighted with himself.

"She really is a wretched woman," he said to his companions as they feasted on huge salmon served on yew-wood platters. "She's had count-less suitors and given every one of them tasks to perform that were quite beyond them. When a man fails, she sends him away in disgrace, with no saving of his pride at all."

Finn took a handful of boiled eggs from a basket proffered by an attentive servant. "I take it you succeeded, however?" he enquired dryly.

"I did of course. Any man who has met the challenges of Finn Mac Cool can run faster and jump higher and be more agile than mere chieftains and cattle lords," he said contemptuously.

"I took pity on him for the trials you'd given him," Creide said. To the unspoken astonishment of the Fíanna, she had taken her place among them for the feast, rather than eating in a place reserved for women. She sat now as a male host might and entered fully into the conversation. "When Cael told me the things you'd made him do," she said to Finn, "I felt quite sorry for him. I have a tender heart."

"Exactly as tender as a stone," Cael added quickly. He reached out and cupped her breast over her heart as if they were alone. A look so weighted with desire passed between them that the most hardened war-rior dropped his eyes in embarrassment.

After the meal, Creide herself showed Finn and his officers to couches reserved for them. As was the custom, all slept in the one large room, but at Creide's the room was divided into sleeping compartments by carved wooden screens and linen hangings.

Fergus could not resist remarking aloud on the luxury of the accom-modations.

"I earned it," Creide said with unexpected bitterness.

"Earned it?" Fergus started to question her, but Goll Mac Morna dug his elbow into Honey-Tongue's ribs and he closed his mouth.

"Women become wealthy in their own right when male members of the clan die without leaving sons," Goll said smoothly.

That night Finn found himself sleeping on the couch adjacent to Goll's, separated only by a wooden screen. When there was enough snoring to drown the sound of his voice, he put his head close to the screen and called Goll's name. "Are you still awake?"

"I am."

"Why did Creide say she'd earned her wealth? Do you know?"

"I knew a man who carried a spear for Creide's father," Goll replied in his husky whisper, meant for Finn's ears only. "He said the father spent too much time on the couch of the daughter."

"Warming her bed as people do?"

Goll gave a coarse laugh. "I'd say not. Something more. He warmed something more. He supposedly got her with a child, or children, that were immediately put out to fosterage. At last Creide's mother, his chief wife, lost her temper and threatened war between her tribe and his. So he sent Creide away—almost impoverished himself to do it, but it cost him less than a war with his chief wife's people. Everything you see here, Creide earned, if the story is to be believed, by submitting to her father."

"I'm surprised she'll look at a man at all."

"She has no history of treating them well," Goll replied. "Our Cael seems to be the exception."

"Why, do you suppose?"

"Unlike the men of Kerry, he wouldn't have known the story. They probably came at her with a leer in their eyes. He treats her as he treats all women, as boys treat their sisters, and she's obviously comfortable with that."

"She seems a strong woman."

"I'd say she is," Goll agreed. "Did you notice his body when he stripped to bathe? Bruises and claw marks the length of him, and a grin on his face like a hound lying in the sun. And if they marry, he'll be supported by her property, by all of this. Provided he does his share of conserving and defending it, of course. Not bad for a man who was born in a herder's summer hut."

Finn said quietly, "You need not remain where you are born."

"This is true. You left the Bog of Almhain, didn't you? Now here you are in Kerry."

Recognizing the sly insinuation in Goll's voice, Finn knew what direction the conversation was meant to take. He moved back from the screen.

"Do you mean to visit your mother while we're in Kerry?" Goll's disembodied voice followed him. "Do you even know if she's still alive?"

"I wouldn't know," Finn said coldly.

"Your own mother?" Goll's voice pretended to be shocked. "And you not knowing?"

Finn spat out his words. "I've had other things on my mind, Goll."

"But it would be no more than a day's march from here if you wanted to—"

"Leave it, Goll!" commanded the Rígfénnid Fíanna.

Goll subsided, smiling to himself. That subject's still very tender with Finn, he thought, like flesh with a thorn festering. It might be something to use against him some day, some way. It might indeed.

Imagining stratagems, Goll was slow to fall asleep.

Finn did not sleep at all.

Crossing his arms behind his head, he lay and watched the play of firelight and shadows—distorted shadows—on the walls. As in all prosperous households, a few candles were left burning throughout the night, but nothing could chase away the shadows.

Finn could see faces in them. Women's faces.

A deer's face.

A worm of pain twisted in his belly, gnawing.

Speculation was rife in the morning. "Why Cael? Is his spear that much longer than other men's?" Red Ridge asked Madan.

"I'd say about average. Perhaps his gift is his tongue."

There was a wave of knowing laughter.

Creide left no doubt that she was willing to marry Cael. She said it right out in front of the Fíanna. "He's such a wretched excuse for a man I might as well take him, no one else would have him," she said, groping beneath his tunic as she spoke.

Finn's mouth went dry, watching them.

"I'll bring some of my women and follow the army," Creide promised. "Women fight. I can fight. Would you like to see me carrying a spear in your wake, Cael?" Her eyes danced.

"I'd rather carry a spear in yours. *This* spear."

"We'd better go away *now*!" Blamec moaned to Cailte, who nodded agreement.

The laws of hospitality required them to stop several days with Creide, however; several days that were a torment for Finn's men, being forced to observe the abandoned delight Cael and Creide took in one another. Creide kindly offered those of her bondwomen who wished to partake, but Finn gave strict orders that his rígfénnidi refuse. "We can do better than bondwomen," he told them. "Look at Cael."

Looking at Cael was almost painful, however.

They were very glad when their commander announced that the visit was concluded and they must return northward. When they left, Creide stood in her gateway promising Cael she would follow him with a band of women as soon as she could equip them.

"And she will," Cael assured his companions cheerfully.

Midday found them climbing a heathered hill with a soft wind at their backs. The air was sweetened with birdsong. On a day so radiant, Finn's companions expected him to recite a poem of his own composition. They kept cutting their eyes toward him expectantly.

But though he chewed on his thumb as if deep in thought, he said nothing. His face was closed.

At last Goll remarked, "That trail off through the heather would take us eventually to the stronghold of Gleor Red-Hand. We could demand hospitality for the night and you could enjoy a reunion, Finn."

Finn turned his back on the indicated trail and set off in the opposite direction. Beneath his billowing cloak, his shoulders were rigid.

"Who's Gleor Red-Hand?" Blamec wanted to know.

"Just someone Finn knows," Goll replied. "At least, Finn knows his wife. Knew her intimately at one time."

Finn whirled on him, his face livid. "I told you before, Goll: leave it! That's an order!"

As Goll had intended, Blamec misunderstood. "So you've enjoyed the welcome of a Kerry woman's thighs also, Finn?" he asked innocently.

The next moment Blamec found himself lying on his back in the heather, gazing up at a sky so blue and bland he could not understand why it was also filled with whirling lights.

He saw a circle of faces looking down at him. "What happened?" he asked his friends. "Was I struck by lightning?"

"As near as makes no difference," replied Cailte. "Finn hit you. You said something he didn't like."

"And he hit me for *that*?"

"Look at that sky. You weren't struck by lightning."

A member of Blamec's company extended a hand and helped him to his feet. He was excruciatingly embarrassed. Being struck by the Rígfénnid Fíanna in front of his own men was almost unprecedented. What could have come over Finn? he wondered. But he did not ask, nor did he argue.

It seemed prudent for once to say nothing.

The army marched on, though not into the territory of Gleor Red-Hand.

Goll was pleased with himself. It was a petty satisfaction, but that did not make it less pleasant. Wounding Finn and letting someone else suffer the punishment improved the game considerably in his opinion.

Two nights had passed before Blamec regained sufficient confidence to complain, "I thought the king promised us horses. Seasons ago. Whatever happened to them?"

"They'll be waiting for us at Tara," Finn assured him. "Cormac wants to make something of a ceremony of their presentation, I believe."

"I'd be happier with less ceremony and less walking," Blamec replied. "Couldn't he have given us horses at the start of battle season this year?"

"He could have. But he wants to do it at the Great Assembly, where everyone will see. His will be the first army to have all of its officers mounted; it's an important occasion, and sure to impress the other kings and chieftains."

Fergus wanted to know, "Will we be expected to ride them right away? In front of everyone?"

"I suppose so," Finn told him. "That's the point."

"But I've never been on a horse."

"Anyone," Madan declared, "can ride a horse. You've seen Cormac do it, it's just like sitting on a bench."

Fergus looked dubious. "I don't think that's all there is to it."

"It is of course. Just watch me when I get my horse."

Cailte enquired, "Have you ever ridden a horse, Madan?"

"I have not. But I know I can."

"Your men are too arrogant, Finn," Goll remarked, "and you've made them that way. But I suspect your first experience with horses will teach you all a little humility."

Finn did not reply, but later in the day he ordered Cailte in a confidential tone, "Send Taistellach ahead to locate the next noble stronghold along our way that has some riding horses."

Swift-footed Taistellach sped away, to return in due course with reports of the stronghold of a wealthy chieftain on the banks of the Blackwater. The man, who was called Dorbha, had some cattle, flocks of sheep, and a herd of horses penned near his fort.

"He appears to be very proud of his horses," Taistellach said. "And of his women, for that matter. His household's full of them. He keeps them warm with cloaks of otter skins so there must be good hunting along the banks of the river. He has vats of ale and buttermilk, almost like a hosteller, and a fine reputation for generosity among his tribesmen."

"The very man we need," replied Finn Mac Cool.

He picked up the pace.

Dorbha was at first alarmed to find the majority of the fíans of the Fíanna descending upon him, but relieved when Finn requested quartering and hospitality only for himself and his officers. "The rest of my men provide their own beds and feed themselves," he was assured.

His alarm returned, however, when a thin man with hair just beginning to turn grey said quietly to him, "The Rígfénnid Fíanna has a mind to try one of your riding horses. Only for himself, you understand. Out of sight of the others."

"The Fíanna are going to take my animals," Dorbha predicted gloomily to his senior wife.

She glared at him. "Don't let them!"

"This is the Fíanna we're talking about, woman! They could take the hide off your body and mine if they wanted. We should be thankful if we lose only the horses to them."

To his surprise, however, they did not lose any horses. While the other officers were eating and drinking in Dorbha's banquetting hall, Finn and Cailte slipped away to a hidden copse, leading a single grey horse.

Cailte held the animal by its bridle while Finn vaulted aboard. The horse did not move and seemed unaffected by the clamping of a stranger's legs on its sides.

"This isn't so hard," Finn said. "Give me the rein, Cailte."

"Are you sure?" Cailte was watching the horse's eyes.

"I am of course. I could almost put my feet down and touch the ground; what could possibly happen?"

Shrugging, Cailte surrendered the single rein. Finn, seeing Cormac in his mind's eye, gave the animal a kick.

Nothing happened.

"We should have brought a horse-goad," Cailte said.

"Nonsense. I can make this creature go, just with the strength of my legs." Finn kicked again—and this time he kicked as hard as he could.

The astonished grey let out a great *whoosh* of air, then threw its head down between its forelegs and gave a mighty twist to its back.

Finn found himself in exactly the same position Blamec had occupied a couple of days earlier, examining an equally blue sky similarly spangled with whirling lights.

"I don't think," Cailte drawled, "that you've perfected the art of riding yet, Finn."

Finn laughed in spite of himself and got to his feet. "Madan seems to have underestimated the difficulties," he admitted. "Let's try it again."

They spent the evening with the grey horse, the long summer evening of Erin that faded only into a semi-darkness, then brightened again. By the time Finn felt confident he could at least stop, start, and turn a horse under normal circumstances, Cailte was eager to try his own luck, so they changed places.

"Don't ever tell anyone I let you do this, though," Finn cautioned his friend with a wink.

Cailte replied, "I never tell anyone anything. I'm famous for it."

They spent several more nights with Dorbha. During the day, the other officers joined their fíans hunting around the Blackwater, but Finn and Cailte used the time to practice riding in secret. If they sat down a little more gingerly than usual, no one noticed.

At night, the women of Dorbha's household offered the visiting rígfénnidi every form of Gaelic hospitality, including the welcome of their thighs; their noble thighs. The Fíanna were no longer men to be despised.

Excited by the recent example of Cael and Creide, Finn's officers responded enthusiastically. "The voice of the cuckoo is sweet in our ears," Fergus Honey-Tongue claimed rapturously.

On what was to be their final night with Dorbha, Finn's officers were given a woman for every lap. The woman who came to the Rígfénnid Fíanna was the finest the household had to offer, one of Dorbha's own daughters, a supple-hipped woman with long, shapely hands. She approached Finn diffidently, half-expecting he would turn away, as he had not yet shown any interest in women, unlike the rest of his men.

But Finn could no longer avoid being aware of humid looks being exchanged, ardent caresses, sudden catches of breath. All around him, his men were enjoying themselves. Life was being lived. Life . . . the word made him ache.

He experienced a sudden, startling sense of bilocation. He seemed to become a passive observer watching a second Finn. He tried to have some influence over this second Finn, but could not reach him.

Between them was a crystal wall. Nothing passed through.

Finn the observer watched a flushed, sweating warrior called Finn Mac Cool take the proffered woman by one of her long, pale hands and pull that hand down to his lap, deliberately inviting her to fondle him.

The woman complied, dropping to her knees in front of Finn's bench. Her eyes, the observer noted, were blank and blue. Eyes should not be blue. Eyes should be brown. Sive's eyes were brown.

Does the Finn on the bench with the woman's hand at his crotch remember Sive? the observer wondered. Does he have my memories at all? Do we dream the same dreams? Or are his different from mine? When I go to sleep, is he awake?

This different person who is also me—where does he go when I can't see him?

Am I inside, and he outside?

Or is it the other way around?

The blue-eyed woman reached under Finn's tunic and smiled with astonishment. Over her shoulder she called, "This man deserves to command armies! This man deserves to be king! He is mightily armed!"

The Finn on the bench laughed and rumpled her hair and swept her into his arms, pressing her body against his. Dorbha looked on, approving.

At some point, observer and observed became one again, but a fracture had taken place. Insulated by pain, the man who loved Sive hardly felt what was happening. His body responded as nature dictated it must, but with neither joy nor grace.

In the false glow before dawn, Finn sought his bed and took with him the blue-eyed woman.

Her name, he learned tardily, was Manissa. She had strong white legs to wrap around his waist and she clutched him with rapturous delight, pulling him deeper and deeper inside her.

The observer returned. He seemed to be hanging in space somewhere above them, slightly to the left and behind Finn, looking down. Listening to the repetitive slap of flesh against flesh and the expected moanings and praisings. With a cold mind he judged the quality of the passion the woman appeared to display, and found it lacking. She was not Sive. She was not anyone. Just a woman.

He wanted to cry, for her and for Finn.

In the morning, as the Fíanna were preparing to leave, Finn took Manissa aside. "I need a wife," he said bluntly. "A marriage of the first degree, that's what's appropriate for the Rígfénnid Fíanna. Your father is a man of rank and prestige, so we would have equal status, you and I. You would be my wife of equal dignity. Shall I arrange it?"

Manissa was taken aback. From a man known as a warrior-poet, she had expected something less brisk, less bald. But Finn stood before her with his face closed and his eyes guarded, obviously eager to be on the road, giving her this one chance to become a wife to the famed Rígfénnid Fíanna or probably never see him again.

"I . . . I am willing to be your wife," she said with a dry mouth.

"Good," he said briskly, as if concluding a negotiation for a hunting dog. "Next Beltaine, then. We take no property with our women, so you won't require a dowry, but I shall offer your male kin appropriate coibche. What is your honour price?"

Under the circumstances, Finn announced they would stay with Dorbha for one more night. It seemed discourteous to rush off so abruptly after agreeing to marry the man's daughter. Dorbha was delighted with the arrangement, already imagining the benefits that would accrue from being the father of the Rígfénnid's wife. No one would ever dare raid his herds again!

Finn's men, of course, were equally delighted to enjoy one more night of Dorbha's hospitality.

A fine banquet, surpassing those previous, was hastily arranged in Finn's honour. Dorbha gave him his own carved bench to sit upon, and Manissa seated herself on the floor between his knees, occasionally favouring the other women with a small, smug smile.

She wondered why he did not touch her as she sat thus.

When the first hunger was sated and the men were beginning to pick marrow out of bones and look for forgotten scraps of bread to throw the hounds, Dorbha ordered another log placed on the fire. "I have no bard of my own," he lamented, "although my daughter is about to enter a society where every household has a bard. But I myself am able to recite a—"

"I can be your bard for the night," said Finn Mac Cool.

2 1

GLANCING DOWN INADVERTENTLY, FINN'S EYES FELL UPON the mantle of otter skin Manissa had draped around her shoulders against the cool of the evening. Then he cleared his throat.

His men exchanged knowing glances. "It's a long time since we heard him recite," Blamec whispered to Conan.

"He saved all his pretty speeches for Sive, I suspect. But he's not saving any more!" the bald man sniggered.

Finn drew back an imperceptible degree from the woman at his feet. The silent observer who was also Finn understood and approved. He began speaking in a tightly controlled voice from which he withheld any trace of emotion, a voice that somehow made the story more powerful by contrast.

"Abhainn Mor, great river of black water, knows no time," he said. "Rivers cannot die, so they need not measure nights and days. But there are spirits living in them that do recognize time, and for some of those, its passage is an agony. As it is for some of us," he added in that uninflected voice.

"There is a story told of one such creature who lived in the bitterest loneliness in the darkest depths of the black water. Once the creature had walked the fern-soft earth of Erin in the sunlight, as one of the Tuatha Dé Danann. But when the Dananns were defeated by the Milesians, this particular spirit transformed itself and took refuge in the river rather than be slain or driven from the land.

"It lives there still.

"In order to experience some of the life it had once enjoyed, the creature assumed a body of muscle and bone. The Dananns had that gift, you know. They could take shapes for themselves. This particular one chose to appear as an otter, most of the time."

The hunters exchanged a different sort of glance now. There was not a man among the rígfénnidi who had not speared at least one otter during their stay at Dorbha's fort.

Glas the Grey whispered urgently to Fergus Honey-Tongue, "Is Finn trying to tell us we've done something wrong, killing otters?"

"You never know exactly what Finn's saying with these stories," Fergus replied. "Just listen to him. I think they have hidden meanings only he knows."

Goll said nothing, but kept his eyes on Finn.

"The Danann became a she-otter," Finn was saying, "a supple, shining animal with large . . . brown . . . eyes. But it was not like the other otters and they recognized this; none would mate with it. The Danann otter remained alone and lonely in her river.

"Then one day a shepherd drove a flock of sheep to the Blackwater for a drink, and knelt on the bank himself to cup his hands in the water. From concealment beneath an overhang, the otter saw him. There was something almost familiar about him, some plane of cheek or brow she thought she knew from another time.

"She swam to him and lifted her head above the water very close to his. They stared at one another. The shepherd's first thought was of the value of an otter skin. He had no weapon within reach, but she seemed almost tame; he began to hope he could lure her onto the bank and catch her there.

"He spoke softly to her and she moved closer, trying to remember when she had seen him last. When she had loved him last, in what lifetime . . .

"He made a grab for her but she grabbed him first, with a hand that closed over his wrist as no otter's ever could. She held him fast and began to pull him into the water with her.

"The shepherd struggled but it was of no use; the creature who was not an otter was incredibly strong. He began to shout then, but all he did was frighten his sheep and they bolted. There was no one close enough to hear his cries for help and save him.

"The creature who was not an otter drew him deeper, deeper into the water, and even though he was beginning to drown, he did not know he was drowning. A wild joy overcame him. He allowed himself to be locked in her embrace and it felt like coming home. He surrendered everything to her.

"And she took him down, down into the black depths of the black water where she had once fled for sanctuary. She took him with her, but at some point she must have decided he was not the one she remembered, not one of her own kind after all, and she released her hold on him.

"She abandoned him to the current and he began to move upward again, borne by the water. But it was too late. The life had already gone out of him, and when his body reached the surface, it floated lifeless on the breast of the river."

A stunned silence followed.

Members of Finn's audience looked at each other as if uncertain of how to react.

"What sort of tale is that?" wondered Fidach the Foreigner. "I was expecting a bardic epic."

Conan said tersely, "You didn't get one."

Rousing herself with a little shiver, Manissa half-turned so she could look up at Finn. Unshed tears glittered in her eyes. "*Ochone*, alas! What a terrible story. Where did you learn it?"

Finn did not look down at her, but instead gazed straight at Goll Mac Morna. "My mother taught it to me when I was a child," he claimed. "She taught me all the legends of the Tuatha Dé Danann, which she knew well, being descended from that race herself."

Contradict me if you dare, his eyes coldly challenged Goll.

The one-eyed man refused to accept the bait. Who would choose to believe him over Finn Mac Cool? "You have a very interesting genealogy," was all he said. "When the historians recite it, do they mention your mother's descent from the Sídhe?"

Without hesitating, Finn answered smoothly, "I've not requested the historians to recite my genealogy yet, as until the last few years I've had no property that my offspring might someday inherit, nor have I inherited any from my ancestors. With the exception of the treasure bag of my father's clan, of course." He smiled with one side of his mouth. "And it also contains magic," he said softly.

Watching him, listening to him, assessing his words, Goll was convinced that Finn really believed what he was saying; believed it totally, no matter how preposterous. And if he did, he was mad. Surely, truly mad.

But he was not always mad, Goll had to admit to himself. As commander of the Fíanna, he was sharply sane, a brilliant strategist and gifted leader of men in spite of the shadows at the edges of his mind.

If Finn is mad, I will someday replace him, Goll thought. And if Finn is mad, what a waste, what a loss!

As always, Goll was torn between love and hate when it came to Finn Mac Cool.

With some reluctance, the army got underway next morning. Finn was not the only one who had found himself a woman, and there were several painful farewells. To Manissa's disappointment, however, Finn seemed able to leave her without regret. In fact, his last words were not to her, but to her father. "I'll arrange for the coibche to be sent to you as soon as I get to Almhain," he promised. "I'm stopping there before we go on to Tara. And you're to send Manissa to me next Beltaine. We'll wed then because it's a contract marriage."

Manissa was not pleased to think she must wait through autumn and winter before joining Finn, but he obviously had no intention of taking her with him now. Though there were women with the Fíanna, as she knew.

She thought, briefly, of disguising herself and joining these women, going to Tara with them as just another of the army's followers. Then she recalled that she was a chieftain's daughter and restrained herself.

"I must behave with dignity," she assured herself, gazing into the polished metal mirror her mother had given her on her Day of First Bleeding. "Finn Mac Cool's a self-controlled man, an unemotional man. He will want the same of me. He will want a wife of calm demeanor, nothing impetuous, nothing wild."

Pleased with her judgment of the man, Manissa settled herself resolutely to await the passing of the seasons.

As the Fíanna swept northward, they fought one more battle, a brief, bitter skirmish on a morning of alternating rain and sun, when shadows chased golden light across the rolling grassland and birds flew up in alarm at the clash of swords.

For Conn Crither, the battle seemed only the continuation of a dream. Together with his three nines, he had spent the previous night bedded down in a hollow a little distance removed from the main body of the army. The night had been disturbed; he saw visions of three women in battle dress approaching him, promising to create additional warriors for him out of stalks of grass. His brain was still cobwebbed with sleep when a hostile band encountered the encamped Fíanna and battle broke.

Yelling at his men to follow, Conn Crither ran to join the fighting. He somehow thought he had more men behind him than just his three fíans, and ran into the very thick of the battle as if he were invincible. So boldly did he attack that he found himself facing the leader of the opposition, and without pausing to draw breath, he beheaded the man with his sword.

It was an act of conspicuous bravery.

"I thought I was leading a whole army," Conn Crither told Finn later. "I had this dream, you see . . ."

Finn listened sympathetically. He knew about dreams and how they impinged on reality.

Reaching Almhain, he paused only long enough to ascertain that no one had heard anything of Sive, and to send the coibche to Dorbha.

Then, ordering Red Ridge and Donn to leave enough men behind to guard the fort and follow him themselves, he set out again for Tara.

Everyone of any importance must be at Tara this year for the Great Assembly.

"There will be a fortnight of sport before the Assembly itself begins," Finn reminded his men, "and I expect the Fíanna to win every contest. The serious part of the Assembly starts three days before Samhain and lasts three days after, and every king in Erin will be there, in addition to all the brehons and the chief poets and historians . . . anyone who matters. I want every officer of the Fíanna there too, very much in evidence. We can hold our own with the nobility."

"Arrogant," said Goll to himself, since no one else was interested.

No sooner did they arrive at Tara than Finn began telling a highly coloured version of their most recent battle, one in which Conn Crither's dream became part of the reality and the battle took place partly in the Here and Now and partly in the Celtic Otherworld. It was a spectacular tale, making of Conn Crither a hero out of legend, and he was the last to contradict Finn.

Goll did not attempt to correct Finn either. He merely listened, his one eye narrowed thoughtfully.

Feis Teamhrach, the Great Assembly of Tara, was an occasion for arguing and proclaiming law, for making new regulations when required, for updating tribal history by having recent events related by the participants, and for correcting and adding to the all-important genealogies upon which rank and inheritance depended. The entire proceedings were scrupulously committed to memory by professional poets steeped in the oral tradition, using the rhythm and metre of their art to carve words ineradicably in the mind.

At the Great Assembly, Finn would be expected to relate the activities and victories of the Fíanna, to become part of the history of Erin.

After debating with himself for some time, Goll went to see Cormac, whom he found with Flaithri, inspecting the Fort of the Synods. "Now that I've built a similar fort for the poets," Cormac told his chief brehon, "I want to be certain the structures reflect the exact status and prestige of the two professions."

Flaithri, scowling at an iron door hinge that seemed slightly less elaborate than those on the Fort of the Poets, was about to comment when Goll joined them. Instead of criticizing door hinges, the brehon said acidly, "There is nothing in the law that permits rígfénnidi access to this building whenever they like."

"This is important," Goll said. "I need to speak to the king."

"Ah, isn't it always important?" Flaithri rolled his eyes roofward and turned his palms up in an eloquent gesture reminiscent of his father.

Studying Goll's face, Cormac gave a short, sharp nod. "This is important," he decided. "Wait for us, Flaithri." He followed Goll from the fort.

A thin, cold wind was blowing across Tara. Goll turned his back to it deliberately, letting the king take it in the face. Cormac smiled. "You interpose your body between me and the wind," he said. "A thoughtful gesture."

Disconcerted, Goll blinked rapidly and regathered his thoughts. "What I wanted to say to you is . . . is . . ."

"About Finn Mac Cool?" Cormac guessed.

"About Finn Mac Cool," Goll conceded. "Are you aware that he's . . . not himself?"

Cormac smiled again. "On the contrary, I think he's very much himself. He's strutting around Tara and boasting like a rooster that's laid an egg. Isn't that the Finn we know?"

Trying not to feel disloyal, Goll said, "Those boasts are lies, Cormac. Outright lies, most of them."

Cormac's face was impassive. "Are they?"

"They are. I was there, I know. He's telling these outrageous stories and—"

"He's always done that, it's part of his attraction."

"But he hasn't always believed them! At least, not fully. He does now, though. And he'll tell them to the poets and believe he's describing events accurately. I can't let that happen."

"You have a laudable sense of honour, Goll."

"Are you patronizing me?"

"I am not, I was paying you a compliment. Are you so rarely complimented that you can't tell the difference?"

Goll was embarrassed. In a voice made hoarser than usual by the emotion, he muttered, "I don't need compliments. I'm just doing my duty."

"You call that doing your duty? Accusing your commander of . . . of what, Goll?"

Goll threw a furious look at Cormac. "All right then, defend him! But don't say you weren't warned!" He spun on his heel and strode away. Cormac was a player of games himself, but the king's games were too subtle, too shaped by the folds of the man's mind, for Goll to enjoy them.

Cormac returned to the Fort of the Synods and Flaithri. But later that day he drew his chief historian aside and had a few words with him in private. "My Rígfénnid Fíanna is a very brilliant warrior," he said, "but he has a tendency to exaggerate even more than most. It might be wise to remember that when committing his descriptions of events to memory. His are splendid tales for telling around a campfire, but I cannot vouch for their accuracy, and our children's children might not be well served if the more outrageous stories were made part of our history."

The chief historian, a thin-legged, round-bellied man with a prodigious memory, found this an astonishing conversation. "Are you telling me Finn Mac Cool would lie about the achievements of himself and the Fíanna?"

"He would not lie, I think. But he . . . adds colour. A great deal of colour. He introduces elements into his narratives that exist only in his imagination."

"What elements?" the historian wanted to know.

"I can't even tell you, I'm not certain myself. With him, it's hard to know what might be fact and what might be his own creation."

The historian pondered the king's words in private, and made his own decision. He thereafter listened to the stories told by and about Finn with a critical ear. Only the bare facts, such as recountings of battles won and hostages taken, were memorized to be incorporated into the histories handed down from generation to generation. The tales in their vivid entirety became the property and pride of the bards, whose creativity fed upon them.

But no matter what version of the Finn Mac Cool stories was being told, there was one eager listener. Cruina of the Questions spent little time in the Grianan after the Fíanna arrived. She could usually be found within eye-distance of Finn, a rather forlorn shadow hoping to attract his attention but unwilling to come forward and demand it.

Finn knew she was there.

He had sent the agreed coibche to Lochan the smith every year; as far as he was concerned, he had done his duty by Cruina. She represented a bruise on his memory that he preferred to forget. Manissa was better; he was in control of the situation with Manissa.

"She's still there, you know," Cailte remarked to him one day.

"Who?"

"The smith's daughter."

"Is she?" Perhaps I should speak to her, Finn told himself; it would be kind. But he did not really want to.

As he had expected, Cormac had arranged for horses to be presented to the officers of the Fíanna during the period of the Great Assembly. The king summoned Finn to accompany him to the stables for a personal tour of inspection.

"They are very fine animals," Cormac said proudly. "As good as a chieftain might ride."

"Grand animals," remarked Finn, recalling the shorter, sturdier horses Dorbha possessed. These were leggier, with finely carved heads and tapering muzzles. Their eyes were as large and liquid as a deer's. The

horses were tied by means of rope head-collars to iron rings set in pillars
the length of the stable. The nearest animal to Finn was a sleek chestnut
mare who turned her head as far as she could at the sound of his voice
and looked at him.

"Where did you get them?" he asked Cormac. "I've seen no horses
like these in Erin."

The king grinned. "They didn't come from Erin. After you threw such
a fright on the raiders from Alba, a tribe of Britons sent a delegation over
here to discuss peaceful trade with me—while you were in the south this
summer, in fact. They brought horses and left with hounds instead, and
thought themselves well served. They had seen nothing as large and fine
as our hounds, which they say will be prized among the Britons."

Finn looked the length of the stable. "You have only ten horses of this
breed?"

"That's all they were willing to trade me. But I have a selection of
good strong hill ponies for the rest of your officers. Every man will be
mounted, I promise you."

Without waiting for Cormac's permission, Finn began untying the
chestnut mare. "I'll take this one." He led her outside.

The king followed. "I've spoken to one of my kinsmen about demon-
strating the finer points of riding to you."

"Och, he'd waste his breath entirely. Didn't you know? I can ride as
well as you."

Cormac said sternly, "There's just yourself and myself here right now,
Finn, so don't tell your tales to me. You've never sat on a horse in your
life and I know it."

"Have I not?" Finn gave Cormac a smile so dazzling, so full of youth
and joy and mischief, that the king was momentarily disconcerted. In
that moment Finn gave a leap and threw one leg across the mare's back.
He tugged her head around with the rope affixed to her head-collar and
tightened his legs on her sides, at the same time thrusting his pelvis
forward against her spine.

The mare obediently moved off in a soft little jog-trot, with Finn
sitting as relaxed and boneless as a sack of meal on her back. He looked
like a man born to ride.

Cormac stared after him. "What to believe?" the king murmured to
himself.

A horseboy emerging from the stable overheard him and asked anxiously, "Did you speak to me?"

"I spoke to myself," Cormac replied gently. "I was telling myself not
to be too quick to judge others."

Perplexed, the horseboy went on about his affairs, wondering at the
inscrutability of kings.

Finn galloped the mare in and out between the forts and halls and limewashed walls of Tara, glorying in the sensation of control she gave up to him so willingly. Even with no bit in her mouth, the mare obeyed every pressure of his legs and shift of his weight. She was lighter on her feet than the grey horse had been, and her supple joints cushioned the impact of her feet with the earth. Riding her was almost like floating. In one circuit of Tara, she taught Finn why kings ride horses.

He guided her back to the stable. Cormac was gone, but his chief horsemaster was soon located and ordered to bring the horses designated for the rígfénnidi down to their training ground.

It was only a short distance, but Finn rode.

He assembled his officers and arbitrarily assigned a horse to each. One tall grey stallion he indicated, with a nod of his head, was for Cailte. "You're both lean and grey, it's a good match," he said, neglecting to add aloud that the animal was obviously the pick of the lot.

Cailte obediently took the rein from the horseboy holding the grey and vaulted aboard. The other rígfénnidi watched, awaiting their turn.

"I told you it was easy," Madan said to Glas. "See how Cailte did it?"

They soon discovered it was not as easy as it looked. The horse assigned to Glas tried to kick him when he missed his first jump and kneed the animal in the belly.

Blamec's horse tore its rein out of its horseboy's hand and ran backward with Blamec running after it, shouting slanders on its ancestry.

The unfortunate Conan Maol was given the sturdiest horse, a broad brown animal with a convex nose and a bristling mane, but the two took an instant dislike to one another. Conan made repeated attempts to vault onto the horse, but each time it sidestepped just out of his reach. "Go around to the other side and swing him toward me," Conan ordered the horseboy.

The attendant complied. The horse swung too far and trod heavily on Conan's foot, crunching bone. He howled in pain and outrage.

"Your turn, Madan," said the implacable Finn Mac Cool.

Madan Bent-Neck surveyed his new mount. A brown mare so dark she was almost black, she looked back at him with equal curiosity.

Cailte said, "It's easy. Like sitting on a bench."

Madan swallowed hard, caught hold of the short black mane and swung himself up. The mare stood like an oak tree. When he found himself aboard her with no difficulty, he grinned hugely. "It is easy!" he agreed.

At that moment the mare decided she disliked the whole procedure and gave her head such a toss she jerked the rein out of his hand. She promptly lowered her neck so she could begin grazing the sweet green grass of Tara. Madan found himself sitting on an unfamiliar animal over which he had no control. The rein trailed beside her head, on the grass.

"What do I do now?" he asked the horseboy. "Hand me that rein again."

But the boy, who was enjoying this as much as Finn and Cailte were, began an intense conversation with his nearest fellow and pretended not to hear.

Meanwhile, Finn closed his legs on the mare and urged her forward. "Right, you lot," he said to the others. "Follow me." The chestnut mare broke into a trot.

Cailte's grey followed close behind. The other horses, obeying their herd instinct, set off after them, subjecting their unprepared riders to a torment of jouncing and bouncing. Some dropped their reins; some grabbed hold of the mane for support. Some slid to one side and some to the other. Madan, who had never got hold of his rein in the first place, had the alarming feeling of being on a runaway and emitted a tiny squeak that would embarrass him in memory for years afterward.

For the first time in history, a mounted company of rígfénnidi rode across Tara—in wildly haphazard fashion while following a silver-haired man who was fighting hard not to laugh aloud.

By the end of the day, almost everyone but Finn and Cailte had fallen off at least once. As Goll had predicted, the horses were excellent for teaching humility. Goll, who had fallen like the rest, remembered those words ruefully as he rubbed his bruised backside.

But the relentless Finn kept after them, and within seven nights, his rígfénnidi could ride, if not like princes, at least as well as himself and Cailte. Humility evaporated and arrogance returned, stronger than ever.

"It should be the natural heritage of every man in Erin to ride a horse!" proclaimed the delighted Fergus Honey-Tongue.

Finn wove a great tale around the acquisition of the horses, one in which the son of the king of the Britons had kidnapped Finn's hounds and the Fíanna claimed them back, and the horses as well. It made splendid telling around the hearthfires of Erin, and in time was taken as truth by most people who had not been at Tara.

Each accomplishment by himself or one of his Fíanna earned a tale by Finn. Every one was told as fact. The battles they fought grew larger in the telling, involving more enemy and more casualties, often including elements from the Otherworld, spangles of magic. Finn and the Fíanna won with incredible feats over impossible odds, or so the stories claimed.

But no member of the Fíanna denied the tales. Indeed, Fergus Honey-Tongue, who recognized creative talent when he heard it, reworked the narratives into his own style until his recitations were considered works of art, and Finn named him officially as chief poet to the Fíanna.

The truth, in the high summer of the Fíanna, took on a very strange shape.

As Cormac commented to his latest wife, "It does no harm. Indeed, it does a great deal of good. The Fénian stories win battles for me without us even having to fight. The royal historians know the facts and the ordinary people know the wild tales, and that's as it should be. It keeps both happy."

Finn married Manissa and installed her at Almhain, but spent little time with her. There was no repetition of the idyll with Sive. In his mind, he considered her as a requirement for the Rígfénnid Fíanna, as essential to the status of that office as the other aristocratic trappings he was accruing.

In addition to a druid, a physician, a steward, and a chief poet, he had cupbearers at Almhain and doorkeepers and horn players and sewing-women and an official candlemaker, and assistants to all of them. His pack of dogs was enlarged to include a fine selection of greyhounds, not as large as Bran and Sceolaun but better for hunting small game.

When Finn was not fighting, he was hunting. Manissa complained that he hunted to excess. "It is not normal," she told her attendants, "for a man of rank to spend all his time out on the bog or the mountain, following hounds. Surely he has plenty of others who could keep us well supplied with game."

When she said the same thing to Finn, he gave her a look so chilling she never mentioned it again. There was something wild in his eyes, something she could not begin to understand.

She was not sure she wanted to. Living with Finn Mac Cool was like living with something only half-tamed, elusive and unpredictable—and probably dangerous.

Manissa was careful not to rouse his temper.

Sometimes he was gone for a fortnight at a time, with just Caurag his chief huntsman and the hounds. He did not take porters on these expeditions, nor did he bring back game. But Manissa, fearing him though he had never raised a hand to her, did not question him. "There are some things," she advised her attendants, "it's better for a wife not to know."

Even Caurag did not know the entire reason for those driven, solitary forays. He knew only that he had strict orders about what hounds to bring, and how to treat any animal they flushed. He knew that Finn continued, summer and winter, to search with an unreasoning passion for a particular red doe.

When Cainnelsciath informed Finn, "Bebinn says your wife is with

child, and the portents indicate a daughter," Finn's reaction was typi-
cally unpredictable. He went at once to his chief huntsman.

"Prepare for a long hunting trip," he ordered Caurag.

He did not want to watch Manissa swell with his child. He remembered Sive carrying Oisin. That was the image burned in his brain. He
was, he realized, pleasantly fond of Manissa; she was warm and kind and
calm and undemanding. He had no quarrel against her, and he would
be proud to have children.

But she was not Sive.

The anguish flared up in him, the need to know if Sive lived, if she
had been taken from him, if she had deserted him. He had never stopped
asking himself those questions. Only in the heat of battle was he able to
forget them, but on starry nights or full-moon nights, or when the soft
green wind blew in the tops of the trees, pain came flooding back. Pain
and the need to go on looking for her.

Over a long period of time, Finn had been systematically quartering
Erin, seeking some trace. Although she had never been willing to talk
about her people, her accent was undeniably western. So when he sought
Sive, he always faced the setting sun.

Having exhausted the midlands, he determined this time to go all the
way to the great sea, the western coast of the island, and follow the
limestone north from the Burren and Galway Bay, through the home-
land of Clan Morna and even farther north. It was late in the year; he
expected no battles to break out to interfere with his plan.

Having horses to ride made such long journeys easier. He rode the
chestnut mare and took a second horse to be a pack animal so that
Caurag could devote all his attention to the hounds.

"Are you certain you don't want at least an escort of three fíans?" his
steward asked worriedly.

"I do not, Garvcronan. Do you think there's a warrior in Erin by now
who doesn't know who I am? I'm safe enough, particularly so because I
travel alone. It's obvious I'm not seeking battle."

Garvcronan was not reassured, but like Manissa, he did not argue. He
had seen Finn angry and did not want to repeat the experience.

It was the season when flax was rotting in the ponds preparatory to
being gathered and separated into strands for weaving into linen. The
appalling stench of the disintegrating fibres hung in the air like a
miasma as Finn made his way west across the central plain, then slanted
northward.

"Have you a particular hunting ground in mind?" Caurag asked,
thankful that his bandy legs were tireless. The hounds trotting in a pack
around him lifted their ears at the sound of his voice.

Bran was closest to Finn's horse. Rather than look back at Caurag, the hound automatically looked up at Finn's face, anticipating an answer.

Finn half-turned on the mare's back. "I've heard talk of fine herds of red deer around *Beann Gulban,* Gulban's Mountain," he said.

"Ben Bulben?" Caurag repeated in his own accent. "That's a desperate long way to go for deer when there are plenty to be found closer to home."

"We've spoken of this before," Finn said over his shoulder. "The true hunter is always seeking something . . . exceptional."

"Exceptional." Caurag said under his breath to the pack of hounds surrounding him, "By the seven stars, I hope someday to see the deer exceptional enough to satisfy Finn Mac Cool."

The hounds laughed up at him.

As they approached the northwestern coast, Finn chose to go as far as the sea before turning to travel northward. The limestone Burren and Galway Bay lay behind him, and dark clouds were massing in the north, but the sky over the ocean was still clear, its Atlantean light illuminating the green-and-grey hills as they rolled toward Gulban's Mountain, which waited like a crouching lion with its feet buried in heather.

They camped for the night beside a narrow strip of white-gold beach and moved on with first light. Finn rode slowly as the day grew brighter, enjoying the late-season beauty of the countryside. A poem began to stir in him. It struggled to break through the trapped pain that was always inside him; always Sive.

He held the mare to an easy walk so he could take time to appreciate the moss campion and mountain avens, past their bloom but still interesting to him in structure and shade of leaf. His eyes delighted in the brilliant purple saxifrage contrasting with rich green ferns. Immersed in beauty, he began to weave words in his mind as the flax-makers would weave flax.

The chestnut mare snorted loudly and shied to her left. Finn halted her and stroked her neck while his eyes searched for the source of her fright.

"What is it?" called Caurag, hurrying up to him.

"I don't know, I don't see . . . I do! There! Over there, trying to hide in the heather!"

Finn slid from his horse and walked forward very slowly, holding out his hand. At that moment Bran and Sceolaun bonded past him, barking with recognition and joy.

A small figure emerged from concealment in the heather. It was a nearly naked little boy . . . with Sive's features.

22

 CAURAG HAD NEVER SEEN—OR EVEN IMAGINED—FINN Mac Cool crying. He stared thunderstruck as Finn swept the boy into his arms and wept uncontrollably.

At first the child struggled, but when his strength could not prevail against Finn's, he subsided. Caurag glimpsed the curve of his brow and one huge dark eye peering past the man's heaving shoulder.

Sceolaun stood on her hind legs with her forefeet braced against Finn's body as she attempted to lick every portion of the boy's uncovered flesh. Bran, more dignified, waited quietly, but the hound's feathery tail was waving a wild welcome.

"Do you know this little lad?" an astonished Caurag asked.

Finn did not hear him. He was aware of nothing but the child in his arms who smelled like Sive. Something tore in him, a sheet of white pain like ice breaking on a frozen river.

"Where is your mother?" he asked through his tears.

The boy began to squirm again. "Put me down."

Finn struggled to regain control of himself. "Where is your mother?" he asked again, more insistently.

"Put me down!" The boy's piping voice was clear and sharp with a note of command out of all proportion to the speaker.

"You must have a mother. Tell me where she is so I can take you to her."

The child redoubled his efforts to break free. With calculated cunning, he drove one knee into Finn's midriff and kicked hard lower down with his other foot.

The child was stronger than he looked. Finn grunted with pain. Caurag fought to keep from laughing, but Bran, whose loyalties were never divided, snarled at the boy.

Keeping a tight hold on the child's arm, Finn set the boy down. "I must know where your mother is," he demanded. "I have to find her, don't you understand?"

The little boy whipped his scrawny body back and forth in Finn's grip until the single piece of deerskin clumsily arranged around his hips fell away.

"Bring something to wrap him in and something to tie him with," Finn ordered Caurag.

When the child was bound with leather thongs and enveloped in Finn's spare tunic, which was large enough to hobble him effectively, Finn vaulted back onto the mare and Caurag handed the boy up to him.

He sat the boy crosswise on the mare's withers and fixed him with a stern look. "Now direct us to your people. I am Rígfénnid Fíanna, and I command it."

The term obviously meant nothing. The child glared at him.

Finn tried a change of tactics. "How old are you? Six winters? Seven summers, would that be right?"

"Don't know," the lad muttered.

"Seven summers," Finn said as if to himself, his thoughts drifting. "Seven summers since Sive . . ." She ran through his mind in a shaft of sunlight, and the pain that leaped in him was so sudden and sharp he winced.

The boy took advantage of Finn's lack of concentration to hurl himself from the horse. But Bran instantly caught him by the back of Finn's tunic and held him until Caurag picked him up. This time, once the boy was seated in front of him, Finn took an additional strip of leather and bound the two of them together.

"You wanted something exceptional," Caurag commented. "I would say you've found it."

"Tell me where you live, and with who," Finn asked the boy one more time. "I mean you no harm, nor them either. Just take me to them. To your mother. I beg of you, take me to her!"

The child stared up at his face and said nothing.

"We'll find them on our own, then. Bran! Sceolaun! I need your noses! Backtrack this child!"

Had any other man issued such an order to any other hounds, Caurag would have laughed. But he had observed Finn's relationship with these two over many hunting seasons and he knew they understood him as if all three spoke the same language.

Bran and Sceolaun promptly began quartering through the heather, searching. When Bran gave tongue and set off at a run, the others followed, Caurag running almost as fast as Finn's galloping mare.

The trail flanked Ben Bulben and led at last to a wide, well-concealed valley fringed by trees, with a small stream fed by a waterfall at its head.

As Finn galloped into the valley, he saw the last of a herd of deer scattering into the woods beyond the waterfall.

"My people!" the child cried.

Finn reined in the mare. "What do you mean, your people?" His heart shook his body with its thundering.

The child clamped his stubborn little jaws and did not answer.

"Have you a name?"

Continued silence.

Finn drew a deep breath. "If I called you Oisin, would it mean anything to you?"

Caurag came panting up just in time to hear this last. "Do you think it could be?" he gasped, gulping air.

The child, silent, fiddled with the knots of the thongs.

Finn and Caurag and the hounds methodically searched the valley and the woods beyond, but the only trace they found of any human agency was a smear of soot on stones where a fire had once burned. A few charred sticks, a couple of gnawed bones, and broken nutshells were all that remained of whoever had camped there. The ashes were cold and scattered.

But Bran sniffed around the site a long time. Then the great hound sat down and emitted a howl that raised the hackles on Caurag's neck.

"What happened here? You must tell me!" Finn demanded of the child.

Something in his tone at last loosened the little boy's tongue. "There was . . . a man," he said slowly, searching for words from a limited vocabulary. "A dark man. With us. Sometimes. He had a stick. He hit her . . ."

"Her!" The word leaped from Finn's mouth. "Who? Your mother? What was her name? You must tell me her name! And who struck her? *Ochone,* who could ever strike her!" The very thought was a torment to him.

The child frowned in concentration, pleating with wrinkles that forehead so like Sive's. "The man . . . shouted at her. Sometimes. He went away. He came back. He hit her. One day . . . he made her go with him. She did not want to. He hit her, he made her go and leave me. She looked back at me with rain on her face." His narrative powers exhausted, the child fell silent and stared up at Finn.

The tortured man wanted to beat his head with his fists. But he fought to remain calm as he asked, "Do you think he killed her? That dark man who took her away?"

"Don't know," the boy muttered. He seemed to shrink into himself. "She never came back for me."

"Fire and water, earth and sky!" groaned Finn Mac Cool.

In spite of their most diligent searching, he and Caurag could find no trace of the child's past, or of his kin. At last, defeated by time, Finn knew they must return east and prepare for the winter to come.

He took the little boy with him.

Time spent in Finn's company began to smooth away some of the child's wildness. He grew accustomed to having enough food to eat, and to sleeping beside Finn at night, the two of them wrapped in one mantle. He spoke little, but he listened to the two men talking and began to add some of their words to his own small supply. The woman he referred to as "her" he never called by name, as if unaware she had one.

He accepted Finn's calling him Oisin.

They took him home to Almhain of the White Walls.

On the way, Finn told the boy stories. The child sat on the mare's withers and listened, absorbing everything.

"Almhain will be your inheritance," Finn promised. "It was mine. I am entitled to build my stronghold there because it comes to me through the blood. That entitlement will be yours. We shall tell the historians your genealogy, so you can prove your right to all that is mine.

"You will be a man of high rank, Oisin. I've made certain of that, even before I knew there was . . . an Oisin. As son of the Rígfénnid Fíanna, you will be welcomed in every dwelling in Erin and permitted to stand at the right hand of every king. Och, you're going to have a good life!"

The child listened gravely, his huge eyes never leaving Finn's face.

When they reached Almhain, Finn proceeded to introduce Oisin as his son. He explained, "A dark druid stole Sive and her infant from me, but I never ceased looking for them. The druid put her under an enchantment to hide her from me, but I knew Bran and Sceolaun would recognize her no matter what shape she took. When at last they did find something of her, it was this boy they found, however. Oisin, who was born here, has come home!"

Cainnelsciath was not totally happy with this version of recent history. He approached Finn in private and told him, "You make a mistake by accusing a druid of stealing your wife. Why are you doing that?"

"I'm only telling what I know," Finn explained patiently. "Sive, like me, has the blood of the Tuatha Dé Danann in her. She must have; it's the only thing that explains her magical abilities."

"Magical abilities?" Cainnelsciath raised an eyebrow. "I never saw any indication that—"

"She could shapechange," Finn confided.

"She could? How do you know?"

"And me married to the woman? I knew everything about her!" Finn declared hotly. "Because she was of Danann blood, the druids feared her. Not you, I'm not blaming you for any of this, Cainnelsciath. Other druids." Finn waved his hand vaguely. "They took her from me with a powerful enchantment. She would never have left me otherwise.

"The dark man who held her and made her abandon our child struck her with a stick, Oisin tells me. It must have been a druid's rod; nothing else would have had power over her. They made her abandon the child because it was my child. But I found him anyway, and I've brought him home. Rejoice for us, Cainnelsciath!"

Later, speaking of this to Red Ridge, Cainnelsciath said, "I've read the signs and I find nothing in them to confirm this tale of Finn's. It doesn't even make sense . . . except to him."

"If it makes sense to him," Red Ridge replied, "then I accept it."

So did Manissa. While she was astonished to see her husband arrive at Almhain with a little boy riding in front of him, she was mindful of the law. "I shall foster this child as if it were my own," she promised Finn.

Under Brehon Law, the institution of fosterage underpinned much of Gaelic society. The personal relationships upon which both tribal and military alliances depended were developed and reinforced through fosterage. Members of the warrior aristocracy routinely exchanged children, and foster parents were often regarded with more affection than birth parents. The lower classes also practiced fosterage, however, including the taking in of orphans. Gaelic society, in which clan and tribe became extended family, was structured to prevent any child's living as an orphan. Even Finn Mac Cool had been fostered by two old women.

There were two forms of fosterage, fosterage of affection and paid fosterage. In either case, the fosterers were required by law to maintain and educate the child according to its rank in society.

Determining Oisin's rank in society provided a problem for the brehons. When the situation became known, Flaithri had a private discussion with Cormac Mac Airt.

"Your Rígfénnid Fíanna insists the boy is a child of his siring," the chief brehon said, waving his hands in the air. "We accept his word, of course. Normally, any claimed child of a father begins life in the same level of society as that father, and may expect to command a commensurate honour price. However, with Finn Mac Cool, we have something of a problem."

"Always," Cormac interjected dryly.

"Finn began life as a Fir Bolg," Flaithri continued, "member of a subjugated race, commanding no higher honour price than one of the unfree. When he joined the Fíanna, his honour price increased to the value of his weapons, but his rank in society did not increase. Even a Rígfénnid Fíanna had never been accorded the privileges one of the nobility expects.

"But Finn Mac Cool has drastically altered the standing not only of

the Fíanna, but of their commander. His men are respected and welcomed everywhere, and he is given hospitality by princes. He lives and
behaves like a member of the nobility. Furthermore, Cormac, you have
made no effort to discourage this behaviour. If anything, you have
encouraged it."

"I need Finn," Cormac said simply. "I do what I can to reward him
for his services."

"Your rewards are quite unprecedented, if I may say so."

"It is not the function of the brehons to criticize my handling of the
Fíanna," Cormac replied, his voice hardening. "You make and interpret
law, you do not run the military."

Flaithri nodded. "Agreed. But the law permeates society and regu-
lates its members at every level. In order to be of valuable service to the
people for whom it was designed, the law must be flexible; it must grow
and change with changing circumstances. Finn Mac Cool is a perfect
example. We need to rethink his personal position, as well as that of
members of the Fíanna. Until a new definition of rank applying to him
and to them is determined, we cannot assign rank and honour price to
his claimed son."

"People have often moved both up and down within the levels of
status," Cormac observed.

"Indeed. But this is the first time in the long memory of the poets that
some Fir Bolg have become equal to the Milesians."

Cormac stiffened. "They are not . . ." he began angrily. Then he
paused. As Flaithri waited, he forced himself to examine reality. "In
fairness, they are," he said at last. "And I would rather be remembered
as a fair and just king than as a successful warlord and bloodletter."

"So you shall," Flaithri affirmed. "Until the mountains fall and the
seas rise, the poets will celebrate you as the wisest king ever to rule in
Erin, a man who cherished the law as much as the brehons do and let no
person be treated unjustly.

"But as to this matter of Finn Mac Cool . . ." Flaithri's voice abandoned hyperbole and turned practical, "is he entitled in your judgment
to what he claims?"

"He is, through his own achievement."

"Including his claim to Almhain through inheritance? I thought you
gave it to him."

Cormac lifted one eyebrow. "Through inheritance?"

"He has informed the genealogists that his mother was of the Tuatha
Dé Danann—and his wife Sive also. He says his son Oisin is thus doubly
entitled to Almhain after him."

Cormac's second eyebrow joined the first. "Do the genealogists accept this?"

"They will if the brehons do. But, as you know, we are prohibited from making any judgment on the word of one man only. Will you support Finn's claim?"

The king stroked his beard, where silver threads now outnumbered the gold. He gnawed his underlip, realized it looked like the mannerism of a worried man, and stopped.

Flaithri cleared his throat.

Cormac continued to stroke his beard. Then he drew a deep breath. His expression cleared as if his troubled face was wiped calm by a resolute hand.

"It may happen that even a wise man erects an edifice upon a single pillar," Cormac said. "Having done so, he would be unwise to fail to reinforce the pillar in every way he can. Tell the genealogists I vouch for Finn's claim. He once revealed his history to me."

Bowing, Flaithri left the king's chamber. When he had gone, Cormac sat for a long time stroking his beard. "That wretched Finn," he said at last, heaving a sigh.

At the next Assembly, that wretched Finn sat on a carved bench in the Banquetting Hall. The upper end of the hall was reserved for poets—and for historians and brehons and genealogists—as well as the noblest of the noble. Finn Mac Cool sat between them and the king.

Flaithri himself made the announcement. "The brehons here convened, having examined and debated the law as it pertains to the last year, have found areas where change is needed.

"Therefore, tonight we announce a change in the rank and privileges of the Rígfénnid Fíanna. From this time forth, the man who commands the army of Tara is entitled to receive fifty swift riding horses, fifty milch cows, fifty heavy beeves, fifty sheep with the fleece on them, and fifty deep-bellied hogs each year, as his share of the tribute paid to the king of Tara from his tributaries.

"Likewise, he shall be given twelve gold cups, twelve drinking horns, and twelve high-sided carts with sufficient oxen to pull them, and stores of corn to fill them. Barley and wheat and oats are his to the value of six bondwomen."

Before those assembled had time to express their surprise at this enormous largesse, Flaithri continued, "Furthermore, from this night forward, the honour price of the Rígfénnid Fíanna, the price that must be paid to his family for damage done to him, is to the value of twelve bondwomen."

There was a concerted gasp the length of the hall. "The king my father only commands an honour price of fourteen bondwomen!" cried a prince of the Laigin.

Cormac fixed him with a stern eye. "You question this judgment?"

In an eyeblink, the rígfénnidi stationed around the great hall had their hands on the hilts of their swords.

The Laigin prince hesitated.

Cormac gave a crisp nod to Flaithri, who went on smoothly. "In accordance with this rank, the sons of the Rígfénnid Fíanna are to be educated in the skills to which princes' sons are entitled. They are to learn chess and board games, horse riding, and swimming in lakes, and to sing with a clear voice. His daughters are to be taught sewing and flower plaiting and to embroider with fine needles. They are also to be allowed property sufficient to make them wives of equal dignity for chieftains and princes of the tribes."

The prince of the Laigin drew in a sharp breath. As one man, the rígfénnidi turned their heads toward him.

He bit his lip and said nothing.

"He's not quite as stupid as he looks," Conan said in a low voice to Red Ridge.

The other replied, "He can't be too pleased to learn there's what amounts to a new king in his territory."

Conan grinned a rare grin. "but what can he do about it? Apply to the king of Tara?"

Those nearest them laughed outright.

As he listened to Flaithri, Finn had closed his eyes. In the darkness behind his lids, she came to him. Sive. Sive, he said, I have given our son the status of a prince.

There was, of course, grumbling and resentment in some quarters. Warriors who did not belong to the Fíanna hated seeing others of their kind advanced so far above them. But they did not openly rebel. The unprecedented step of allowing members of a subjugated tribe to move so far up the social scale meant new opportunities for everyone of ability. This lesson was not lost on the meanest leather-tanner in the most stinking pit. What Finn Mac Cool had done, others might do. Achievement would be rewarded, whatever its source.

To Cormac's delight, this conferred new admiration on him. "Cormac Mac Airt is the most noble, the most generous, of all kings!" poets claimed the length of the land. "He shares his prosperity as no man has done before him!"

Finn actually had Fergus Honey-Tongue compose a long, highly coloured praise-poem to this effect and recite it everywhere they went.

Manissa was pleased with the inflowing of wealth to Almhain. She expanded the household at Almhain of the White Walls to take in more fosterlings. "Look around," she would say complacently to visitors. "Can you tell which of these little ones was born to the wife of a chieftain and which to the wife of a woodcutter? We have both here. Finn insists we foster them without regard to their rank, except in the matter of their education. He is a good-hearted man," she added proudly.

Sometimes when she was not aware he was watching, Finn stood in the shadows, gazing thoughtfully at Manissa. "She is a good woman," he remarked to Cailte. "She does everything a chief wife should do."

"But . . . ?" enquired Cailte, always sensitive to the tone of Finn's voice.

"But." Finn looked away, shadows in his eyes. "But."

But there had been only one Sive. And there was only one Oisin. When Manissa bore him one daughter and then another, he was pleased and proud. But it was Oisin he took with him everywhere, Oisin who sat at his feet and listened to his tales at the end of every battle season.

Highly coloured tales they were, in that high summer of the Fíanna. As the king of Tara subdued the other kings and forced submission from them, an increased prosperity made the island of Erin more tempting to invaders from the western coasts of Alba and the land of the Britons. Foreigners crossed the sea in wooden boats, intending to plunder and pillage.

But Finn continually enlarged the Fíanna until Cormac's army was an armed presence the length of the coast, meeting beaching boats with irresistible battle-lust.

"The greatest kings in the world send armies against us!" Finn boasted in the hall when he had been drinking ale throughout the night from one of his gold drinking cups. "But we defeat them all! No king can stand against us!"

No one contradicted him publicly. Historians elicited and memorized carefully reported, less florid versions of events. But Oisin sat at his father's knee and drank in Finn's words instead of ale.

To Manissa's sorrow, she seemed able to bear only daughters to Finn. When their fourth was born, she told him, with tears in her eyes, "I wanted to give you a son."

"I have sons," Finn replied, swinging his arm wide to indicate the fosterling thronging his fort.

"I meant a son like . . . like Oisin. A son of your heart."

He was surprised that she understood this. He had not looked for sensitivity from her. He no longer looked for sensitivity from anyone. It was the source of too much pain.

"You should take another wife to give you sons," Manissa insisted, mindful of her duty.

"Cormac Mac Airt has only a few sons, though he has many wives. Most of his children are daughters. Don't fret about it, Manissa."

But for once, she could not obey. She kept on bringing up the subject until at last Finn mentioned it to Cormac himself.

"My chief wife thinks I should take a second wife."

Cormac lifted his eyebrows. "You're lucky in your women," he remarked enviously. "Have you a woman in mind? The smith's daughter was finally forced to take another man for husband, you know, but—"

"My chief wife is of noble blood," Finn said. "And my honour price is the equivalent of twelve bondwomen. I don't think it appropriate to marry a smith's daughter now." His voice was cool. He had not realized Cruina had married someone else.

"The arrogance of princes," Cormac commented as if to himself.

"What?"

"Nothing. I was just . . . you want a noble wife, then?"

"I didn't say I wanted one at all, I merely said Manissa keeps suggesting it."

"She feels guilty for not giving you sons and this is her way of easing that guilt," the king told Finn.

"Are you sure?"

"I have an instinct about people," Cormac said, though he wondered silently just how good his instincts were when it came to Finn Mac Cool.

"If it means so much to Manissa, I'll take a second wife," Finn subsequently told Cailte.

The thin man bit back the impulse to laugh. "Kind of you to do it for her."

"I think so," Finn agreed in all seriousness. He did not, in spite of what Cailte thought, long for a new woman. Women were not uppermost in his thoughts at all—with the exception of Sive, who was always there, her face softened by time, the memory more beautiful than the person had been. The pain unfaded.

But he set himself to the task of selecting a second contract wife as zealously as he did everything else. She must be an enhancement to the new prestige of the Rígfénnid Fíanna. She must be a statement flung in the teeth of the world.

"She must," he told Cailte, "be at least as good as Cael's Creide."

"Perhaps one of Creide's sisters?"

"My rank is now higher than Cael's," Finn reminded Cailte, dismissing the idea.

Winter was drawing down. At Almhain of the White Walls, the druid Cainnelsciath would be bringing boughs of holly and yew inside to keep the spirit of the evergreens alive through the cold season until time to burn them in the springtime bonfires. On the day before Finn planned to leave Tara for home, he was hurrying across the lawn—in reality a sea of mud churned by many feet—when he bumped into a slender figure hurrying in the opposite direction, talking to itself and unaware of him.

Finn paused to extend a steady hand. His fingers touched an arm in a pleated linen sleeve, and a bright face peeped out at him from beneath a blue hood.

"You've made me forget my poem," the girl chided him.

She was some fourteen winters, just reaching the age for marrying, and her accents were purely Milesian. Finn dragged his thoughts back from wherever they had been to put a name to the face.

"Ailvi! You've grown so I hardly recognized you. It *is* Ailvi?"

"It is," she said softly, suddenly shy.

"What are you doing reciting poetry?"

"I'm not reciting, I'm composing. Or trying to."

"And you a woman?"

"Women can be poets. They can even be satirists."

"Some of the most cruel satirists are women," Finn agreed. "I trust that's not your intention?"

She smiled. "Not at all. My poems are about the way the birds sing and the shadows race each other across the face of the mountains. I love beautiful things. I try to capture them in poetry." Her voice faded. Suddenly she was aware she was talking to the fabled Rígfénnid Fíanna himself and babbling on like a child.

But Finn did not seem to mind. His eyes kindled with interest. "Would you recite one of your compositions for me?"

Ailvi stared at the sea of mud on which they stood, afraid to meet his eyes. Finn in turn studied the sweep of her lashes against her cheeks, seeing another form of beauty and, as always, captivated by it.

For Finn's final night of the year at Tara, the king had ordered a special banquet served to the commander and his officers. To no one's surprise, Cailte Mac Ronan was the first of the rígfénnidi to arrive at the Banquetting Hall, carrying a hollow belly full of appetite. But though the trumpets were blown again and again and the servitors waited impatiently, Finn Mac Cool did not appear.

At last Cormac sent a runner to find him. "I will take no insult from any man, not even him," the king said through tight lips.

But at that moment Finn entered the hall—through the Door of Equality, customarily used only by kings.

Without apologizing for his tardiness, he took his seat on the carved bench and signalled to a cupbearer to serve him. Only when he had taken a brimming drink did he turn toward Cormac with a broad smile.

"It's been a good day for me," he announced warmly.

His voice infused with a commensurate degree of coolness, Cormac replied, "How very pleasant." He surveyed the contents of a huge tray being proffered by two bondwomen: stewed eels, ham and bacon, pots of curds and cheese, cakes of oats and barley, blood puddings, and sausages of boar meat from the autumn's hunting. He selected a sausage and a honey-cake filled with crushed nuts, took a bite of the cake, chewed, swallowed, washed it down with mead from his cup. Then he turned toward Finn. "And was your day so grand you forgot about the night entirely?" he enquired.

"Och, I didn't forget." Finn stretched out an arm and boldly helped himself to the tray being held for Cormac. He took the largest slab of bacon. "I've been looking forward to it because I have an announcement to make."

Rising to his feet, he shouted to be heard above the din of feasting, "I'm going to take a second wife!"

Some people stopped in mid-chew to listen.

"I'm going to marry the High King's daughter!" cried Finn Mac Cool.

23

 CORMAC CHOKED ON A MOUTHFUL OF SAUSAGE.
Before he could stop himself, Goll Mac Morna laughed out
loud.

A wave of astonishment swept the hall like air rushing to the eye of
a storm.

At its centre stood Finn Mac Cool, clearly enjoying the moment.

Cormac spat the offending morsel into his palm. "What did you just
say?" he asked in disbelief.

"I thought I spoke loudly enough for everyone to hear. I said I shall
marry your daughter Ailvi." Spreading the sweetest of smiles across his
face until even his savage cheekbones seemed softer, Finn added in a
carrying voice, "If you think me worthy of her, of course."

His eyes locked with Cormac's.

People held their breaths to listen.

I brought this on myself, the king thought ruefully. Goll warned
me—how many seasons ago? That's why he laughed just now, and I don't
blame him.

Finn knows perfectly well that after all he's accomplished for me, I
can hardly refuse him publicly. I've set the precedent of giving him
anything he asks.

But . . . Ailvi! A girl I might happily have married to a foreign king,
perhaps forming bonds with the tribes of Briton.

Ailvi married to a man of the Fir Bolg.

Cormac writhed inwardly.

A second thought came hard on the heels of the first. If Finn's claim
was true—and by now no one knew for sure—then Cormac's daughter
might someday bear a child with Danann blood. An infiltration of the
enemy into the royal family of Tara . . . where they had once held sway.

There is a dreadful inevitability to this, Cormac told himself, if Finn is to be believed.

Is Finn to be believed?

He stared at his Rígfénnid Fíanna, who stared back placidly.

"Have you any objections?" Finn enquired. "I assumed I had your support in all things." He opened his eyes very wide.

Deep within them, something . . . shifted.

Cormac saw it.

Now is my chance, he thought. Now is my chance to put him in his place and keep him there, before he makes my place his. My Tara his . . .

The Thing in Finn's eyes shifted again. Cormac had the sudden chilling conviction that the Rígfénnid Fíanna was reading his thoughts as a wolf reads the thoughts of the stag at bay.

The assemblage in the crowded hall leaned forward to a man, waiting to hear what the king would say.

Cormac was skewered by his own sense of fairness. Finn had done nothing to merit either distrust or abandonment. In fact, he had behaved exactly opposite. No king with a reputation for justice could deny him now.

"I have no objections," Cormac said in a voice that did not quaver. "If she is willing, my daughter Ailvi may be wife to Finn Mac Cool."

The news would sweep the land like flame. The Rígfénnid Fíanna was marrying a king's daughter—and not just the daughter of a tribal king, a ríg tuatha, but the daughter of a man he had publicly described as the High King. The *Ard Ríg,* overlord of Erin. King of the kings.

In one bold step, Finn had elevated Cormac to unprecedented rank, then claimed kinship with that rank through marriage. He had changed Erin as surely as Cormac had done.

"We're all princes now!" Donn boasted to Cael.

"Fosterlings of the overlord Finn Mac Cool," growled Conan.

Fergus reproved him. "That's an incautious and ungrateful remark."

"We don't have to be cautious. We're the Fíanna."

"You're what Finn made you," Goll interjected, deliberately leaving himself out of that description. "And you need to be more cautious than ever now. Finn's given you a lot to live up to. You can't just bash right and left with no thought of the consequences, any more than Cormac can."

Blamec laughed. "I wonder if Cormac considered the consequences when he began being so generous with Finn."

Goll said soberly, "He did, but not thoroughly enough. Now Finn's outplayed him. Step by step and move by move—and it looking almost accidental—Finn's outplayed him. I am frankly astonished."

"You always did underestimate him," Cailte remarked.

"Did I? I don't think so. I knew from the beginning that he had a certain wild cunning."

"He has more than that. He's very clever."

"And he can do magic," Cael asserted. "He could not have accomplished what he has without the aid of magic."

All the while, the stories told of Finn and his Fíanna were multiplying. With each telling, the storyspinners—who had not the noble poets' obligation to truth—added their own vivid imaginings, making of Finn and his companions the men they would like to be themselves. So the tales grew.

It was told as truth that Finn fought a great battle on the White Strand against the Dog-headed people and the Cat-headed people and defeated them every one with tricks and guile.

It was told that his rígfénnidi, Dubh and Dun and Glas, attacked the stronghold of the Sídhe on the river Boyne and seized a bottomless cauldron, which they gave to their commander.

It was told that for Finn's wedding, the fifty best sewing-women in Erin were put into a fort with a thousand beeswax candles and were labouring night and day to make new garments for Finn and all the Fíanna.

It was told, and told, and told . . .

Finn took Ailvi as a wife of the first degree on Beltaine. No one challenged his claim to equal rank, and if he had demanded equal property of her, Cormac could have provided it, though he was glad the demand was not made.

Manissa was not displeased with the match. She liked Ailvi, who was cheerful and young and would be a great help in caring for the children who multiplied like Finn Mac Cool stories, with more fosterlings coming to Almhain every season.

"I wish Finn really had been given a bottomless cauldron," she confided to Garvcronan the steward. "Sometimes I think we have enough children to make a new army."

"If we do," the steward told her in his rasping voice, "young Oisin will be its commander."

Oisin attended Finn's wedding to Ailvi. In that moment when Finn joined the young woman and the brehon beside the Beltaine pole, his eyes inadvertently fell on Oisin's face.

Sive's face.

The words he meant to speak dried on Finn's tongue.

"Are you ill?" the brehon asked, seeing him go pale.

The reply was swift and harsh. "I'm never ill. Proceed!"

Finn made his vow to Ailvi in a tight, clipped voice, not lingering over words or meaning. She took more time with her vows, savouring them. From time to time she glanced up at him, admiring the magnificent Rígfénnid Fíanna with his colourful cloak trimmed with wolf fur, his massive brooch on one shoulder, his startlingly silver hair. His strong, weathered face.

"She looks like a child beside him," one of her attendants murmured to another.

"Och, he's old, that one. I've been hearing stories about Finn Mac Cool for years."

Finn's keen ears heard them. Old, he mused. And I a young man still.

Almost. Thirty winters. Is that old?

Is that old, Sive?

That night he stayed at the wedding feast until almost dawn. When at last he went to the new house where Ailvi was waiting, his path led him past the door of the house still occupied by Manissa. He found her standing in the doorway, watching for him. "I wish you joy of her," she called softly to him, "and many sons."

Finn walked over to her. Feeling slightly awkward, he said, "You're a good woman, Manissa."

Her voice was wistful in the fading night. "Is that all I am? A good woman?"

He did not want to hurt her, so he chose not to understand. "That is everything a woman should be," he said positively. "Go back to your bed now. It may be Beltaine, but there's an edge to the wind and I don't want you chilled."

She turned obediently and went inside. The oak door creaked on its iron hinges.

There was a calm pool at the center of Manissa that reminded Finn of Sive, but she was not Sive. This new one . . . would he find something of Sive in her?

His steps quickened as he approached the new house.

Ailvi had fallen asleep waiting for him. She lay stretched on the bed with her head pillowed on one outflung arm. Befitting her new married status, her attendants had bound her hair. As she waited during the long night, her hair had become disarranged, and curls and tendrils were escaping the thin gold fillets that circled her brow.

Gold because she was a king's daughter.

I have married the daughter of the High King of Erin, Finn reminded himself, exulting.

He studied the lines of her body, revealed by the light of bronze lamps and the dying fire on the hearth. Lying on her side, Ailvi was a mountain range, with shoulder and hip for peaks and a deep valley at the waist.

The silent observer in Finn dispassionately considered the slight roundness of her belly, evidenced by the shadowing of the fine linen gown she wore. Her hips were wide, her belly deep; she could bear many children. She shifted in her sleep as if subliminally aware of his presence. Her eyelids fluttered as she rose toward wakefulness, and her movements caused her gown to drag slightly over what must be a bush of pubic hair.

The silent observer in Finn noted the stirrings of lust.

Finn strode to the bed and rested one knee on it as he leaned forward to take her by the shoulders. "Ailvi? Wife?"

Her eyes opened. They were very large, and for just a moment he thought they were dark brown.

He swiftly closed his own eyes before he could see that they were dark blue after all.

She was not like Manissa. Her textures were different, her responses her own. The entrance to her body was guarded by a dense thicket, and he remembered suddenly, agonizingly, that Sive had scant body hair.

Then he plunged into Ailvi and sought forgetfulness.

The silent observer watched. Saying nothing. Feeling little. Watching.

Finn was a mature man by now, with more control of his physical passion, and he took time with Ailvi. He could feel when she wanted him to be gentle and he obliged her; as she grew more accustomed to him, he could tell when she wanted strength and he gave that too. She was good in bed, he found; better than Manissa, her dimensions more suited to his.

But she was not Sive. He could almost hate Sive for having been so perfect for him that no other woman could equal her.

Or did he just remember her that way? Was time blurring truth, so that he was remembering his own version of Sive, as he remembered his own version of so many other things?

The silent observer seemed to be inside him now, thinking these thoughts to the exclusion of everything else, until he found himself lying on his back with one forearm across his eyes and Ailvi leaning over him anxiously, saying, "What's wrong? Did I do something wrong?"

"Nothing's wrong," he replied thickly. "I'm just catching my breath." He moved his arm and made himself smile up at her. There was strong sunlight filtering through the cracks around the closed door. It must be morning.

"Ah." She accepted his words. She nestled into his shoulder sweetly and he put his arm around her, grateful that she had not chosen the side Sive liked to lie on.

I have to stop this, he thought. It's no good. It wasn't good for Manissa either.

Perhaps these are just the wrong women. Perhaps the bits of Sive I find in them aren't enough. No! Stop that!

Finn Mac Cool lay on his back in the new house at Almhain with a king's daughter in his arms and tried to convince himself he was happy.

Next day he took the hounds and went hunting.

Life at Almhain settled into a new routine that was but an extension of the former one. Ailvi blended seamlessly into Finn's household, which was not so very different from the one she had known at Tara. The Rígfénnid Fíanna was becoming very prosperous, enabling her to continue to live in much the same style she had enjoyed at Tara. The attendants she had brought with her were augmented by Finn's own bondwomen. The only labour required of Finn's second wife was embroidery or helping Manissa with the children.

"So many children!" Ailvi said laughingly to the older woman. "How many of these are Finn Mac Cool's?"

"Most of them are fosterlings," Manissa replied. "The lad called Oisin is his, as are my own brood. Perhaps one or two from marriages of lesser degree, I wouldn't know and he never says. Oisin is his unquestioned favourite, though."

"Is he not fond of children, to have so many fosterlings?"

Manissa considered the question. "I could not say that either. He doesn't talk to me about his feelings. The majority of the fosterlings are the children of chieftainly families who hope sending a son or daughter to Finn Mac Cool will give them advantageous ties with the Fíanna. But that one . . ." she pointed a henna-stained fingertip, "and that one there, and those three over there . . . they are motherless.

"When Finn hears of a child who has no mother, he insists on it being sent here, even if the child's father and kin are able to care for it. Under the law it should go to the father, but Finn insists, and who's to stand against him?"

"Why, I wonder?"

"I don't know that either," Manissa sighed. In silence, the two women watched the scurry of children through Almhain. Then Manissa said softly, "If Finn is fond of me at all, I think it is because I am good at mothering."

With the exception of Conan Maol, Finn's original nine had by now taken wives. Conan responded predictably to the jibes they made at his expense. "Women are nothing but trouble," he insisted, "and I get enough trouble following Finn Mac Cool's banner during battle season."

But he seemed to like Ailvi, to his friends' amusement.

During the winter Finn invited his first companions to make their homes at Almhain and garrison their fíans beyond its walls. The famous white walls were opened again and yet again to allow for expansion as new dwellings were constructed and wives and households installed.

Ailvi enjoyed the company of Finn's men and their women. As a child growing up at Tara, she had been familiar with the names and faces of the more famous members of the Fíanna, but they had not seemed quite real to her, their lives being too different and separate. Now, meeting them in a domestic setting, she found them to be human. She liked surly Conan best of all, for he was a challenge. In an effort to win him and make him smile, she recited bad poetry and told bad jokes until he was devoted to her as he would never be to any other woman.

Of the officers' wives, Ailvi was most intrigued by Creide.

Creide was a woman quite outside the experience of a king's sheltered daughter.

"She carries weapons like a man," Ailvi commented to Conan one day as he watched her carding wool to loom a square for her embroidery. "Yet she talks and behaves like a noblewoman and her clothes are as fine as my own."

Conan, who was sprawled on a bench in the sun outside Ailvi's house, shifted position and pulled away a wisp of wool a passing breeze had stuck to his lip. "Creide likes fighting. I vow by the seven stars, she actually enjoys bashing men. I couldn't tell you why. Most other women who accompany the army are content to forage for us and bind up our wounds, but Creide will wade into a battle as readily as into a river, and she's more ferocious than anyone but Finn himself."

"Yet she's so loving with Cael!" Ailvi marvelled.

"Ask her about it sometime. I suppose women speak of things like that among themselves, don't they?"

"They do," Ailvi agreed. "Sometimes."

"Do it soon, though. Cael and Creide will return to Kerry soon. Theirs is a marriage of the third degree, you know, the Marriage of the Strong Woman, and he has to defend and maintain her property for a certain portion of every year."

"Would you like such a marriage?"

"Not me," the bald man assured her. "I want a marriage where the woman does all the work and I don't have to do anything but watch her do it."

"You're working now. You're helping me."

"I'm sitting down," Conan pointed out.

When Ailvi emerged from her house one morning to find Cael and Creide organizing porters and pack horses for the journey to Kerry, she hastily ordered Garvcronan to supply two bowls of hot broth and some honey-cakes, then invited Creide to sit with her beside her hearth for a time while Cael completed packing. "Let your man do the work," Creide was urged with a smile.

They chatted of running households and of dealing with servants and of the scarcity of good wolf pelts the winter before. When Creide began to stir restlessly and glance toward the doorway, Ailvi summoned enough courage to ask, "Why would a woman as independent as yourself marry at all? Why did you marry Cael?"

Creide sat still, her dyed eyebrows furrowing her forehead in thought for a moment. Then she smiled, and Ailvi realized she was beautiful.

"Because he makes me laugh," she said. "I never laughed before he came to me, and if he were gone from me, I would never laugh again."

That night as they lay in bed together, Ailvi said to Finn, "Do something for me."

"What? This?" His hands moved on her.

"That too. But . . . mind Cael, will you? Don't let anything happen to him."

Finn stopped caressing her in surprise. "I don't let anything happen to my friends," he said.

But such confidence belonged with youth—and the years were passing.

Next battle season saw the boats of the foreigners beaching again on the coasts of Erin, with renewed hopes of conquest and plunder. That summer saw the hardest fighting the Fíanna had done in years. Although he had not reached fifteen winters, the customary age for taking up arms, young Oisin was aglow with the desire to take part and so Finn let him accompany the Fíanna, though with strict orders to stay out of spear distance.

"If you are killed, you'll die twice, because I'll be so angry I'll kill you again myself!" he warned the lad.

A great battle was fought on the White Strand, and Goll Mac Morna distinguished himself above all others on the first day of it. "Sing praise-songs of him," Finn commanded Fergus Honey-Tongue.

On the second day of battle, Finn realized Conan Maol was not actively leading his fíans but seemed to be hovering at the edge of the conflict. "Conan is resting more than he's roaring," Finn told Fergus. "Go to him and urge him into the heart of the battle. He's setting a bad example to the other rígfénnidi. Men won't follow a man who won't lead, and if my officers get in the habit of being in the rear, the only move we can make is to retreat . . . and I won't retreat."

Fergus sought out Conan and did everything he could to urge the hairless man to action, but at best, Conan's response was desultory. "I'm getting too old and too heavy for this," he muttered to his second-in-command. "I'm going to have to let out my belt any day now."

But there was no question of Cael Hundred-Killer letting out his belt.
He was here, there, everywhere, sword flashing, voice shouting encour-
agement to his fíans. Because Creide was with the army to see and
admire him, he excelled himself, desiring to hear Fergus sing praise-
songs of him at the end of the day.

Sometime during the hottest part of the battle, Finn lost sight of him.
There was a fierce skirmish fought above the beach, where trees gave way
to sand like a receding hairline. Eventually the Fianna drove the foreigners back into the surf, where they clambered frantically into their boats
and lifted their oars, anxious to escape. But they left a number of bodies
littering the beach and the woods above.

The women went out to claim them, to tend the wounded and mourn
the dead and dying. Finn was crouching on the beach cleaning his sword
of blood and gore by driving it repeatedly into the sand when he heard
the terrible cry.

It splintered the air like the scream of the Sídhe.

He was on his feet in an instant. "Who's dead?" he cried, fearing the
answer. He had recognized that voice.

She came walking down from the woods alone. On battle days Creide
dressed for fighting, in a tunic like a man's rather than in long robes that
would hamper her movements. Her bare legs and feet were very white,
but her face was paler still.

With her two hands she was pulling the hair out of her head in great
bloody clumps.

Finn ran toward her. Her unseeing eyes looked through him.

He took her by the arm, fearful that she would walk past him into the
sea. Her arm felt like cold stone. "I should never have let you come with
us," he said, as much to himself as to her.

When she spoke, her voice was as hollow as a cry from the depths of
a cave. "And I not to have the dying of him?" she asked reproachfully.
"And I not to take the last breath from his mouth into my mouth to keep
safe for him?"

She shrugged free of Finn and walked back up the beach toward the
trees. Helplessly, Finn followed her. There were other men dead and
other women keening over them, but somehow the members of Finn's
original fían materialized, one at a time, and joined them, until they
entered the sparse strip of woodland and came to the body lying there.

Creide dropped to her knees beside it. With pain etched on every
face, Finn and his companions formed a protective circle around the
pair of them.

Cael's upturned face was calm, the fury of battle wiped clean. Creide
had paused only long enough to straighten his limbs and spread his

cloak over his body, leaving his sightless eyes uncovered to stare up into the branches of the trees. Then she had fled her pain.

But the pain had gone with her. Now she brought it back, brimming. If she bent over him, it would spill out.

She touched his sweat-soaked hair with a tentative hand. Turning her palm upward, she trailed her fingers down the side of his cheek in what was an old gesture between them.

The watching men felt the fingers and the pain.

Even Conan winced.

Creide was of the Gael, and poetry lay deep in her bones. For Cael, for what was loved and lost, she brought it to the surface. Bending over him so that pain poured from her with her tears, Creide wept her lament.

> *The harbour roars, the gulls cry, the waves are keening on the strand.*
> *The hero has drowned in blood.*
> *Sweet-voiced the crane, but she cannot save her nestlings.*
> *The wild dogs take them.*
> *Sorrowful is the wren in the meadow. Her mate lies dead on the grass.*
> Ochone, ochone, *grief to me! My mate lies dead on the grass.*
> *He lay living beside me, and his white body was my joy and delight.*
> *His sweet mouth laughing.*
> *Now waves weep on the shore, and my beauty flows away with the tide.*
> Ochone, ochone, *song of grief! I will love no man after.*

Creide bent lower still, so that what remained of her torn hair fell like a curtain. Stunned by the beauty of her poem, Finn noticed too late that there was a movement behind that curtain. His reflexes were fast, but not fast enough.

Creide drew not her shortsword, but Cael's, and plunged it deep into her body before anyone could stop her.

24

"WE BURIED THEM BOTH IN THE SAME GRAVE," A GRIEV-
ing Finn told Manissa and Ailvi later.

"Many are killed in battle," said the pragmatic Manissa. "It was
a noble death."

But Ailvi's eyes glittered with tears.

The first death of one of his closest companions shook Finn more
than he was willing to admit, even to his women. During the good years,
the years of triumph, he had come to believe they were indeed immortal.
In his imagination they would go on forever, fighting great battles and
always winning, wading through blood and carnage and coming home
unscathed—or at least not fatally wounded. There was not one of them
by now who did not carry many scars. The women tended them and the
physicians treated them and the druids implored the forces of nature on
their behalf, and in time they healed to fight again. Finn's fían, the heart
of the Fíanna.

Until Cael.

His death was like a fatal tear in the essential organ.

Unconsciously, Finn began being more careful with his men. They
began losing occasional battles, mostly small skirmishes that were not
important in themselves, but denied the infallibility of the Fíanna and
encouraged their enemies.

Cormac criticized Finn and they argued, not once but several times,
with increasing rancour.

"I won't sacrifice my men just to please you!" Finn shouted at the
king.

"They're warriors, Finn! Spear targets! That's what they're for, to
fight and die if need be."

"If need be. But not when I can save them by being more careful with
my strategies."

"Being more careful is losing you battles."

"We come back the next day and win."

"Be certain you do," said Cormac Mac Airt.

Winning got harder to do; wounds took longer to heal. When Finn inadvertently glanced into one of Ailvi's mirrors, he saw a man he did not recognize, a man with his seasons carved on his face and reflected in his tired eyes.

But when he looked at Oisin, he saw himself renewed. He began spending much of his time training the boy, making of him as fine a warrior as Finn Mac Cool ever was.

Trying to make him immortal.

He took Oisin everywhere with him, except hunting. A certain sort of hunting.

Like Manissa before her, Ailvi had learned that there were times when a silent mood overtook Finn and he left Almhain without saying good-bye to anyone, taking only his huntsman and his hounds with him.

He never stopped looking for her. As the years passed, the hunt became more dreamlike, less immediate and urgent, a sort of ritual to which Finn was addicted. He could go for a cycle of the moon or more without thinking of Sive if battle season was sufficiently demanding, but then she would drift through his thoughts like a stray beam of sunlight and he would stop where he was, transfixed, and have to fight his way back to the matter at hand.

As soon as circumstances allowed, he would go hunting for her again.

Though the years were passing for Finn, he never imagined Sive as other than he had seen her last. In his mind, she was caught like a fly in amber, glowing with youth. With Bran and Sceolaun, he scoured Erin for a young doe, never an aging one.

Bran and Sceolaun were aging too. They were not as quick to pursue anything that ran; time had substituted wisdom for impetuosity. When they did give chase, however, nothing escaped them. Working together, they were an invincible pair.

Even Caurag, whose favourites were Finn's pack of greyhounds, had to admit that Bran and Sceolaun had no equals in Erin. Because he was an experienced huntsman who took pride in his profession, he could also admit what Finn would not.

"They're getting old," he began telling the Rígfénnid Fíanna. "Grand dogs they are and they've outlasted any I ever heard of, but just look at them, Finn. Sceolaun's gone quite grey around the face, and as for Bran—"

"Bran is perfect," Finn said shortly.

"Perfect indeed, but stiffer on every cold morning. The dawn will come very soon when I blow the horn and old Bran there will not get up."

"Bran runs as fast as ever."

"Because Bran's heart is as big as ever. But it will burst, Finn. Mind my words. Let that dog stay at Almhain by the fire the next time you go hunting, or prepare for sorrow."

But Finn could not leave Bran and Sceolaun behind. Only they could be trusted to recognize Sive in her deer shape. Other hounds might kill her before Finn could stop them.

Together they had hunted her from Ceshcorran to Glenasmole over the years; from the hogback hills of Ulidia to the wolf's tooth mountains of Muma. There were few trails left in Erin that had not felt the feet of Finn Mac Cool, and stories sprang up behind him like crushed grass springing back where a giant has walked.

But he had not found Sive. Of her he had only Oisin, who was dearer to him every day. Even when Ailvi bore him a son they called Cairrel, Oisin was still first in his heart.

After Sive.

Autumn found him in the west again. In the Burren, he and Caurag claimed hospitality of Iruis in his fine stone fort atop Black Head, but Finn was restless. When Iruis asked him to tell stories of the Fíanna to entertain the women and children, Finn responded halfheartedly.

"Is he ill?" Iruis asked Caurag privately. "This is not the man I remember."

"He's not ill with any ailment the physicians can identify," the huntsman replied. "Our Bebinn back at Almhain is as fine a healer and herbalist as any in Erin, but when Finn gets in one of his moods, there's no helping him. It's up then and away, and we must hunt from dawn till dark until he's worked it out of him somehow."

"Hunt for what?"

"A red deer. A doe, to be precise."

"Surely you've found hundreds upon hundreds of deer almost anywhere you looked. This island teems with game."

"It does. But none of them good enough for Finn. He'll go out in spitting sleet or howling wind when the mood is on him," Caurag said sadly, hunching closer to the fire while he had the chance.

Next morning the sleet was indeed spitting. Finn was no sooner awake than he was preparing to go out. Iruis, taking pity on Caurag, took Finn aside and said, "Your man there is exhausted, Finn." He did not point out that Finn's face was also grey with fatigue. "Would it not be wise to let him stop inside on a day like this?"

Finn seemed surprised by the suggestion. He reflected a moment, looking over Iruis's shoulder. "I suppose it would," he decided. "Have your women get some hot broth into him, would you? I'll be back . . . later." He strode through the door with his hounds at his heels before Iruis could think of any other protest to offer.

The day was bitterly cold, precursor of a hard winter. Bran and Sceolaun struck off toward the southeast, and twice they seemed to hit on some sort of spoor only to pull up again, looking back at Finn apologetically.

He was on foot. It was foolish to ride a horse in the Burren, where a misstep could break a leg, so Finn and Caurag had left their animals with a fisherman whose hut was on the black, stony beach of Galway Bay. But as the great broken cakes of limestone receded and Finn and his dogs advanced onto hilly grassland, he began to wish he had the mare under him.

"Once," he confided to Bran when they stopped to make camp in the lee of a hill, "I could have run twice this far by midday and still fought a good battle. But now . . . now it seems wiser to stop for the night and start fresh in the morning, if you're convinced we're going in the right direction."

Bran, who had collapsed at his feet, looked up adoringly at Finn and waved a feathery tail in agreement. Sceolaun already lay stretched with her head on her forepaws, snoring in little snuffles.

Her face was very white, where once it had sported strong red markings from the ears to the eyes.

Finn slept fitfully. In his dreams he was in bed with Sive and her hot hands moved over his body. He groaned once, softly. With a deep sigh, Bran arose and came over to lie down close against him, sharing comfort and warmth.

They renewed the hunt at first light.

Late morning found them rounding the flanks of heather-carpeted Mount Callan. The dogs were panting and slow. Finn reluctantly paused to camp again for a time and let them rest, but then he insisted they push on. He could feel Sive's presence very strongly for some reason, as if she had followed him to this remote place where she had never been and was now experiencing it with him. Was now standing almost at his shoulder, if he could just see her . . . around a hill . . . look along a stream . . .

The day passed fruitlessly. Toward evening Finn had to admit to himself that the chase was accomplishing nothing, merely frustrating him and exhausting his dogs. He resolved to cast them one final time, then make camp for the night and return to Black Head.

But when he whistled and signalled with his arm, Sceolaun merely looked at him. Her expression was eager enough, but her body was past obeying. She sat down on her haunches and whined.

Bran went to her and sniffed her solicitously. Then, with an effort, the giant dog moved off alone in the direction Finn had indicated.

A moment passed before Finn trotted after. "Wait for us here," he ordered Sceolaun. She lay down with a grateful sigh.

Finn followed Bran as dusk settled around them. The sense of Sive's nearness returned. Once or twice Bran looked back, but each time Finn gave the signal to go on. Just beyond this strip of trees, only a little farther . . .

A range of hills called Ceentlea, tree-mantled and craggy, rose before them. Bran stopped, head lifted, then gave tongue again with such rising excitement that Finn began to run.

Following his hound, he bounded up the slopes like a young man. Ahead of him in the twilight, he caught a flash of red.

Red deer, red deer!

He ran faster.

Bran was belling with every stride, the deep, melodious voice of the true hound that knows the reason for its creation. No horn designed by man could match that song of nature, of freedom and excitement. Finn's heart leaped in response.

Running cleared his brain. He told himself quite sensibly, even if we don't find Sive, we'll have had one last good hunt together, the old dog and I. I shan't ask this of Bran again.

He burst through a stand of pines to find himself approaching the summit of a steep slope. Ahead, the ground soon fell away abruptly to form the brow of a crag that overhung a small lake far below. Beyond that point there was only empty sky.

And the deer.

She stood on the very brink of the abyss, silhouetted against the lingering light of the twilit sky.

From the size and shape of her, Finn recognized a young doe, hardly more than a fawn in spite of the lateness of the season. Her slim legs were bunched under her in arrested flight. She was staring fixedly toward the hound racing up the summit to her.

"Sive!" Finn cried with all the power in his lungs.

The deer turned her head toward him. Though he could not possibly have seen her eyes, he thought she looked at him. Then she whirled in one smooth motion and leaped, leaped for freedom, out into space to plunge into the lake fatally far below.

Bran hesitated for a sliver of an instant. The great hound glanced back one last time at Finn, made an assessment of the man and the situation and the agony that only Bran could know, then bounded after the deer again.

Bounded out into space.

Finn's second cry was not remotely human.

He raced forward to fling himself belly-down at the edge of the precipice. He was in time to see the second splash subsiding. Concentric circles spread out and out until they vanished and the surface at last became a smooth, dark mirror, glimmering faintly. Undisturbed.

When Finn had not returned after three nights, Caurag asked Iruis to organize a search party.

"If any man in Erin can look after himself," Iruis replied, "I'd say that man is Finn Mac Cool."

"It is," Caurag agreed. "That's why I'm worried. If something had not happened to him, he would have been back here by now."

"How do you propose to find him in an area so large?"

"Och, that's easy enough. He took Bran and Sceolaun with him, but his other hounds, Lomair and Lomluath and Brod, can track them, no matter where they've gone."

"Across the stone of the Burren?"

"Across the water of the great sea!" Caurag claimed. "These are Finn Mac Cool's hounds we're talking about."

They set off at dawn. The party consisted of a number of armed men and several porters to carry supplies, in case the trail led them far from Black Head, or in case they found Finn injured somewhere and in need of tending.

"I can apply a poultice or bind a broken bone if need be," Caurag assured Iruis. "Finn likes us to be resourceful."

"I hope he's resourceful enough to get out of whatever trouble has been keeping him," Iruis replied.

The sleet Finn had encountered initially had been replaced by a few days of false warmth. Autumnal sunshine poured like honey over the grey slabs of the Burren as if promising that no matter how bleak the winter to come, the days of light would eventually return.

At Caurag's signal, the hounds cast and cast again for a trail. When they found it, they set off toward the southeast, the men following eagerly.

Eventually they found Sceolaun. Starving, shivering, but true to her god, she was sitting on her haunches in the place Finn had left her, waiting for his return.

Caurag was horrified both by her condition and by finding her alone. "This is bad, very bad. Finn would never have gone off and left her like this without returning for her. I knew something had happened to him." He crouched down beside the bitch, who weakly licked his face. "Where is he, Sceolaun? Do you know? Can you take us to Finn? And Bran?"

She got to her feet, painfully. When she tried to walk, she was un-steady. Caurag gathered her into his arms. "We can follow the direction of her gaze," he told Iruis. "She knows which way they went, she can show us that much."

Using Sceolaun's head as a guide, they followed the way Finn had taken. When they neared the region of Ceentlea, she squirmed and Caurag put her down. The search party followed her slow progress as she made her way step by step after Finn. The other hounds stood back and let her lead them, though they could have run ahead easily enough.

At the edge of a small dark lake below an overhanging crag, they found him. Like Sceolaun, he was just sitting. His arms were wrapped around his legs, knees bent, feet flat on the earth. His unmoving gaze was fixed on the surface of the water.

His face was stone.

"What's wrong with him?" Iruis asked in a whisper. "He doesn't seem to see us."

Sceolaun went to Finn and licked his face, but he paid no attention. She stood beside him with her head cocked, studying him. Then she followed the direction of his gaze.

Slowly, one step at a time, she left him and waded out into the lake.

The men paid no heed to her, being preoccupied with Finn. He seemed unhurt, he was not visibly ill—he was just absent. There was no spark of life or recognition inside the strong body. Caurag and Iruis both tried to talk to him, but it was useless.

Finally Cuarag said, "Help me get him on his feet, will you? I'll have to take him back to Almhain, there's nothing I know to do for him here."

But at that moment Finn's eyes focussed. "Sceolaun," he called in a rusty voice.

They turned to look then at the hound neck-deep in the lake. She had advanced as far as she could without swimming and was just standing there, undecided.

Finn pulled away from the men holding him and staggered a few steps forward. "Come away," he told the dog. "Come away. There's nothing for us here. She gave me Oisin and she's taken Bran. It's compensation. Compensation."

In the lake, her head seeming to float on the surface of the water like a disembodied creature, Sceolaun lifted her muzzle skyward and began to howl.

To the horror of all who heard him, Finn howled with her.

"I thought I was hearing wolves," a shaken Iruis confided later to his friends. "I thought I was hearing a pair of wolves on a cold winter night."

Finn was strangely docile during the return journey to Almhain. He had bidden a perfunctory farewell to Iruis and instructed Caurag to fashion a sling so he might carry Sceolaun on his horse instead of making

her walk. But aside from that, he said nothing as they crossed Erin—
except, occasionally, to murmur, "Compensation."

Forming the core of Brehon Law, the laws of compensation and
distress affected every aspect of Gaelic life. The honour price a man must
pay for injuring another, or for taking a woman against her will, was but
a small example of the way in which retribution was attained for every
injustice, down to the smallest insult. The point of compensation was not
to punish the wrongdoer, but to re-establish amity between himself and
the person he had wronged, or their family, so there would be no need
for the acts of revenge that were a legacy of man's more savage past.

It did not always succeed, of course. The feud between Clan Baiscne
and Clan Morna was an example, though one exacerbated by an outside
force for personal reasons.

As a result of hearing the brehons adjudicate matters of compensation at the Assemblies for many years, Finn had the concept burned into
his brain. It made sense to him in a world in which little made sense
anymore.

The more he thought about what he had seen at Ceentlea—and he
was thinking of nothing else—the less he was certain of the evidence of
his senses. Had it been Sive out there on the brink of eternity? Had Bran
ceased baying before running out to her, going in glad silence instead?
And if it was not Sive, why had Bran followed her over the edge?

If it was Sive, why had she not given Finn some signal, some ease for
his pain?

Compensation.

She had given him something. She had given him Oisin. By that gift,
Finn had contracted an obligation, however, and Bran had paid his debt.
Compensation.

That must be it.

Must be.

Must.

He rode with blank, unseeing eyes, and after a time a worried Caurag
took the rein out of his hands and led the horse himself to keep it from
wandering off with Finn and Sceolaun.

As they entered the territory of the Laigin, Finn became agitated,
rubbing his hands together, chewing on his thumb, casting wild glances
to left and right. Caurag began to fear he would not be able to handle
him. He took a small diversion to the stronghold of Sciathbracc of the
Speckled Shield, an old ally, to ask for help.

"His mind is troubled," Caurag explained to Sciathbracc, a broad,
stout, freckled man who claimed with some justification to have three
hundred children. "I'm afraid I may not be able to get him the rest of
the way to Almhain without help."

Sciathbracc looked at Finn, sitting on his horse with the old bitch riding comfortably in her sling across the animal's haunches. "I'd say his mind is troubled. Whoever heard of carrying a hound on a horse?"

"He won't hear of her walking," Caurag replied. "She's very old and footsore."

The freckled man shrugged. "We all get old and footsore. What do you want of me?"

"Send a runner on to Almhain to request that some of Finn's men come here to escort him home."

While they waited, Sciathbracc offered what hospitality he could to Finn, who seemed unaware of it. He was seated on a bench by the hearthfire and given food and drink he did not touch. Sceolaun lay at his feet and he fed the food to her in tiny morsels.

Sciathbracc was concerned. To be seen as failing in hospitality was to dishonour oneself. "Suppose Finn someday tells that he was a guest in my fort and did not eat? He must take something." From one of his women came the suggestion, "Have a fair young girl serve him, he won't refuse from her."

The chosen servitor, a plump and pretty person called Dairann, stood in front of Finn holding out a cup to him. "Drink this for my sake," she urged.

With an effort, he collected himself enough to accept the cup. "What is it?" he asked as he stared down into a dark liquid.

"It's very strong mead, the best we have."

"Mead is gold. This is dark, like a dark lake . . ." Finn took a sip. Then another. Then he threw back his head and tossed off the contents of the cup with desperate gulps as if he could not get enough, as if he would drown himself in the dark liquid.

By the time a party arrived from Almhain, he was roaring drunk and abused each of his men in turn, quite publicly.

They were horrified.

Only Cailte stayed close beside him, ignored the curses and insults hurled indiscriminately from the drunken mouth, and urged the others to do the same.

"I don't have to stay with him and take this," argued Blamec. "Did you hear what he said? He just told me I have a face like toad shit."

"You do," Cailte replied amiably. "So it isn't an insult. Help me get him on his horse, will you?"

Sciathbracc watched them ride off. "I never thought I'd be glad to see the back of Finn Mac Cool," he remarked to the wife standing nearest him.

At Almhain, Bebinn the physician ministered to Finn while Manissa and Ailvi hovered in the background, feeling superfluous.

"He's very drunk," was Bebinn's uncontested opinion, "and because he's got drunk on mead, he'll be very sick when it passes off."

"But will he be himself again?" Manissa asked anxiously. "His men say he's been acting very strange."

The three women looked at Finn, who by this time had been laid on a bed in Manissa's house and was muttering to himself soddenly.

Bebinn, her professional expertise impugned, raised herself to her full height and said stonily, "The treatment I am going to give him has never been known to fail!"

As Finn's wives watched, she prepared a decoction of masses of dried peppermint mixed with the crushed flowers of cowslip and camomile and arnica. To this she added an infusion of willowbark and thistle, then poured the result into a silver cup. Sitting beside Finn, she held his nose until his mouth opened, then she poured in the drink.

Choking and spluttering, Finn sat up. His red-rimmed eyes glared at Bebinn. "Poison!" he accused thickly.

"Nonsense. Have another drink."

He tried to avoid her but found Manissa holding one of his legs and Ailvi the other. Normally he could have thrown them both off with no effort, but he was very drunk. He could not coordinate his legs.

Bebinn pinched his nose again and got another drink down him.

Allowing him to fall back on the bed muttering more darkly than before, she then instructed Manissa to have a quern brought to her. "And a raw liver," she added.

Garvcronan the steward was embarrassed to admit there was no raw liver at Almhain of the White Walls.

"Then slaughter an ox!" Bebinn ordered impatiently.

She ground the hot, steaming liver, fresh from the ox, in the stone quern, turning it into a paste. This time she actually had to sit on Finn's chest while his wives held his arms and Cailte and Red Ridge held his legs, but they finally managed to force the liver paste down his throat.

He vomited violently.

Bebinn gave him another dose.

Afterward, Finn curled into a ball with his back turned toward them and was totally unresponsive.

"Let him sleep," Bebinn advised. "No matter how bad he seems now, he'll be all right when he finally wakes up."

Finn lay on the bed through three nights and three days, until, as Manissa said with distaste, "He has made the whole house stink of himself and his sickness." On the fourth morning he awoke feeling as weak as an infant, but with a clear mind.

He lay watching a thin sliver of light filter in through a chink in the wall.

It's day out there, he thought.

He could hear sounds: the rumble of cart wheels, a man shouting orders, the murmur of women to children, the gabble of Manissa's hens outside the doorway.

It's day and I'm alive, Finn thought regretfully.

He sat up very slowly, waiting for the headache to thunder through his skull.

When it did not come, he got to his feet like an old, weak man and tottered to the doorway, holding on to things as he went. When he pushed the door open, he expected the sound of the iron hinges would make him cringe, but it did not.

He held on to the sides of the oak doorframe with both hands and looked out. The sky was grey-white, banked with clouds. Finn knew the weather too intimately to mistake them for snow clouds, but their appearance confirmed his inner conviction.

"The summer is truly over," said Finn Mac Cool.

And so it was. For a long time no one else realized that the high summer of the Fíanna had slid into autumn, but Finn's internal season had changed and he would carry the Fíanna with him.

Sive, he believed, was truly lost to him. The hope that had kept him roaming Erin with Bran was dead, as dead as Bran.

An end to it, then.

A different future to face, with other possibilities.

So long as he had believed Sive just might be his again someday, he had been able to float on the surface of life in a sense, living in a state of expectation, making the best of things until his real life began again.

But now he saw he had been living his real life all along. Manissa and Ailvi were real women, his women. If he took more women, they would be real too. And they would be all he had.

There would be a huge lacking in his life, always. Like a scar—like Goll's missing eye, it could not be repaired. Goll's scar was on the outside, Finn's on the inside, but of the two, Finn's was worse, he knew.

Under the law, a man with a blemish could not be a king.

Oisin was becoming a young man. He was being trained as if he were a Milesian. Finn insisted the finest poets tutor the youth in the art of training his memory, the best horsemen perfect his riding, the purest voices teach him to follow them in song. Long before he would be permitted to take part in battle, Oisin had mastered the skills of sword and shield and javelin and talked continually of the battles he would someday win. But he always wore the clothes of a prince.

Finn's companions welcomed him into their circle as if he had been one of the original nine. "He's so much like Finn was when we first knew him," Cailte observed. "Merry and full of himself. Finn was a joy to be with in those days."

"Is he not now?" enquired a new rígfénnid.

"Och, it isn't the same. We've seen a lot and done a lot and it changes a man.

"Funnily enough," he went on, "somehow I never thought the passage of years would change Finn Mac Cool, though. It's only now, looking at Oisin, that I realize how much it has done."

Fergus Honey-Tongue interjected, "We thought Finn would always have a wild young heart."

"If that is gone out of him, then a light has gone out of the world," said Goll, to everyone's surprise.

25

THE BATTLES WERE AS FIERCELY FOUGHT AS EVER, WITH as much style as any particular situation allowed, but there were fewer of them. Fewer men, native or foreign, were willing to defy the power of the High King of Erin as represented by his Fíanna. As a result, the fénnidi had more time to spend hunting during battle seasons.

Finn, once the most devoted of hunters, rarely joined them, however.

"He lost his pleasure in the chase when Bran died," Caurag sadly concluded.

To tempt Finn, Caurag acquired other hounds for him of the same type as Bran and Sceolaun, huge animals bred to hunt wolves or take down grown stags. Finn responded to only one of them, an animal known as Conbec of Perfect Symmetry, who looked something like Bran. When the Fíanna were on the move, Finn took Conbec into his bed on cold nights to keep him warm.

When Sceolaun died quietly in her sleep, having attained an unprecedented age for a hound, Finn wept for one of his dogs for the last time. "I called her Survivor, and survivor she was," he told Caurag. "Bury her deep and put a cairn over her."

"Like a person?" The huntsman was surprised.

"Like a person."

Season gave way to season, and the tales told of Finn Mac Cool multiplied in inverse ratio to the number of adventures he had and battles he fought. The length of Erin, storyspinners heard men and women alike clamouring for new tales of Finn Mac Cool and complied with *Finn and The Pigs of Angus, Finn and the Phantoms, The Red Woman, The King of the Foreigners, The Giantess, The Cave of the Sídhe* . . .

. . . and, and, and. There was no end to the stories, or to the young men who, hearing them, longed to join the Fíanna and flocked to Almhain for testing and training.

Among them was a youngster called Dairmait, who was not many seasons older than Oisin, being the first son of Donn. Lugaid also sent his oldest son to Finn as he had promised, and the two young men arrived together on a wet morning at Almhain of the White Walls.

"What are you called?" demanded the sentry at the gate.

"Cormac Mac Lugaid," was the first reply.

The sentry looked the lad up and down. "That's awkward," he decided. "And I don't think anyone should be called by the name of the Ard Ríg but the man himself. We'll just call you Lugaid's son. And you . . . what's your name?"

"Dairmait Mac Donn Mac Duibhne."

"Mmmm. Dairmait. That'll do us. Open the gates for this pair," he bellowed over his shoulder, "and tell the commander that Dairmait and Lugaid's son have come to him for training if he wants them!"

The two young men entered together. They had attained the age for taking up arms, but neither had yet reached the age of beard encirclement and their faces were relatively smooth, save for the moustaches they were frantically trying to grow. Lugaid's son looked very like his father, but Dairmait looked only like himself.

Donn's son had thick brown curling hair, and eyelashes longer than any woman's. From the moment he entered Almhain, he swam through a sea of admiring female eyes. Every woman in the stronghold, from the oldest bondservant to the youngest girl child, turned to watch him stroll by, though he was quite oblivious to them.

His thoughts were on Finn and the Fíanna and the future stretching before him, bright with glory.

Donn himself proudly introduced his son to Finn. "Dairmait was fostered in a noble household," he boasted, "and has all the arts and skills of a chieftain's son."

"Noble households clamour for the privilege of fostering the children of rígfénnidi now," Finn said calmly. "Once, Donn, you'd have been fortunate to have him taken in by a stonemason."

"We all know what you've done for us. Now do something more and take my son and train him as you would your own."

"I show no favouritism, Donn, you know that. I shall accept him and Lugaid's son if they prove themselves, but they will have to pass tests to justify being here at all."

The first tests were the easiest, but even they weeded out many applicants. During Finn's long years as leader of the Fíanna, he had devised a series of steps by which a prospective warrior could prove himself, and then a second series by which he could qualify as an officer. Neither was dependent on age or birth rank; what a man could do on the day was sufficient. But the tests, particularly for officers, had grown more demanding with the years.

Several days later a proud Donn was able to tell Madan Bent-Neck, "My son has recited his twelve poems already, not a word put in, not a word taken out. And he's won two footraces and one javelin-hurling."

"Did he outrun Oisin?"

"He wasn't raced against Oisin," Donn said tightly.

Lugaid's son proved himself adept with the sword and the sling, and though his mastery of poetry was obviously more difficult for him than for Dairmait, he succeeded in reciting to satisfaction. Both young men defended themselves successfully in the trench when attacked by nine, and removed thorns from their feet while running. They also demonstrated their ability to ride horses, swim rivers, and cobble together footgear for themselves, if necessary, from pieces of untanned leather.

They passed the first tests; they were put into fíans, though not into the same bands.

Oisin also was in a different fían. Finn sprinkled the sons of himself and his companions impartially through the army. Yet almost from the first, the younger generation seemed drawn together as if by invisible bonds and were often to be found in one another's company.

Dairmait was popular with everyone. He was so unaware of his physical beauty, so eager to please, so full of gentle laughter, that even older, hardened warriors enjoyed being with him.

On the day when the newest members of the Fíanna were given swords of their own to carry in Cormac's service, they gathered afterward for a private and impromptu feast to celebrate the event. But nothing at Almhain could ever be kept secret. Lugaid's son had taken a bag of hares with his slingshot, and they had begun to roast the meat on spits over a small fire when someone noticed the smoke and ran to see what was happening.

"You can't cook here!" protested an outraged Garvcronan.

Lugaid's son looked up at him from where he crouched on his heels, rotating a spit over the flame. "Why not?"

"Look over there, you fool. That's thatch on that house. One spark and it goes up like the sun. If you want your meat cooked, take it to a proper firepit."

"This is just for ourselves," Dairmait said. "We didn't want to bother anyone."

"You mean you didn't want to share. Don't you understand what it is to be one of the Fíanna? You share, young man!"

"We only have four hares!"

"Then offer your four hares to everyone at Almhain."

Dairmait and Lugaid's son exchanged dismayed glances. Then they realized Garvcronan had put one hand over his mouth to stifle laughter. "Finn used to have an officer who played tricks like that," he told them. "Cael, his name was."

The two young men laughed with him then. "It's not a bad idea, sharing," Dairmait admitted. "We should. Is there anyone who will eat with us, Garvcronan? Not too many!" he added hastily.

Smiling, the steward left them. He soon returned with Finn and Cailte—probably the last men with whom the two newest warriors expected to share a meal.

What had seemed a feast when they were planning it for just the two of them seemed embarrassingly humble when offered as a meal to the Rígfénnid Fíanna and his favourite companion. Dairmait blushed. Lugaid's son mumbled. But Finn and Cailte crossed their legs and sat on the ground as if they were the lowest-ranked of warriors and gobbled the meat and wiped their mouths on their arms and had a wonderful time.

Soon the four were laughing and talking together as if they were of an age and a rank.

At one stage Finn got to his feet, brushed himself off and went away, only to return with Oisin. "There are enough scraps here to feed a fifth," he told the others, adding his son to the circle.

Firelight gilded their faces and returned Finn's silvery hair to its old lustre. Sitting there, he could almost imagine he was back in the beginning, on Black Head perhaps, with the future in front of him and all the victories yet to win. In that moment he envied Oisin and Dairmait and Lugaid's son as he had never envied anyone.

Mellow with the mood, Dairmait held up his new, unblooded sword. "I'm going to call it *Liomhadoir,* the Burnisher," he said.

Finn was taken aback. So many battle seasons, so many swords . . . he had never thought to name one. They got lost or stolen or broken, or given away, and another was forged, and then another. To name a sword was like naming a hound, making it a friend. A permanent memory.

"Mine is called *Mac an Luin,* Son of the Waves!" he cried spontaneously. "I wear the bag that once belonged to Manannán of the Sea!"

He fingered the ubiquitous neck bag that he still wore with a perverse pride, and the tale came flooding back to him. He told it again beside the small cook fire as he had not told it in years, and the others leaned on their elbows and listened with shining eyes, dreaming of Manannán Mac Lir.

"You've never told it better," Cailte said as the two men walked toward their own dwellings later.

"I haven't told that particular story in a long time. Not even to Oisin, though he loves hearing my tales."

"He does of course. We're all interested in our histories," Cailte responded.

Finn stopped walking and turned to look at the thin man. "Is that my history?"

Cailte's face was devoid of guile. "You said it was."

They walked on.

The infusion of a new generation into the Fíanna brought new energy. There was a veritable spate of naming weaponry, which until then had merely been the tools of war. Finn entered into the spirit by calling his shield Storm Shield and his golden banner Sun Shape. Oisin proclaimed that when he became an officer, his banner would be known as the Dark Deadly One, but happy-hearted Diarmait said his would be the Shining Silver.

But before the young men fought in their first battle, Almhain of the White Walls was attacked by an enemy against which swords and spears were useless.

One of Garvcronan's children was the first to fall ill. Bebinn worked frantically with the little boy but could not save him. Like a fire in dry grass, the illness spread. It sent a dry cough rattling through the youngest and the weakest, though the strong were able to throw it off.

Unfortunately, Ailvi had just given birth again and did not have the strength to resist. When both she and her baby began to cough and choke, Manissa joined Bebinn in caring for them and worked untiringly to save them.

She saved the baby.

"I did all I could," she told Finn. The first tears he had ever seen her shed were running down her cheeks.

Finn took his wife into his arms and patted her shoulder distractedly. "I know you did. You are . . ."

". . . a good woman," she finished for him. To his surprise, he thought he heard a note of bitterness beneath the sorrow.

Finn grieved for Ailvi, for her brightness and her sweetness. But the silent observer in him noted dispassionately that he did not mourn her as he had mourned Sive. Ailvi was not irreplaceable.

Then Manissa began to cough.

Within a fortnight of Ailvi's death, Finn found himself wifeless.

When the two women were gone, he discovered he missed them more than he had expected, and valued them more than he had realized. Particularly Manissa. She seemed, in retrospect, to be the mother he had never known, though he could hardly articulate such a thought even to himself. But there was a hole in the world and he did not know how to fill it.

At the bottom of night's well when he lay sleepless, he imagined that hole as a small, dark lake into which had fallen Sive and Bran and Ailvi and Manissa, a lake that would swallow everyone in time, himself also.

Manannán Mac Lir, he thought. The waves reclaiming their own.

Because Ailvi had been Cormac's daughter, Finn announced funeral games to be held at Almhain in her honour. Cormac sent word that he would attend. It was a singular mark of honour. Never before in the memory of the poets had funeral games been held for the wife of a Fir Bolg.

But before they could take place, Manissa died, and Finn announced that the games would now be held as a memorial to both his wives.

Goll Mac Morna protested. "You can't do it, Finn. Manissa was only a chieftain's daughter. Her rank doesn't entitle her to any sort of funeral games."

"I demand it by right of my own rank."

Goll shook his head. "You can't. As long as you were married to the daughter of the High King, you could. But you aren't husband to the High King's daughter anymore. With Ailvi, you lost a certain rank. Surely you know that. If you don't believe me, ask the brehons, they'll tell you."

Finn was coldly furious. "Everything I have I won for myself. Nothing depended upon the women I married. I did not even take property with them."

"Still," Goll insisted, "your situation is not quite what it was when Cormac was your father-in-law."

An angry Finn consulted the local brehons, who confirmed what Goll had told him.

Ignoring them, he ordered the funeral games held in the names of both women.

When he was informed of this, Cormac refused to attend.

The High King had never acquired the soul-friend and confidante he had once envisioned, the position to which Finn had once aspired. It just never happened, the right man did not appear at the right time. He found no Cailte Mac Ronan to love him and trust him implicitly and guard his secrets, so over the years he had been forced to keep his own counsel. There were many matters he could not discuss beforehand with the brehons, for they must remain objective. And the men who were officially designated his counselors would, he had learned, say whatever they thought he wanted them to say.

So Cormac found himself considering this latest problem over Finn Mac Cool alone. At the bottom of the well of night.

"There has to be a point at which I stop giving in to Finn," he said aloud as he sat on a bench staring into the banked fire in his firepit. His voice was pitched low so the many other occupants of his lodge could not hear him, but he found its human resonance gave him a certain comfort.

"This is that point," he decided.

Later he would justify his decision to those around him by saying, "In the heel of the hunt, Finn shows his origins. He does not have the same innate sense of what is appropriate that a Milesian would. If he did, he would realize I cannot honour his other wife equally with my daughter—nor should he do so. The very fact that he has developed outside the bounds of society and rank makes it all the more important that I, as king, uphold such values and set an example. Without a clear understanding of each person's place in the whole, Erin would disintegrate into chaos, with bondservants demanding to be treated like princes and no man certain of his honour price."

His court, of course, agreed. "He is wise!" they said.

When Finn was told that the High King would not attend the funeral games, he took the news in a silence so cold, so furious, that the messenger turned heel and ran. The expression in Finn's eyes terrified him.

"The games proceed as planned," Finn announced with no further comment. But as he strode through Almhain, people stayed out of his way.

Lugaid travelled to Finn's stronghold for the event, where he joined the other original companions, plus Red Ridge, to serve as judges of the games. He and the others exempted themselves only from those contests in which their sons were taking part. At the start of the games, there was considerable boasting and wagering by the various rígfénnidi, each man backing his own sons, but it soon became obvious who would do the most winning.

Finn did not act as a judge. He stood watching on the sidelines while Oisin won one competition after another.

The first man to congratulate him was always Diarmait.

"Was ever a young man so generous and so beautiful?" Donn asked the other spectators.

"He may not be able to defeat Oisin," Blamec conceded, "but he's already made himself very popular."

The women, watching, were of the same opinion.

When the games were concluded and the poets recited the last praise-poems in honour of Finn's dead wives, Finn sadly gathered their trinkets and treasures. Had either wife brought property to the marriage, he would under the law have been entitled to keep it now, but all that remained were their personal jewels and ornaments, their mirrors, their clothing, their jewelled cups, their looms and needles.

Manissa's things Finn returned to her family, together with a gift the equivalent of her father's honour price, quite astonishing the old chieftain.

But he sent nothing to Cormac Mac Airt.

They sat each on his respective hilltop, with a sea of anger between them.

"I fear you made a mistake," Fiachaid told Cormac. "You appear to have alienated your commander. What if war breaks out? What if—"

"There is peace," Cormac said firmly.

"This is Erin," Fiachaid replied.

And so it was. The Ulidians broke the truce at midday on the longest day of the year, storming down from the north with painted faces and howls of fury to attack Tara in force.

Fiachaid, who had grown paunchy and forgotten his battle skills, found himself thrust unprepared into the heart of war, and without even waiting for Cormac's authorization, sent a desperate message south to Almhain. "Come to us!"

Finn sought out Cailte. "Walk with me."

"Where?"

"Just . . . out. Outside the walls. Under the sky."

Leaving Almhain of the White Walls, they strolled out across bogland, drifting aimlessly while Finn's sentries stood at his gates, weapons at the ready, and waited. The Fíanna waited also.

Finn walked for a long time without speaking, but Cailte was a patient man. At last Finn said, "He insulted my wife, Cailte."

"I don't think he meant to insult Manissa. I truly don't. Cormac isn't like that and you know it."

"I wanted her to have the same honours Ailvi received."

"And she did, you saw to it."

"The Ard Ríg himself should have wept over her!" Finn cried suddenly.

Cailte waited a moment before replying in a gentle voice, "You didn't."

Finn turned toward him. "Didn't I? Just because you don't see my tears, Cailte, doesn't mean they are unshed. The bitterest weeping happens inside."

Cailte changed the subject. "What will you do now? You command the Fíanna and the king has sent for you, for you and the army. Without you . . ."

Finn nodded. "Indeed. Without me . . . Cormac knows that. He chose to forget it for a time, but now he remembers. I suspect that right this moment he wishes he'd come to the funeral games."

"He was doing what he had to do, Finn. That's what it means to be the nobility."

"How would you know?" Finn asked harshly.

"Because you've made us nobility too," Cailte told him. "You've put obligations on us we never had before, so I can recognize those on Cormac. And you can too, if you think about it."

Finn gave the thin man a long, searching look. "And the obligations on myself," he said at last. "I recognize those."

He sighed, a sound dragged up from the bottom of his spirit. "It would be a good day to take the greyhounds and chase hares," he said wistfully, his eyes sweeping the horizon. Then he turned around and set his face toward Almhain. "Come on, Cailte," he said in a changed voice. "We're needed."

Before the sun set, Finn and his men were armed, organized, and on their way to Tara.

Oisin and Diarmait were aglow with excitement. "This will be our first really big battle!" they told each other repeatedly as they trotted among the other fénnidi, spears in hand. The time had come to kill and be killed; to live and know that you were alive, because you could so quickly die.

The two young men tingled with the knowledge, like wine coursing in their blood.

In an unprecedented move, Finn kept his warriors traveling through the night. They reached Tara in time to be guided by the glow of Ulidian campfires ringing the ridge and its stronghold.

The very sight brought back Finn's youth in a flood. All the old dreams of triumph and glory, the old joy of being responsible for the king's safety. He forgot his quarrel with Cormac as if it had never been. Compared to the sight of hostile campfires, it seemed no more than the squabbling of two birds over one nest.

The war drums were silenced by Finn's order; he wanted to surprise the enemy. But he could feel the drumbeat anyway, coming up his spine from his groin, into his heart, into his brain.

He reined in his horse and gave her to a horseboy to hold. "Don't let her whinny," he cautioned. "Pinch her nostrils . . . like this." He started forward on foot.

The Fíanna followed.

By Finn's order, they separated into different streams that snaked across the plain of Míd, seeking to encircle the Ulaid. "Are we going to attack them in the dark, do you think?" Diarmait whispered excitedly to Oisin.

"I'd say not. There's no style in that, it wouldn't be fair to them. They have to have a chance to fight back or when we win, it will be a pitiful victory at best."

Diarmait nodded, understanding. He was about to become part of the legend; everything must be done right.

Because Finn had summoned them to attend the funeral games and do honour to his wives, the majority of the Fíanna had been encamped beyond the Hill of Almhain when Cormac was attacked. Ordinarily, Finn might have had to summon them from the four corners of Erin, but the timing was fortuitous—for him, not for the enemy. He was bringing a total of more than three thousand warriors to hurl against the northern insurrection.

"I suspect," Finn had remarked to Cailte, "that the Ulidian princes heard through their spies that Cormac and I were, ah, not as close as we once were and thought it an ideal time to try to regain Tara." He smiled thinly. "Their spies did them a disservice."

The might of the Fíanna silently surrounded the encamped Ulidian forces during the night, careful that no twig snapped under any Fénian foot to give them away. Then they waited.

Battle broke with the dawn. The first Ulidian sentry to realize he was looking not at a forest of trees but a forest of men gave an alarmed shriek, but it was too late. The Fíanna were upon them.

The war cries could be heard at the gates of Tara.

Diarmait and Oisin were in the front rank of the warriors. Holding their shields in front of their bodies, they raced forward screaming. Everyone was screaming. Battle was cacophony. Cries of rage drowned howls of pain—at first.

Finn's choice of weapon was no longer the shortsword, but the latest in a series of greatswords first forged by Lochan the smith. Finn's own smith at Almhain made them now. Son of the Waves had been precisely shaped to Lochan's original model, however.

With two hands firmly grasping its massive hilt, Finn began hacking his way through the ranks of the Ulaid. A shieldbearer ran beside him, holding up the Storm Shield to protect Finn as much as possible, for a man wielding a two-handed sword could hardly manipulate a shield as well.

Only Finn's original companions carried greatswords, a symbol of status. Everyone else, including Oisin and Diarmait, used the shorter blade, and privately they assured each other that it was a much more modern design.

"You!" Oisin was now screaming at every man he attacked with his sword. "You! You! You!"

He had been well trained. His blade flashed in the light of the rising sun until it was too bloody to reflect light at all. The Ulidians carried yew-wood shields bound in bronze, hard to damage, but Finn's warriors had been taught numerous ways of going over or around such shields— and under them when all else failed, attacking the genitals, though that was not considered good style.

Afire with youth, Oisin felt as if his sword were wielding him rather than the other way around. He had no sense of time passing. He fought. Men fell. It was glorious. Diarmait fought with equal brilliance, clearing a space around himself, as Finn Mac Cool was doing elsewhere.

Finn was seeking the commander of the Ulaid. He would be recognizable by his face-paint. The Ulidians had never abandoned the old wild custom, or begun identifying themselves in the Milesian style, with banners. Only their commander would wear the sun's colour on his face, however.

The Rigfennid Fíanna had a sun-gold banner.

Gold met gold as the sun gleamed golden on the thatched roofs of Tara.

The Ulidian commander had a name Finn knew but chose not to remember. He had a face Finn had seen gilded by firelight at friendly feasts, and hands that had shared meat and fruit in the Banquetting Hall at Tara. Now he was simply The Enemy. He could not be considered in any other way.

Finn looked at the face-paint and not at the man behind it, and with one terrible, angled downstroke of his two-handed greatsword, tore open the man's body from heart to groin.

Blood geysered. Intestines erupted from the body cavity like huge glistening worms.

The Ulidian gave a frightful groan and clutched at his belly. He staggered forward. Finn stepped back to give him room to fall, which he did, when the combination of pain and shock reached his brain. He was cut almost in half.

It had been an awesome blow, forcing the already battle-blunted iron sword blade through highly resistant skin and tough muscle fibers to grate, ultimately, on bone. It was the sort of blow a man might manage once in a battle without doing his own shoulders and back muscles damage.

Finn had been known to do it four times in one day, but that day was far in the past. As the Ulidian fell, spasming in his death throes, agony flamed through his killer's body.

Finn gasped for breath and almost dropped the sword. His shield-bearer reached out to steady him, but he brushed the man aside. Shaking his head defiantly, he blinked back pain. Something was torn somewhere, back near his shoulder blades. He could feel his fingers going cold.

"Gutting this one's ruined my blade," he croaked to his shieldbearer. "Needs a new edge." He managed to give the man the sword just before he lost the ability to grasp anything with his rapidly numbing hands.

"I'll see to it and get you another."

"Don't think I'll need another," Finn replied thankfully.

As was customary with battles in Erin, when a leader fell, his men were swiftly disheartened. Ulidians who saw their commander receive his fatal wound shouted the news over their shoulders so it spread rapidly to the outer fringe of the fighting. The northerners either surrendered on the spot or turned and ran.

The battle was over before the Ulidian leader's dying organs had finished gurgling.

Goll Mac Morna joined Finn to stand looking down at the ruin of a man. "You're as fast as ever, I see. Well done, this. The blow would have cut the side off a wild boar."

"Enough style for you?" Finn asked through gritted teeth. He was determined that Goll should not know what it had cost him.

"Brilliant. I used to do it myself."

"But you can't now."

Goll's lips tightened. "I can't now."

Something of the old merry spirit leaped in Finn's eyes. He took a step closer to his longtime rival. "I'll tell you something," he said in a voice pitched for Goll's ears alone. "Neither can I. This is my last one."

Before he could stop himself, Goll gave Finn a look of comradely understanding.

Runners were dispatched to search the area and bring Finn the names of the slain. The Fíanna had come so quickly there had been no time to bring women for tending the wounded, so anyone not able to walk would have to be carried back to Tara on a litter by his uninjured companions. Finn, hiding the fact of his own injury, walked around the battlefield assessing the damage done to his men. His hands hung at his sides, but no one noticed.

He was relieved to hear that Oisin was uninjured, though he tried to keep his face impassive. "Donn's son Diarmait has received a blow to the head, however," the runner reported.

Finn went personally to check on young Diarmait's wound, since Donn was off somewhere on the far side of the battlefield and did not yet know of it. He found Diarmait and Oisin together beside a small stream. Blood from a dead warrior was staining the water farther down, but Oisin knelt on the bank above it and tore a strip of his princely linen tunic to use for bathing his friend's wound.

Diarmait had taken a nasty cut to his cheek, close to his mouth, rather than the head injury Finn had feared.

"There's your beauty spoiled," Oisin was telling him laughingly as he wiped away the blood.

Finn crouched on his heels to inspect the injury, being careful not to bend his back. "Perhaps not," he told Diarmait. "It isn't deep."

"There'll be a scar."

"Och, there are always scars," Finn assured the youngsters. "Scars are a warrior's beauty marks."

True to Finn's words, when the scar healed, it drew up one corner of Diarmait's mouth in the faintest hint of a mysterious smile. Women ever after would find it irresistible.

26

The victorious Fíanna ran roaring toward Tara, waving their weapons aloft and shouting Cormac's name.

He met them in the open gateway.

The Ard Ríg, now—and for a while—undisputed High King of the kings of Erin, was splendidly attired and gleaming with gold ornaments. At his shoulder stood his eldest son, a youngster just entering manhood, who rejoiced in the name of Cairbre Mac Cormac. The boy wore almost as much gold as his father and stood as tall, as handsome.

He had, however, his mother's eyes. Like Ethni the Proud, he disliked seeing honours go elsewhere. He watched with unspoken jealousy as men and women swarmed forward to praise Finn Mac Cool.

"Cormac sometimes treats Finn like his own son," Ethni had said more than once to Cairbre as the boy was growing up. "Watch that he doesn't get what should be yours."

Cairbre was watching now, through narrowed eyes.

In the light of Finn's impressive victory, Cormac could hardly be less than gracious, even effusive. Whatever rancour had lain between them must be forgotten. Finn had never betrayed him, he had to admit honestly to himself. Indeed, Finn had come to him and fought for him when he could just as easily have kept the Fíanna at Almhain and let the Ulaid seize Tara, then sold his services to them. He had made the Fíanna strong enough to be an independent force. And whoever had the Fíanna, had Tara.

Cairbre watched as Finn was shown to the place of honour second only to the king's in the hall. Finn sat down carefully, refusing to wince in spite of the pain of torn back muscles. Later he would have the king's physician, Eogan, look at them. For now, he just wanted to enjoy his triumph. He did not notice the hard stare the king's oldest son was giving him.

But Goll did. With only one eye, Goll Mac Morna saw more than many men with two. He edged closer to the young man to take a good look at him, measuring him as he would measure an opponent over his shield. Cairbre had his father's sharply moulded, aristocratic features and deep-set eyes. There was something a little weak in the shape of his mouth, however; something a little petulant in the jut of his chin.

Goll concluded Cairbre might be more easily manipulated than Cormac Mac Airt. "It's a grand victory," he said aloud in a conversational tone. "It's a pity Finn claims all the glory for himself, though."

Cairbre turned to look at him. "What does that mean?"

"Och, nothing. He's always been like that. He's of Clan Baiscne, you know, and they're a greedy lot. If Finn has his way, this won't be remembered as a victory for Cormac at all, but for Finn and his Fíanna. The High King will be lucky if his name is mentioned by the poets."

"But the Fíanna is my father's army!" Cairbre protested.

Goll allowed himself the slightest sneer, an expression made sinister by his scars. "It's Finn's army. Ask your father, he knows. When Clan Morna led the Fíanna, things were different, of course. My men and I always gave our total loyalty to the kingship.

"If you ever succeed your father as High King, young Cairbre, you might want to keep that in mind. You'd be better served with officers of Clan Morna."

Then, before Cairbre could do too much thinking or ask too many questions, Goll changed the subject. The youth could brood on this in private. The seed had been sown. Smiling at Cairbre, Goll enquired, "Are you a good games-player, by the way? I happen to possess the Gold and Silver Chess Set—I'm sure you've heard of it. Now that we're in for a season of peace, apparently, I would enjoy a game or two with you."

Cairbre was startled, and then flattered that a man of Goll's generation was making such an offer. "I would like that myself," he said.

Finn Mac Cool had never paid much attention to Cairbre.

Finn was, even now, smiling at his son Oisin, and Cormac Mac Airt was positively beaming on both of them.

Cairbre observed this, then stared into his cup. My father is too impressed with Finn, he thought.

It was only much later, as he lay in his bed too tired to fall asleep, that Goll Mac Morna thought over his conversation with the king's son and asked himself a question: why did I do that?

Does the habit of playing games for the sake of playing games never die?

The celebration lasted for days. Finn graciously accepted the accolades heaped upon him, not once mentioning the recent coolness between himself and Cormac. But there was one thing he never forgot.

"You aren't husband to the High King's daughter anymore," Goll had told him.

The terrible drive to achieve that had characterized Finn's earlier career had abated with the loss of Sive and the establishment of the Fíanna in its final form. He could have accepted the diminished status implied in Goll's remark—had it not been for Oisin.

For Oisin's sake, Finn wanted everything.

For Sive's son.

There must be no loss of prestige.

He waited until he knew Cormac had reached the maximum mellowness of mood, with just enough mead in his belly and just enough rich food slowing his thought processes. Then, on the third night of the celebratory feasting, Finn leaned across to the king and said quietly, "Both my contract wives are dead, you know."

Cormac frowned. *Is he going to start in on me about not attending the funeral games?*

But instead, Finn said, "Such a loss has been terrible for me, of course. I need a new wife, would you not agree?"

With a sense of relief, Cormac nodded. "I would of course."

"An appropriate wife. Someone you would approve of, to enhance the position of your Rígfénnid Fíanna."

"Indeed." Cormac took another drink from his cup and held it up for refilling. "Indeed."

"Then I ask for another of your daughters, since we are agreed," replied Finn Mac Cool with a radiant smile.

Cormac almost dropped his cup.

His gesture was so unexpected that the servant pouring the mead poured it down his arm instead.

Cormac jumped to his feet, shaking his sodden sleeve. Finn continued to sit smiling on his bench. There was a flurry of excitement as servants ran in every direction, finding cloths to mop the king with, bringing more mead. Cormac resumed his seat, but not his serenity.

"Are you serious?" he demanded of Finn.

"I am of course. Would I joke about women? Cael Hundred-Killer was our prankster," Finn added with a touch of sadness in his voice that disconcerted Cormac, recalling yet another loss the commander had suffered. "I do think," Finn went on, "that since I was married once to the High King's daughter, I can hardly marry a woman of lower rank now. How would it look? And you do have so many daughters," he added truthfully.

Cormac Mac Airt had a well-earned and cherished reputation for wisdom. It was only in combat with Finn Mac Cool that he doubted himself. Finn was surely not as intelligent as a prince of the Milesian race—yet somehow he won. He always won.

Cormac shook his head, trying to clear it of the golden lustre produced by too much mead. He wanted to think sharply and clearly. But there had been three long days and longer nights of celebrating, celebrations that included the captured officers of the Ulaid, as was traditional. Everyone had drunk and eaten and sung too much, and shouted too much, and enjoyed too much. Thoughts were no longer clear and sharp. Wise arguments and clever rebuttals did not leap to the tongue.

Cormac found himself trying to remember if Finn had refilled his cup as often as the rest of them.

"My men have claimed the Ulidian weapons abandoned on the battlefield," Finn reminded the king in a calm, relentless voice, "but I have asked for no reward for myself. Nothing at all." The thought lay unspoken on the air between them—I did not have to come and fight for you this time.

Honour compelled Cormac's reply. "I shall give you whatever you think appropriate as a reward." A muscle jumped in his jaw. "I take it, that means my daughter."

"If you have a daughter who is willing to marry me."

"What if I don't?"

Finn's smile was as guileless as a child's. "Surely you have some influence with your daughters, Cormac?"

How does he do this to me? wondered Cormac Mac Airt.

By the light of the following day, the king surveyed his unwed daughters. They were a comely lot. Ethni had borne many girl children, but the loveliest of all was Carnait's daughter, the one called Grania.

Cormac looked at her, went on, came back to her. She had her mother's slightly exotic cast of feature, with tilted eyes and a creamy, poreless skin. Carnait had made Cormac happy. Perhaps her daughter would do the same for Finn.

If Finn is happy, the king told himself, he might be less of a thorn in my foot.

Cormac broached the question tactfully but got no response. Grania did not seem interested.

He spoke to her mother. "Finn wants a daughter of mine as wife, Carnait, and for various reasons, I need to give him what he wants. Our Grania is perfect for him in my judgment. Can you not bring a mother's influence to bear on her? Remember, it was through Finn's intercession that the mill down below was built and you ceased being Ethni's grinding-woman."

Carnait could hardly argue. She spoke long and earnestly to Grania, who at last approached the king. "I'll talk with Finn Mac Cool," the girl agreed. "But if he doesn't please me, I won't marry him!"

Cormac was relieved. "That goes without saying, and he knows it."

He offered them the use of the House of the King for their first interview. Servants were ordered to keep out of sight. A huge fire was built in the central firepit, every bench was hand-rubbed to be certain there were no splinters, and cups of both mead and wine were poured out and left waiting beside platters heaped with apples.

Grania, attired in her second-best dress, waited for the Rígfénnid Fíanna with barely concealed impatience, tapping her foot and taking one bite out of every apple. None of them were sweet enough.

When Finn arrived at the House of the King, he paused for a moment in the open doorway, letting his eyes adjust to the change in light. Against a rectangle of sunny sky, he stood in huge silhouette, his silvery hair like a crown.

Grania stopped chewing her apple.

He strode into the room. The light of fire and lamp and candle was kind to a face scored by weather and war and the pillage of seasons.

As Finn looked down at Grania, sitting on her bench and staring up at him with a bulge in her cheek from uneaten fruit, he was struck by the difference in their ages. She was hardly more than a child.

But she was very pretty, as pretty as Carnait had been when she first attracted the High King's attention.

It was almost too much to hope that Carnait's daughter would prove to be an intelligent companion as well.

"What do you know of me?" Finn asked the girl.

She gave a couple of quick chews, swallowed the apple. "My father says you're his sword arm." She peered up at him; her eyes were slightly tilted, a pale grey-green. "Who do you say you are?" she asked disconcertingly.

Finn was pleased. She was quick. On long winter nights he would not be bored. "I'm a warrior," he told Grania. "And a poet. And commander of the Fíanna. And a man with no wife. And possessor of a fine fort on a hill, and enormous prestige."

"All of that? How impressive."

He could not tell if she was really impressed or not. Her young face was as bland as the surface of an apple. She studied her fingertips, dyed with berry juice, then looked back up at Finn. "And are you a skillful lover?"

He was disconcerted. "I know how to pleasure a woman," he replied gruffly. He undertook to sit down beside her and put an arm around her by way of a beginning. But when he raised his arm and tried to encircle her with it, the pain of damaged muscles ripped along his nerve endings. He could not complete the gesture.

She felt him hesitate and gave him a sharp look. Seen up close, his face was older somehow, with lines of tension around the eyes and mouth.

Finn forced himself to clasp Grania with his arm. The pain was intense. "It will pass in a few days if you keep hot compresses on your back," Eogan had told him, but the injury was taking longer to heal than he had anticipated. In his youth, he had seemed to heal almost overnight.

He must not be old and crippled with this young one.

He squeezed her, hard. "I can give you all the pleasure you can stand," he said.

In his youth, he would not have been so blunt. He would have used poetic phrases; he would have tried to read her eyes and see what she responded to, as he had always done with Sive. But seasons had passed and he was no longer young. He was impatient, and in pain.

"If you don't give me sufficient pleasure," Grania reminded him, "under the law, I can seek it with another man."

"You can," he agreed gravely. "But the other man must be of rank equal to mine, so that any children you bring into our family will be a source of pride." He would show her he knew the law as well as she did.

By now, Finn Mac Cool knew the law very well indeed.

"When you marry me, you will be chief wife of the Rígfénnid Fíanna," he said, "as I have no other living contract wives. If I take any more women, I must have your permission to do so, and they will be second in rank to you. No one will stand above you. At Tara, you are just one of the king's daughters. At Almhain of the White Walls, you will be the most important woman, with many bondservants to do your bidding and complete authority in the Grianan."

"You have a Grianan?"

"I do of course. I have every luxury," Finn boasted.

"Musicians? I love music."

"Then we shall acquire more musicians," he promised her. "You will have whatever you want, Grania."

She sat in the curve of his embrace, warmed by his body, and considered.

Her sisters would be very jealous.

She tilted her head back and looked up at the massive cheekbones, the gentle mouth. "I shall be wife to you, Finn Mac Cool," she promised.

Finn returned to Eogan. "You have to do something about my back. It still pains me, I can't move freely, my fingertips are often cold and numb. I'm planning to take a new wife, Eogan, I can't disgrace myself on my marriage bed!"

The royal physician laughed. "Your fingers aren't your most important parts, not in the marriage bed. How's your staff?"

"Nothing wrong there," Finn assured him. "But how can I hug a woman, lift a woman, pleasure a woman, with a damaged back?"

"It will heal, I assured you it would. You're just rushing the season. We can strap you up, though, with linen bandages, to keep you from moving those muscles more than you need to. That will help you heal faster."

Eogan duly applied a broad webwork of linen to Finn's torso, binding him tightly. It did ease the pain.

But the next time Finn put his arms around Grania, she felt the bulky bandaging under his tunic and knew a sudden stab of revulsion.

He's old! she thought. He's so old they've tied him together like a pudding for the boiling!

The enormity of the promise she had given and the life it presaged began to frighten her.

Whenever she saw Finn in daylight, she looked not at his broad shoulders or his gleaming hair, but at the lines in his face and the careful way in which he moved. And every time, he seemed older to her.

She was relieved when he bade her farewell and returned to Almhain for the winter.

"I'll be back to marry you at Beltaine," he promised.

He decided to leave an honour guard of the Fíanna at Tara as a tribute to his intended wife. Cormac was pleased by the gesture. "A large honour guard," he said to Finn. "Enough men to discourage any more uprisings like the last one."

Finn grinned. "The Ulidians won't make another attempt on Tara for quite some time."

"Even so. From now on, I want a lot of your men here in every season, Finn." Cormac spoke firmly, enforcing his authority. The garrisoning of the army must not be left up to its commander, not entirely. He was resolved to take more of the control of the Fíanna into his own hands, being all too aware of the danger of losing it to Finn entirely.

By mutual agreement between commander and king, Conan Maol and Conn Crither were senior officers for the garrison left at Tara. Finn returned to Almhain for the winter, taking with him, among others, Cailte and Oisin and Donn and Donn's son.

The days of winter, usually so brief, seemed long to him as he waited for spring. The nights were endless and leaden. He thought of taking various women to warm his bed, but the thought never prompted the deed. It almost seemed too much trouble, though his body was eager enough. Still, the burning hunger he had known for Sive was only a memory now, a memory of youth.

On a night when the wind howled and beat against the white walls and his hounds piled atop one another to keep warm, Finn lay sleepless as so often before. Memory stirred and rustled in his mind like insects in thatch.

Once this fort smelled new, he thought. Dazed wood, limewash. Clean, fresh smells. Now it seems musty. The very air feels tired.

Why doesn't it smell new anymore?

He longed to sleep out under the windblown stars and awake in a wild world that always smelled new.

But when he went to the doorway, the young fénnid standing sentry looked at him quizzically. "You wouldn't go out on a night like this surely," the sentry said. "The wind would blow your eyeballs to the back of your skull."

Once Finn would have laughed and strode past him into the full force of the gale. Now he hesitated, considered, then at last shrugged and went back inside.

But once he was lying on his bed under piles of fur and woven wool, he was angry with himself for having given in. He fought off the covers and whistled softly. "Conbec!" he called to the Hound of Perfect Symmetry. "Here to me now!"

The great dog, so like Bran, eagerly joined Finn in his bed and nestled close against him with a contented sigh. Finn stroked the coarse-haired skull absentmindedly and dreamed of the old days' hunting. Of the red deer . . .

Winter passed, as it must. But never a winter so slow as that one.

The Festival of Imbolc celebrated the lactation of the ewes, return of life to a slumbering world. Beltaine loomed on the horizon three cycles of the moon later.

Finn began preparing for his marriage to the High King's daughter.

Cailte, as always, was with him. One night the thin man reported back to his wife, "Finn's more nervous about this than he was about the first one."

"Nervous? Of taking a wife? Why should any man be nervous of something so natural?"

"Och, Finn isn't like any man. He always wants everything to be perfect. And in his control, that's very important to him."

Cailte's wife laughed. "No man who wants everything under his own control should have anything to do with a woman!"

The passage of the seasons had given Finn time to ponder on Grania, time to recall her every gesture and word to him. Again and again he heard her asking, "Are you a skillful lover?"

The question was a reasonable one. In Gaelic society, women, especially of the upper classes, had as much sexual freedom as men. Young women often sampled several suitors before agreeing to a contract marriage. Such behaviour was not discouraged. If a woman knew what to expect in the marriage bed, she would be more likely to please her husband—and less likely to want other lovers after marriage, because her youthful curiosity had been satisfied while at its peak.

So, young as she was, Grania might well have welcomed one or more men into her bed already. Finn did not begrudge them. He did, however, feel the gnawings of his own curiosity. How would he compare with other, surely younger, men she might have known?

At last he brought himself to broach the subject with Cailte, obliquely. "What do you know of the arts of pleasing a woman's body?"

"What any other man knows, I suppose," the thin man replied.

"Would you say some men are better at it than others?"

Cailte considered the question. "I suppose some would be, just as some are better at running and others excel at spear throwing. Why?"

"No particular reason. I just wondered. Ah . . . who would you say, among the men here at Almhain, is most expert at pleasing women?"

Cailte gave Finn a long look. "Are you seeking a tutor?"

"Of course not! I need no help there, or anywhere else. I mastered all physical skills long ago. I was just asking. For the sake of curiosity."

Cailte was astonished to think that Finn—the Finn he had known for the better part of his life, the man he had followed and admired and tried to emulate, the man who had proven himself superior in any way, again and again—would now be looking for instruction in so simple a thing as bedding a woman to her satisfaction.

With a stab of alarm, Cailte wondered if he himself had been as good at it, all these years, as he had assumed.

Would the wife tell him?

Aloud, he said, "The man at Almhain who has the most women following him is young Diarmait, Donn's son. Every female old enough to bleed sighs when he walks by, and I know for a fact that he spends very few nights sleeping among the unmarried warriors. He appears with the dawn and disappears at sunset. I'd say he's an expert, in spite of his youth."

"Or because of it," Finn said gloomily. Somehow he could not bring himself to go to Diarmait Mac Donn and ask for his secrets for pleasing women.

As Beltaine approached, he turned his mind to other matters, to the acquisition of fine clothing for himself and his party, to the collection of an acceptable coibche to give to Cormac, and to the assigning of companies of Fíanna around the periphery of Míd to assure that no unwanted hostilities broke out while Finn was occupied with marriage. He drove himself relentlessly.

Cailte was not the only one observing the excessive activity the prospect of marriage had engendered in the commander. The officers and men talked of it among themselves, with wry and ribald commentary. When Oisin overheard one man saying to another, "You'd think the commander had never had a woman before, he's making such an effort to impress this one!", Finn's son caught the offender by the neck and bashed his head against the nearest post until the man howled for mercy.

Within half a day the incident was the talk of Almhain. Hearing of it, Finn thought bitterly, I'm making a fool of myself. It isn't as if I never took a wife before. I must be more casual about the whole thing.

But with the single exception of Sive, Finn had never known exactly how to behave toward women. His contemporaries, nurtured by the many female members of their clans almost impartially, slid without difficulty into comfortable relationships with bedmates and wives. But Finn's sole female contact during his childhood had been with two leathery old women who never caressed him, never sang to him, hardly even talked to him, because they did not know how to talk to a young boy. They merely kept him alive.

Finn had been nurtured by the hills and forests, the wild places. Only wild Sive fitted the shape of his soul. Otherwise, women would always be a mystery to him.

When the time came to depart for Tara, he found himself growing increasingly tense. He hid the tension behind a grim visage, refusing to give anyone reason to laugh at him again. From his horse's back he talked to his men of war and weaponry throughout the trip northward, as if women were the farthest thing from his mind.

A welcoming party, alerted by runners, was at the Slige Dala gate to meet them. Finn sent back an order to the fénnidi to halt and stand, and prepared to ride forward the last little distance alone to meet his intended wife. He could see her waiting beside Cormac.

Not entirely alone, he decided. In a harsh whisper, he called, "Cailte, ride with me! I should have an attendant."

Cailte was hardly the appropriate choice for an attendant, being a senior officer of the Fíanna. But he understood. He kicked his horse forward until it was shoulder to shoulder with Finn's.

"There she is," Finn said in a low voice. "Gowned in yellow, with flowers in her hair. What am I going to say to her, Cailte?"

"Try hello," the other advised seriously.

They rode forward.

Grania watched their approach, shading her eyes with her hand against the strong sunlight of imminent summer. She let herself look at

Cailte first, thin and grey-haired and easy on his horse. Then she slid her
eyes sideways to Finn Mac Cool.

He was dressed as splendidly as a king, with a fur-lined cloak in spite
of the warmth of the day, and a great golden torc around his neck. But
he looked so . . . so grim! So forbidding!

Grania glanced toward her father for reassurance, but Cormac was
already hastening forward with his hands outstretched in welcome.

Finn gave Grania a brief greeting with all emotion strained from it.
Appearing casual.

She murmured something in return, then fell to talking with her
sisters and female companions, "Isn't the Rígfénnid Fíanna magnificent!" one of them enthused. But another, stung with jealousy, hissed to
Grania, "He's old enough to be your father."

Grania promptly looked at Cormac and then back to Finn, compar-
ing the two.

Cormac Mac Airt was older than Finn but had spent his recent years
in the ease and luxury of Tara for the most part. Finn had spent the same
years either fighting or hunting. His face chronicled the weather of Erin.
The two men looked to be of an age. If anything, Finn looked older at
the moment, his features deliberately set in a stern mold.

Grania bit her lip.

As he had done before, Finn delivered the coibche to Cormac Mac
Airt in a formal ceremony, then met with Grania at the ritual Beltaine
pole to recite their promises to each other. As before, it would be a
marriage of the first degree, though with the man claiming no property
with his wife.

Finn did not want property. He wanted to be married to a daughter
of the High King.

And, looking down at her piquant face in the sunshine, he realized
he really did want her, want her body.

He could feel a welcome stirring below his tunic, as if something long
hibernating were coming to life again.

He smiled down at Grania, but she did not notice. Her eyes were fixed
obediently on the brehon, Flaithri, as he recited their obligations to each
other. Only once or twice did Grania look away. She briefly peered from
beneath her eyelashes at the ring of spectators attending the ritual. As
if against her will, her eyes were drawn to the youngest, freshest faces.

27

THAT NIGHT CORMAC MAC AIRT ORDERED A GREAT FEAST served in honour of his daughter and her new husband in the Banquetting Hall. In anticipation, Finn had brought a change of clothing for every member of his party who would have the rank to attend. He himself put on a new tunic of softest linen, girdled with leather set with precious stones, and used a massive brooch of bronze and gold wire to fasten a flowing blue mantle around his shoulders. He knew—because Sive had once told him so—that blue was the perfect complement to his silvery hair.

The other rígfénnidi chosen to accompany him on this occasion were dressed in almost equal finery. Donn wore gold ear rings. Cailte had a fox-fur mantle. Fergus Honey-Tongue was resplendent in dyed wool and silver ornaments.

The newest heroes of the Fíanna were also invited to attend, though they had not yet received the rank of officers. Oisin and the sons of Donn and Lugaid were in the crowd that night in the Banquetting Hall, to drink wine and mead and sing songs in honour of Finn and his new wife.

Due to the occasion, Grania was given a seat beside her husband rather than one with the other women. She sat demurely, enjoying being the centre of attention. Her hair was newly bound to indicate her married status, and around her neck she wore a chain of gold, Finn's gift to her.

But from time to time she glanced through her eyelashes at the others in the great hall. The other men; the young men.

In spite of her question relative to Finn's skill, she had not yet bedded a man. She was very young, merely playing at being older and more experienced. She had heard other women talk.

She was curious. And though she would not admit it even to herself, she was more than a little frightened of the prospect of having her body invaded by the toughened, fabled, weatherworn man sitting beside her, exuding a male aura of power.

Her eyes repeatedly sought the younger and gentler faces among his men in the hall.

As the meal was devoured, bones were thrown to the ubiquitous hounds, who followed their masters everywhere. The king's chief poet was actually reciting Cormac's lineage and deeds as a compliment to Cormac's daughter when a fight broke out between two of the dogs. The king scowled. "Make them be quiet!" he roared. "Do it!" Finn echoed.

The two nearest fénnidi ran to separate the snarling hounds, but the dogs evaded them and scampered across the rush-strewn floor, ducking under the many low tables holding food, scurrying behind benches, growling and lunging at one another the entire time.

The two young men—Oisin and Diarmait—ran after them, aware that Finn would be furious if they did not put a stop to the fight at once and please the king.

The dogfight boiled its way almost to Grania's feet. There Diarmait succeeded in interposing his body between the quarrelling hounds, caught each of them by the scruff of the neck, and pulled them apart with an act of brute strength that surprised himself.

Panting and flushed with triumph, he looked up to find his face no more than a forearm's length from that of Grania. He smiled, delighted with himself.

She smiled back.

He was young, barely bearded yet, with soft lips and smooth skin and a beguiling curve to one side of his mouth, and when Diarmait looked at Grania, she thought the rest of the room went away.

They stared at each other in the golden light of torch and candle.

Finn at that moment was speaking earnestly to Cormac about provisioning the outlying garrisons for the summer and did not notice the exchange between Donn's son and his new wife.

But from twelve spear-lengths away, Goll Mac Morna noticed it. He dug his elbow into Cailte's ribs. "Look there," he commanded. "There's trouble."

Cailte followed the direction of Goll's gaze. "Och, Diarmait. They all look at Diarmait."

"She's doing more than looking at him, Cailte."

"She can't do more, not on the very night she's married Finn."

Goll unconsciously rubbed the scar below his eye. "Have you seen a woman turn away from Diarmait yet? They all love him."

"Everyone loves him. He's as popular as Oisin, perhaps more. And he's beautiful, even with that scar. It makes him more beautiful than ever. You can't blame the child for looking at him."

"I don't blame her for looking," Goll said, "but they're doing more than looking, those two. The king's daughter's laying an enchantment on him with those slanted eyes of hers. Mark my words, Cailte, and remember them."

Cailte, troubled, felt his appetite fall away and sat toying with his food, his gaze repeatedly returning to Finn. And Grania. And Diarmait, hovering close.

The feasting continued until the first streaks of salmon-coloured light appeared in the eastern sky. Abandoning the positions in the hall assigned to them according to rank, the guests mingled freely with one another as time passed and wine flowed. The assemblage became much less formal, louder, rowdier. Cups were filled and refilled. One by one, heads nodded, eyes shuttered closed. The first to weaken slid down with their backs against the wall and fell asleep, leaving others to step over them until they in turn collapsed as well.

It was Finn's wedding night, but he was drinking as much as anyone else. More. It helped forestall the moment when he would have to prove whether or not he was a satisfactory bedmate for a very young wife. He did not want to disappoint her. He ached to have this most recent, perhaps this last, marriage go well. He did not want to have to seek another woman, not ever.

He took one cup too many, even for him, and against his will, his eyelids drifted down. He did not realize he was leaning forward, did not know his head was pillowed on folded arms on the nearest table. But Grania knew. Looking down at him, she thought with contempt, he's old. Old!

Then she looked up and her eyes met those of young Diarmait Mac Donn.

She summoned him without making any physical gesture at all.

"Will you keep me safe company to the nearest doorway?" she asked. "I need to breathe cool air."

Diarmait willingly complied, hoping his companions would notice he had been chosen to escort Finn's new wife. But his companions, like most of those in the hall, were past noticing.

Diarmait walked with Grania to the Doorway of Kings and stood beside her as she gazed out into the breaking dawn. She was very aware of his proximity. He was young and fresh; he was able to stay awake through a long night, as she had done. He was not sleeping with his head down amid the rubble of the feast.

She turned toward him. "Will you take me away from here? Now?"

The request startled him. "To your house? I mean, to the house where you and Finn are to . . ."

"Take me *away,* I said. Away from Finn Mac Cool, away from Tara. I don't want to be here. I don't want to do this."

Diarmait stammered, "I don't understand."

"I think you do. I want to go away from here with you."

Diarmait had grown accustomed to having women desire him. It was pleasant and natural, and he invariably responded with delight. But this particular situation was unique in his experience.

He was tremendously flattered to have such a proposal made to him by the brand-new wife of Finn Mac Cool. At the same time, he was shocked by it.

Pleasantly shocked.

Grania, in Diarmait's opinion, was beautiful. And the deed she was suggesting was so daring it surpassed all the acts of courage he had yet committed.

He drew in a sharp breath.

"I can't take the commander's woman . . ."

"You can." Her pale eyes sparkled with excitement and mischief. "You can! Do it now!" She caught his hand in hers and pressed it between her breasts, so he could feel the soft mounds of flesh and the beating heart behind them.

Diarmait had drunk a lot of wine that night, and sung not a few songs. The roistering atmosphere of the banquet had seeped into his bones. All around him, members of the Fíanna had been telling lurid stories, boasting of great deeds to impress the poets in the room, as Finn's men had always done. There had been an atmosphere of unreality in the Banquetting Hall at Tara that night. The unfettered Fíanna . . .

What would be more appropriate in such an atmosphere than to commit the most spectacular of kidnappings and run off with Finn's wife? Just for a little while?

Had Diarmait been four seasons older, or four cups of wine less drunk, he might not have done it.

But Grania tugged at his hand and pleaded with her tilted eyes, and a wildness seized him. "While Finn Mac Cool's at Tara, he has men on all the gates," he said. "We couldn't get out past them."

"We can of course. I'll take you through the Grianan, there's a hidden entrance there."

"For what purpose?"

Grania's laugh gurgled like water running over stones. "Women always insist on having a secret entrance to their Grianan, didn't you know? Come with me now." She tugged at his hand more insistently. "Come quickly!"

Afterward, Diarmait never knew just why he gave in, or at what moment. He only knew they were outside the hall and running across the muddy lawn, slipping through the shadows of lodges and walls, pausing with pounding hearts to let a sentry walk by, then running on again until they came to the oaken door of the Grianan and Grania led him inside.

She did not give him time to examine the women's sunny chamber, much as he wanted to, but led him across it to a hanging of woven wool on one wall and pushed the hanging aside.

There was a small, low door.

Bending, Grania shoved at the door, but her strength was not enough to open it. "Help me," she pleaded with Diarmait.

He drove the door open with his shoulder and they stepped through it.

They found themselves in a narrow, chokingly dark passageway that seemed built inside one of the palisades of Tara. They had to feel their way step by step, like blind people. Grania, who seemed to know where she was going, had one hand extended in front of her and with the other was holding fast to Diarmait's arm.

How strong it is! one part of her mind thought. How firm the muscle!

A narrow crack of light appeared ahead and she hurried toward it. "Push here," she instructed Oisin.

He lent his shoulder to the task and grunted.

Nothing happened.

"Hurry!" Grania urged, making him fear someone was coming behind them.

Diarmait gave another, mightier heave, and this time rusty hinges creaked in protest and a door slowly grated open, revealing space beyond. The pair slipped through.

They found themselves outside the walls of Tara, facing south.

Diarmait straightened and looked around. His head was spinning from the fumes of wine and the atmosphere of the hall and the flight and the exertion. And the nearness of Grania, pressing herself against him.

She was tingling with adventure.

"What do we do now?" he asked her.

"Run, of course!"

"Run?" The word began to soak into his consciousness, bringing additional ramifications. "Run where? How?" He glanced around. "Do you not think we should go back?"

"Go back? Go back!" She sounded shocked. "Of course not! I have chosen you for myself and you've just stolen me from the Rígfénnid Fíanna. We can't go back. We can never go back. We have to make a new life for ourselves, you and I!" She was aglow with the fanciful excitement of a child playing. Before he could stop her, she darted away into the brightening day and he had no choice but to run after her.

Grania was laughing and as light-footed as a butterfly. She sped over the dew-wet grass as if she had not just spent a sleepless night in a crowded hall, breathing fumes of mead and wine. Her hair had pulled loose and tumbled about her face in tempting tendrils; her tilted eyes were glittering and thoughtless.

Diarmait pursued her wholeheartedly. He did not dare stop to think. This was an adventure, the greatest of all adventures! What a tale it would make to tell around the campfire later . . .

. . . later. He brushed the thought away.

He was young. They were young, and the world was newly made.

Grania ran until she was gasping for breath, then sank down, laughing, into a leafy hollow and held out her arms toward Diarmait. "I am your prize!" she called to him. "Your trophy of the chase!"

He stood over her, legs apart, looking down. She was flushed and very beautiful. In the hall, the others were probably still asleep, unaware. He could take her here and now and then sneak her back inside. No one need ever know.

He bent toward her, fumbling with his clothes. Grania's eyes opened wider. "Not yet!" she cried in sudden alarm, leaping to her feet. Before he could grasp her, she brushed past him and ran again. "We have to get farther away!" she called over her shoulder.

Diarmait ran after her.

He did not know if it was a game, or serious. There was no time to think. He knew only that it was very exciting and that he was having a wonderful time.

He caught her and tumbled her gently to the ground. She looked up at him. He could not tell if he saw fear or desire in her eyes, or some other emotion he did not know. "We have to keep running," she said breathlessly. "We must not stop now. They'll catch us. Later, though. I promise you. Later."

"You really promise?" He clutched her shoulders and squeezed, hard.

"I promise. Now let me up."

He helped her to her feet and they set off again, running shoulder to shoulder this time, with Diarmait holding back so she could match his pace. He thought at any moment they would turn around and go back.

They must go back.

This could not be serious.

At some time, though, it began to be borne in upon him that it was serious. Grania had no intention of going back. She was fleeing Finn Mac Cool, and he had got caught up in the momentum of her flight.

Diarmait felt as if a cold hand clutched his heart. He stopped running between one stride and the next. "The sun's up," he panted. "We must go back right now, we're in enough trouble as it is."

But she ran on.

"Grania!" he shouted. "Listen to me, we have to return to Tara! Your husband's waiting!"

"I've taken you for my husband," she called over her shoulder, running.

Diarmait stared after her in consternation.

"Come on!" she called urgently.

She was intoxicated with her first true taste of feminine power. Marrying Finn Mac Cool was surely prestigious, and pleased her father, but it was nothing compared to snatching up this beautiful young man and making him turn his back on his commander and his oath of loyalty and run away with her. She felt blazingly alive. Her thoughts did not go so far as to tomorrow, or even to the night to come. She knew only here and now. Here and now was thrilling and she wanted it to last.

"Come *on!*" she cried again.

Diarmait, torn, looked back toward Tara. The golden thatch, illumined by the early morning sun, glowed like lost treasure. Banners were fluttering in a rising wind. Clear and terrifying to his ears came the sound of a horn, a hunting horn.

They had been missed already. Someone was after them.

With a cry of anguish, Diarmait set off after Grania.

If he had not heard the horn, he could have gone back, he thought. But somehow that one sound, trumpeting his betrayal, had cut him off from hope of return. If he did go back, he would be seen. Questioned. Everyone would know of his foolishness.

It was too much; he had to keep running.

Then too, she was so beautiful. Her eyes had said magic things to him, and Diarmait came of a race that believed in magic.

At last they found a small cave in a riverbank, its mouth well-screened by alders. Slipping inside, they lay breathless and listened to the thudding of their hearts.

"We've done a mad thing," Diarmait said at last. "There will be no forgiveness for either of us. Och, the king may forgive you, you're his daughter, but the commander never will. And what he will do to me doesn't bear thinking about. I've stolen from him and disgraced the name of the Fíanna."

The full meaning of his deed swept over him like dark floodwater.

"Disgraced the Fíanna," he repeated in a whisper of disbelief.

She was afraid he would leave her to her fate. She rolled over against him, pinioning him with her body, and pressed herself against him. "But I can't go back," she said. "Not to that old man."

"What old man?"

"Finn Mac Cool, of course!"

Diarmait pushed her off and sat up. He stared at her in the dim, watery light filtering through the mouth of the cave. "Finn isn't old."

"He is! He's generations older than I am."

"You and I are only two years apart, I'd say," Diarmait replied, "and he doesn't seem old to me. He's a strong man."

"You don't see him as I do. I don't want to look at him at all, in my bed or out of it. I only want to look at you." Grania reached for Diarmait, her lips parted and soft. He meant to pull away from her.

Afterward, he could not have said why he went into her arms instead.

Grania made up in eagerness what she lacked in experience. The excitement of the elopement had stimulated her to an almost unbearable pitch. Diarmait's touch made her moan; every movement of his body made her wriggle closer to him until they were locked together so tightly it was hard for either of them to breathe. Her frenzy set fire to him, and he stopped worrying about pursuit or loyalty to his oath or anything else. There was only Grania in a cave filled with watery light, as if they were under the sea. And magic was all around them.

Magic, in time, faded into reality.

Diarmait lay on his back, wondering what to do next. Grania was curled up against him like a kitten, sleeping. Her breathing was shallow and delicate. She seemed fragile. He felt an obligation to protect her against whatever they had brought on themselves.

At last he stirred, adjusted his clothing, touched her shoulder. "Stay here," he whispered.

She awoke and clutched at him. "Don't leave me!"

"I'm not going to leave you. I'm just going back to Tara long enough to find out . . . find out how Finn's responded to this, and try to get some sort of idea of how much trouble we're in. I have friends in the Fíanna, they'll advise me what to do next."

"Don't go!"

"I must, Grania," he said, trying to reason with her. "Maybe there's still time to . . . to make things all right."

"I don't want things to be all right. I want to go on just as we are, you and me together."

"It won't be that simple," he warned her. "We can't just go on together and trust we'll be forgotten. I heard the sound of the hunting horn; that means someone's looking for us already. And Finn Mac Cool's the best hunter in Erin."

"I won't go back to him." Had she been standing, Grania would have stamped her foot for emphasis. "I want you, not him, not that old man. I want to be *your* wife."

Even in his distraught condition, Diarmait was man enough to be flattered, and far enough under her spell to be glad of her words. But he had been thoroughly trained. He knew the demands of honour. He would have to go back, if only long enough to try to explain.

The oath of loyalty he had pledged to Finn Mac Cool lay in him like a stone.

"You can't be my wife, my contract wife, while you're wife to Finn Mac Cool," he reminded her gently. "We can be lovers, we can enjoy a marriage of lesser degree, but a woman can be contract wife to only one man at a time."

"He can have more than one wife, though. Why can't I have more than one husband? And stay with the one I choose?"

"It's the law," Diarmait said.

"I refuse the law, then," she replied. "I refuse all law that keeps me from you!" She threw her arms around him.

It took all the fortitude Diarmait possessed to disengage himself from her embrace. "Try to understand, Grania. I want you too, and I'll come back to you. But first I must return to Tara and undo the damage I've—we've—done. I *must.*"

She had begun to love him, truly love him. She heard the need in his voice and reluctantly submitted. "Go if you must," she said. "But give me your word you'll come back to me."

The return journey to Tara seemed much longer than the flight from it. Twice he had to hide from a search party. With every step Diarmait took, his crime loomed larger in his mind.

He had stolen Finn's wife and the High King's daughter! What compensation would the brehons demand for such a theft? Grania was a princess; under the law, he would owe the injured parties not her honour price, but theirs. Theirs jointly, Finn's and Cormac's together, king and husband.

The combined property of himself and his father and all their tribe would not be enough to pay it. He had impoverished his people.

By the time the palisades of Tara rose before him, he was sick with hopelessness. He actually turned to go back to Grania because there seemed nothing else to do, when the sentry on the Slige Dala gate hailed him.

Fortunately for Diarmait, the sentry was Lugaid's son. "Hssst! Run quick and hide yourself in that hollow! I'll join you!" Lugaid's son, after making sure no one was watching, put deed to word.

"Now, Diarmait, tell me. What in the name of the four winds possessed you to lay violent hands on the High King's daughter and steal her from her wedding bed?"

"Is that what they're saying I did?" Diarmait asked with a sinking feeling.

"That and worse things. No one seems quite sure just what did happen, actually, except the two of you were seen leaving the banquet together, and shortly afterward neither of you was to be found in Tara."

"Is Cormac very angry?"

"It isn't Cormac you need worry about, though he is as angry as a hornet's nest. Your problem is the Rígfénnid Fíanna. You not only took his wife from him, but you know yourself he's always demanded we treat women with the utmost respect and obey every aspect of the law concerning them. Have you not heard him say, time and again, that kidnapping women is strictly forbidden to the Fíanna? But now you've done this. You're in more trouble than a quartered deer boiling in a fualacht fiadh."

Diarmait slumped onto the ground and buried his face in his hands. "I never meant any of this," he said muffledly.

"A bit late now," was the accurate reply.

"What am I to do? I need help, advice. Could you find Oisin inside and bring him out to me? He's my friend, I can trust him."

"Wait here and I'll try," promised Lugaid's son. "But keep your head down and if anyone catches sight of you, run like a hare!"

Hot with shame and cold with fear, Diarmait waited for an eternity. At last Lugaid's son returned with Oisin and some other members of the Fíanna, mostly of Diarmait's own age. They made a circle around the unfortunate man, further concealing him.

Oisin said, "This is a terrible twist you've got yourself into."

"And I knowing it. But what am I to do?"

"Return what you've stolen," said Cailte Mac Ronan, stepping through the circle of younger men. His face was stern, his eyes agonized.

Diarmait shook his head. "I can't. She won't go back to Finn. Nor, to be honest, do I want her to," he had to admit. "She's put an enchantment on me, I think."

Cailte narrowed his eyes to slits, trying to see into the inmost recesses of the other man. Finn believed in the power of enchantments, he knew. It could be possible that something such as had happened with Finn and Sive had happened again with Donn's son, and if it had, there was no fighting it.

Cailte gave a weary sigh. "I see." He sounded almost envious. "You don't mean to return her, then."

"I can't. I just came back myself to . . . to find out what had happened when our absence was discovered, and to try to explain."

Oisin spoke up then. "Does Grania want you, Diarmait?"

"She says she does."

Oisin sounded openly envious. "I would never dare take a woman promised to Finn Mac Cool, but if she wants you and you want her, then neither the sky nor the sea should stop you!"

Cailte whirled on him. "Don't encourage him, do you not realize what he's letting himself in for? Himself and the girl too?"

Diarmait said, "What am I letting us in for, Cailte? How has Finn reacted?"

The agony in Cailte's eyes grew more pronounced. "You had not been gone for very long before those who were still awake, and saw you leave together, made Finn aware of the fact."

"They would," commented Lugaid's son. "Conan, I suppose?"

"Indeed. You know him. But others too, whispering, speculating. At first Finn tried to shrug it off. He said you had undoubtedly escorted the girl to her bed to wait for him. He left the hall then and went to join her.

"He came back with a look on him such as I have never seen, and I've seen him in some bad times. He stood in the Doorway of Fate . . . of Fate! . . . and cried aloud like a man in mortal pain."

Diarmait was almost afraid to ask. "What did he say?"

"He said 'Abandoned!' in a terrible voice, like a voice issuing from a tomb. He cried the word aloud three times, then he collapsed in the doorway. We carried him back to what should have been his marriage bed, but he refused to lie on it. He seemed in mortal agony, yet he would not let the physician touch him. He writhed from side to side like a chained animal and gave great hoarse dry sobs." The reflected pain in Cailte's eyes made Diarmait wince.

"We only eloped together," he tried to explain. "It wasn't so terrible as that. Men and women have run off before . . ."

"*Women* have run off before," Cailte stressed. "From Finn. And this one was one too many."

"I don't understand."

"You don't have to understand. You have to take the woman and run and keep running if you value your life and hers."

"Would he hurt Grania?" Diarmait asked in disbelief.

"I honestly don't know what he's likely to do. He's gone . . . mad, Diarmait. Quite mad. I've seen Finn disturbed in his head before, but never anything like this. Something seems to have broken inside him.

"He wanted, so much, to have a wife again and a warm bed and a cheerful companion. I know he did. He once had a wife he loved very much—"

"My mother," interjected Oisin, who had heard all the stories.

"—and I think Finn hoped to find something of that again with Grania. Now she's left him too. You could not have done the man as much damage if you'd run your spear through his heart."

Diarmait was appalled. "If I went to Finn right now and asked his forgiveness and mercy, would he—"

"Don't even think it," Cailte warned him. "Just run."

"Where can we go?"

"Anywhere, as far from here as possible."

"There are hounds after us already, I heard them."

"Cormac sent that party searching for you," Oisin explained. "He gave the order while Finn was too upset to issue any commands."

"But Finn will recover," Cailte warned. "He'll recover enough to come after you himself, and then there'll be no tree tall enough for you to climb or sea wide enough for you to swim to escape him. And he won't listen to apologies or to reason, I promise you. I know him. As he is now, he won't listen to anything."

Diarmait said, "Why do you even speak to me, you who are the commander's closest friend, if I've done something so terrible to him?"

"Because I am his closest friend," Cailte replied. "If and when he ever comes to his senses again, he will regret any violence he does to you or the girl. I know him. So until that day comes, I will do what I can to protect the two of you so he will have less to reproach himself for."

"You love him very much," Diarmait said, suddenly aware.

"As you and Oisin love each other, I do. I guard his back," Cailte added simply.

Oisin went to stand beside Diarmait. "And I guard yours," he vowed.

"Even against your own father?"

"We do not choose our parents, but we choose our friends." The words were difficult for Oisin, but he said them. As far back as he could remember, he had been the son of Finn Mac Cool and proud of it. But the man he had seen raving inside Tara a short time ago was not the father he loved and admired. Today's Finn Mac Cool was like a wild animal, terrifying in its unreasoning rage, and he did not want to be associated with such a creature. Diarmait Mac Donn, pale with anxiety but still sensible, still his merry-hearted companion, was his choice of the two.

In the shadow of the walls of Tara, the young men made their decisions. The majority went with Oisin to stand beside Diarmait, silently pledging to him.

We would have so pledged to Finn, Cailte thought but did not say aloud, remembering how it was with himself and the original nine. He respected Oisin for his courage.

Lugaid's son went back to stand guard at the gate as if nothing had happened in order to allay any suspicions, while Oisin and some of the others went to the stables to get horses for riding out across the plain. But they did not mount the horses. Instead, they brought a pair to

Diarmait in his place of concealment and urged him to take one for himself and one for Grania and flee before the sun went any farther toward the western sea.

"You have hardly any chance of escape," Cailte concluded sadly, "but none if you stay here. Go now, quickly, and we'll do what we can to help you."

So Diarmait Mac Donn, bright young hero and most popular member of the Fíanna, was forced to turn his back on Tara and run for his life.

At first he galloped with tears in his eyes. But as he drew nearer the place where Grania waited hidden, he began to feel her calling him, drawing him like a tidal tug, and his pain eased just a little.

He would salvage something. Out of this youthful madness, he would take something of value and hope it made the cost worthwhile.

28

THIS TIME FINN WAS NOT LONG INCAPACITATED BY MAD-
ness. Within a day and a night he was in control of himself
again, or in as much control as he could be of the raging beast
within him. Too much hurt had been done to him, too many times. He
had met the world with a smile on his lips and poems in his heart, and
the world had bashed and battered him and taken from him everything
that mattered, including the hard-won honour of the Fíanna.

Only Oisin was left to him, and when he saw his son's face, he knew
Oisin's sympathies were with Diarmait Mac Donn.

I am alone, Finn thought. I am as alone as I was after I left my foster
mothers and went roaming through the wilderness. Being alone did not
bother me then. It seemed natural. Why should it bother me now?

He thought this with his head, but he did not feel it in his heart. From
some place deep inside him, in the marrow of his bones, rose an ache
beyond endurance.

Once he would have talked to Sive about it, trusting the fact of her
being to soothe away the pain, any pain.

But Sive had left him.

Muirinn had left him.

Now Grania. And when he allowed himself to even think the name of
that slant-eyed girl, black rage rose up in him and choked out all his
rational thinking like briers choking healthy fruit.

Cormac Mac Airt was deeply upset. "I am sorry about this, Finn," he
told his commander. "More sorry than I can say. It appears now that my
daughter went willingly. She may even have enticed young Diarmait,
from what one or two of the servants are saying. If that is true, she has
disgraced not only herself, but me, and I will accede to any punishment
you demand of her."

"Punishment?" Finn's teeth grated on the word. "Revenge? I foreswore revenge a long time ago."

Cormac gave a small, relieved laugh. "It's glad I am to hear you say it, because—"

"But I take back that oath," Finn went on relentlessly. "When I find Diarmait and Grania, *and I will,* I will be revenged on them as no man has ever been!"

In horror of the thing he saw in Finn's face, Cormac took a step backward. "You're very angry and you have every right to be, but I beg you, remember the law. We can work out compensation. In all the years I've been High King, there are hundreds of situations that have been brought before the brehons instead of resulting in bloodbaths. Compensation restores goodwill between people. I've upheld that principle as has no king before me. In this matter too, we can arrange for compensation . . ."

"I cannot be compensated for what's been done to me," Finn said flatly.

"You can of course, there's always a way. We can have my daughter shorn of her hair perhaps, and the young man's clan, even his tribe, will be forced to pay—"

"I cannot be compensated," said Finn Mac Cool. "But I can exact vengeance."

Arguing with him was useless. In the end, Cormac had no choice, as one of the aggrieved parties, but to support him. They would combine forces in the search for the runaways.

What happened when Diarmait and Grania were found was a problem for the future.

An icy Finn Mac Cool, embittered almost beyond recognition, issued orders to the Fíanna. Huge hunting parties were to be formed to comb Erin from north to south and from east to west. Bands were to station themselves at every bay and harbour, denying the fugitives any chance of escape by boat.

"That's not possible," Goll tried to tell Finn. "There are hundreds of hundreds of places around the coast of Erin where one can launch a boat. We can't guard them all."

"Try," commanded Finn Mac Cool.

But Diarmait and Grania were not making for the sea.

When Diarmait returned to their hiding place with the pair of horses, Grania was overjoyed to see him, but puzzled as to why he had brought horses. "So we can flee more swiftly," he explained.

"But I cannot ride a horse, Diarmait. I've never even tried. I'd fall off, I know I would."

He felt young and foolish. "I should have thought of that."

"I can ride in a chariot, though. Can you get us a chariot?"

"I cannot, I don't know where . . ." His eyes brightened. "I do know! There is someone who will give us a chariot! Someone not too far from here. If we travel by night, we may be able to reach his home without being caught."

Under cover of darkness, Diarmait mounted one of the horses, balanced a fearful Grania on the animal's rump behind him, and led the other horse at a careful walk. "Don't go any faster," Grania kept saying, holding him around the waist hard enough to shut off the workings of his gut. It was obvious she would indeed require a chariot, she would never endure a flight on horseback.

Diarmait made his cautious, wary way to the banks of the river Boyne, to the stronghold of the chieftain who had fostered him there in the years of his beardlessness. Angus was a strong, proud man who adhered to the old ways and still kept chariots long after the fashion for using them in warfare had died.

Angus was delighted to see his fosterling. "Come inside and take hospitality!" he insisted. "And your woman too. Who is this? Have you taken a wife?"

"I am his wife," Grania announced, sliding thankfully off the horse.

But Diarmait's personal honour forced him to say, "She is not wife to me. We have a marriage. By abduction."

"By abduction! Good on you, lad! Strong, hot blood in you, then! I thought that sort of thing was forbidden to the Fíanna these days. Come in and drink ale with me and tell me all about it, eh? Eh?"

Diarmait was relieved to know that the full details of his crime had not yet reached far beyond Tara. If they had, Angus might not have given him the same welcome. But he went inside his foster father's hall and drank ale and ate meat by his fire, and let Angus's women tend the weary Grania.

And late in the night, when the shadows of the fire threw grotesque shapes on the walls and the wind rose, he divulged the entire story.

Angus was understandably taken aback. "Not good, this, not good at all. You have the High King and the Rígfénnid Fíanna against you; that's quite an achievement for so young a man. And the debt you owe is monstrous. Neither your sire nor I could ever pay such a price."

"I know that. I'm not asking you to. I'm just asking for what help you can give: a chariot for Grania to ride in and enough food to get us across Erin without stopping if we must."

Angus stared into the fire and considered. He was a beefy, grizzled man with a broad red face and a fringe of whiskers like moss creeping over his features, moss that did not hide his concern as he said, "As your foster father, I shall do what I can for you. And I won't condemn you.

There'll be enough of them to do that. I've always been proud of you, Diarmait, and never prouder than the day I heard you'd been welcomed into the Fíanna and were training as an officer. That's come to be a noble boast, and I've boasted of you."

"I'm sorry you can boast of me no more," Diarmait said sadly.

Angus gathered himself. "Who says I can't? I can indeed! Who else has a son bold enough to steal a king's daughter and a commander's wife?" Determined to convince both himself and Diarmait, he clapped the young man on the back so hard he left a huge bruise that ached for days. "Now get some sleep, and we'll see you away at dawn."

The light of the next day was just creeping into the sky when a grateful Diarmait departed the stronghold of his foster father, equipped with a chariot and two horses trained to pull it, for which he had exchanged the riding horses taken from Tara. Bundles of food were stored in the wicker-sided cart, leaving just enough room for Diarmait to stand and drive, with Grania beside him.

Sleepily, she leaned her head on his shoulder as he waved farewell to Angus and lifted the reins. "I hope I see you again," Diarmait called to his fosterer.

"Here or in the Land of Everlasting Youth," the other replied with a cheer he did not feel.

The fugitives set off for the west, for the empty places.

Diarmait had hunted with Finn and Oisin, he knew how the hounds worked. He deliberately drove the chariot as far as he could along the beds of rivers and streams, destroying the scent for the hounds to follow. Where the water was too deep or the way too narrow, he emerged to drive along the bank, regretting but unable to prevent the ruts the chariot wheels made. It would have been easier riding horses, but he would not chide Grania.

She touched a deep protective streak within him. The enormity of their deed had gradually dawned on her as well, and he knew she was afraid. From time to time she trembled. But she clung to him and reiterated her love for him until he could not doubt her. He could do nothing but go on.

Chariots made for rough riding. They leaped and lurched and threatened to overturn almost constantly. Diarmait, trained to ride horses, was uncertain with the reins, and the team felt his hesitation and took advantage of him. But he continued grimly, determined to save Grania and himself if he could.

It was a large if.

The systematic hunting of the fugitives was underway. Finn himself led the principal team of trackers with his best hounds, and Caurag to tend them. Cailte insisted on accompanying him.

"I could use you better with another company," Finn told the thin man. "I need officers I trust. Too many of the Fíanna seem to be taking Diarmait's part in this."

"The young ones," Cailte assured him. "Diarmait's one of their own, they sympathize with him."

"Some of the older ones too, I'm afraid. There are men who admire what he's done."

"There were men who admired Cuhal Mac Trenmor," Goll could not resist remarking.

Finn tried not to hear.

When he was occupied elsewhere, Cailte approached Caurag. "If the hounds pick up the trail," he said, "see that Conbec of Perfect Symmetry leads them. If you can, send him on ahead and hold the others back. If Diarmait sees him, he'll know Finn is close behind and be warned."

"You're asking me to act against the commander."

"I am not, I'm asking you to act in his best interests. If he catches them while in his current state of mind, he'll do something that will blight the rest of his days."

"Och, I don't think he'd hurt the woman."

"Do you not? Have you looked at him recently, Caurag? Really looked at him? There's nothing behind his eyes but madness. He looks like a wolf with the foaming-mouth sickness. Do as I ask, help me protect him from his own actions."

Reluctantly, Caurag agreed. "If I find out later that I've betrayed him, I'll blame you for it," he promised Cailte.

The hunters found wheel tracks occasionally, often enough to lead them in time to the ford of Luan on the Shannon. There, Diarmait had finally realized the chariot was more trouble than it was worth and abandoned it. The hounds found it lying broken among the reeds by the river, and the horses turned loose to graze.

"From this point, they've gone on foot," Caurag reported to Finn.

"They'll be easier to find, then."

"Not necessarily. They can move in and out of streams more easily now, and climb bare rocks where the scent won't hold."

"The girl could never do that."

"She can if she's determined enough."

She was.

Within herself Grania had found, to an unexpected degree, a stamina and tenacity that surprised both herself and Diarmait. The spoiled and petted child of a king, she stripped her spirit to the bare bones of survival and went on long after a lesser woman would have collapsed.

Diarmait's admiration for her, and pride in her, increased daily.

Within one cycle of the moon she had shapechanged from a plump, pretty girl with a white skin to a thin, freckled woman with ropy sinews in her arms and wild hair snarled and tangled by briers. Yet to Diarmait she seemed more beautiful than ever. He no longer remembered that her first purpose had been to flee Finn. He remembered only that she loved him and wanted to be with him, and was willing to undergo terrible hardships to that end.

His own sufferings seemed meagre compared to hers.

Feeling the hot breath of dishonour on the back of his neck, Diarmait made a point of telling people, whenever they encountered anyone, "This is not my wife. She is my woman, but not my wife." In that way he felt he was to some small degree keeping faith with Finn.

It was the best he could do.

But those words angered Grania. Whenever she heard them, she always announced, "I am his wife! I am wife to Diarmait Mac Donn."

"It isn't true," he told her repeatedly. "We've agreed to no contract, we've exchanged no vows. We've exchanged no vows, Grania!"

"Then let's exchange them now," she would plead.

But he could not take that irrevocable step. The tattered shreds of his loyalty to Finn lay like splinters in his eyes. Grania, seeing them there, wept.

But she went on.

And Finn pursued them.

Across the face of Erin, he pursued them. Soon enough, people in every territory knew the reason for the hunt. It was the sort of story beloved by bards.

Many were sympathetic with the guilty pair. Women especially wept over the imagined fate of Diarmait and Grania, and urged their husbands to hide the two if they saw them.

Men with an eye on their own prosperity and survival were less quick to turn against Finn. As one chieftain remarked to another, "There's no harm in a bit of fun with a woman, but any lad who tries to take the Rígfénnid Fíanna's woman deserves whatever befalls him. I wouldn't care to have Finn Mac Cool angry with me. It would mean having the whole Fíanna against me, and I can't afford it."

"Not the whole Fíanna," said the second man. "From what I hear, some of them sympathize with Diarmait and refuse to join in the hunt."

"A bad thing, that. It could split the army."

It could and did. Finn seemed unaware of the quarrels that sprang up at night when the hunters were encamped. Officers and fénnidi who were accompanying him seemed to have divided loyalties. Many counted themselves among Diarmait's friends, and were with Finn only because of the oath to him that they had sworn. The Finn Mac Cool they found themselves following now was a man they did not know.

Goll Mac Morna was surprised to discover how much he regretted Finn's disintegration. He tried more than once to talk to him. But as he subsequently confided to Red Ridge, "Talking to Finn is like talking to a bull maddened by bees. He hears nothing. He just shakes his head and roars."

Still, Goll tried. One last time.

He waited until the evening of a long day, when he hoped Finn would be too tired to be argumentative. He himself was exhausted, but he knelt by a stream and splashed icy water on his face until he was somewhat restored, then went and sat down beside Finn at the campfire.

When he turned to look at the Rígfénnid Fíanna's profile with his one good eye, he thought at first he was seeing the implacable face of a stony cliff. Even the mouth, once so tender and merry, was a cruel slash.

"Let them go, Finn," Goll said.

Finn did not look at him. "I cannot let them go. Diarmait Mac Donn has disgraced the Fíanna. We discipline our own; it's up to me to catch him and do what needs to be done."

"And what does need to be done? Are you going to hound that lad to death, and the girl too? To what purpose? Men who loved you once are beginning to look at you sideways now. Diarmait's obviously dismissed from the Fíanna, which is the normal punishment. What more do you want to do to him?"

"He owes compensation."

"You know he couldn't pay the compensation in a hundred years. Would you destroy his tribe over this? Donn's been loyal to you all these years, why make him suffer for—"

"I'm not making Donn suffer. You'll notice I haven't included him in the pursuit."

"That's not what I meant and you know it."

"Then I don't know what you do mean," Finn said stonily.

"That this relentless pursuit is nothing more than a lust for revenge! And you telling me for truth, all those seasons ago, that you disavowed personal vengeance. You even made that a rule for the Fíanna. Yet here you are, breaking your own rules just to get even with Diarmait and Grania."

Finn slowly turned the upper part of his body until he was looking at Goll. "I did say that, didn't I? That I would seek no vengeance?" he asked slowly, as if he had forgotten.

"You did of course. And I've relied on your word ever since," Goll added recklessly.

"Have you? Did you really believe me?" Finn asked.

Goll's entire body tensed. I knew it, he told himself, I knew it all along. "Are you saying it was a lie, Finn? A lie you told to get my guard down, so someday you could take revenge for your father?" he asked in the calmest voice he could manage. There was, he felt, a terrible inevitability about the question.

As Goll watched, Finn's features seemed to blur, shift, re-form themselves. A feral light glowed in his eyes.

The hackles rose on the back of Goll's neck. I should have kept my mouth shut, he told himself. I should never have reminded him of Cuhal's death, not in his current mood.

Then Finn smiled. The smile was most frightening of all. "I never lie, Goll. I'm famous for my honesty. What I say, I believe to be the truth . . . when I say it."

"So it was the truth, once. But apparently it's not the truth any longer, because you are seeking vengeance."

"That was then and this is now," said Finn Mac Cool.

Run for your life! cried Goll's brain, trapped inside his skull, peering out through the eye-hole at a merciless face that had its teeth bared in what was not a smile after all, but the snarl preceding the attack.

As a hunter, Goll had faced dangerous wild animals many times. He knew enough not to run. He stood up slowly and carefully, making no sudden move that might provoke Finn. "I'm tired," he said, trying to sound casual. "I'm going to make my bed now."

No muscle of Finn's moved, yet Goll received a sudden impression of coiled intensity. With his good eye he measured the space between them. If Finn leaped, there was no way he could outrun him—and no way he could outfight the younger man either. If Finn leaped, he was dead.

But Finn did not move. He stayed exactly where he was, fixing Goll with that terrible gaze. Through his bared teeth came one word, spoken low. "Compensation."

Goll's nerve broke. He turned and left the fireside at a pace lacking in all dignity. Every moment he expected to be seized from behind.

The love he had borne Finn had always been mingled with resentment and fear, but it had been, in its own way, the proud affection of a father toward a son. Even when Goll plotted against Finn, there had been an element of sport about it, the attempt to regain the Fíanna being a game he did not even need to win, so long as he could play.

But the time for games was over, and so was the love. Finn had destroyed that by revealing Goll to himself as a man who would run if he was frightened enough.

And he was frightened. Goll's legs were pumping with an energy they had not felt for years. He went from trot to gallop in a heartbeat and sped into the woods beyond the campsite, fleeing thoughtlessly, knowing only that he had to get away from the creature with silvery hair who sat beside the fire and grinned at him.

He did not stop running until he was deep into the woods and so breathless he thought his heart would burst. Then he sank onto a rotting log and just sat there for a measureless time, feeling very old and very broken.

29

GOLL STAYED HIDDEN IN THE WOODS UNTIL DAWN, FIGHT-
ing to recover his lost courage. He was furious with himself for
running. Though he tried to excuse his action on the grounds
of age and weariness, when he considered it honestly, he knew he had
simply been afraid.

Any man who had seen the look Finn Mac Cool gave him would, he
told himself, have been afraid.

I could take the officers and men of Clan Morna and pull out now,
he said silently. I should do. I don't owe Finn anything. I could simply
go home.

The prospect was tempting.

But he had already been a coward. He could not allow himself to be
a deserter as well. And so, when the sky began to fill with grey light and
the first sonorous call of Caurag's hunting horn rang through the dawn
air, Goll wearily stood up. Every muscle ached. Every bone rebelled.

But he put one foot after the other and returned to the camp.

To his relief, Finn paid no attention to him. He was busy organizing
the day's pursuit.

Each new day brought new problems. More and more of the Fíanna
were openly reluctant to continue. A team of expert trackers belonging
to Clan Navin approached Finn and told him, "We are friends of Diarmait Mac Donn and resent being made to search for his trail. Get
someone else to do it."

Finn's lip curled. "You swore an oath to me when you joined the
Fíanna. You vowed to obey me. Are you breaking your oath now?"

The young men glanced nervously at one another. "We are not,"
their spokesman said at last. "We just wanted to say—"

"Say nothing to me until you've picked up Diarmait's trail," Finn
snapped.

The party set out again. A thoroughly exhausted Goll gathered his fíans and went with them, thankful that he had a horse to ride and was no longer a foot warrior. He could slump on his horse's back and doze, trusting the animal to follow the line of march, and one of his men to catch him if he actually went to sleep and started to fall off.

His fíans were made up of men from Clan Morna, and he was certain of their loyalty.

The hunt swung southward.

Oisin was increasingly unhappy. Like every member of the Fíanna, he had sworn an oath to Finn, a powerful and binding oath upon which his honour depended. But they were pursuing his best friend, and the man leading the hunt no longer seemed like Oisin's father. He was a stranger with staring eyes, a man who listened to no one and nothing but his own obsession.

"I know where they are!" Finn announced some time later. "They're hiding in an oak forest in the next valley!" He kicked his horse to a canter, riding at speed toward the distant darkness of the trees.

Hurrying to keep up with him, Caurag muttered, "He's like a wolf, he scents his prey when no one else can. Even the hounds haven't got the scent yet, they're trying to go west."

Cailte put a hand on Cuarag's arm. "Whistle in the one called Conbec and direct him into that wood at once," he urged. "He's the swiftest of the hounds and he'll get there before Finn. When Diarmait sees him, he'll know we're not far behind and he'll have time to make good an escape."

Caurag frowned. "In all the seasons I've served him, I've never been disloyal to Finn."

"Trust me when I tell you you aren't being disloyal now. Do this, Caurag. Do it for Finn, even if he can't appreciate it at the moment."

Cailte fixed the huntsman with his grey eyes, and at last Caurag nodded. He whistled to Conbec, who came running up to him. Then he gave a firm directional signal with his arm and the huge hound raced off toward the woods, reaching them well before Finn Mac Cool did.

By the time Finn and his men arrived, there were only cooling embers where a campfire had been, and crushed branches that had once formed a bed for Grania and Diarmait. But the pair were gone.

Oisin commented, openly admiring, "See how he's dragged the limbs of trees after him to obscure his trail! There's no substitute for a training in the Fíanna. Now that they've abandoned travelling by chariot, they'll be harder to find."

"Not so hard," Finn replied grimly. "They go slower on foot. We'll catch them. Soon." He scowled at Oisin, his expression warning his son not to sympathize with the fugitives. But Oisin threw a fearless look back at him. "Diarmait may surprise you," he said. "He's young and strong and clever."

"I'm young enough to take him," Finn snarled.

He drove his men relentlessly. Once they loved hunting; the joys of the chase were their greatest pleasure. Now, increasingly aware of the tragic nature of their prey, they had to be urged forward continually. Even those most devoted to Finn found themselves dragging their feet. Only Finn seemed more determined than ever. Each time Diarmait eluded him he grew angrier.

He began to suspect that his own men were conspiring against him on Diarmait's behalf. His fury flared to singe everyone around him. Only toward Oisin did he temper his anger, with an effort.

His men avoided speaking to him. They proceeded according to his orders, but there was no light in their eyes.

All along their way, people gave aid to Diarmait and Grania. The poetry of their plight ran ahead of them, winning support in unexpected places. More than once some chieftain's women so berated him that he at last took horses and went to bring the pair to his own fort to rest for a night or two, until the runaways learned the Fíanna were approaching and would not stay longer lest they put their host in danger.

That summer, which should have been a battle summer, faded into the russet and gold of autumn, and still the Fíanna had fought no wars in the name of Cormac Mac Airt. They had done nothing but pursue a harried man and woman back and forth across Erin.

"My father has gone mad," Oisin said bitterly to Cailte one long, weary day when the wind from the north had begun ripening the last of the sloes.

"He has."

"Will he recover and be himself again?"

Cailte said sadly, "I cannot tell you. It's happened to him before, and each time he becomes harder to reach. I suspect he will continue as he is until this dreadful matter of Diarmait and Grania is resolved. Be patient with him, Oisin."

But the dreadful matter had not yet run its course. The next day a team of trackers reported to Finn, "In the forest beyond the next ridge is something that looks very like a Fénian hunting booth, the sort of wickerwork shelter we've always built for ourselves when needed. There is a wicker palisade around it too, a flimsy thing that would only reassure a woman, never a man."

"Diarmait and Grania?"

"It could be indeed. The scent blowing from the place excites the hounds."

Finn Mac Cool bared his teeth in what was once a smile.

As for a battle, he divided his men with orders to surround the forest. It was one of those dull, dark days that makes light flat and perspective deceptive. As they approached the trees, the rígfénnidi ordered their men to advance soft-footed, breaking no twig. Only the birds were aware of them. Sensing menace, they sat silent and hunched on their branches.

An eerie quiet descended on the forest.

By the time the fíans were deployed, it was late in the day. Finn sent his orders around by silent, swift runners: surround the area of the hut and wait until morning.

Like trees, the men of the Fíanna waited in the forest, each thinking his own thoughts. It was not an easy time.

Diarmait awoke before dawn. As he did each morning, he turned first to look at Grania, asleep beside him on their bed of moss and leaves. Her face was a pale, featureless oval in the grainy grey light seeping through the cracks of the hut, but he saw it clearly in his mind. She had grown very dear to him.

He lay listening. Something was wrong. There was dawn rising, but he heard no birds.

He slipped from the bed and began gathering his weapons, taking care not to awaken the sleeping woman.

A tiny creak of wickerwork warned him. He went quickly to the doorway and saw the narrow gate in the fence opening. Diarmait had reached it, sword in hand, by the time a lone figure entered.

The man threw back the hood of his cloak just in time to save his life. "Angus!" Diarmait exclaimed, almost dropping the sword in astonishment.

His foster father nodded. "I've come to help you. Are you aware Finn's men have you surrounded?"

A flash of terror shot through Diarmait. He was young and very tired; it was hard to summon courage in the cold grey light of dawn. "Are you certain?"

"I am certain. I was barely able to slip through their line myself without being seen."

"But why did you come here? How did you know?"

"And did I not oversee the raising of you? Are you not dearer to me than the children of my siring? I felt danger closing in on you and I came, that is all I can tell you."

Against his will, tears burned into Diarmait's eyes. They made him feel even younger and more tired. He brushed them away with an impatient hand, but Angus saw, and it tore his heart.

"Come away with me now," he urged. "I think I can get you out of here by the way I got in. There is one place Finn's men haven't covered, and—"

"I won't run from him," said Diarmait Mac Donn.

In that moment the youth was wiped from his face. For the first time, Angus noticed the threads of premature grey in his hair, and lines of strain around mouth and eyes.

"You must come," he urged. "Finn means to kill you. That's what everyone believes."

"I won't run from him any longer. I'll fight him man to man, and if we escape, I'll find a place even more isolated than this and build another shelter for us, and wait. Winter is coming. Soon the Fíanna will have to return to Tara for the Samhain Assembly, then go into winter quarters. It's a rule never broken. Once that happens, we'll be safe for the winter at least, and perhaps by spring we can have made a more permanent escape."

"You cannot possibly defeat him," Angus said sorrowfully. "He has a large force with him, you have no chance, good as you are. I do not think he'll fight you man to man, I think he'll attack you with every warrior he has. You'll be hacked to bits in front of your woman. Is that what you want?"

Diarmait gulped. "He wouldn't."

"I think he would," Angus replied.

"Then . . ." The young man hesitated. "Then take Grania away with you now, so she won't see."

"Never!" exclaimed a voice from the doorway.

Grania stood there, dishevelled from sleep. Her face was puffy and her eyes swollen, but by now she was always lovely to Diarmait. "I won't leave you," she told him, hurrying into the protection of his arms.

"You must." He bowed his head to touch his lips to her hair. But he kept his eyes locked with the eyes of Angus. Then, silently, he mouthed, "Take her."

Suddenly he shoved her away from him with all his strength. Angus caught her and enveloped her in his cloak before she had time to struggle. He thrust a wad of fabric into her mouth and dragged her bodily through the gateway.

She kicked and tried to scream, but even in his middle years, Angus of the Boyne was a powerful man. He held her while Diarmait took thongs from his neck bag, and the two of them trussed the struggling woman like a deer in the thick cloak. Then Angus slung her over his shoulder with a grunt, cast sad eyes on his foster son one last time, and set off, back the way he had come.

He knew it was all he could do for Diarmait.

He took his captive, who fought him all the way, to a little valley beyond the forest. There he waited with a heavy heart, knowing the wind would bring him the sounds of battle. He would not go any farther until he knew if Diarmait had, somehow, survived.

At the same time, Finn and his men were closing in on the hut in the forest.

"I want my most trusted rígfénnidi with me," he decided. "Cailte, you. And you, Goll. Oisin. Gonna of Clan Navin. Madan Bent-Neck. And myself. We six will stand at six points around the hut, so no matter which way he tries to run, one of us can strike him."

Oisin demurred. "You can't ask this of me, Father. He's my best friend."

Finn's eyes were like chips of flint. "I'm Rígfénnid Fíanna. Prove your loyalty now. Do you understand what's brought Diarmait to this? Lack of loyalty to his commander. Now, prove yours." His face was as implacable as his voice.

Oisin glanced toward Cailte. "You'd better do as he orders," the thin man said quietly.

They took their places. At a signal from Finn, his men laid hands on the flimsy wicker palisade and ripped it away, leaving the similarly constructed hut unprotected.

From inside, the sound was like ripping skin. Diarmait braced himself, shortsword in one hand, shield on arm. "Who's there?" he called, forcing his voice to remain steady.

Before Finn could answer, Oisin spoke up. "Oisin Mac Finn of Clan Baiscne. Come out under my protection. Even my own father will not hurt you then."

Finn cast a furious glance at his son.

But Diarmait called, "I dare not. Who else is there?"

To Finn's great anger, Cailte spoke next. "Cailte Mac Ronan. I add my protection to that of Oisin."

Oisin and Cailte. Diarmait began thinking there was just a ray of hope. "Who else?"

"Goll Mac Morna," came the answer in a husky voice.

"Madan Bent-Neck."

"Gonna of Clan Navin."

"Clan Navin have never been friends of mine," Diarmait replied. "Who else is there?"

"The Rígfénnid Fíanna," said a voice.

Diarmait closed his eyes for a moment and swallowed hard. Four who might not be quick to strike the fatal blow, and two who would. One of them Finn Mac Cool.

His fear was so total, so terrible, he knew only one defense against it. Giving a cry of mortal terror, he burst through the wall, rather than the doorway, of the wickerwork hut, attacking the nearest man with all his strength.

The nearest man was Oisin, who fell back before he could stop himself.

There was a wild flurry of flashing swords. Finn had been on the other side of the hut. By the time he ran around it, Diarmait Mac Donn was gone.

Finn's bellow of fury brought the rest of his men flooding in, almost stumbling over one another, but too late. Their prey eluded them, following the route Angus had taken.

Finn unleashed his rage on everyone . . . but Oisin. When he sought to club Oisin with a mad fist, the young man looked fearlessly back at him out of Sive's face, and Finn's arm dropped to his side. A great sob was wrenched from him and he ran from them, going deep into the woods while the rest of his men hunted, desultorily, for the vanished Diarmait.

Finn raged through the forest like a wild beast. In his mind—in the clouded, howling, aching emptiness that filled his mind—he was dimly aware of the goads that drove him.

Duty. Obligation. Both willingly accepted at one time. Both burdens beyond bearing now.

His duty to the Fíanna to punish members who broke the law.

His obligation to his father to at last take revenge for his murder.

In organizing the army to his pattern, it had been Finn himself who appointed the Rígfénnid Fíanna as the ultimate disciplinarian. And it had been Finn who, sometime over the long years, had unconsciously accepted the fact that the matter of Cuhal's killing must not go unresolved.

Goll had been one of those who let Diarmait escape.

Goll, Goll, Goll!

Meanwhile, Diarmait, running for his life in spite of all his courageous intentions, eventually caught up with Angus and Grania. Their relief knew no bounds. But they had no time to celebrate. Driven by the sure knowledge that Finn would be after them again, they provisioned themselves as best they could and set off once more, seeking an even more secluded hideaway where the pair could subsist through the coming winter. Angus did not urge them to return home with him. "Finn sends men to my stronghold every so often, just to make certain you aren't there," he said. "It would be the least safe place for you now."

Finn ordered his men on a great sweep of the region, but Erin was a land of hidden glens and wild mountains and deep forests, and even the full force of the Fíanna would not have been enough to search all of them.

But Finn did not have the full force of the Fíanna.

After the incident at the hut, he did not speak to Goll Mac Morna, nor to Madan Bent-Neck. He stared through them as if they did not exist and no orders were issued to them. Their fíans were not included in any arrangements he made.

At last Madan apologized to him. But Goll did not. Goll treated Finn in kind, keeping his men with the body of the Fíanna only out of his older loyalty to the army and the kingship, but disregarding the commander.

It was a situation that could not last, and both Finn and Goll knew it.

It was different with Cailte. Somehow Finn could not quite bring himself to ostracize the thin man, though they stayed warily out of reach of one another.

Oisin was another matter again. "My father treats me as he did before," he said to Cailte. "He pretends nothing happened. Yet he's furious with the rest of you, though it was I who let Diarmait slip away. Why should I be the only one forgiven?"

"You aren't forgiven," Cailte told him. "It's just the fact that you have your mother's face, I think. Finn can't take out his anger on you, so he takes it out on the rest of us."

But Goll Mac Morna was the principal target. Unfinished business. After Diarmait, Finn silently vowed, Goll.

They ran out of time that autumn. Even Finn in his madness would not disregard the imperative to return to Tara for the Samhain Assembly.

There he reported to Cormac, "We've spent the summer seeking your daughter and the man who stole her. Once we almost had them, but at the last moment they got away. Next summer, however . . ."

Cormac gave his Rígfénnid Fíanna a hard and searching look. Finn seemed to have aged decades that summer. His face was deeply seamed, his eyes sunken in his head.

"Let them go, Finn," Cormac said gently.

"I cannot."

"I have other daughters."

"I took her as wife. She betrayed me. And Donn's son betrayed his oath to me. There is nothing more sacred than an oath, nothing!"

The years had taught Cormac Mac Airt a great deal about compassion. "Did you never break an oath, Finn?" he enquired. "Are you not as human as the rest of us?"

Finn stared at him blankly. "I am of the Tuatha Dé Danann," he said.

"If I accept that, I must at least remind you your father was human, a Fir Bolg."

"I am obligated to be better than my father," Finn replied.

There was no talking to him. Cormac was greatly pained by the change in Finn, but the king's son Cairbre, who had never liked Finn, had less mercy. He began openly criticizing the commander of the Fíanna and saying to his friends, when he had drunk too much, that once he was Ard Ríg, he would have a different leader for his army.

Someone from Clan Morna, perhaps.

Inevitably, someone told Finn what young Cairbre was saying.

Because he had no one else, Finn spoke of the matter to Cailte. "Goll Mac Morna never stops. He's been whispering and promising, and he's convinced Cairbre that Clan Baiscne is no good and Clan Morna deserves command of the Fíanna. He wants my position for himself again."

"He doesn't Finn. Even Goll must bow to the years. He's far too old and he knows it."

"For his kinsmen, then. For the line that murdered my father. It never stops, does it? It goes on and on."

"You stopped it when you swore us all not to seek personal revenge," Cailte reminded him.

"Did I? Then that was a mistake," Finn said flatly.

Cailte tried to reach him with calm and reasonable words, but Finn went deeper and deeper inside himself to a place no one seemed able to reach, that clouded and howling place where he dwelt alone now, living only for vengeance.

On the first day of summer the next year, the hunt for Diarmait and Grania was resumed.

All winter the bards had told their tale in the great halls, and story-spinners had repeated their own versions in humble dwellings. The sympathies of most of Erin were with the fugitives by now. Wherever they fled, there was always someone to warn them and hide them or help them on their way.

Wherever they went, Finn Mac Cool followed.

Fewer of the Fíanna were with him. The number whom he felt he could trust in the situation had dwindled drastically. He tried to take only those from outlying territories who had not known Diarmait personally, leaving Goll and Madan and Cailte, and even Oisin, to conduct the usual battle summer while he pursued Diarmait with a handful of fíans.

Late in bilberry season, he caught up with them again.

There had been many days of unrelenting rain, making tracking difficult. Almost by accident, Finn and his men stumbled across a small hut of wattle and daub, once long abandoned, but now reoccupied. Someone spotted a woman who fit Grania's description trying in vain to dry clothing in front of a fire beside the hut.

"We have them now," Finn said.

Again he ordered his men to surround the area. But this time he went forward alone. He would not make the mistake of taking someone who might betray him at a critical moment.

I will do what has to be done myself, he vowed.

His men let him go gladly. None of them, even the most devoted, wanted to be remembered by the poets as the slayer of Diarmait Mac Donn.

Finn approached the hut through a driving rain, lances of silver water beating against his uncovered head. He did not feel them. He felt nothing. He put one foot after the other and went forward, numb to all but his impending victory.

Drawing near the hut, he found that it stood alone at the edge of a strip of trees. It was otherwise surrounded by meadowland. There was no easy way to approach it without being seen and warning Diarmait, if he was standing watch.

But there were the few trees . . .

Finn had spent a childhood in the wild places. Tree climbing was a skill never forgotten. Selecting a likely specimen that stood tall enough to give a view down onto the hut, he spat on his hands, jumped up to catch the lowest branch, and began climbing.

How strange that something once so easy should be so hard! He had to try several times before he was able to drag himself onto the limb he had chosen and look down. His heart was hammering violently . . .

. . . as he peered through a broken patch of roof directly into the chamber of Diarmait and Grania.

Ignoring the rain, or perhaps to distract themselves from it, they had made a soft bed against the far wall opposite the hole in the roof, and were locked in each other's arms.

Finn stared.

"Diarmait," Grania murmured, running her hands through his hair. It was heavily streaked with grey now, as if denying his youth. She did not feel young herself, not anymore. Youth had been left behind on some mountaintop or in some windswept pass or at a lonely ford.

All they had left was each other.

Diarmait moved against her, growing hard. She smiled dreamily. "Diarmait," she said again. In her increasing passion, she turned her head, her unfocussed gaze sweeping along the ruined roof of thatch.

She drew in her breath suddenly. Diarmait thought it was in response to him as he slid into her warm and welcoming body. But she had seen, framed by dead brown straw, the limb of an overhanging tree. And peering down from that limb, a face she knew.

Over Diarmait's shoulder, Grania gazed up at Finn Mac Cool.

We are dead, she thought.

Like Diarmait breaking through the wall, the acceptance of finality liberated something in her. Holding Finn's staring eyes with hers, she smiled. Slowly. Voluptuously.

Punishing him.

Punishing him with the sight of her body joined with Diarmait's.

She writhed beneath her lover and ran her hands down his back, fingers following the ridges of straining muscle. She groaned louder than she had ever groaned before, so that the sound carried to the watcher above. Shifting her hips, she clutched Diarmait tightly with her inner muscles to squeeze the utmost pleasure from him, abandoning herself to one last glorious, protracted, rippling convulsion of delight.

The cry she wrung from Diarmait echoed primal joy.

Staring at them, unaware that he was simultaneously sweating and shivering, Finn felt a mist come over his eyes. They were so beautiful! He had forgotten . . .

He had not forgotten. The mist softened Grania's piquant features until they . . . changed. Changed subtly into a lovely, eloquent, remembered face, with huge, wide, doe-like eyes.

Sive looked up at him.

And the broad muscular back that shielded her was his own.

30

Finn Mac Cool entered Tara by the Slige Cualann gate. His fíans followed silently.

The sentry on duty lowered his spear in a salute, expecting Finn to return the greeting as he had always done before, but the Rígfénnid Fíanna walked past him with no sign of recognition.

His face was very strange.

As soon as he had disappeared inside the palisade, the sentry called to the nearest guard on the wall, "Did you see that? Finn Mac Cool's back!"

"I see him," the other replied. "He's heading for the House of the King."

"How does he look to you?"

"He's walking very rigidly, I'd say."

"You should have seen his face up close. It would put the heart crosswise in you. Do you suppose it's over? Do you suppose he's . . . killed them?"

The man on the wall could not answer, only stare after the silvery-haired figure in the billowing cloak as it passed through the private gateway to the House of the King.

Cormac Mac Airt was not alone.

Angus of the Boyne had arrived that very morning, having at last decided there was nothing left to do but go to the High King and plead personally for the life of his foster son. Donn had tried it already to no avail, but Angus was a chieftain, a man whose support Cormac needed, and he might be willing to listen.

"If Cormac will agree to forgive Diarmait, perhaps Finn will have to also," he had told his household before his departure for Tara, with an optimism he did not feel.

He had argued throughout the morning, and had finally received

Cormac's agreement when Finn Mac Cool strode through the doorway with a face like death.

Angus's heart sank.

"What have you done to them?" he cried.

At that moment someone else burst through the doorway, ignoring the sentry's challenge. Only Finn could enter at will; even Goll Mac Morna should have waited for permission. But he had not.

Hearing Angus's cry, Goll echoed it. "What have you done, Finn? They just told me you'd arrived. Look at me! What's happened?"

Cormac sat silently on his bench, waiting.

Finn turned to face his old adversary rather than speaking first to the king. "What I've done is no business of yours," he snarled.

"So you have killed them! You've got your revenge, have you? In spite of everything? Then I tell you you've dishonoured the Fíanna more than your father ever did! You made it something special, something magnificent we could all be proud of. You gave us . . . nobility. Now you've taken it away. You've broken the oath you took against revenge and by doing that, returned us all to where we were before, men not to be trusted, men without honour. Oath-breaker. Oath-breaker!" He hurled the name as an epithet.

Cormac's attendants gasped. Angus looked from one warrior to the other, expecting a killing before his eyes. The king rose from his bench, determined to interpose his own body between them if necessary.

Finn had one hand on his sword hilt, but he did not hook the scabbard with his leg and draw the great blade. "I heard you, Goll Mac Morna," he said. "I've heard every word you ever spoke to me, every criticism. Once I tried to model myself on you and win your approval. I actually admired you; can you imagine? But no more. No more. After this, there is nothing but enmity between us."

"Then I'll take my men and leave the Fíanna!" Goll cried. The skin of his scar was livid and twitching as if with a life of its own.

"You'll split the Fíanna permanently!" Cormac shouted. "Stop this, the two of you!"

But Goll said sneeringly, "Split the Fíanna? There is no Fíanna anymore. Finn's ruined it. All that's left are his followers and mine; mine the old, true warriors, his the fawning hounds who lick his fingers!"

In a faraway voice, Finn murmured, "You should have waited."

It made no sense to Goll. "Waited? I'll never wait for you again! We're gone!" Throwing one last arrogant one-eyed glance at Cormac, he bolted from the hall, and a few moments later they could hear him shouting hoarsely for his men.

Cormac sat down slowly, looking at Finn. When he spoke, his voice sounded very tired. "Now see what you've done."

"I've done nothing. I told him, he should have waited."

"What do you mean?"

It was Finn's turn to sit down. He lowered himself onto the nearest bench as if his legs would no longer hold him. At a gesture from the king, a cupbearer brought him wine, but he pushed it away.

"I had them," he said in a low voice, staring at nothing. "Diarmait and Grania; I had them."

"I knew it," whispered Angus, already grief-stricken.

"I had them and I left them," said Finn.

"Left them . . . alive?" Angus could hardly believe his ears.

"Alive indeed. Unharmed. I shall not raise my hand against them again."

Cormac let out a groan and wiped his palm across his brow. Angus was still struggling to understand. "You mean you found them and didn't kill them?"

The awful mask that was the face of Finn Mac Cool seemed to crack a little, just around the edges. For a heartbeat, a merry boy peered out, a boy who said teasingly, "Is there another language you would understand better?"

Cormac said, "It's over, then," with infinite relief.

"It's over," Finn agreed. "They are safe from me."

"And from me," the king told him. "I had already agreed to forgive them. Angus here convinced me."

"But who convinced you?" Angus asked Finn.

Finn Mac Cool reached out then and took the proffered cup, draining it in one long swallow. He held it up for more and drained that too, as if he could not get enough.

"Who indeed?" he said at last.

That was all the answer they got.

News that the terrible hunt was over spread quickly. Oisin was the first to come to the House of the King and hear the tale from his father's own lips, but he learned no more than Cormac and Angus had. His relief was equal to theirs, however.

"You would not have forgiven yourself if you'd done this thing," he said to Finn.

"Who told you that? It doesn't sound like you."

"Cailte."

"Och, Cailte." Finn smiled faintly. "He knows me well, does Cailte."

Cailte arrived soon after Oisin and was heartened to discover that Finn's stony countenance and feral glare had faded, were being replaced by a semblage of the old Finn, though one very battered and aged.

"I think he's coming back to us," Cailte said to Oisin behind his hand.

If so, it would be a long journey. Finn was obviously exhausted, mentally if not physically. Cormac insisted on his being well fed and well rested, given all the time necessary to restore him. The women fussed over him. His rígfénnidi called upon him, one by one, to re-establish the bonds so cruelly strained.

Only Goll did not come to him. Goll was gone.

"Deserted," Finn said to Cailte. He was lying at his ease on a couch in the house set aside for his personal use, and Cailte was lounging in the doorway, eating some of the fruit the women were continually bringing.

"That's a hard accusation," the thin man told Finn. "You and Goll had a quarrel and he left, but that hardly amounts to desertion."

"He took his fíans and the officers from Clan Morna with him, and you know he won't be back. That's desertion."

"I suppose so. But don't think about it now, Finn."

"I have to think about it. I'm the commander. I can't allow desertion."

"What will you do about it?"

Finn closed his eyes and lay back on the couch. "I'll have to go after him," he said.

Cailte felt a pricking of alarm. Was the Diarmait situation beginning all over again? "Surely you won't seek revenge?" he said.

"For desertion? I shall not." Finn sounded painfully, agonizingly tired. "Goll accused me of being an oath-breaker, but I haven't broken that oath, as it turns out, nor do I mean to in his case. Going after Goll won't be vengeance. It's a matter of discipline. Deserters have to be punished, and only I can punish one of my own rígfénnidi. It's as simple as that."

He seemed to fall asleep then. Cailte waited a little while longer, then took a last apple from the pile on the nearest table and sauntered out.

Finn was not asleep. He lay behind closed eyelids, looking at a face, a dear face lately restored to him. A face that watched him, lovingly, from huge brown eyes.

I'm all right, Sive, he said. I think I was . . . away for a while. But I'm all right now.

Yet he was not purged of the bitterness. It returned at unguarded moments in waves of anger and resentment directed not at Diarmait specifically, nor at Goll, but at the chaos known as *fénnidecht,* the condition of being a Fir Bolg warrior before Finn Mac Cool had reshaped the Fíanna. Fénnidecht meant running headlong and heedless through life, taking what you wanted, refusing responsibility for your actions, everything out of control . . . as Diarmait and Grania had been out of control, as Goll was now beyond Finn's control.

As Cuhal Mac Trenmor had been out of control.

Chaos.

It lay like a dark pool at the bottom of Finn's mind, waiting. As long as he could hold on to his vision of Sive, he could push it down and back. But when he lost contact with her . . .

Now that he had the High King's daughter, Diarmait applied to Cormac for property suitable to her rank on which to build a fort. Cormac consulted with the brehons at some length.

"She is contract wife to Finn Mac Cool," they reminded him unnecessarily.

"Finn has relinquished his claim and forgiven them."

"But the Fíanna does not take property with its women," Flaithri pointed out.

Cormac replied, "Diarmait is no longer one of the Fíanna. He has a right to ask for property with her, and I want to see my daughter well cared for."

The brehons shut themselves away in the Fort of the Synods, consulted long and diligently, and at last announced they saw no impediment.

To spare Finn the painful reminder of seeing them together, Cormac gave Diarmait and Grania a landholding at Ceshcorran in the far west, making an arrangement with the king of Connacht in order to secure his daughter's future there. After a complicated exchange of cattle and bondwomen and sureties, Diarmait was informed it was safe to take Grania away and build a new home for her.

They left without Finn ever seeing them.

But he could not forget them.

Once the pursuit was officially over, chieftains and tribal kings who had helped Diarmait decided they needed to restore themselves to the good graces of the Rígfénnid Fíanna.

They began visiting Finn, one after the other, each disavowing any sympathy with the former fugitives. "Diarmait Mac Donn brought shame on the Fíanna!" they proclaimed stoutly. "We gave them no help at all. Our sympathies were always with you, Finn."

Finn listened with increasing cynicism. The bards were already commemorating the dramatic pursuit, and listing the names of those who fought for Diarmait and those who fought against him. The tale was becoming an epic in its own time, and with every telling it grew, so that common storyspinners in humble huts were soon claiming the terrified lovers had slept "in that very glade beyond this hill!"

"Diarmait and Grania appear to have visited every clanhold in Erin," a wryly amused Blamec remarked to Fergus Honey-Tongue, who was telling his own version of the story, replete with new details as they occurred to him.

But no one told it in Finn's hearing.

On the surface, things returned to normal. Ignoring Cormac's offer of another daughter to be his wife, Finn threw himself into the familiar business of leading the Fíanna. There were always young warriors to be tested, sporadic skirmishes and battles to be fought or quelled, depending on the politics of the moment, and in the high, hot days of summer or the crisp days of autumn, there were the hounds and the chase.

He no longer watched for a singular red doe. He did not think he would find her again in that guise. She was back in his head, safe there. At least she was there sometimes.

Other times he could not find her but felt the dark pool instead, waiting to rise and flood over him.

"Your father is permanently changed by what happened," Cailte advised Oisin.

"We are all of us permanently changed," Oisin replied coldly. He had grown; he was a man, his bones long and slabbed with powerful muscle, his sinews taut and hard, his voice resonating in his chest. Among the fénnidi, he had no equal as an athlete, and his successes in battle were already inspiring the bards. Since the pursuit of Diarmait, he and Finn had been estranged, however. He followed the Rígfénnid Fíanna and obeyed orders, but the old closeness of father and son was gone, which saddened Cailte.

Finn never spoke of it, one way or the other. But Cailte fancied he could see pain in his eyes when he looked at Oisin.

"Finn was doing what he had to do," the thin man tried to explain. "His duty, as he saw it."

"He saw killing Diarmait as his duty? Have a brehon recite for me the law that made it so."

"Och, Oisin, don't be so hard on him."

"And why should I not? Finn's hard on everyone else."

"Hardest on himself," Cailte replied, but Oisin did not seem interested in continuing the discussion; he walked away.

Regaining his prestige within the Fíanna was proving a challenge for Finn. Not only Oisin still bore a grudge, but many other fénnidi and officers had been alienated during the pursuit and must be won back. He tried in the old ways, challenging them physically and inspiring them intellectually with spectacular boasts and claims of magic.

Some listened, believed, responded.

Oisin did not.

He no longer saw Finn Mac Cool as magical and magnificent. "Why does he keep on telling those lies?" he asked Fergus Honey-Tongue in disgust.

Fergus was shocked. "They aren't lies! No one questions Finn's honesty."

"So I've always been told. But I'm no fool, Fergus. I don't believe that story about the salmon and being able to stick his thumb in his mouth and know things—not anymore. I don't believe any of his stories anymore."

"But you must. We all do—especially Finn himself. They are part of him, they make him what he is."

"Perhaps. But he's not the man I once thought he was," Oisin curtly replied.

At the back of Finn's mind lay an awareness of Goll Mac Morna. The matter of his desertion was unresolved; it must be faced eventually. But Finn found himself putting it off.

He did not know how he felt about Goll.

The one-eyed man had served him long and well under the most difficult circumstances. They had always been rivals, but it was a rivalry grown comfortable, a defining fact in both their lives. Goll had been, in many ways, Finn's standard of honour, though he would never have told him so.

For that reason if none other, the desertion rankled. And it must be punished, there could be no doubt. Otherwise an unfortunate precedent would be set and Clan Morna would not be the only company of men to simply walk away from the Fíanna when they felt like it.

But one season passed and then another, and still Finn did not go after Goll.

Cailte began to hope he never would.

Oisin took a wife. In far Ceshcorran, Diarmait and Grania had a son, and then another.

In his own stronghold in the west, Goll Mac Morna began to relax and quit looking over his shoulder every time he thought he heard someone behind him.

Diarmait and Grania had a daughter, then another son.

Finn's silvery hair faded into white almost unnoticed.

But his vigour was undiminished. He still loved to hunt. When he could, he ranged farther afield, leaving Almhain behind to explore the remotest reaches of Erin with his hounds and his huntsmen. Sometimes some of his rígfénnidi accompanied him, as much for the sake of hearing him tell his tales beside a campfire as for the thrill of pursuing stag or boar. They were older, as he was older, and knee and hip joints were stiffening. Going hunting was becoming an exercise in nostalgia, though none would admit it except Conan Maol, who flatly refused to go at all.

Even Oisin went hunting with Finn from time to time. But he did not ride at his father's side on such occasions, or sit next to him by the campfire. He always found someone else to talk to and be with.

He might have been a stranger rather than the son of Finn Mac Cool.

Brooding behind his eyes, Finn observed, and spoke of it in his head to Sive.

He hates me for what I did to Diarmait. But I really did nothing to him, no lasting damage. And look what he has now!

Indeed.

Look what he has now.

There were times when Finn could not help brooding over Diarmait's success in spite of the dishonour he had committed. It seemed to negate the very concept of honour.

Early one autumn, Cuarag purchased a new pair of dogs for Finn, a sturdy, broad-shouldered, thick-chested pair that had been bred in the land of the Britons and could, it was claimed, bring down the largest boar between them.

"They aren't as handsome as our staghounds," Cuarag apologized to Finn, "but if they're half as good with boar as they're reputed to be, it would be a treat to watch them in action."

Before Finn had a chance to try out the new boarhounds, a messenger from Tara brought word from the High King.

"Grania and Diarmait wish to put aside old enmities and make things smooth again," the messenger reported, "and they have invited both Cormac Mac Airt and yourself to attend a great feast at their stronghold in Ceshcorran. The king sends me to inform you, and to ask you and your officers to travel there with him."

Finn started to answer, then became aware of Oisin's eyes on him, watching. Such large, dark eyes beneath a crop of golden curls.

"I'll go of course. Return to Cormac and tell him we are preparing," Finn said.

"Good," Oisin said. It was not much, but it was a small thawing, and Finn essayed a small smile at his son. Oisin looked away at that moment, however—perhaps unintentionally.

The journey west to Ceshcorran was a long one, allowing considerable time for speculation. Finn and Cormac rode side by side. "I suspect the invitation was initiated by Grania," Cormac said. "That's the sort of thing women do, trying to make peace."

Finn's brooding eyes stared over his horse's pricked ears, watching the road ahead. "Perhaps the idea began with Diarmait, who might be afraid I haven't forgiven him after all. He was always clever, was Diarmait."

Cormac shot a look at the Rígfénnid Fíanna. "Are you saying you haven't forgiven him?"

"I'm saying he always was clever," Finn replied calmly.

When they at last reached the fort Diarmait had named Rath Grania in honour of his wife, they learned that she indeed had been the instigator. Grania, older, plumper, ran forward eagerly to throw her arms around Cormac's neck and shower the side of his face with kisses. Then she drew back to look at him. "But you've gone entirely grey!" she protested.

Then her eyes slid sideways toward Finn, who sat unmoving on his horse. The years had not changed him since last she saw him. Finn had reached an apparent age that, thanks to his bone structure, he would retain until he died. He would never look less than strong.

Diarmait, on the other hand, had grown thin with the passage of time, and fretful under the continuing yoke of exiled domesticity. They had few visitors at Rath Grania. Local chieftains were wary of incurring Finn's anger by being too friendly with Diarmait Mac Donn.

So he was quite fulsome in his welcome to the Fíanna, and to Oisin in particular. The two linked arms and went swinging off long-strided together, talking as they had in the old days.

Grania was left to guide her father, Finn, and the other officers into the fort and make them welcome. "I did so want to see the pair of you together under my own roof," she told them, "and to know there was no anger left among us."

Cormac, who was already knee-deep in grandchildren, smiled fatuously. "And how could I be angry with you?" he asked Grania fondly.

"And you, Finn?" she enquired, looking toward the white-haired man who was watching her silently, his thoughts hidden behind his eyes. "Have you any anger left toward me?"

She licked her lips. She smiled. Grania could never bear to think any man could resist her.

She remembered Finn staring down at her through the hole in the roof of the hut, and she thought, with a guilty thrill of delight, he still wants me! I know he does!

"I was never angry with you," he said.

She tried to interpret the inflection of his voice, but could not. Finn kept his words as expressionless as his face. Whatever Grania found in either, she imagined.

She had had years to perfect her imagination, years in exile with Diarmait Mac Donn, years far away from the luxury and excitement of Tara.

To entertain the king and the Rígfénnid Fíanna, she and Diarmait had made the most elaborate preparations possible. But both men had brought sizable retinues. Food for feasting ran out all too soon.

"I brought some new boarhounds with me," Finn announced. "Who would like to go out with me tomorrow and give them a run, see if we make a kill?" He made it an invitation to all present.

There was a unanimous male shout. Cormac, whose years lay like frost in his bones by now, said nothing, but even his eyes gleamed just a little at the prospect, and he was almost tempted.

That night in their bed, however, Grania pressed against Diarmait and urged, "Don't go hunting tomorrow with Finn."

"Why not? It's glad I am that he's willing to have me. It tells me the old trouble is behind us."

"Just don't go." But she could not tell him why.

Suddenly she felt guilty for having flirted, however mildly, with Finn. Diarmait had thrown away everything he had for her sake and risked his life; there was no way she could equal such a gift. She snuggled loyally against him and let her hand slide down his belly, tempting him with warm fingers. "Don't go," she repeated softly. "Stay here with me. Let the others hunt."

She did not dare tell him she was afraid for him. That would have challenged his maleness and driven him to join Finn in pursuit of the boar. But she was afraid, though she could not say why.

The hunting party set off at dawn, riding out on the clarion call of Cuarag's horn. The boarhounds were fresh and overeager. They had to be restrained with collars around their necks and leads, and they almost pulled the arms out of the sockets of Cuarag's assistant huntsmen.

The other hounds followed, and were followed in turn by Finn, Oisin, and the other rígfénnid, on horseback.

Diarmait stood in the gateway and watched them go, then turned back toward Grania with a brave, false smile. "I don't much care for hunting anyway," he lied.

She saw the lie in his eyes.

He hesitated, torn, until the hunting party disappeared behind the nearest hill.

They rode for quite some time, giving the boarhounds an opportunity to cast back and forth in search of a scent. Like Grania, Finn found himself invaded by a growing gloom. The sun was bright and the wind off the sea was tangy with salt, but he was nagged by a persistent melancholy. Perhaps seeing Grania was the cause.

He tried to push her out of his mind. But the more he tried to grapple with his thoughts, the more unbidden thoughts rushed in to join the chaos.

A low bank of dark clouds materialized on the western horizon. As he rode, Finn stared at it, deaf to the sound of the hounds and the horn and the conversation of his companions.

He drew rein abruptly. Cailte, following close behind, signalled for the others to halt. The huntsmen and the hounds went on without them.

Keeping his eyes on the dark clouds, Finn began to recite.

Woman . . .

He paused, shook his head, began again.

Two things have overcome me. A vision of shapes appeared to me, and took my strength and vision.
Now I see other visions. A man with shorn hair will come to us and tell us of wonders, but will not harm us.
Other foreigners will also come.
Listen to the prophecy of Finn.''

He paused again, and quite unconsciously put his thumb into his mouth.

Oisin watched his father with wide eyes.

When Finn removed the thumb, he said,

Listen to the prophecy of Finn.
Grey-faced foreigners will come, and myself and the Fíanna not here to drive them out.
The foreigners' gardens will flourish here, and many a tree of their planting.
Kings will advance and break battle, and a High King will leave the battlefield red with blood.
Men from the east and the west, the north and the south, will struggle against the foreigners.
But I shall not be here to lead them.
I am Fionn son of Cuhal, and this is my prophecy.

He fell silent, his eyes still staring into the west. His men shifted uncomfortably on their horses' backs and looked at one another.

"That doesn't even sound like one of Finn's poems," Red Ridge said.

Blamec agreed. "When I was first with him, his poems were about blackbirds and red deer and wild geese and foaming waterfalls."

"Now," said Fergus Honey-Tongue portentiously, "he has the prophetic gift of the druid. Remember that he carries the blood of the Sídhe."

Oisin swung his eyes toward Fergus. He frowned, unsure of what to believe.

But before he could decide, the voice of the hounds came clearly to them. They had picked up the trail of a boar and were in hot pursuit. Even Finn was startled out of his reverie, and they all set off at a gallop.

As the horses thundered up a rocky incline, Oisin found himself riding knee to knee with his father. The younger man's blood was running hot and high, infected with the excitement of the hunt. Without intending to, he grinned at his father.

Finn's answering grin was so radiant Oisin could not help challenging gaily, "I'll race you to the boar!"

"Done!" cried Finn Mac Cool.

He clamped his legs on his horse's sides with such force the animal leaped to the front and held the advantage. Oisin did his best but could not catch up. Finn raced away from the others and soon disappeared over the crest of a hill.

Meanwhile, Diarmait Mac Donn had succumbed to temptation. Giving a half-apologetic and rather sheepish smile to Grania, accompanied by a hasty hug, he had gathered his weapons and set off after the hunt himself.

Grania stood in the gateway, watching him go.

Her stomach clenched into a hard knot.

Diarmait knew the land as the others did not. Guided by the sound of the hounds, he took a shortcut through a narrow valley that led, eventually, to the flanks of Gulban's Mountain. There he found the boarhounds, which had outrun their keepers once the leads were slipped from them.

And there he also found Finn Mac Cool.

As Diarmait rode up, Finn warned him back with an impatient gesture. "He's just in there," he said, pointing toward a stand of hazel. "The hounds drove him to cover, but it's not enough to protect him and he knows it. He'll come charging out soon enough."

Diarmait slid from his horse. "I'll face him on foot," he boasted.

"You'll do no such thing. He's my boar!"

Diarmait tensed, an inward clenching that reflected itself in fist and jaw. "I have the hunting of this territory," he said.

Finn glared at the younger man, the man who had taken his wife. "It's my boar," he repeated, deadly quiet. "Don't try to take this from me."

The hounds bayed their warning, but the boar was very fast. It broke from cover and charged toward the nearest figure with the blind rage of its kind, a murderous attack that could not be deflected.

"Behind you!" Finn roared at Diarmait. But even as Diarmait was turning around and hefting his javelin, the boar was upon him.

The hounds sprang upon the creature, trying to pierce its thick, leathery hide with their fangs, but it ignored them. It flung itself at Diarmait with a grunting squeal, seeking his body with its tusks. He tried to dance out of the way but felt the great curving, yellow tusks rip into his lower belly.

Cursing at his terrified horse, who was trying to run backward out of reach, Finn slid to the ground. His great sword in its sheath banged against his leg, almost tripping him as he sought to draw it and attack the boar. There was a moment of frenzied confusion, with a blade flashing and the animal screaming and a man screaming too, high, terrible sounds that rang through the clear air.

But it was Diarmait's shortsword that somehow found its way into the boar's throat, inflicting a fatal wound.

And it was the tusks of the boar that tore out Diarmait's guts.

31

THE BOAR WAS ON THE GROUND, THE BOARHOUNDS WORRY-
ing it while red froth bubbled from its mouth and nostrils. Finn
drove the hounds back and finished killing the animal with a
powerful blow from Son of the Waves. Then he dropped to his knees
beside the crumpled body of Diarmait.

One glance told him the damage was mortal. The younger man's
intestines lay glistening on the bloody earth like twisted grey snakes.

Finn seized them in his two hands and tried irrationally to stuff them
back into the gaping belly wound, but he stopped when Diarmait
groaned in agony.

He put his face close to Diarmait's. "What can I do for you? Tell me
something I can do for you!"

The dying man opened his eyes to find the world had shrunk to a dim
grey whirlpool with Finn Mac Cool's face at its vortex, slowly receding.

"Water," Diarmait gasped.

Finn scrambled to his feet and ran in search of water. He had nothing
on him to carry it in; he did not know where it might be found, but water
had become the single imperative. His breath sobbed in his throat.

He burst through a tangle of scrubby undergrowth to find Oisin
sitting on his horse, staring down at him. "What happened?" his son
wanted to know. "There's blood on you!"

"Diarmait's," Finn replied distractedly. "Which way to water? I must
find water."

"Diarmait! Where?" Oisin leaped from his horse and grabbed Finn's
arm in iron fingers. "Where? What have you done to him?"

"I've done nothing, I have to get water—"

"Take me to him," Oisin grated. He forced Finn to lead him back to
where Diarmait lay.

At the sight of his friend on the ground, Oisin gave a cry of pain. "So you've finally done it!" he cried at his father. "You finally achieved what you failed to do years ago!"

"Not me," Finn protested. "It was the boar—"

"Water," came Diarmait's hoarse gasp. They both turned to him. "Please . . . water . . ."

Oisin's face was terrible to behold as he shouted at Finn, "Get him water, then! Bring it back to him in your two hands! You claim to be of the Tuatha Dé Danann, you claim to be magical. Well then, use your magic to heal the damage you've done this good man! There's a stream not a spear's throw from here." He pointed the way he had come. "So bring water!"

Finn forced his legs to run once more. He came to the stream soon enough and knelt beside it, filling his cupped hands. Then he ran back. But as he ran, the water, against his will, trickled through his fingers.

By the time he reached Diarmait and knelt beside him, his hands were empty. He held only moist fingers to the dying man's mouth. Diarmait's lips almost touched them . . . then he gave a soft sigh and seemed to grow smaller.

Finn and Oisin looked at each other across his dead body.

"I did not want his death," Finn said, willing his son to believe him.

"Did you not? But it was very convenient, wasn't it, the two of you here alone, no witnesses—"

"Look there, there lies the boar that killed him!"

"His guts could have been torn out by any weapon," Oisin replied. "Tusks or a blade. Who's to know?"

"*I* know. I don't lie!"

"Do you not? I've heard the stories you tell!"

They were shouting at each other. Then Oisin broke. He dropped down beside Diarmait and gathered the dead man's head in his arms, cradling it against his breast and weeping.

That was how the rest of the hunting party found them.

"The boar killed him," Finn said dully. He would not look at Diarmait and Oisin, nor at anyone else, until Cailte stood beside him. Then he turned agonized eyes on the thin man. "The boar killed him!"

"I know, Finn."

"You believe me?"

"I do of course."

Finn drew a deep breath. "We'll have to take him back to . . . to Grania. I hope she'll believe me."

"Does it matter?" Cailte asked.

Finn was surprised at the question. "It does, very much. My own son somehow does not seem to believe anything I say."

They carried Diarmait Mac Donn back to Rath Grania across the back of a horse, his legs dangling on one side and his arms on the other. It was not a noble carrying, but at least he was on a princely horse—Oisin's own.

Oisin insisted on leading the animal himself. When the horse shied from the smell of death and excrement and would not let them put the body on it, Oisin tore a strip from his own tunic and bound it over the animal's eyes, blinding it to make it docile.

It was a sombre party that returned to Diarmait's fort. Grania met them at the gate as if she had been waiting for them. Her small children clustered about her, staring with wide eyes at the still body, the dangling limbs protruding from beneath a covering cloak.

"What happened?" she asked in a whisper.

"The boar killed him," Finn said. "But he killed the boar."

"Where is it?"

"We didn't bring it back. We didn't think you would want it," Cailte told her gently.

She went to the horse and felt beneath the cloak for Diarmait's dead face. "His skin is not yet cold," she said, wondering. With a sudden impulse, she threw back the cloak and pressed her mouth to the dead mouth.

Finn and Cailte exchanged stricken glances, but it was Oisin who put his arms around her and pulled her away.

That night she sat beside the body until dawn, keening. The rise and fall of her voice rubbed Finn's nerves raw. He had to leave the fort and stand beneath the Connacht stars, looking blindly into the sky. "I didn't kill him," he told the moon.

I did not kill him, Sive. But he could not find her face in the sky.

Diarmait Mac Donn was buried beneath a cairn, and a stone each was taken from the cairn to be given to Donn and to Diarmait's foster father, Angus.

"He was the noblest of us all, and the most fortunate," Oisin said. "Everyone who knew him loved him." He paused. "Except one."

His words were a stone in Finn's heart. I have lost Oisin forever now, he thought.

I'm sorry, Sive.

When they were preparing to leave, Finn went to Grania. "The fort is yours, of course, and the landholding with it. When we return to Tara, I can have whatever you need sent to you, and I shall leave some men here with you to be your guards and sentries since you have no man now."

Her face was puffy and her eyes red and swollen from weeping, but underneath the soft skin were hard bones, and a strong, practical woman's mind lived inside her skull. Grania pushed her hair back from her brow and straightened her posture. She had no intention of being left alone in the wilds of Connacht with Diarmait gone.

"I have a man," she said to Finn. "I was your contract wife."

He was astonished. "You can't mean that you—"

"I simply mean I expect you to be responsible for me now and take me back east with you. I don't want to stay here alone and my heart's blood dead and gone."

I will never, Finn told himself, understand women. They seem soft and men seem hard, but in truth, it may be the other way around. Is it, Sive?

"I will deliver you safely to your father the king, if that is what you want," he promised.

"It is what I want." Her head was high; her slanted eyes met his with an inscrutable look that made him uncomfortable. "And I want my children . . . Diarmait's and mine . . . to be fostered by chieftains. Can you see to it?"

"I can of course," Finn agreed. He waited for her to continue, with the firm conviction there was something else she wanted to say, but she clamped her lips together and turned away from him as if she did not want him trying to read her thoughts.

What had she not said? I hate you?

On the morning of departure, Finn made a point of speaking with Cuarag. "As soon as we get home, I want you to send those so-called boarhounds back to the Britons. They failed miserably, they did nothing I expected of them. If we'd had Bran with us, Diarmait would be alive today."

During the journey eastward, Finn, trying to keep from thinking too much about Diarmait, regaled his companions with one tale after another about Sceolaun and Bran and other hunts with happier outcomes.

Only Oisin did not listen. His ears were stoppered against anything his father might say.

They were on the Slige Asal almost within sight of Tara when Finn realized something was seriously wrong. They had begun meeting the usual sentries at intervals—and none of them were his own men. Or Fiachaid's.

None of them were men he knew.

He signalled for a halt, then led his party off the road altogether and across a sweep of grassland to shelter behind a belt of woodland, out of sight of the road.

Grania was indignant. "What's this about? I demand to be taken to my father now!" She was tired and querulous.

"I'll take you to him," Finn told her, "but not until I'm certain it's safe. Red Ridge, you and Blamec will be in charge here. Cailte, I want you and your men to come with me." He kicked his horse and rode away.

Cailte galloped beside him, their fíans, afoot, trotting after. The closer they got to the great stronghold on the ridge, the more apprehension Finn felt.

Unfamiliar sentries manned the gateway and scowled at him suspiciously as he rode up. "The Rígfénnid Fíanna is here to report to the Ard Ríg!" he cried formally.

For a moment he thought they would not open the gates to him. Then there was a creak of timber and a groan of iron hinges, and he and Cailte were allowed to enter. But the foot warriors were held outside.

"Trouble," said Cailte softly. It was not a question.

They rode forward at the walk. Finn's eyes flicked continually from right to left and back again, noting every change. The most troubling one was the fact that the banners of Cormac Mac Airt no longer flew from ridgepoles. New banners had replaced them, gaudy with fresh dye.

He halted his horse at the gateway to the House of the King and dismounted, giving a surreptitious hand signal to Cailte, warning him to stay on his animal and be ready.

The sentry on duty passed Finn into the House of the King without challenge. But the man was another stranger.

The man who waited inside, sitting at arrogant ease on the carved bench Cormac had occupied for so long, was no stranger. Finn knew the proud eyes and the petulant mouth all too well.

"Cairbre," he said tersely, the least possible greeting. "Where's your father?"

"Not here, obviously," Cairbre replied, enjoying this.

"You should not be sitting on the High King's bench, whether he's here or not."

"He's not High King anymore."

Finn felt as if someone had hit him in the belly with a knotted fist. "What?"

"While you were away, doing whatever it is you went to the west to do—"

"Cormac dispatched the Fíanna to settle a quarrel, you knew that."

"And did you bring Goll Mac Morna back with you, since you were in his territory?"

"We did not go to Goll."

"Pity. I should have liked to have him here now. He's a man I feel I can rely on."

Finn's temper flared. "Where's Cormac?" He took an angry step toward Cairbre. At once three spearmen had the points of their weapons aimed at the throat of the Rígfénnid Fíanna.

Finn's shock was enormous.

Cairbre made a gesture of studied magnanimity. "Let him go, I'm sure he won't hurt me. Finn would never lay hands on the next High King."

Watching Finn's eyes, Cairbre's bodyguards were not so sure. They lowered their spears reluctantly, but only halfway.

"What happened to Cormac, and what makes you think you can replace him?" Finn demanded to know.

"While you were not here to defend him, as you should have been doing, there was a battle. A small rising, nothing important, but my father felt it incumbent upon himself to defend Tara and his kingship and prove he was still the man he used to be. He rode out with the warriors, he got embroiled in the fighting, and he took a slingstone in the eye. He's as blind as Goll Mac Morna now. And no man can be king who is so blemished, according to the law.

"Even as we speak, Finn, I'm waiting upon a gathering of the elders of our clan and the brehons to elect Cormac's successor. I expect they will choose me. I am the eldest of his sons, the one with the most experience acquired at his elbow, and the other eligible men of our clan know much less about the kingship he's created here.

"You know how devoted he's always been to the law, how he's made it central to his rule and spent the better part of his time with the brehons, learning, discussing, enlarging the body of the law. I was privy to much of that. I can continue where he left off."

Cairbre spoke so smugly it set Finn's teeth on edge. And the central question was not yet answered. He repeated it once more, very softly. That softness was deadly. Cairbre's bodyguards recognized the danger implicit in the tone and raised their spears again.

This was the fabled Finn Mac Cool. He might do anything.

If Cairbre was frightened, however, he gave no sign. He had studied his father and learned well. "When it became apparent the blemish was sufficient to deny him kingship, Cormac wisely retired to a holding at Cenannus. Flaithri went with him, in fact. I daresay they are there this moment, still discussing the law. He seems content enough. He's an old man anyway, Finn. It's time he rested."

Cormac Mac Airt, old? It was not a concept Finn had ever considered, though he knew the number of the High King's years and had watched his hair go white.

Cairbre gave him ample time to digest the information, then said, "What of you, Finn? Will you serve as Rígfénnid Fíanna under me? For the time being, at least? At some future date I may make another appointment. You're not young either, you're—"

"I am able to serve as Rígfénnid Fíanna for as long as you or any other man holds Tara," Finn said icily.

For the first time, Cairbre's arrogant mask slipped. In Finn's eyes he saw something he did not care to challenge. "Well then," he said as if to himself. "Well then. That's settled, I suppose. I, ah, am relieved to hear you'll serve me. I know it's what my father would want," he added as a sop.

Finn stared at him stonily, then turned on his heel and left the House of the King.

Cailte was waiting for him, holding his horse's rein. Finn did not even bother to vault onto the animal. He needed to feel solid ground underneath his feet. The earth seemed to be tilting crazily, threatening to spill him off.

He stalked across the royal compound with Cailte and the horses following. Livid with inheld anger, he crossed the lawn below the Fort of the Synods and was heading for the nearest gate when yet another strange warrior barred his way.

"Where are you going?" the man challenged.

Finn's jaw dropped. "Who are you to challenge me?"

"I serve Cairbre Mac Cormac, and I have orders not to let you leave Tara."

"I am Rígfénnid Fíanna!"

"I know that. I mean no disrespect. But Cairbre feels that you should stay here now, within these walls."

Instantly, Finn understood. The last thing Cairbre wanted was for him to get back to the Fíanna. The army was the strength of the king, and that same strength meant control of Tara. It could also be turned against anyone who tried to seize the kingship. Finn had only to utter one word. Cairbre must be very afraid he would utter that word.

But Cairbre, for all his cunning, must not realize that the Fíanna was no longer as solidly Finn's as it had once been.

Finn pretended to accept the situation. He turned back toward Cailte and said calmly, "You are not needed here. You might as well go."

Cailte understood. He started to turn the horses and ride toward the gate, but the guard cried, "Stay!"

"Have you any orders concerning this man?" Finn asked.

"Och, I have not, but—"

"But he is under my command, not yours. Go, Cailte."

The thin man took advantage of the guard's obvious confusion to ride swiftly away, out the gateway and back to the waiting warriors beyond the trees.

Age had taken a toll on Cailte's legs, but not on his wits. With his old rapidity he outlined the situation for Finn's men, sent messengers to bring reinforcements from loyal Fénians beyond the plains of Míd, dispatched an armed escort to convey Grania to Cormac at Cenannus, and organized a rescue of Finn Mac Cool.

When what appeared to be the majority of the Fíanna came marching toward Tara along every one of the five roads, holding their weapons aloft and shouting Finn's name, Cairbre had no choice but to let him go.

"I was only offering you hospitality," he tried to claim. "You misunderstood me, Finn."

Finn's face was stone. "While we await the decision of the electors as to the new High King, I prefer to take hospitality from Cormac at Cenannus."

Seeing Cormac almost broke his heart. The former High King was truly old, with an empty eye socket and a haggard face. His fingers continually made restless, twitching gestures. But he seemed genuinely delighted to welcome Finn, and glad to have Grania back. "My daughter is welcome to live in my household for the rest of her life," he said. "My circumstances are somewhat reduced, of course, but—"

"But you belong at Tara," said Finn.

"Ah, Finn, I don't. Not at all. I have obeyed the law, as we all must if there is to be order rather than chaos. I'm aware you don't like Cairbre very much, but I've been preparing him for a long time. He is the most intelligent of my sons and the one best able to replace me, if he is chosen."

"He may not be," said Finn hopefully.

"I think he will be. He's the best of the litter."

Cormac's assessment was correct. Within a few days, the decision was made and word brought to Cenannus. Cairbre Mac Cormac was king of Tara, High King of Erin.

Finn grieved in his heart. At night, lying on his bed in Cormac's guesthouse, he spoke of it to Sive. The high times are truly over, I fear, Sive. Cairbre is not the man his father was. Who could be? Cormac and I had our differences, but he has been extraordinary. We'll not see another like him.

Now this new one. He expects me to serve under him and lead the Fíanna to his order, but I don't know, Sive. The army has changed too. My fault, my doing. If you had been with me to talk things through with me, support me . . . but. But.

He sighed in the darkness. But everything changes.

Sive did not deny it.

Finn fell asleep and tried to find her in his dreams, but they were clouded and filled with undefined turmoil.

He could not find Sive, but in the morning there was Grania emerging from the women's chamber, plumped with maturity, mellowed by tragedy. Finn found himself hungry for a woman's voice and fell into step beside her, discussing recent events pertaining to the kingship, and also to her future.

On the journey from Rath Grania, Finn had hardly said three words to the woman. The very sight of her made him feel guilty for Diarmait's harrying and, to some extent, for Diarmait's death, whose details became increasingly blurred in his mind as the days passed. Grania had not openly accused him of killing Diarmait as Oisin had done, yet he had begun to wonder. Did he do it?

Did I, Sive?

So he was pleasantly surprised that Grania was being friendly toward him now. She walked with him and talked with him, and her female presence was curiously comforting.

He did not see, hidden behind her slanted eyes, the plan in her mind: the slow and subtle and very female revenge she had long since determined to take on Finn Mac Cool.

Later, she found her father closeted with Flaithri the brehon, discussing some obscure point of law pertaining to the size of outbuildings. She asked Cormac to dismiss the brehon, then got straight to the point.

"I want you to ask Finn Mac Cool to accept me back as his wife, Father."

Cormac could not hide his astonishment. "You do?"

"I do. When my period of mourning is over. Will you ask him to do it . . . as a favour to you?"

When Cormac made the request of him, Finn was equally astonished. But the former king asked so beseechingly he could not refuse, though his every instinct was to do so.

"Take care of my daughter for me," Cormac said pleadingly. "She's had a terrible time these past years, and only you can make it up to her."

"I should think I'm the last person she'd want to make it up to her."

"I would have thought the same," Cormac agreed, "but apparently not. She seems to feel she should in all honesty revert to her former position as your wife. She actually seems to feel some guilt for having been disloyal to you all those years ago, and says she wants to make it up to you. So if you come together again, you can bind each other's wounds and wipe away the past."

Finn gave Cormac a dubious look. Once the former king would have been too wise for such fatuous talk. But he was old . . . changed.

And he did seem to desire the reconciliation.

As if he could hear Finn's silent thoughts, Cormac said, "It will be the last formal request I ever make of you, Finn. It will put my mind at ease, knowing the two of you have forgiven one another."

Finn started to put his thumb into his mouth before answering, then dismissed the idea. It seemed childish at the moment, a silly prank. "If that's what you really want," he said stiffly.

Cormac smiled, a faint light briefly glowing in his one remaining eye like an echo of an ancient sun. "It is what I want, because it is what my daughter wants," he said.

So it was agreed between them. When Grania ended her season of mourning, she would move into Almhain. Finn would care for her and protect her for Cormac's sake.

He was not entirely comfortable with the idea, but he accepted it.

It did not matter very much. Nothing seemed to matter as it once had. He was going through the motions more out of habit than conviction, even when it came to commanding the army.

But Cairbre made it obvious from the beginning that he wanted an energetic, dedicated Rígfénnid Fíanna, and that Finn Mac Cool was not his favourite in that position. There was frequent friction between them.

It came to a head when Finn learned that Cairbre had secretly sent to Connacht for some of Goll's own kinsmen, promising the men from Clan Morna they could be officers in the Fíanna if they were loyal to him.

Finn stormed into the House of the King with some of his old authority and a face like thunder. "The rígfénnidi don't give allegiance to the king, you fool!" he shouted at Cairbre. "They swear their loyalty to me. *I* swear to the king of Tara!"

Cairbre tried to stare him down. "Do you call the king of Tara, to whom you have sworn your loyalty, a fool? That sounds like the act of an oath-breaker to me."

The mention of that epithet, last heard from Goll's lips, enraged Finn. He almost repeated Goll's action and deserted Tara then and there. At the last moment he caught himself and realized what he would throw away.

The Fíanna. Not the Fíanna it had been, but still . . . his creation. Shaped to his desire. If he left now, by sunset Cairbre would have given it to someone else to command.

So with an effort as mighty as any of his feats in battle, Finn choked back the furious response and stood his ground, meeting Cairbre's challenge unblinkingly. "I lost my temper," he said.

"You owe me an apology."

In all their long years, Cormac Mac Airt had not asked Finn for an apology.

But everything changes, Sive.

"I apologize." The words hurt him. His tongue did not know their shape.

Life changed like a river, shifted in its bed, flowed in a different direction. Finn Mac Cool served as Rígfénnid Fíanna, but the army he commanded was only nominally his; he did not employ his entire will and energy in welding them into one weapon. Old arguments surfaced, factions developed. The men Cairbre had brought from Clan Morna kept apart from the others, causing problems.

Finn felt the subtle dissolution as he felt the dissolution of his own body.

He tried hard to care. But more and more he lay alone in the dark and talked to Sive in his head.

Grania was not proving to be the feminine companion he might have hoped. No sooner had she moved into Almhain than she began making changes. Their lodge was too small, it must grow this way and that. The roof should be higher, more visible from a distance. More bondservants were needed. The midden heap should be moved farther from the door.

Finn's old companions should spend less time lounging around his guesthouses, or drinking ale in his banquetting hall.

Only the most loyal ignored Grania's increasingly sharp tongue and stayed with Finn whenever they liked. Cailte could be relied upon, always. Blamec and Fergus Honey-Tongue would not be driven away. And Oisin, though married and with a new son of his own now, came on occasion to Almhain of the White Walls, though Finn rightly suspected it was out of a sense of duty and not through any desire to be with his father.

More and more frequently, Finn escaped by going off into his head with Sive.

The others noticed, commented on it to one another. "He's gradually slipping away from us," Cailte said sadly to Fergus Honey-Tongue, but Blamec refused to accept it. "He's tired and distracted, as who wouldn't be with a wife who constantly demands this and that? It was a cold, wet night for Finn Mac Cool when he brought that woman to his bed!"

In truth, Finn did not take Grania into his bed very often. Once or twice, more out of curiosity than desire, but he soon abandoned the habit. She was more grasping than responsive. She made him pay for his small pleasure.

She was not the woman he had watched through the hole in a thatched roof.

Where was that woman?

In his head, he wandered off in search of her.

But he was brought rudely back by a messenger from Tara. "The High King desires that his Rígfénnid Fíanna effect a reconciliation with the former Rígfénnid Fíanna, Goll Mac Morna, so that Erin will be a peaceable kingdom in the reign of Cairbre Mac Cormac."

"I can't believe it!" Cailte exploded. "The man has a brass neck, suggesting such a thing! Did Goll put him up to it, Finn? What do you think? Is this the same old Goll we always knew, trying to worm his way

back into power? You should have pursued him long ago as you meant
to do, and punished him for desertion."

Finn sighed and ran his fingers through his hair, still thick on his
head but pure white now, as gleaming as the walls of Almhain. "Pursue
him. Punish him. Why, Cailte? In the heel of the hunt, what would it have
accomplished? Just what did those summers of pursuing Diarmait ac-
complish?"

"It isn't the same thing and you know it."

Finn shrugged.

But Cairbre's command would not be ignored. He sent a second
messenger and then a third, so that at last Finn felt obliged to respond.

"My joints are too stiff in the mornings for this exercise," he admitted
to Cailte as they mounted their horses and set off to ride to Connacht
for a formal meeting with Goll Mac Morna.

The meeting was a tense one on both sides. Goll had had considerable communication from Cairbre, but Cailte was wrong in his surmise.
Goll had no desire to become Cairbre's Rígfénnid Fíanna. He knew
himself to be too old. Finn's fires were banked. Goll's had gone out. He
only wanted to be let alone with his old wife and his sturdy fort and a few
friends to challenge him to a game with the Gold and Silver Chess Set.

It was not much to ask.

But there were harsh words remembered and anger unforgotten
lying between Finn and Goll, and they circled one another warily like a
pair of hostile dogs, hackles erect as they assessed the situation. Go for
the throat? Or wag the tail?

In a few terse words, Finn explained his mission.

"It is friendship between us, then?" Goll said. "Cairbre wants us to
be . . . to be what, Finn?"

"Not enemies."

"Were we enemies?"

"Were we friends?"

Both questions were unanswerable. Fortunately, however, the Gaelic
laws of hospitality were strict, and even men whose relationship was as
undefined as Finn's and Goll's could share a cup of ale and sit together
by a fire. In fact, it was mandatory that they do so.

Goll's wife, a stringy old woman with a permanently pursed mouth,
served them herself, while several of Goll's daughters and other female
kinfolk served the warriors accompanying Finn. There was hardly room
in Goll's small fort for more than the senior rígfénnidi. The others made
camp for themselves beyond the walls, listening tensely for any signs of
trouble within.

Goll and Finn discussed everything but the subjects that mattered.
They spoke of Cormac and Cairbre and the new king's rule; they talked

of the Fíanna and politics and battles. Goll never said "oath-breaker," and Finn never said "deserter."

But the words were in the air.

At last Goll could not stop himself from saying, "I heard you killed Diarmait Mac Donn after all, and took his woman."

Finn's eyes flashed. "That's a lie. He died in a hunting accident. Afterward, Cormac asked me to take Grania under my protection and I agreed, though it was not what I wanted."

"Really?" Goll's lip curled just enough to be insulting.

"Really."

"Even if what you say is true, Diarmait was a fool to go on a hunt with you."

"He didn't go with me, he joined us later. He caught up with us just in time to encounter the boar, in fact, and he was dead before I could save him."

"Ah. I repeat, he was a fool to go on a hunt with you."

Finn's eyes narrowed to slits. "Would you be afraid to go on a hunt with me, Goll Mac Morna?"

Goll meant to scoff at the very idea, but he had been a warrior all his life, responding to challenges. "I wouldn't be afraid of anything you might throw at me, Finn Mac Cool."

"Then let's do it. To show Cairbre and the others that we are not enemies."

At once Goll was apprehensive. Here was, his instincts assured him, a most blatant trap, the trap he had expected from Finn for decades.

In a way it was almost a relief to say, "I shall go hunting with you, Finn. whenever you say and for whatever game you choose."

Goll's response was so unhesitating that Finn felt an old surge of admiration for the man. Whatever his faults, Goll had courage.

There was no trap involved. A hunt was simply the most obvious step to take, in Finn's mind; a way of re-establishing the best of the past and summoning back, if possible, some rapport with the man who had been his best teacher. Finn no longer had the enthusiasm for tricks and manipulations. He longed for things to be simple.

He longed for yesterday.

They agreed upon a boar hunt, which struck both men as truly Gaelic irony. But even as they were setting out in search of their prey, Goll's men and Finn's fell to quarrelling. At first it was over little things, but the argument soon heated. It was as if every old grudge of the last three generations surfaced.

Men of Clan Baiscne heard Cuhal's perfidy recited with relish. Men of Clan Morna were accused of failing to meet their obligations. Blows were soon exchanged.

The boar was forgotten.

At the end of the day, an exasperated Goll came upon Finn's favourite hound, Conbec of Perfect Symmetry, alone in a glade, and chopped him down with his blade for no reason at all other than an excess of anger.

Cailte was nearby and heard the dog's last, truncated cry. He knew the voice. "Conbec!" He ran forward, spear in hand, in time to find Goll straightening above the body. The one-eyed man liked dogs and was instantly remorseful, but the damage was done.

Cailte hurled his spear straight at Goll's head.

32

GOLL MAC MORNA WAS A SURVIVOR BY NATURE. WHEN on a boar hunt, he wore his old bronze helmet from his days as Rígfénnid Fíanna, just in case. Cailte's impulsive spear throw missed his one good eye and glanced off the helmet with a clang, making his ears ring but doing no damage.

Goll reached down with a grunt and hefted the spear. "You want me dead, Cailte?" he asked in his shredded voice.

"You murdered Finn's hound. You owe compensation," Cailte replied, already regretting his unthinking deed.

"Is my life the compensation? I do not think so, under the law."

"Finn will demand—"

"I know what Finn will demand. Not compensation. Revenge. He's waited a long time for it, and nothing will deny him. He had his revenge of Diarmait, didn't he?"

"It wasn't like that."

"Och, you'd defend him no matter what really happened. He's going to need you to defend him again the next time he and I meet, Cailte. Tell him that when he's ready, I'll be waiting for him. We might as well get it over." Goll smiled thinly, broke Cailte's spear shaft across his knee, tossed the two halves to Cailte, and walked away with more dignity than one scrawny old man should possess.

Cailte went to find Finn. "There will be no peace between you now, and I'm to blame."

"You are not to blame. It was impossible in any case. Come with me and we'll bury Conbec, then prepare ourselves."

Cailte did not need to ask what they would be preparing for.

At Finn's command, his men buried Conbec deep in the soft earth of Erin and erected a stone cairn above the hound. As the stones were being piled high, Finn twice referred to the dog as Bran, but no one corrected him.

Meanwhile, Goll returned to his fort. His wife knew by the look on his face that something had gone wrong. "What will you do?" she asked.

"Fight. It's all I know how to do."

"But are you certain he wants battle between you?"

"From the moment I killed his father, it was inevitable."

It was the first time she had ever heard Goll say his was the hand that struck down Cuhal. The words were like a sentence of doom; the outcome now seemed inevitable indeed.

She began gathering her cloaks and linen.

"What are you doing, wife?"

"Going with you, wherever you go."

"I won't hear of it. I'll gather the men of Clan Morna and we'll make a stand against Finn and his men. There are enough of us for a good showing, I won't embarrass you in the manner of my dying."

She threw him a fond glance. "You have never embarrassed me," she said. "You never will, I know."

But she went with him.

Finn and his followers encamped in a ravine amid slabs of massive grey stone. Sentries were posted at either end of the ravine, anticipating some effort on Goll's part at a surprise attack. Finn crouched beside a small campfire, warming his hands. The night air was chill.

His thoughts were colder, and darker.

I did not mean it to come to this, Sive. I honestly did not. Had so much anger been festering between us for so long that we had no other choice?

But I don't have to kill him, Sive, do I?

Finn stood up. He brushed off his hands, very methodically, and began kicking dirt on the fire. Lugaid's son came to him.

"What are you doing?"

"Breaking camp. We're going to pull out and go back to Almhain."

The younger man was distressed. "Without punishing the deserter? I thought that was the point of this exercise! You'd let him kill your favourite dog and do nothing, would you? Sneer at you, laugh at you? Where's the Finn Mac Cool my father spoke of?"

The others, overhearing, crowded around, adding their arguments to the dialogue. Everyone seemed to want to go after Goll. Denied the boar hunt, they hungered to hunt a man.

The old dark chaos rose up in them, demanding.

Soon enough they were shouting and pounding their spear shafts on the ground. If he were younger, wilder than they, Finn would have roared them into submission. But for some reason, he could not. They would not listen. The yelling and the pounding and the noise went on and on until it lifted him like the crest of a wave, then dropped him back into the dark trough of chaos and madness, and by morning they were hunting Goll Mac Morna in earnest, all of them.

Hunting him to the death.

Led by Finn Mac Cool.

Later, looking back, there was much of it Finn could not remember. He knew the details of that final pursuit only through the tales of the storyspinners, the poems of the bards. There would be many versions, some of them the creations of the men who were with him. Fergus Honey-Tongue would become famous for his.

But for Finn it would remain an episode shrouded in darkness, a clouded time, like the harrying of Diarmait and Grania. The darkness was relieved by a few brightly lit, specific moments: a skirmish on a cliff top with some of Goll's men, a spear wound in Red Ridge's thigh that would ultimately cripple him, three old women of Clan Morna who conspired to mislead Finn and tried to trick some of his men into falling into the sea.

And Goll. He would remember seeing Goll far ahead of him on the skyline, turning to look back. And himself shouting, "Goll!" And Goll, just for one moment, half-lifting an arm to wave, then turning and fleeing instead. And standing to fight later in a desperate battle Finn would hardly remember at all. The battle took place in a stony field called Corcomrua, and afterward there were more men dead than Finn wanted to think about.

Goll fought hard for his life at the end of it.

One night in camp, Oisin approached Finn. He would not meet his father's eyes, but looked over his head as he spoke. "Do you want me to go to Goll and effect a truce? This is a mad thing we are doing, killing good men. You and he were friends once. Can't we end it now, before one of you kills the other?"

Finn's heart leaped in gratitude. He stood up, wishing to embrace the young man with Sive's face, but Oisin pulled away before his father could touch him.

At once Finn drew back as well. "Go and effect a truce if you can," he said in a formal voice, the order of an officer. "You have my permission."

Taking Lugaid's son and two fíans with him, Oisin made his way through the night to Goll's camp. But they were not as careful as they should have been. A warrior in one of the fíans made a noise that Goll's men heard, and a spear was thrown.

It arced through the night and struck, quivering, into Oisin's shield.

The men with him interpreted this as an attempt to kill Finn's son and fell on Goll's camp with savage cries. Goll barely escaped with his life that night.

So there was to be no truce. Everything conspired against it.

"I am the hunter, yet I feel like the prey," Finn confided to Cailte. "I'm being driven into this."

"Refuse. Turn around. Go back."

But Finn knew that was impossible. He was the commander; duty and obligation demanded he lead, not retreat.

Men were dying. Men he knew. Sons and foster sons on both sides were slain; blood cried out for blood until the air was thick with the smell of it, and still the hunting and the fighting went on. Goll's supplies were almost gone.

Sometimes Finn did not know if it was night or day, or who he was fighting or why. When he was least himself, Cailte stayed with him and cared for him, but eventually he would gather his weapons and go on again.

The old quarrel between Clan Morna and Clan Baiscne had been revived at the rim of the world, with new and younger men carrying on the enmity when older men were gone.

Against his wish, Goll's wife stayed with him. She made nothing easier, but she would not leave. In camp she fussed over the wounded and complained of the lack of food, the weariness, the danger. But she stayed.

One night when Goll could not bear to hear her asking him yet again if he was all right, he slipped away and went down by the riverbank to sleep in peace.

That same night Finn, tormented by his own thoughts, rose and wandered along the riverbank, seeking some surcease. By the light of the stars he spied a form huddled by itself on a bed of moss. At once he rose onto the balls of his feet and advanced in the Fénian way, soundless.

He stood silently over the huddled figure and looked down at Goll Mac Morna.

The one-eyed man lay curled into himself like an infant, with his cloak dragged around his shoulders for warmth. Seen that way, he was smaller than Finn had ever thought him.

And he was totally vulnerable. His weapons lay beside him. His hand had even slipped from the hilt of the sword he held next to him.

Finn's hand strayed to the hilt of his own sword, drew back. He turned, still on the balls of his feet, and moved away.

The hoarse, familiar whisper floated to him on the night air. "Good style, that, sparing a sleeping enemy. Well done, Finn Mac Cool.

"But the next time we meet, the circumstances will surely be different, and I advise you to kill me then if you can."

Finn froze. His back was toward Goll, but he did not turn around. He knew with perfect certainty Goll would not put a spear in his back.

He waited until the echoes of the whisper had died, then made his way back to his own camp. Once he got there, he realized he was shaking all over, as with a fever.

For years he had tried to fight back the chaos, in his head and outside it, in every way he knew. Sometimes he had won. More recently he had lost, and the battles were harder. With Sive beside him, he could have won them, he believed.

But even if he killed Goll Mac Morna, he would not win this one. He would lose.

Either way, he would lose.

With a sense of sick despair, he prepared himself to end it.

Goll knew what was coming. After the night on the riverbank, he returned to his camp to tell his remaining followers and his wife good-bye. His men cried openly. He turned his wife to face the sunrise, so he could see its roseate glow give her face one last semblance of youth and beauty as he said, "My curse on the Clan of Baiscne, my blessing on the Clan of Morna. I have fought all my days, and the battles I won are without number. Remember them.

"Woman, take my best tunic with you and go now. You are lovely . . ." He traced his gnarled and roughened fingers down the side of her seamed cheek, and she seized them and pressed them against her face so her tears could flow over them.

Goll swallowed hard and went on. "When it is over, go to the camp of Finn and ask mercy of him. He is courteous to women. He will not harm you. You may even find, among his rígfénnidi, some strong man who will take you and protect you for the rest of your life, and if you do, I wish you joy of him."

Goll's wife was shaking her head in anguished negation. "What man would I wed? Who would I accept after you? It is harder for me to leave you than for you to leave me. From this night forward, I will be heavy-hearted and heavy-footed. I will belong to no man on the surface of the earth.

"Try to save yourself, my husband! If they attempt to starve you, eat the bodies of the dead on the battlefield, but live. Oh, do live!"

He thrust her away from him more violently than he intended. "Take her home," he ordered his men in a choking voice.

When she was out of his sight, he gathered up his weapons, ate the last pitiful crumbs of food they had left, and set off again, knowing Finn would soon be after him.

For no reason he bothered to articulate to himself, Goll struck off toward the west, back toward the cliffs above the ocean. Death and sunset and old age and the sea all came together in his mind. It was a fitting place for dying. Such a death would have style, like the swoop and sweep of blades in a beautifully fought battle.

The old one-eyed man smiled slightly as he trotted with the last of his strength toward the rim of the world, where the ocean breakers rolled, white-crested.

Finn's men had long since slain his horses. His food was gone. He was alone. And in this solitude he found himself strangely content, accepting.

There are worse ways to die, he thought.

Finn also knew it would be the last day. He had already begun grieving for Goll in his heart, even before he caught up with him.

I am forced to do this, Sive; it is my duty to the men who follow me and demand his death.

My duty.

In a haze of pain, Finn followed Goll westward. He held his horse to a walk, forcing his followers to the same pace. There was no need to hurry. Let Goll get to wherever he was going, his chosen place for his final stand.

As they neared the cliffs, Finn understand how Goll wanted it.

I am still learning from him, he thought.

Turning his horse around, he held up his hand to signal a halt. He commanded his officers and men, "Stay here. I want none of you to come with me. This is between himself and myself, and you are not to approach until it is over."

"A single combat, a battle of champions!" breathed Fergus Honey-Tongue, awed.

"A last meeting between two . . . friends," Finn said.

He slid from the horse and handed the rein to Cailte, who was as always close beside him. "See that they obey my order," he said.

During the day of leisurely pursuit, the sun had passed them and was now edging down toward the sea. Its light made a golden road from the rim of the world back across the water to the land. According to tradition, heroes passed after death along that road to the Land of Everlasting Youth.

Unexpectedly, Finn felt as if a dark cloud was beginning to lift from his spirit. Like the merry boy he had once been, he could see something ridiculous about the situation: two old men battering at one another like a pair of fighting dogs past the age for fighting, toothless and grizzled, comic and pathetic.

He wondered if Goll could see it too.

Silhouetted on the edge of the cliff ahead of him was a single dark figure. Finn blinked, reminded of a deer above a pool. But when he blinked a second time, he saw it was a man.

Goll Mac Morna lifted his arm to wave, completing the gesture he had aborted earlier. "Finn!" he called almost cheerfully.

"Goll." Finn advanced slowly. He could see that Goll was drawing his sword. He paused to take Son of the Waves from its scabbard. He went forward again, carrying the weapon in front of him almost like a cup-bearer with an offering.

When they were three strides apart, he stopped. He worked his throat, trying to summon a battle cry. Nothing happened. His mouth was dry.

"How can I kill you?" he croaked despairingly to the man who had his back to the setting sun.

Goll studied Finn's face. He found no hatred there, no lust for vengeance; only regret.

"How can you not?" he replied in a hoarse whisper.

Finn did not move.

Goll waited.

The sun sank imperceptibly lower.

"Lift your sword in your two hands," directed Goll Mac Morna.

Finn shifted weight slightly.

"Lift your sword, I say!" Goll cried in the tone of a man accustomed to being obeyed.

Finn lifted the sword.

Goll removed his bronze helmet. He fingered the worn leather chin strap almost lovingly before tucking the helmet beneath his arm. "Now strike, Finn. A mighty blow the poets will retell for centuries." He stood with neck bared for the blade.

Finn raised the sword higher, then froze. His eyes glittered wetly.

"Strike now!" roared the unmistakable, irresistible bellow of command, the voice of a Rígfénnid Fíanna.

Finn brought the sword down in a great whistling arc.

His tears blinded him. The blow was not a clean decapitation as he intended, but glanced off Goll's bony shoulder, sending up a spray of blood as it skidded across the collarbone.

Goll made no sound, delivered no counterblow. He simply tumbled backward over the cliff.

Finn leaped to the edge. Goll's body was rolling down the steep face, rebounding from projecting ledges, twisting and turning on its way to the white foam of the sea.

Finn stared down. He had fulfilled his obligation at last. His oldest obligation.

Revenge.

Revenge.

You are revenged, Cuhal Mac Trenmor. Father.

But Cuhal had never been a father to him.

The nearest thing he had to a father had been Goll Mac Morna.

Finn felt empty. Burned out, scooped out, hollow.

Then into that void flooded the greatest loneliness he had known in his life.

33

Finn returned to his men, carrying a dented old bronze helmet by its worn leather strap. He spoke to no one, but took the rein of his horse from Cailte, mounted, and turned the animal's head east, toward Almhain.

His men followed him in sombre silence. When it was too dark to go farther, they stopped and made camp.

Finn slept by himself, far from the fire.

Cailte kept an eye on him but said nothing to him. Oisin also said nothing to his father. He avoided him as he would avoid something rotten. "I follow the commander because I am sworn to," he said through gritted teeth to Lugaid's son, "but I am no kin to that liar and murderer who calls himself Finn Mac Cool."

He never knew if Finn heard him. Nor did he care.

Finn did not go to Tara, but sent Cailte there for him to relate the manner of Goll's dying. Cailte reported it in simple syllables to Cairbre, who was obviously angered. "Finn has killed a better man than himself out of pure spite and jealousy!" he complained.

Fergus accompanied Cailte to Tara and recited his own colourful version of that last pursuit and battle to all who would listen. The historians discounted it, but the common people swallowed it whole and repeated it with delight.

Finn did not tell anyone what had transpired on the edge of the sea. When he reached Almhain, he wanted only to go to bed and pull the covers over him.

But Grania would not hear of it. She saw his haggard face and bloodshot eyes and had no mercy. She started on him at once, urging him to do this and that, complaining about the other, her voice an irritant that forced its way into his mind like sand shifting between cracks of stone and wearing down the surfaces.

She never criticized Finn to others. Grania was a king's daughter, and her father had been the ultimate supporter of the law. She gave Finn not the slightest reason for setting her aside as wife, not the slightest reason under the law.

But she had her revenge in full measure. Loyal, loving, devoted Grania, who had forgiven her lover's killer and so was admired by everyone, tormented Finn to the fullest in ways only he and she knew.

"Finn, don't just sit there! The limewash on the walls is badly stained and you know the men will obey only yourself. Get someone out there or we will no longer be known as Almhain of the White Walls.

"Finn, those wretched hounds of yours are quarrelling again and Caurag can't seem to do anything with them. Go at once and stop them. I have the most dreadful headache.

"Finn, since Donn left you, no one can prepare food my stomach will accept. You have to find someone for me, I can hardly cook my own food, I'm the daughter of a king!"

She goaded and prodded until they snapped angrily at one another from dawn until dark, but she always kept her actions within those permitted by the law. She supported him before others. She never denied him her bed, though he no longer sought it.

When he was at Almhain, he began sleeping outside on the ground in all weathers, making his bed of branches in the old way. He could lie in the quiet night and if there were no clouds, look at the stars.

But he was less and less frequently at Almhain. He spent his time with the Fíanna, or with what the Fíanna was becoming, and there too he had little sense of being at home.

Loneliness bit deep into him. Even Cailte's company did not relieve it. "I seem to be growing morose with age," he once admitted to the thin man.

"Och, not at all. You've just been through a bad time."

"My whole life," Finn replied, knowing it was not true.

He did not know what was true. When people asked him to tell of his adventures, he told increasingly florid tales, piling exaggeration upon exaggeration because that seemed to be what they wanted to hear.

Oisin was silently, icily scornful. "Finn Mac Cool is an echoing cave," he told his wife. "The man is empty, he has no heart. All he contains is a lie."

Finn returned to Almhain at the end of a battle summer marked by frequent bloody skirmishes on Cairbre's behalf, arguments Cormac would have resolved by negotiation. He was weary beyond measure, but knew Grania would give him no peace. Still, he must be seen to keep Almhain as his stronghold. He really had no other.

He entered his dwelling to find Cormac's daughter busily directing her servants in yet another refurbishment and rearrangement. All the familiar furnishings were gone, even cook pots and benches that had been there since the place was new.

Grania wanted everything different.

"Where's my favourite bench?" Finn asked, looking around.

"Burned," was the crisp reply. "A leg was broken and the seat was a mass of splinters."

"The seat was worn smooth by my rump, and it fitted me."

"You're mistaken." She turned her back on him and went on ordering the servants.

Finn, head down, wandered out of doors. He drifted aimlessly across the footbeaten earth, wondering if it was worth fighting about.

Probably not.

What was worth fighting about?

Probably nothing.

He did not notice Oisin enter through the gateway, glance coldly at his father, then turn and go in the opposite direction. But he did hear Grania's carrying voice escape the confines of his lodge and come to him like a knife to the brain. "Throw out that and that and that," she was saying. "Take it all away. Throw it out on the midden where you put those smashed pots and baskets and that broken comb."

Finn stopped walking. He felt as if a cold wave flooded over him.

"What broken comb?" he said aloud to no one.

What had Grania found in her relentless emptying of his house?

He reached to his throat, found the worn leather thong and followed it down to the crane-skin neck bag, thin with decades of abrasion against his chest, under his clothing.

With fingers that trembled, he opened the bag and drew out his own comb. His broken half of a comb carved of bone and snapped in two long ago while taking the tangles from a woman's hair.

If Grania had found a broken comb, it must be the other half.

Sive's half.

Somehow lost and overlooked all these years in the accumulating rubble of a Gaelic fort.

He knew this with as much certainty as he knew the weather and the shape of the hills.

"Sive!" he cried in sudden agony.

Like a young man, he sprinted across the open space toward the midden heap beyond the stables. He flung himself upon it, digging furiously. He tossed aside broken vessels and scraps of food and gnawed knuckle bones and wicker baskets too frayed for use. He dug like a hound seeking a choice morsel. He dug with a frenzy he had not felt in years.

Coming around the corner of the stables, Oisin was startled to see his father there, grubbing in the rubbish. Had the man finally gone completely and permanently out of his head?

From a sense of duty rather than love, Oisin hurried toward him. But just as he reached Finn, his father seized a fragment from the midden and held it aloft in triumph.

A radiant smile lit the face of Finn Mac Cool.

"It's hers!" he cried.

Then he realized Oisin was beside him.

He twisted his body to hold up the comb so the younger man could see it. "This was your mother's," he said in a voice softened by love. "It was mine once. Just after you were born I used it to comb her hair for her—her hair was so thick and heavy—and the comb snapped in two. She kept this half for herself and used it ever after. I thought it had vanished with her, Oisin, but she's left it here for me to find, to have, to keep. She's left it here for me!"

Finn drew a deep breath then. The light in his eyes was not mad, but sane. "She left me this comb . . . and you," he told Oisin.

"My mother's comb?"

"Indeed. Here. Take it." Finn pressed it into Oisin's hand.

What a tenuous connection with the past, the younger man thought, turning it over in his palm. Yellowed with the years, the carving worn dim along its spine, it still showed clearly where the fracture had taken place. When he held it up to the sunlight, he discovered a few strands of hair caught in the teeth.

My mother's hair.

Hair the exact colour of a red deer's coat.

Sive had not been real to him until that moment. She had been one of Finn's wild tales, magical entertainments that became increasingly discredited as he grew older and lost faith in Finn.

Now he held her comb in his hand. Now he was looking at her hair.

Finn was musing aloud, "So many women have been in the fort since then, changing it to suit themselves. So many people coming and going. Yet no one found the comb before, isn't that extraordinary? It wasn't found until now. Now when I need it most." His voice caught in his throat. "But that's Sive. She always has been magic."

She always has been magic. Oisin lifted his gaze from the comb and met his father's eyes.

In them was wildness and sanity and total belief. In them was magic.

Reluctantly, Oisin held out the comb. "You may have this back now," he said.

Finn closed his fingers over his son's hand, trapping the comb in Oisin's palm. "You keep it to remember her by," he said. "I have you."

Their eyes held. A great bubble rose in Oisin's chest, threatening to cut off his breath. It made an aching at the base of his throat. He closed his eyes for a moment.

Then he said, "Indeed, Father. You have me."

Oisin did not return to his own fort and family until ice glittered on the bog pools below the Hill of Almhain. Instead, he found himself increasingly shouldering many of the responsibilities Finn was increasingly willing to shed. It was Oisin who saw to the winter's provisioning of Almhain, assigned housing for the season's guests, tested applicants for the Fíanna, led the hunt in search of game.

Finn was still Rígfénnid Fíanna and did what was required of him, but he was inclined at the end of the day to wander off across the bog, living in some reality of his own.

When Finn did not return until extremely late one night, it was Oisin who, quite unintentionally, overheard Grania berating him in private as she never would in public.

The next morning Oisin called on Grania in her lodge and gave her a tongue-lashing such as he had never given anyone. For many nights thereafter, she walked softly around Finn and his son both.

"You're a good son to him," Cailte told Oisin approvingly.

"I wasn't."

"That was then and this is now," said the thin man.

When Oisin knew he must stay at Almhain no longer, but return to his own family, he made his preparations with mixed feelings. Cailte and the other old companions of Finn's held a last feast in his honour in the old Fénian way, building a huge fire outside the walls of Almhain to keep from setting thatched roofs afire, and cooking enough meat to feed half an army, or so Fergus claimed.

Though they would not eat until after sunset, the cooking went on all day. Grania, who was not eager to cross swords with Oisin again, stayed within the walls and let the men do everything in their own way.

Finn was with them, more or less. He was in one of his distracted moods and kept wandering away from the cooking area, then sauntering back again. "Smells good," he commented once or twice.

Cailte said anxiously, "I hope there's enough."

Finn chuckled. "There's not enough food for you on this whole island, my friend. I've never dared get an arm too close to your face for fear you might gnaw it off."

In spite of his seeming cheerfulness, Finn grew increasingly restless as the day wore on. He paced back and forth as if to keep himself warm, even though he was wearing a great heavy mantle across his undiminished shoulders.

One of the newer recruits called out to him, "Tell us a story of your victories in battle, Commander!"

Finn did not seem to hear. He kept wandering about aimlessly, his thoughts far away.

There was a murmur of disappointment among the men waiting for the feast. It was the sort of cold grey day that made men hunger for vivid, hot-blooded tales of adventure.

Unexpectedly, Oisin cleared his throat.

"I'll tell you a story," he ventured. "What would you like to hear? My father's victory at the Battle of the White Strand? Or how he outsmarted the Sídhe in their hidden stronghold?"

The other men turned to him eagerly. Their eyes glowed. One enquired, "Do you know the story of the Battle of the Sheaves?"

"Or the House of the Quicken Trees?" another asked.

"I do of course, I know them all. Am I not the son of Finn Mac Cool?"

They gathered around Oisin in an expectant circle, and he began to recite the tales they loved to hear.

Meanwhile, the hero of the stories wandered farther and farther from the cooking fires. He would go back eventually, in time to share the meat and the crisp skin and the foaming ale sent down from the fort on the hill.

But not just yet. Not for a little while. Not while there was open sky ahead of him and soft land beneath his feet, luring him onward.

Concluding one story and already urged to tell another, Oisin looked up to see where his father was. At first he could not find him. Then, as he narrowed his eyes against the silvery light of a winter afternoon, he made out a distant figure walking along slowly as if deep in thought.

As Oisin watched, a red deer emerged from a clump of hawthorn and glided gracefully forward to walk beside Finn Mac Cool.

BIBLIOGRAPHY OF PRINCIPAL SOURCES

Adamson, Ian, THE CRUTHIN, A HISTORY OF THE ULSTER LAND AND PEOPLE, Pretani Press, Belfast, Northern Ireland, 1974

Byrne, Francis John, IRISH KINGS AND HIGH-KINGS, St. Martin's Press, N.Y., 1973

Comyn, David, THE YOUTHFUL EXPLOITS OF FINN (from the Saltair of Cashel), Gaelic League Series, Dublin, 1904

D'Alton, E. A., Rev., HISTORY OF IRELAND, The Gresham Publishing Co. Ltd., Dublin & Belfast, n.d.

Dames, Michael, MYTHIC IRELAND, Thames & Hudson, London, 1992

Goode, William J., THE CELEBRATION OF HEROES: PRESTIGE AS A CONTROL SYSTEM, Univ. of Calif. Press, Berkeley, 1978

Gregory, Isabella Augusta Persse (Lady), GODS AND FIGHTING MEN, Colin Smythe, Buckinghamshire, England, 1976

Hickin, Norman, IRISH NATURE, O'Brien Press, Dublin, 1980

Hogan, F. Edmund, THE IRISH PEOPLE, THEIR HEIGHT, FORM, AND STRENGTH, Sealy, Bryers & Walker, Dublin, 1899

Jackson, Kenneth Hurlstone, THE OLDEST IRISH TRADITION: A WINDOW ON THE IRON AGE, Cambridge Univ. Press, Cambridge, 1964

Joyce, Patrick Weston, HISTORY OF GAELIC IRELAND, Educational Company of Ireland, Dublin, 1924

———, SOCIAL HISTORY OF ANCIENT IRELAND, Vols. I and II, Arno Press, N.Y., 1980

———, STORY OF ANCIENT IRISH CIVILIZATION, THE, Longmans, Green & Co., London, 1907

Macalister, R.A.S., Ed. and Translator, LEBOR GABALA ERENN, PART V, Irish Texts Society, Dublin, 1956

———, ARCHAEOLOGY OF IRELAND, THE, Arno Press, N.Y., 1977

———, TARA, Charles Scribners' Sons, N.Y., 1931

MacKillop, James, FIONN MAC CUMHAILL, Syracuse University Press, N.Y., 1986

MacKenzie, Donald A., DIARMAID AND GRÁINNE, The Celtic Review, 1909–10

————, FINN AND HIS WARRIOR BAND, Blackie, London, 1910

MacNeill, Eoin, CELTIC IRELAND, Martin Lester Ltd., Dublin, 1921

————, Translator, DUANAIRE FINN, THE BOOK OF THE LAYS OF FIONN, Irish Texts Society, London, 1908

MacNiocaill, Gearóid, IRELAND BEFORE THE VIKINGS, Gill & MacMillan, Dublin, 1972

Matthews, John, and Stewart, Robert, CELTIC BATTLE HEROES, Firebird Books, Dorset, England, 1988

Nagy, Joseph Falaky, THE WISDOM OF THE OUTLAW: THE BOYHOOD DEEDS OF FINN IN GAELIC NARRATIVE TRADITION, University of Calif., Berkeley & London, 1984

Neeson, Eoin, A HISTORY OF IRISH FORESTRY, Lilliput Press, Dublin, 1991

O'Cathasaigh, Tomas, THE HEROIC BIOGRAPHY OF COMIC MAC AIRT, Dublin Institute for Advanced Studies, Dublin, 1977

O'Curry, Eugene, MANNERS AND CUSTOMS OF THE ANCIENT IRISH, Williams & Norgate, London, 1873

O'Donovan, John, ANNALS OF THE FOUR MASTERS, THE, Vol. I, De Burca Rare Books, Dublin, 1990 reprint

————, LEABHAR NA G-CEART, or, THE BOOK OF RIGHTS, The Celtic Society, Dublin, 1847

O'Grady, Standish, FINN AND HIS COMPANIONS, T. Fisher Unwin, London, n.d.

————, SILVA GADELICA, Williams & Norgate, London, 1892

Ó hÓgáin, Dáithí, THE HERO IN IRISH FOLK HISTORY, Gill & Macmillan, Dublin, 1985

O'Rahilly, Thomas F., EARLY IRISH HISTORY AND MYTHOLOGY, Dublin Institute for Advanced Studies, Dublin, 1946

Redlich, Anna, THE DOGS OF IRELAND, Dundalgan Press, Dundalk, Ireland, 1981

Rees, Alwyn, and Rees, Brinley, CELTIC HERITAGE, Thames & Hudson, London, 1961

Rolleston, T.W., THE HIGH DEEDS OF FINN, George C. Harrap & Co., London, 1910

Scott, Michael, Ed, IRISH HERBAL, AN, Aquarian Press, Northamptonshire, England, 1986

————RIVER GODS, THE, Real Ireland Design, Ltd., Bray, Co. Wicklow, Ireland, 1991